The Incidental Legacy Of Carlo Negrini

D B Minter

Copyright © 2024 D B Minter

ISBN: 9781917293402

The book is dedicated to Deirdre, my beautiful wife, who is the love of my life and my musical soul-mate.

If music be the food of love, play on.
Shakespeare.

I will arise and go now, and go to Innisfree,
And a small cabin build there of clay and wattles made;
Nine bean-rows will I have there, a hive for the honey-bee,
And live alone in the bee-loud glade.
W. B. Yeats.

Leading Characters:

Stephen Zandors: English operatic administrator

Helen Mentones: American but English-born musician

Simon Negrini: English – with musical aspirations

Carl Warringson: American business tycoon

Freddy Wakeson: English sports journalist

Dov Katz: Israeli schoolboy friend of Simon Negrini

THE INCIDENTAL LEGACY OF CARLO NEGRINI

PART ONE

CHAPTER 1 – Dublin 1983

The date was 17 March, which of course was Saint Patrick's Day – a Bank Holiday in Ireland, and as was often uncannily the case on this special day of Irish celebrations, the weather was absolutely glorious – sunny and warm for early spring.

Stephen Zandors, a thirty-five year-old single man from Suffolk, on the English east coast temporarily living and working in Dublin, woke up in high spirits on that particular morning. His Central Dublin bohemian-style apartment on Lower Leeson Street with its many Parisian prints of Montmartre hanging on the walls was especially fetching, with the bright sunshine streaming through the large windows.

Stephen was in the second of a three-year contract, working for the Dublin Grand Opera Society, an old-fashioned opera company that needed help with marketing and writing programme notes. The pay was quite modest, but the accommodation was included in the contract and the work was not too stressful, with plenty of free time to enjoy the delights of Dublin's city life and to explore much of Ireland's scenic beauty spots.

With the day off and without a plan on how to spend it, a visit to the National Gallery of Ireland in nearby Merrion Square seemed a good way to start the day, and then maybe a nice lunch somewhere in one of the city's Italian restaurants. The gallery founded in 1854 housed one of the great collections of Europe and one of the finest for its size. Famous artists in the collection included Velazquez, Rembrandt, Vermeer, Turner,

Monet, Caravaggio, Degas, Picasso and the Irish artist Jack B Yeats, the brother of the poet William Butler Yeats.

The gallery was very quiet, and Stephen took his time viewing some of his favourite paintings without crowds of noisy people surrounding him. A couple of paintings featuring Venice caught his eye, as amongst so many dark and gloomy canvases the brightness of the sky above the Venice Grand Canal put him in the positive mood of earlier that morning. The name of the French artist, not a particularly well known-figure, went by the name of Felix-François-Georges-Philbert Ziem. The one with the brightest sky was titled – *'Venice: A Sailing Ship'* dating from 1883, and Stephen stood mesmerised by the simplest of scenes – just the ship in the water underneath the most blue of skies imaginable.

Being so absorbed in the painting, Stephen was unaware of the person standing quite close to him who was also viewing the same work. Without thinking, Stephen blurted out, 'The sky in the painting is even bluer than the one we are lucky to have outside today.'

The young woman glanced at Stephen and responded with a wry smile.

'Yes, it's an amazingly blue sky.'

Stephen detected a soft American accent and immediately regretted not having said something more original to the woman, whose physical appearance was immediately appealing – medium height with an upright posture, making her seem taller than she actually was. She had a beautifully shaped face with a perfect aquiline nose, blue eyes and long dark brown hair conveying a mix of determination and sensitivity. Despite his less than perfect opening line, Stephen managed, very hesitantly, to develop some sort of conversation before the woman would move away to another section of the room and then be lost forever.

With his right hand fully outstretched, Stephen said with more confidence than he felt, 'Bye the way – my name is Stephen.'

For one second, Stephen thought he was being rejected as the woman did not respond, but then with a warm smile, she responded, 'pleased to meet you, Stephen, and my name's Helena.' The ice was broken and they started to walk round the gallery together, discussing the various artists and their particular works.

It was strange that at home earlier that morning, Stephen had a premonition that not only something special and positive was going to happen to him that day, but subconsciously he had also sort of known that the special thing would be him finding love. The feeling was similar to the scene in the Leonard Bernstein musical, *West Side Story,* where Tony sings 'Something's Coming' before he goes off to the dance where he meets Maria for the first time and they instantly fall in love.

When Stephen and Helena felt that they had done justice to the collection at the National Gallery and had viewed and discussed paintings of many different schools and periods, Stephen felt relaxed enough in Helena's company to ask her if she would like to join him for lunch with the comment, 'I don't know about you, but all those paintings have given me a tremendous appetite and I was thinking of an Italian restaurant for lunch, so if you've no other immediate plans I would be delighted if you could join me.' Helena graciously accepted and off they went to the Donizetti Restaurant in Kildare Street.

During lunch of pasta fagioli, veal chop served with a green salad and ice cream to finish, all washed down with a nice bottle of Soave, Helena talked about herself – her background and her career as a classical music cellist. Stephen mainly listened, feeling increasingly attracted to this beautiful woman.

Helena Mentones, aged twenty-three, was visiting London for an audition with the Royal Symphony Orchestra, and whilst there decided to fly over to Dublin for a few days to see the sights; she was fascinated with Ireland having read a lot about Irish history whilst working as a librarian in New York.

On leaving the restaurant, Stephen suggested a cup of tea or coffee at his flat. Helena hesitated for a moment, perhaps not wanting to appear too forward. She agreed to join Stephen but added that she would not stay long.

Over a pot of tea and a piece of fruit cake, Helena, having admired the flat, quizzed Stephen about his job in Dublin.

With a brief peck on the cheek, Stephen escorted Helena out of the flat into Leeson Street to the appropriate bus stop nearby that would take Helena back to her guest house. Although Helena was staying on the north side of the city (Leeson Street being on the south side) at a bed and breakfast, it was not too far away as Dublin was a compact city, certainly compared to the huge sprawl of London. Helena and Stephen arranged to meet up again the following day.

Irish people are known for their friendliness and have a wonderful way of expressing themselves, but perhaps sometimes a friendly chat, although well meaning, could be a little too inquisitive. Mrs Macklin, the landlady of the guest house that Helena was staying at, had given Helena a traditional warm welcome and treated her like a long-lost relative not a paying guest. When Helena arrived back from Leeson Street, Mrs Macklin inquired about her day – where she had been etc. – and during the chat it sort of came out that Helena had met a man whom she had spent time with and was meeting again the following day. Mrs Macklin made Helena aware of her disapproval about young women consorting with strange men and gently warned her not to let the young man take advantage of her.

Helena thought that Mrs Macklin was a lovely woman but she had outdated views about modern romance. Stephen seemed to her totally genuine and being twelve years older than her, he looked young for his age and she thought him to be quite handsome; whereas she was usually attracted to men taller than Stephen – he being about five foot eight. The only serious boyfriend Helena had ever been involved with was just over six foot. Stephen though had attractive dark features and a winning smile, reminding her of a young Paul Anka, the Canadian pop singer. In any event, she was open to a romantic adventure as she was travelling alone and it had been over six months since she had split from her boyfriend. In fact, Helena couldn't wait to meet up with Stephen again – he was on her mind all through the night.

As well as visiting all the cultural and touristic sights in and around Dublin, Helena wished to experience places Dubliners frequented in their leisure time. Dublin was world renowned for its pubs where often one could hear live Irish music, and there were many famous one's around the city. That being the case, Stephen suggested a non-touristy pub which was located around the corner from the Gaiety Theatre; the Gaiety being the home of the Dublin Grand Opera Society, where Stephen worked. Dublin did not possess a purpose-built opera house but shared the theatre with all types of theatrical offerings, from drama to musicals, revues, comedy shows and classical concerts. Stephen had to work at the Gaiety during that morning, but as it was a Friday, he had the afternoon off. The arrangement was for Helena to make her way to the theatre, which was in South King Street, close to Grafton Street – Dublin's main shopping thoroughfare – at 1pm so that they could spend the afternoon together.

The pub was Fogans in South William Street which had become a sort of local for Stephen.

Fogans diverse clientele ranged from working-class Dubliners, office workers and local business owners (South William Street being the centre of the Irish fashion industry).

The pub also attracted political activists, Irish writers and a smattering of Dublin's celebrated intellectuals. Upstairs, the pub rented an office to a well-known art dealer, Paul Dellans, a specialist in Irish contemporary artists, and Paul, who was a loquacious figure, held court in the pub and conducted his art business over a few pints of creamy Guinness.

Stephen found the mixed crowd at Fogans very stimulating, even if conversations occasionally become somewhat heated between the contrasting groups of drinkers. That was all very different from the London scene, where individual pubs traditionally hosted a specific tribe of clientele and people generally stuck to pubs that attracted their own kind. It was all very congenial but missed out on the eclectic atmosphere of a typical Dublin pub.

Fogans interior was very basic: dark brown banquettes in the front bar section led to tables and chairs at the back end of the pub – the so-called lounge, with toilets at the very back area; the less said about them the better. The two gentlemen who owned and ran the pub were both somewhat dour individuals, with the taller thin one sporting a wig that was always skew-whiff, which made him rather a figure of fun with the regulars. However, they knew how to look after those regulars, serving pints of Guinness, Smithwicks, bitter and Harp lager that were second to none in the great beer city of Dublin. Food wise, all that was on offer was a lump of cheddar cheese served on its own. Musical entertainment of any sort was discouraged. Nothing at Fogans got in the way of good drinking and stimulating conversation, and for the regulars it was home from home.

The pub was an eye opener for Helena – the atmosphere of Dubliners having serious conversations whilst knocking back pints of beer, some with whisky chasers by the side of their pint glass, absolutely fascinated her, and it was just the sort of establishment that she wanted to experience. After a few pints, Stephen and Helena were starving, having passed up the lump of cheese. Stephen offered to prepare some food back at his place and off they went, slightly light-headed and hand in hand.

As soon as they arrived back at Stephen's flat, they indulged in a little light kissing before he went to the kitchen to rustle up some food. As Stephen was preparing salmon steaks with a homemade hollandaise sauce – boiled potatoes and broccoli, he took a bottle of pinot grigio from the fridge and filled a couple of glasses – handing one to Helena, leaving her to her thoughts as he prepared the food.

Whilst sipping the wine, Helena pondered on the unexpected chance meeting with Stephen; and now in his flat, she was nervously anticipating carnal pleasures to follow their late lunch. Was that what she wanted? Yes, she told herself – a sexual adventure with such a lovely man was exactly what she desired. Although Stephen was still a virtual stranger, her instincts led her to believe that he was completely trustworthy and that he would only make love to her with her total consent. Those thoughts, as she sipped her wine, were giving her sexual frissons that went right through her body.

And so it came to pass; lunch was eaten and enjoyed – with Helena complimenting Stephen on his cooking abilities. He stroked her hand gently at first, then with a firmer grasp leading to a clinch which developed into passionate kissing as Helena parted her lips, inviting Stephen to explore her mouth with his tongue. As they made their way into the bedroom, they undressed each other slowly and fell onto the bed – the sex for both of them felt totally natural, as if their bodies had been old friends reuniting with each other after time spent apart.

CHAPTER 2

Twenty-five years earlier – Northwest London, July 1958

With much anticipation, Simon Negrini finally had a weekend all to himself – to eat whatever he fancied and at unfixed times to suit his appetite. Of course he would miss his wife Felicity, who was visiting her parents at their new home in Brighton on the Sussex coast. Simon got on well enough with his in-laws but had managed to duck out of this visit due to him having to go to work on the Saturday morning and Felicity wanting to make an early start driving down to Sussex to avoid the traffic through south London. It was Saturday afternoon – Simon was now back at home with work over until Monday. Simon was looking forward to playing a complete long-playing record of an opera on his hi-fi system in peace and quiet without domestic interruptions. Simon chose a recording of Claude Debussy's opera *Pelleas et Melisande* dating from 1902. Unlike the famous Italian operas of Verdi and Puccini, Debussy's French opera, adapted from Maurice Maeterlinck's symbolist play of the same name, was all of a piece and was a play with music without separate arias and ensembles. The opera required full concentration to appreciate it fully, but with the right conditions it creates a magical atmosphere of heartbreaking beauty as the tragic story unfolds.

Simon and Felicity lived in Wembley, a north west London suburb that was close to the most famous football stadium in the world, and the small house within a modern housing estate was an ideal starter home for a young couple in their twenties hoping to have a family. They had made friends with other young couples who lived in the same estate, which was most convivial, and one older couple, Freddy and Susanna Wakeson, whom they looked up to, as Freddy was a successful sports journalist, with football being his special interest, and had travelled extensively.

Simon had settled down with a sandwich and a glass of white wine – with the Debussy opera on the turntable, and as he was just beginning to immerse himself in Debussy's sound world, the front door bell rang.

With some irritation, Simon turned the music down and opened the door. It was Freddy, who asked if he could come in for a chat.

'Of course, Freddy – please come in.'

During the football season Freddy would be at one of the first division matches on a Saturday afternoon reporting for the newspaper he worked for, which was the popular daily '*The Planet*,' but this being out of season he had the afternoon off. Freddy apologised for disturbing Simon as he took a seat, and offered Simon a cigarette which he refused, whilst Freddy lighted-up one for himself – accepting, with thanks, the glass of wine that Simon had put down in front of him. As both men were Arsenal football supporters with Freddy naturally being the expert, the conversation opened with the usual moan about how poor the Gunners were doing in the league finishing twelfth in the table at the conclusion of the season.

'Jack Crayston was fine as the assistant to the manager Tom Whitaker, but he can't quite cut it as the main man,' mumbled Freddy.

'Yes, poor old Whitaker, dying of a heart attack at aged fifty eight,' chipped in Simon, as the chat about Arsenal, always a safe subject between them, continued its usual trajectory as they both crowed about the three trophies won under Tom Whitaker's management – two First Division titles and one FA cup trophy. 'We definitely need a new manager,' said Simon, as the football chat sort of petered out.

'What's the opera you had on when I called?'

Simon gave Freddy a quixotic glance, as he knew that Freddy had absolutely no interest in opera.

'An opera by Debussy, but I didn't think opera was your thing?' Simon knew that Freddy was only filling in the gaps in the conversation but went with the flow nevertheless.

'Well, that's true Simon, but I do know some of the famous Italian arias. Actually, now that I think of it, I did go to a complete opera performance when I was in Milan for a European football match.'

'Oh yes?'

Simon was now showing a genuine interest in what Freddy was saying, 'Do you remember which opera it was Freddy?'

'Well, it was a journalist colleague who dragged me along and I found it disappointing, even though it was by Verdi.

'The opera was *Simon Boccanegra* and although it was sung in Italian, the programme book contained a full English synopsis. But even having read the story before the performance, I found the plot incomprehensible. And I must have missed the bit in the text that tells us that following the short prologue, we skip twenty-five years before the main Act One properly gets under way, so I got totally confused. Besides, the opera lacked good tunes and the music generally was very dark and gloomy – so I was decidedly underwhelmed.'

Simon was amused by Freddy's rant and responded by pointing out that if he was asked to recommend an opera for opera novices – he would certainly not suggest *Simon Boccanegra* as he agreed it did lack the big tunes of other Verdi operas, such as

La Traviata and *Rigoletto,* but as far as he was concerned, the revised version of the opera dating from 1881, was one of Verdi's greatest works which moved him to tears in its portrayal of love, hate and reconciliation in a historical context.

Freddy was looking distracted and showed a disinclination to continue talking opera, and he changed the subject to inquire about Felicity's trip to Brighton and what plans they had for the following weekend.

'Nothing planned as such,' said Simon, who sensed that Freddy had something on his mind.

'Look, Simon – the reason I popped in to see you is that I've something to confess.'

'Oh yes?' Simon had a sudden lurch in his stomach and a premonition that his life was about to change.

'Felicity and I are in love and are having an affair,' Freddy blurted out, not looking at Simon. A stunned silence pursued with Simon responding by asking Freddy to leave the house immediately.

'Sorry Simon.'

Freddy, feeling hugely awkward and embarrassed made a hasty exit.

Simon slumped in the chair, in total shock and feeling utter despair as well as anger that he had been betrayed without ever having a notion that a liaison had been going on behind his back. It was uncanny that he had chosen *Pelleas et Melisande* to play that afternoon – the story of love and betrayal in the opera had suddenly become Simon's own personal sad tale.

As Simon sat and reflected on the shock news of Felicity's infidelity, he began to feel that actually it was his fault as he had encouraged Felicity to be flirtatious with other men and that he wouldn't object to her enjoying a little fun outside marriage, as he himself would have liked to indulge in a little flirtation or two, albeit in a loose and casual way. But Freddy was a friend of theirs and mentioning the word 'love' in his confession had put everything into a new and very disturbing context. And how did Felicity feel about betraying Susanna? After all, their marriage was of fairly recent origin. Simon realised that he had been hoisted with his own petard. He should have realised that it was much easier for men to compartmentalise flirtations and faithlessness within a relationship, whilst women needed to totally fall in love with another to justify straying from one's husband.

However, whilst acknowledging his own part in the situation that now arose, he was still deeply hurt but decided that he would live with the consequences and not jeopardise their marriage, provided of course that Felicity wanted the same outcome. And of course, that would give him the license to continue exploring the options of other women – but for him, love meant Felicity and her alone. Simon decided to be conciliatory with Felicity when she arrived back home from visiting her parents and try to work things out between them with love and understanding.

But in reality, it didn't quite pan out the way Simon had hoped it would. Felicity had fallen head-over-heels in love with Freddy and would have left Simon for him if Freddy would do the same and leave Susanna. But Freddy had no intention of leaving his wife, and Felicity had to accept that if she wanted Freddy, and she definitely did, she would have to accept it on his terms and be content with an affair. This was all too much for Simon and he decided to cut loose and leave Felicity, but his decision was made with good grace and the couple split up on good terms and remained in love, albeit in a brotherly-sisterly manner, for many years.

Felicity, following their eventual divorce – when 'no-fault' divorce became available, – went on to marry an old acquaintance of Simon's, once her affair with Freddy, which had become quite intense, eventually petered out, but Simon's feelings towards Freddy hardened and he blamed him for breaking up his marriage.

Freddy, although friendly enough with Simon, and as a foursome (Freddy, Susanna, Simon and Felicity) socially, they all gelled together positively, considered Simon to be a bit of a cultural snob, especially for his love of opera and in particular his championing of difficult (in his view anyway) composers such as Debussy and Wagner, and even those ghastly moderns – Schoenberg and Berg. Freddy was a very clever guy and had done really well in life, but not only did he not have intellectual or cultural aspirations, he also thought that men (it was more acceptable in women) who did have those aspirations were a bit suspect in manly terms and even potentially closet homosexuals. A grammar school boy from a tough London east end background, Freddy had pulled himself up by his bootstraps, and his knowledge of sport was second to none. Being well travelled for his newspaper, covering major tournaments at home and abroad, he was an interesting man in his own way, and being older than Simon he was considered the sophisticated one of the foursome. Freddy was tall, dark and rugged in build and although not particularly handsome, one could see why women found him attractive. Simon was also reasonably tall, but his fair hair and slim figure gave him a somewhat vulnerable appearance that women wanted to mother rather than lust after.

Susanna was Freddy's second wife and was from the USA. He had met her during his coverage of the Olympics in Melbourne, Australia, during 1956. Susanna's brother was part of the USA's boxing team, and Susanna had travelled to Melbourne to cheer him on. Other than football, Freddy covered boxing for his newspaper and was a real enthusiast for the sport. Whilst Simon, who loved football, had no time at all for boxing and could not understand the attraction of people hitting each other as a sport.

Other than football, what Freddy and Simon had in common was politics. Both were on the left of the political divide and supported the Labour Party – thinking the Conservatives were full of privileged individuals – privately educated people who looked down on anyone not from a similar background. Despite the Suez crisis of 1956 which led to the change of prime minister from Anthony Eden to Harold Macmillan, the Tories were still firmly in power and were hoping to win another term – keeping the Labour Party, led by Hugh Gaitskell, in opposition; although the polls were looking favourably for Labour, who had been out of office since 1951.

Felicity's background was decidedly middle class and reasonably affluent – her parents, Ruby and Edward Koskie, both English by birth but with Jewish East European backgrounds, had done well in life, with Ed rising to a top job in industry. Whilst young they had been extremely left wing, but like many people of their generation, as their own financial status dramatically improved, their political views moved towards the right. Felicity was the eldest of three children with two younger brothers and was the apple of her father's eye. A dark eyed beauty, Felicity was a young ballerina and a dancer with the Vic-Wells Ballet Company, the forerunner of the Royal Ballet. Felicity, aged nineteen, and Simon, aged twenty-one, married in 1956 in a traditional Jewish ceremony, followed by a big dinner-dance at a leading London hotel – all paid for by Mr Koskie.

Simon's background was very different from Felicity's and much less stable. His father, Arnold Negrini, had been killed during the 1939 – 1945 war in a London bombing raid – his mother, Louise, struggled financially to keep her head above water. Arnold and Louise were also from a Jewish East European background. Arnold had Italian ancestors, and, like the Koskies' – they were English by birth. But unlike the Koskies'– they lived a kosher life and were regular synagogue attendees although they would not have been considered traditionally Jewish orthodox either in dress or in lifestyle. However, Louise's parents were orthodox and took Simon, an only child, under their wing, and fed him with a fire and brimstone religious philosophy that frightened him with concerns of the afterlife and what would happen to him when he died if he didn't follow all the religious laws to the letter. When Louise lost her job and was unable to keep up the rent of their flat in Camden Town north London, they moved into her parents' home in the ultra-Jewish orthodox district of Stamford Hill, about five miles away, but an altogether different world.

Simon was very unhappy living at his grandparents ramshackle house which he disliked intensely for its unkempt rooms, shoddy bathroom and a kitchen with a toilet closet by the side of the main kitchen area, leading to the courtyard with a garden shed used for the autumn harvest festival of *Succoth,* where one eats all one's meals in a semi-open dwelling covered only in a grass roof. Simon's grandfather, Issac Feltstein, was a commercial agent for the *lulov* – a long green branch bouquet of palm, myrtle and willow together with an *esrog,* which is similar to a large lemon in appearance. With the *lulov* and the *esrog* – off one went to the *shul* (synagogue) during the festival, and at specific moments in the prayer sequence one shook the *lulov* – so one needed to be carefully strung together to avoid bits of green leaves flying all over the place. It was a strange sight to see all those men, and only men of course, with their big hats, some big-brimmed black felt ones and others with the full *Hasidic* gear of shiny black gowns and fur hats; full-bearded men hugging themselves in woollen prayer shawls and all of them holding long green branches in the one hand and yellow lemon-like fruit in the other hand, shaking their *lulovs'* and swaying in a prayer-like trance as if their life depended on it.

Simon found the whole thing hilarious, but his *zaide* (grandfather) was hugely fussy about the quality of the *esrog* in particular, and if they weren't up to scratch he would return them to the supplier demanding replacements. This was a serious enterprise for Isaac Feldstein both commercially and spiritually.

Simon's barmitzvah at the age of thirteen took place in the same *shul*, a few doors away from his grandparents' house with a congregation full of *Hasidic* men, whom he felt totally alien from, but nevertheless he conducted himself in an exemplary fashion to please his *zaide*, who was an official of the *shul*. Simon recited the full *parshas* (portion) for that particular Sabbath including the *maftir* (the final lines of the *Torah* portion followed by the *Haftarah* (readings from the Prophets). That in itself was rare enough as most barmitzvah boys recite only one portion, which is usually the *maftir*, but Simon capped his performance by giving a *Talmudic* discourse in the language of *Yiddish*. Although he was word perfect in his various renditions Simon also knew that he did not belong there, but for the moment he was trapped in a world that he found totally claustrophobic.

Chapter 3

Greenshead, North east England, 1948

Following Simon's unhappy barmitzvah experience, he felt that he must get away from his grandparents and the stale ghetto-like atmosphere of Stamford Hill. His local secondary modern school was a dump and he was doing badly there, having failed his 11-plus exam two years earlier. His grandpa suggested a Jewish boarding school five hundred odd miles away in north east England on the south bank of the River Tyne. When he was told that the school was not *Hasidic* but run by orthodox Jews originally from Lithuania, known in Jewish parlance as *Litvaks'* and did not wear the full ghetto gear of the *Hasidim* but everyday contemporary clothes, Simon was convinced that it was the right move for him. What Simon did not quite appreciate was that the *Litvaks'* were if anything more religious than the the *Hasidim* and very dour in their demeanour – lacking the joy of celebrating Jewish life, which was the hallmark of the *Hasidim* custom and one of their more attractive traits.

It was a five-hour train journey there from London's Kings Cross station to Newcastle upon Tyne where he was met by one of the school teachers, a Mr Sherman, who was welcoming enough and looked normal in his suit, tie and trilby hat. Mr Sherman drove a small vintage black Ford car for the short drive over the river to the town of Greenshead. During the journey he gave Simon a brief history of the school. It was started by Lithuanian refugees escaping the rise of the Nazi's in the 1930s – and they chose Greenshead because it was not a Jewish town; they did not want their boy pupils to be contaminated by mixing with non-religious Jews one finds in the big cities, especially London. The city of Newcastle had a small Jewish population which was not particularly orthodox and the Greenshead hierarchy made a point of having nothing to do with the Jewish community of Newcastle. The teacher explained that the school was very small at the start but since the end of the war in 1945, a big influx of boys from families that had somehow escaped the horrors of the Nazi regime had enrolled, and so they had expanded the school from one large house to a second one next door to the original building.

'Had you thought about taking in girl pupils?' asked Simon.

Sherman looked at Simon as if he was quite mad. 'Girls?' he stuttered with a look of distaste.

'Of course not, as they don't require being educated in the same way as boys – they need educating to be good wives and mothers only.'

Simon did not utter one more word during the rest of the car journey.

Simon's first impression of Greenshead was of a grey dull-looking town without any redeeming features, and he wondered why they had chosen such an uninteresting place to open their school. The two houses comprising the school looked as grey as the rest of the town and not at all inviting. Once installed in his dormitory on the first floor, to be shared with nine other boys, he was ushered into the principal's office on the ground floor next door to the synagogue, obviously the most important room in the two buildings, where was sat a grim-looking rabbi Moshe Shwabb, the school principal, at his desk, who hardly looked up to greet him and where three other new boys were standing. Shwabb, unlike Sherman, was a no-nonsense humourless man whose appearance was quite intimidating.

The boys introduced themselves to each other quietly saying their names and all looking nervous and a bit anxious. They were Dov from the brand-new state of Israel; Michael from London; Alex from Vienna and Pinchas from Amsterdam. They seemed like a nice bunch of boys of a similar age to Simon. Swabb addressed the four boys in a matter-of-fact manner, distinctly lacking in any personal warmth, and not even a hint of a smile crossed his face. Starting with a very perfunctory welcome, he was keen to let the new boys know the rules of the school.

'All food served must be eaten; lights out at night means exactly that; all prayers are compulsory and every service must be attended. Teaching Hebrew, Torah, Jewish history and religious subjects are the main focus of our school, but to satisfy the authorities you will receive a small amount of secular teaching comprising English, maths and science. But the reason you're here is to develop into religious and upright Jewish men going forward as religious adults. If you take unauthorised holidays during term time, your parents or whoever is paying your fees will be heavily fined. Radio and gramophone records are all strictly forbidden and so are newspapers, magazines and secular books other than books relating to class work. If you're out walking in town on your Friday afternoon off school and you see a female on the road, you must cross over the road, and it is strictly forbidden to engage in any conversation with someone from the opposite sex. I wish you well here in our marvellous school and will be keeping a close eye on you all. Now off you go.'

The four boys left the room rather dazed, having expected a more friendly welcome, but the general feeling amongst them was that they were there now and had to make the most of the situation. The four new boys were all accommodated in the same dormitory which pleased them. The housemaster, Mr Finton, was another dour individual who was a stickler for the rules, but as he was elderly, the gossip around the school was that he was soon to retire.

During their first term, the four newbie's stuck together and became good friends. Simon was particularly fond of Dov, a good looking-boy, and had developed an innocent schoolboy crush on him but was never sure that it was reciprocated.

Simon, being a resilient boy, settled down to school work, taking an enthusiastic interest in Jewish history. He did OK with Torah and Talmudic studies but lacked real motivation in those subjects. The problem with the secular subjects was that the teachers themselves showed little commitment to advancing knowledge for anything that wasn't Hebrew or religion orientated. Simon enjoyed the prayers and looked forward to the three-times-a-day religious services, especially in the singing episodes of the various sections, in which Simon sang out in his developing young tenor voice.

Outside of school work, life around the school was very dull with no sporting activities other than table tennis for the young men to let off steam. The food was dire and the dormitories lacked any sort of heating facilities to cope with the north of England's winter's weather.

Simon looked forward to Friday afternoon as before the Sabbath the boys had free time and were allowed to leave the school premises. Although leaving the town was forbidden, Simon ignored that rule and would walk over the Tyne Bridge to the city of Newcastle. He loved the crowds and buzz of city life with its shops, stores and cafes. For a few short hours, and longer in the summer months, Simon felt he was back in the normal world and understood that this was the world he wanted to rejoin as soon as he was old enough to leave the school.

As expected, Mr Finton retired at the end of Simon's first term at the school and was not missed by the boys. The new housemaster, Mr Ronald Don, was like a breath of fresh air.

At the age of twenty-five, he was young for the appointment, especially compared to his predecessor Finton. He was also the complete opposite in temperament – instead of strict and unsmiling, Ronnie not only asked the boys to call him by his first name, but he was also friendly, cheerful and treated the boys like they were his younger brothers. He was fair-haired, of medium height with a slightly pudgy but not an unattractive face – had a rotund figure and appeared somewhat older than his age. He dressed more like a middle-aged man rather than as a young one, with a sober three-piece suit – shirt, tie and a large trilby hat.

Being an orthodox Jew was a given, but Ronnie conducted his religious life with a light touch. He liked to enjoy himself and started up a table tennis tournament within weeks of taking up his post. The boys who played the sport were favoured and that included Simon, who had spent his first term playing table tennis with any of the boys who showed an interest in the game. Simon would give Ronnie a good game and even win sometimes. A routine started to establish itself in which after lights out Ronnie would wake Simon up and they would head downstairs to the table tennis room and play a few games together. Ronnie always made sure that he had a few tasty snacks with him which he would share with Simon. All in all – life at the school picked up considerably for Simon in his second term.

One night following a few games together, Ronnie suggested that instead of eating the snacks in the play area, they should enjoy them in his own bedroom. Ronnie's single bedroom was at the end of the corridor near the various dormitories and it was a cosy room with a single bed. Whilst enjoying crisps and chocolates, Ronnie was telling Simon about his life.

'I miss my fiancée' said Ronnie, 'but this was a good job offer and I felt that I couldn't turn it down'

'What was your job before coming here?' asked Simon.

'I was a teacher at the new Carmel College Jewish boarding school in Oxfordshire.'

'What subjects did you teach?'

'It was English and modern Hebrew. I got the position through family connections when the school first opened at the beginning of this year, but I only stayed two terms.'

'Why did you leave? I heard that it was a posh and expensive place, replicating the English public school formula.'

'Unfortunately I had a disagreement with the head, and yes, Simon, it was a lovely school and I could get home to London every weekend, whilst here is so far away we're stuck at the school for the whole term – and this is such a long term from October through to April without a winter's break. It must be tough for you boys being away from home for so many months?'

'Well, yes it is, and to be honest I do sometimes get homesick, mainly to see my mother as I hate our home which we share with my grandparents.'

'Oh... Simon – you must tell me all about it?'

Simon explained his home situation to Ronnie, who listened carefully and showed understanding and compassion with Simon's story about losing his dad, his mum being short of money, living with grandparents and having that crazy barmitzvah.

Chatting with Ronnie alone gave Simon a feeling of close friendship, even though Ronnie was twelve years older and had authority over him. It was great to unburden himself with an adult who was experienced in life. The tête-à-tête between them in Ronnie's room late at night became a regular occurrence and they both talked to each other about their respective lives in a relaxed and convivial manner.

It started with Ronnie casually putting his arm around Simon's shoulder and lightly stroking his arm. Simon found this comforting and certainly non-threatening as he missed the cuddles with his mum. In fact, he felt privileged that Ronnie

had chosen him to be friends with and wanted to please him –
so he reciprocated by holding Ronnie's hand. The light touching
of each other continued over time when they had their secret
get-togethers at night in Ronnie's bedroom.

At age thirteen, Simon had been totally unaware of the sexual
act, although he felt his body was changing and his emotions
had been all over the place – up one minute and down the next.
When out walking with his three friends, the boys started to
discuss sex and what physically actually occurs between a man
and a woman. Pinchas, who was slightly older than the others
and the most confident of the four boys in his manner –
presumed knowledge of personal things, did most of the talking
and explaining – his friends becoming somewhat in awe of
him. Dov, who usually was fairly opinionated, kept very quiet
throughout the conversation and Simon was curious as to
whether he knew more about these things than was letting on.

Simon secretly loved Dov but had no idea how that love
manifested itself – he certainly did not associate his feelings for
him with anything physical that Pinchas had been going on
about. There was something about Dov who, although generally
less overall confident than Pinchas with a certain shyness and
reserve in manner, had strong ideas especially about Israel, as
he felt extremely proud of his country and suggested that they
all eventually emigrate there as the new state was now the home
to Jewish people from all over the world. It was his generous
smile and languorous gait that captivated Simon, but his
admiration for the boy was totally innocent and his own kept
secret.

Ronnie started becoming bolder in his touching of Simon and
began to put his hand on the boy's penis, which startled him.

'What are you doing Ronnie?'

'Oh sorry I didn't mean to touch you there – but did it feel
nice?'

'No!' Simon responded emphatically – and that's a very rude thing to do'

'Oh – so sorry – I promise not to do it again,' said Ronnie rather sheepishly.

Later in bed on his own, Simon thought about Ronnie's action and also about the chat relating to the physical side of sex, and he started to see a sort of connection – but that was about men and women – Pinchas never said anything about sex between two men.' It was all very confusing but although he hated what Ronnie did – the thought of doing something similar with Dov excited him, and his penis suddenly felt hard – a weird sensation that had never happened to him before.

Over time, Ronnie became more physically bold with Simon and eventually some sort of actual sex took place. Simon was confused about exactly what was happening to him but let it happen nevertheless, feeling guilty that he had actually led Ronnie on. He only protested mildly, which Ronnie ignored by smooth words of endearment and promises of everlasting friendship.

Simon never told a soul about his experiences with Ronnie, which went on for a year and a half. He just tried to block the whole episode from his mind, but when he did think about Ronnie and what had gone on between them, he felt greatly ashamed.

As soon as Simon reached the age of fifteen during the summer of 1950 – he left the boarding school and went back to live with his mother who by that time had got a good secretarial job and managed to rent a small flat in Chalk Farm north London.

Hindsight is a wonderful thing and in later life Simon's overall negative view of his time in Greenshead softened somewhat – although certainly not with Ronnie, whom he felt had abused a naive boy of thirteen. After all, Ronnie had a duty of care towards Simon. But the softening attitude to the school in general was partly because over the long term his experience there did no permanent harm to his development as a mature adult or to his love life. But more importantly, he came to understand and feel great sympathy for the Lithuanian Jewish teachers whom he encountered during his time there. They were obviously traumatised by the Nazi atrocities and they must have lost relatives and friends to the Holocaust. Simon's immediate family was unaffected by the Holocaust but more distant relatives of his from France and Belgium had been. The Holocaust was hushed up in the Jewish community immediately after the war, and the true horror of the six million murdered Jews only came to light following the Adolf Eichmann trial in Israel during 1961.

Chapter 4

Venice 1857

Giuseppe Verdi's opera, *Simon Boccanegra*, with a libretto by Francesco Maria Piave, first saw the light of day on 12 March 1857 at the Teatro La Fenice, Venice. The cast was as follows: Leone Giraldoni in the title-role, Luigia Bendazzi as his daughter, Carlo Negrini as Gabriele Adorno, Giuseppe Echeverria as Fiesco and Sgr. Vercellini as Paolo. The opera was a flop – the critics found the subject gloomy with a lack of attractive arias and melodies. The Naples production in 1858 went better with full houses, but the *La Scala Milan* production in 1859 was a huge fiasco and the opera fell into neglect.

The one bright spot of the Venice premier was the performance of the tenor Carlo Negrini creating the role of Gabriele Adorno. Negrini, who was actually born Carlo Villa in 1826, was a star *spinto* tenor and had already sung several Verdi roles, including Gaston in *Gerusalemme* (Jerusalem), The Duke in *Rigoletto*, Carlo V11, (King of France) in *Giovanna d'arco*, Rodolfo in *Luisa Miller* and Jacopo in *I due Foscari*, before Verdi chose him for the tenor role in *Simon Boccanegra*. In London at Covent Garden, Negrini sang the role of Pollione in Bellini's *Norma* and Carlo in Verdi's *Ernani*. The Musical World in 1854 wrote 'Negrini is the most perfect Carlo in *Ernani* that can be imagined'

Negrini was married to a Clelia Bonola daughter of Giovanni Bonola; we have no record of them having children together. However, the name Negrini was common enough in Italy, the name travelling to Eastern Europe and later to Great Britain. Tragically, Carlo Negrini, the star tenor died from a stroke in 1865 aged only thirty-eight.

The opera was based on a play by the Spanish playwright Antonio Garcia Gutierrez, the author of *El Trovador* which, a few years earlier, had been the basis of one of Verdi's most popular operas, *Il Trovatore.*

Following the premier productions the opera fell into neglect. In 1880, the composer/librettist Arrigo Boito worked with Verdi on a revised libretto of *Simon Boccanegra,* fleshing out various characters and adding a completely new central scene, known as the 'Council Chamber scene'. Verdi's musical revision was extensive, adding music of great beauty and transforming the work into an opera of absolute tragic nobility.

The revised version received a successful first performance at La Scala in 1881, but even so, the revised version of the opera, which became the standard version, took a long time to establish itself in the international opera repertory. The British premiere took place in 1948 at Sadlers Wells in London, and Covent Garden did not stage the opera until 1968, with the great Tito Gobbi in the title role. The Dublin Grand Opera Society staged *Simon Boccanegra* in 1956 and again in 1974.

Simon Boccanegra was an historical figure, becoming the very first leader of the Republic of Genoa who had been given the title 'Doge' when elected in 1339. Previously, the leader was known as either 'Captain of the People' or 'Abbot'. Early in the twelfth century, the rulers of the city were split between the noble houses of Doria and Spinola, known as the Ghibellines, with the noble houses of Fieschi and Grimaldi, known as the Guelphs. (The Grimaldi name survives to the present time, as it the name of the ruling family of the Monaco Principality) The quartet were the big four families (Magna Quator Prosapiel). The families constantly quarrelled with each other and over time the city struggled for naval supremacy with Venice which led to instability and citizen unrest, culminating in the election in 1257 of Gugliemo di Boccanegra as 'Captain of the People'. A distant ancestor of the later Simon, Gugliemo unfortunately developed into a tyrant and was finally overthrown with the Magna Quator retaking control of the city.

Fast forward to 1339 – the people of Genoa won the right to elect their own leader and chose Simon Boccanegra. Simon was initially reluctant to accept the leader's role – but the people bore Simon aloft to the church of San Siro and proclaimed him 'Doge'. (Although many of the dramatic incidents in the Verdi opera are fictitious, the conclusion of the opera's prologue where Simon becomes Doge by the sheer will of the people, does indeed bears some real historical truth)

Simon restored order to Genoa. He banished the Magna Quator and dismissed all the patricians from the council. He was a popular leader and stopped rioters attacking property belonging to the nobles, and he was instrumental in saving a member of the house of Grimaldi. As a statesman, he made a peace treaty with Genoa's enemy, Pisa. He led successful navy engagements against the Turks, the Tartars and Moors. Following a plot on his life Simon invited some of the nobility back on the council but excluded the Grimaldis', who had been exiled to Monaco. The disconnected Grimaldis', aided by the Visconti family of Milan, stirred up trouble in Genoa, and in 1344 a frustrated Doge went into voluntary exile with his family to Pisa. Chaos followed in Genoa, and at sea it was defeated by Venice, leading to a plea for Simon to return to Genoa.

In 1356, Simon was elected Doge of Genoa for the second time and was feted by Charles 1V of France who made him a chevalier. Whilst the King of Cyprus was on a state visit to Genoa in 1363, the Doge fell ill and died a few days later. Rumour had it that he was poisoned. Whilst ill another revolt took place in Genoa led by a new group of merchants who sought power. Simon's relatives were made prisoners and a plebeian named Gabriele Adorno was elected Doge.

All the successes of Simon's rule were negated by Adorno, and Genoa was forced to accept the protection of Charles 1V of France. Following the execution of Simon's son, Giovanni Boccanegra, the family name of Boccanegra ceased to have a further involvement in the politics of Genoa.

The poisoning of Simon features in Verdi's opera, as well as the character of Gabriele Adorno, who plays a major part in the dramatic events of the opera.

Chapter 5

Dublin and London 1983

Helena stayed with Stephen at his flat for the remainder of her short visit to Dublin. She telephoned her landlady, Mrs Macklin, to let her know that she would not be coming back to the house and would collect her belongings on the way to the airport in a couple of days. Mrs Macklin tut-tutted away at Helena's plans – conveying her disapproval of the state of affairs and warning Helena to be careful and not to let a man seduce her. But Helena was certainly not being seduced as she was as lustful towards Stephen in re -discovering her sexually as he was with her. Helena's sexuality had lain dormant for six months, and in truth she had never really enjoyed the sex with her ex-boyfriend as it had never felt natural in the way it felt so compelling and beautiful with Stephen. She loved the weight of his body on top of hers, the hardness of him pushing into her softness and gently rocking together – she loved the passion – the climaxes' and the loveliness of lying still together afterwards.

The few days with Stephen at his flat flew by in a flash and it was soon time to face the world again – Helena was flying back to London for a master-class with the great French cellist Paul Tortelier, before heading back to New York which was her home city. Expressions of love, hugs and kisses were exchanged between them before parting with promises to see each other again soon, either in Dublin, London or New York.

Helena was born in London during 1960, but it was a tragic beginning as her mother had died in childbirth and she never found out who her parents were. She was adopted by a wealthy established couple from New York, Mr and Mrs Mentones, a childless couple who had met and married in their late thirties. The Mentones' were having difficulties adopting in New York because of their senior age and by the time they got into their mid-forties they had almost given up.

A lifelong friend, Carl Warringson, was a wealthy gentleman from New York but had lived in London for some years. Carl Warringson had been an American GI – a rather mature one of thirty-one when arriving in Britain during 1942. Carl met, fell in love and married a young nurse, Shelley Lambit, who came from a London Jewish family prominent in the ladies clothing industry. On leaving the American army, Carl joined his wife's family clothing business and expanded it greatly – outsourcing the manufacturing to factories in Hong Kong, which could produce the clothes at a fraction of the cost of manufacturing the clothes in London, and this policy, made Carl Warringson a very rich man. Shelley was unable to conceive children and so they thought about adopting. Carl did some research and realised that there were more babies in Britain that needed adopting than people willing to do so. The war had left many abandoned women, as the American GI'-s had eventually gone back home, leaving pregnant women, whose boyfriends had refused to use condoms; the availability of the contraceptive pill still being a few years away.

Unfortunately, Carl's marriage to Shelley had broken down, so all thoughts of adopting faded. But he remembered that his dear friends in New York were desperate to adopt but were unable to go-ahead with an adoption there. So he contacted his close friends Mr and Mrs Mentones'– recommended them to adopt a British baby, which would be a lot easier for them than to keep on trying to persuade the New York authorities, that, despite their age, they would be fit and responsible parents. And so it came to pass – the British authorities approved the Mentones' adoption application and they adopted a little orphan baby, naming her Helena, who became Helena Mentones. The deliriously happy couple brought up Helena in New York – totally doting on her; it was a loving childhood. They were forever grateful to their great friend, Carl Warringson, who had given them the idea of adopting a British baby and who had helped with all the bureaucracy. Carl visited the Mentones' whenever he was in New York – making a point of visiting often – with Helena growing up knowing Mr Warringson as Great Uncle Carl. He kept an eye on her and always showed a keen interest in her education and development – spoiling her with regular presents.

Helena, on her way back to London from her unexpected romantic long weekend in Dublin – her eyes closed on the short flight – was reliving the beautiful lovemaking she had experienced and wanted to repeat that experience with Stephen again and again before returning home to New York – but she secretly hoped that Stephen would visit her there as soon as he could. But meanwhile, Stephen had promised to see her in London the following weekend.

Helena played the Elgar cello concerto, with piano accompaniment, during her master-class in London with Tortelier. The cello and piano went extremely well together, and Tortelier even mentioned that Helena's playing reminded him of the famous English cellist, Jacqueline du Pre, the great interpreter of the Elgar, (who unfortunately was suffering with multiple sclerosis, which had tragically had cut short her career.) Helena brought such passion to the slow movement, which prompted the master to make the Du Pre comparisons. Attending the master-class was the musical agent Keith Foes – on the lookout for new talent in the classical music world and he made contact with Helena – being very impressed with her playing.

Unfortunately, her audition with the Royal Symphony Orchestra was unsuccessful – so she had no professional reason to stay on in London – unless of course Keith Foes took her on and arranged a London debut recital for her. But she was well aware that recitals and concerto concerts were planned years ahead, unless there was a need for a late replacement due to an artist's indisposition.

Helena was desperate to have an excuse to stay on in London to be able to continue seeing Stephen, either in London or in Dublin. But with the orchestral post not now available, it was hard for her to justify remaining in London as her family would expect her back home in New York.

Stephen flew over to London to be with Helena for the weekend as promised and stayed with her at the small flat that she had rented in Shepherd's Bush, west London. It was a blissful weekend – constant lovemaking, only breaking for food shopping and eating, with Stephen taking charge of the kitchen as Helena's cooking skills were fairly basic.

'I love you so much,' said Helena, as Stephen was stuffing a chicken with lemon and garlic. She watched him with admiration as he was gently depositing the stuffed chicken into the oven to slow roast for a couple of hours.

'I love you too,' replied Stephen as he was on his knees guiding the chicken into place with a tea towel slung over his shoulder. Turning around, seeing Helena's beautiful face looking at him with such love, he immediately got up and took her into his arms. He grabbed her hand and led her gently into the bedroom which was close to the kitchen, so they would get a whiff of the cooking aromas as they undressed each other.

Maybe it was the heady smells wafting from the kitchen, or it might have been that Stephen was beginning to overcome some initial caution in their lovemaking that he had been conscious of during their early sexual encounters in Dublin – knowing that besides her one steady ex-boyfriend, she was sexually inexperienced. Stephen, being twelve years older, although never having been in a serious relationship – had experienced many short-term affairs and casual sexual encounters – consequently gaining an understanding of the wonderful variety of the sex act. Sex depended on the chemistry of the people involved – and that chemistry had nothing to do with the type of relationship involved. Good or even great sex could be enjoyed by couples into a long-term relationship, a short-term affair or even in a casual pick-up. It's called being on the same sexual wavelength; or not, as the case may be.

Helena and Stephen professed love for each other which was completely genuine, but this was pure lust – almost animalistic with both of them losing all inhibitions during the sexual act. Neither dominated the other but took it in turns to be the dominant partner and then to be the submissive one. They were loudly vocal, telling each other what they wanted the other to do, which enhanced the lust element, as they passionately kissed and licked each other in every orifice of the body before he penetrated her.

Stephen looked at Helena's perfectly shaped face with absolute awe, deep inside her gorgeous blue eyes, seeking a union of souls to join them together. Helena discovered a sexual self she hadn't realised she possessed, with Stephen encouraging her all the way.

Jointly experiencing orgasm, they lay back in each other's arms and, without uttering a word, became aware that a threshold had been crossed between them, and there was no turning back.

The cooked lemon and garlic chicken in the oven was devoured by two hungry mouths. They drank two bottles of red wine between them and then went to bed, snuggling in each other's arms, experiencing blissful deep sleep – sensuously dreaming of their love.

Darling Stephen,   *2 April 1983*

Today was a bright sunny day and you were in my thoughts continuously. When I think of your smile I go weak at the knees, and when I think of your arms around me and you kissing my neck I get dizzy in the head – I'd better sit down before I fall down!
I was just thinking that I've dedicated my life to building a career in music and yet I would not be truly happy unless I could have both you and a successful career. Just a successful

career would be meaningless on its own. Since you have come into my life my cello playing has so much more life and joy. – There is a new spontaneity – that special something that cannot be learned, only experienced, but it's hard to put into words those exhilarated feelings.

Surely there must be a way for me to stay in England, and I can only cross my fingers for something to develop.

I love you so much, with a passion that reaches deep into my soul, but with a simplicity that is perfectly natural. I don't have to show you my love – it's just there. A fact like the sky is blue. The thing that astounds me the most is that my love for you is not possessive. Whilst I miss you, I can be content with the warmth of the memory of when we are together. I want you and need you, though possibly I may never get to have you, but I can be satisfied in knowing that you really exist – that you are a dream come true.

With this letter I'm sending you lots of kisses and a big hug – I can't wait to see you

Love

Helena

Stephen was back at work in Dublin – reading Helena's letter whilst having a coffee. The post arrived in Lower Leeson Street just as he was leaving the flat, so he grabbed it from the postman and stuffed it into his pocket. The letter overwhelmed him with its heartfelt sentiments and proclamations of love. He felt the same way about Helena and had to kick himself to believe that this love had unexpectedly come into his life. However, part of him felt nervous that it had gotten serious so quickly – putting his mind in turmoil about how the future for them would pan out as she lived in New York, whilst his life was in England and Ireland. And although they were both part of the classical music world, their career trajectories were very different. Helena was a young talented cellist trying desperately to break into a position in a leading orchestra, or even to try her luck as a soloist. This meant travelling to wherever an engagement happened to be, or living in a country where a particular orchestra that engaged her was based. Stephen, on the other hand, had no ambition to work outside the British Isles and would only accept work from one of the UK's or Ireland's opera houses. And being financially secure with family money meant he wished to take his career at a pace he was comfortable with. And certainly, if Helena became a famous soloist travelling the world, he had no wish to become her agent or even worse, her bag carrier.

But maybe he was jumping ahead too quickly. He told himself to let things take their own course and that they should just see each other as much as possible before Helena went back to New York.

'Hello – is that Helena Mentones?' the male voice announced on the telephone.

'Yes – it's Helen speaking.'

'Oh, hi, – this is Keith Foes here. Remember I introduced myself as an artist's agent to you at the Tortelier master-class where you played the Elgar cello concerto and I was mightily impressed.

Helena, surprised and a bit flustered, responded. 'Yes of course I remember you and thank you for calling.'

'Helena, um... for how much longer will you be staying in London?'

'Hmm –I'm not quite sure. But why do you ask?'

'Well, if you could stay on until early May, I could have an engagement for you – would you be interested?'

Helena was now really flustered and excited about a possible performance, but the first thing that entered her head was that this was a chance to stay longer in London and have more opportunities to see Stephen. 'What's the engagement?' blurted out Helena trying to stay calm and sound professional.

'It's the Bocca String Quartet and they are scheduled to play Schubert's great string quintet in C major at the Wigmore Hall on the tenth of May, and as you may know – the Schubert quintet, unlike the Mozart's string quintets with an extra viola, Schubert's is scored for a standard string quartet plus a second cello. Unfortunately, Janet Shall, the British cellist, has been involved in a car accident and is unable to perform for a couple of months. The Bocca's, who I represent, have asked me to urgently find a replacement. I racked my brains but all the cellists on my roster were unavailable – and then I thought of you. What do you think?'

Helena, trying to control her excitement, shot back. 'Of course, Mr Foes, I would be delighted to step in and actually I've played the second cello part of the quintet in a student performance. 'But quickly adding – 'I'm really sorry to hear about Janet Shalls' accident, and please convey my best wishes to her'

The rest of the call was spent chatting about the practicalities of arranging for Helena to meet the quartet and to discuss rehearsal dates.

Helena telephoned Stephen immediately to convey her excitement about her upcoming totally unexpected Wigmore Hall debut and the equally good news that she was staying on in London for at least another month.

'That's wonderful Helena, and I will definitely be there for you – booking a ticket at the hall as soon as we're off the phone!'

She then telephoned her parents in New York gushing about her lucky break, and they were absolutely thrilled for her.

Once Helena had calmed down and had absorbed the seriousness of the undertaking she had just agreed to, she realised that between now and the concert date she would be totally absorbed in relearning her part in the quintet and attending rehearsals with her new musical colleagues – so all thoughts of spending the month in Stephen's arms would be out of the question – but he said he would be there at the concert, and that was wonderful!

Hi Stephen   13 April 1983

I'm sitting in the little French cafe at Shepherd's Bush, where we went together when you were in London. I'm looking at the empty chair across from me, and wishing, like crazy, that you were here. It's funny, the time is going both slowly and quickly – don't ask me to explain that one! When not absorbed in Schubert – all I can think about is seeing your face and being in your arms – kissing you etc. – etc. – etc. The end of this note has been censored!
Love to you,
Helena

Darling,   18 April 1983
I have just read your letter and it is with tears of joy that I express my reaction.

There are no words to express the throbbing heart and tingling spine – the pure emotion that is running down my cheeks.
Stephen, you are the love of my life. Yes, it is true, and I want to shout it to the world. I have found home and heavenly rest, and I am satisfied.

By the time you receive this I'll be on my way to be in your arms.

Love

Helena

Despite Helena spending every hour of the day either practising the Schubert quintet or rehearsing with the Bocca String Quartet, she reasoned that she had earned a short break to visit Stephen in Dublin without taking her cello with her. They enjoyed a magical few days together before Helena returned to her cello and Schubert back in London. The weekend with Stephen was so joyful that it enhanced her cello playing, which even the Boccas' noticed – the leader/first violinist at the rehearsal, following the weekend away, made a comment that he had noticed that Helena was playing with more assurance and passion. Helena blushed but did not enlighten them about her love life.

Hi Stephen   3 May 1983

Just one week to go before the concert next Tuesday and six more days to wait for us to be together again! I'm nervous and excited about the concert but so thrilled that you'll be in the audience, so I'll be playing especially for you, conveying all my love through the music.

Talking on the phone with you yesterday was such fun. I love laughing with you – you put a smile on my face and fill my heart with joy.

Monday won't get here fast enough; I'm going to have to practise non-stop to make the time go quickly.

I can't stop thinking of you for even a second – as the song goes, "I've got you under my skin."

See you soon - love,

Helena

On the concert day, Stephen accompanied Helena to the Wigmore Hall and she introduced him to her new musical colleagues and to the revered long-standing artist director of the hall, William Lyne. The Bocca String Quartet played string quartets by Haydn and Dvorak in the first half of the concert, with Helena sitting it out alone in the artist's room with a study of the score, checking the tuning of her instrument – making sure she remembered all the intricate details of the second cello part of the Schubert quintet.

Stephen enjoyed the first half of the programme and thought the Boccas' were a superb ensemble. The four musicians were listening and responding to each other, and the Haydn was played with verve and imagination – bringing out the composer's sophisticated and witty writing, whilst the Dvorak captured the music's wonderful lyricism and bohemian atmosphere. He went backstage to wish a nervous Helena luck and to re-assure her that she would be a great success.

The Schubert is a long piece in four movements with the most heavenly second slow movement; the second cello giving the quintet that extra depth the music demands. It's one of the great masterpieces of the chamber music repertoire. It contains Schubert's composing hallmark of moving from joyous lyricism to tragic depths of despair in an instant, which can be quite disconcerting to audiences. The musicians need to convey the sudden change of moods without disrupting the overall structure of the whole piece. The Boccas' and Helena captured these mood changes admirably and moved smoothly from the serious first two movements to the more cheerful moods of the latter movements, ending the finale with a flourish depicting great joyfulness. Helena was a bit nervous at first but gradually grew into the ensemble as the quintet progressed, and by the end it felt like an established quintet and not a quartet with an added guest artist.

Backstage was all hugging, backslapping and congratulations. Musician friends and family of the quartet mingled with William Lyne and his team as well as fans of the quartet seeking autographs of the quartet members. Everyone was on a high following the enthusiastic applause and some cheering from the packed hall, with a section of audience giving the artists a standing ovation. Helena was very much part of the scene, the Boccas' making sure that she was being introduced to everyone in the room – She received accolades for her performance and was thanked for saving the show by stepping in late in the day, due to Janet Shalls' accident. Stephen, having kissed and hugged Helena, telling her how proud of her he was, stayed out of the limelight, not wanting in any way to overshadow all the attention Helena was receiving.

Stephen observed how different Helena seemed there in the artists' room, as up until then, he only knew her as a younger woman full of passion and love but perhaps a little unworldly. Here he saw her in a professional environment – where she was full of confidence and self-assurance. He also realised what a good musician she was and he could envisage a great future career ahead for her.

Amongst the crowd surrounding the musicians was the agent Keith Foes, who approached Helena and who was full of praise for her playing and thanking her profusely for digging him out of a hole by agreeing to the engagement. He then mentioned the long-standing musical competition in Munich, named ARD, which started in 1952 and suggested Helena applied for the following year.

'Did you know that the Great Russian cellist, Natalie Gutman, won first prize in 1967? I know you hugely admire Gutmans' playing.'

'Yes I do absolutely adore her playing' replied Helena.

'I'll tell you what' said Keith. 'If you win a prize at ARD next year, I would invite you onto my roster of artists and that would ensure you received lots of engagements, both concerto and recital gigs.'

'Thank you Keith and I'll have a serious thought about applying for ARD.'

Helena drifted back to the others in the room and thought that Keith was full of himself. If he had immediately offered her a place in his agency she would have jumped at it, but if she became a prize winner at ARD, or especially if she won first prize – lots of agents would be chasing after her!

Stephen took Helena for a late celebration dinner at the famous Ivy restaurant, indulging in champagne and oysters followed by lobster spaghetti and finishing with an apricot soufflé. Helena was telling Stephen about the ARD competition and Keith's proposal – mocking the agent for his arrogance. Stephen was thinking that perhaps he had misjudged Helena, as she was certainly not sounding at all unworldly in her description of Keith.

Their lovemaking that night was more tender than passionate – Stephen thinking that all of Helena's passion had gone into Schubert that evening, which he totally understood. He smiled to himself at his good fortune in having met Helena.

Stephen came from a very old establishment and wealthy family going back to Edinburgh in the late nineteenth century as incredibly successful soap manufacturers. The family moved down to Suffolk and bought the 7,500-acre Rudbourn Park near the beautiful small town of Orford by the rivers Alde and Ore. A 1,200-acre part of the park that had a group of redbrick farm houses which were converted into contemporary homes in the 1950s and became the Filleswood Lodge Estate. The Zandors' family lived in the biggest house on the estate and sold off the other houses to well-to-do Suffolk families. The properties became extremely well sought after and, when one came onto the market, they were auctioned off to the highest bidder, but the Zandors' had the final say to who the buyers of the properties were. They had to be the right sort of people with proper English accents.

Stephen's childhood was very privileged indeed – going to the best local prep school and then on to Eton College as a boarder.

However, he found it all a bit stifling with very set ideas about society and politics. Unlike his two older brothers, Stephen questioned the family's superior attitude towards people who had been less fortunate than themselves. His father Kenneth hated the Labour party and took an automatic dislike to anyone who had voted for them. Kenneth was a Margaret Thatcher supporter through and through and praised her to the sky – he particularly celebrated her victory in the 1982 Falklands war.

Kenneth was not really interested in music but owned a box at the Royal Albert Hall in London. However, the only annual concert he attended with his wife, Mary, was the *Last Night of the Proms*. There they would be in their box waving madly their Union Jack flag and singing in their loud voices, "Rule Britannia" and "Land of Hope and Glory."

At Cambridge University, Stephen came into contact with budding orchestral conductors such as John Eliot Gardiner and Andrew Davis, and although they were both a few years older than Stephen, he hung onto their coat-tails somewhat as a sort of follower and they both inspired him into music – although he had never learned to play an instrument as a child, much to his regret. The two musicians were kind to Stephen and encouraged him to study music, even if he didn't play an instrument. They made him believe that he could be involved professionally in the musical world in various ways, either in arts administration or as a writer/critic on music. The second option appealed to Stephen as he was reading English and history at Cambridge, and it was a natural enough development to add music theory and music history to his curriculum studies.

Helena spent another weekend with Stephen in Dublin which was gloriously happy but also sad – not knowing when they would be seeing each other again. Following the success of the concert with her London debut noted positively in the musical press, no other engagements followed and she was unable to afford to stay on in London, and as her parents were expecting her to fly home to New York. Stephen promised to visit her there but was vague on specifics. There were tears, hugs, kisses and proclamations of undying love at Dublin airport on Sunday evening as they reluctantly parted, not wanting to let each other go.

As Helena headed through the departure gates she proclaimed in a loud voice 'I love you' with Stephen responding in kind. Other passengers had noticed the love birds and were smiling at them with typical Irish curiosity, and perhaps silently wishing them well.

A week later, Helena, with her cello, boarded a flight from London's Heathrow airport back to New York.

Chapter 6 - SCENE ONE

North London, 1950

When Simon Negrini left Greenshead Boarding School under a cloud if not in outright disgrace, and wholly uneducated in all subjects except Hebrew, religious matters and Jewish history, he needed to find employment; although only aged fifteen, his mother was struggling financially and he felt obliged to help pay for his keep. He noticed an advert in the local newspaper, which was delivered free of charge to their home, for a showroom assistant to a clothing manufacturing company in Eastcastle Street, just off Oxford Circus, which was the main area of the clothing trade wholesale businesses.

Simon bucked up the courage to telephone the company and spoke to a young lady who took his address details etc. and said she would send out an application form. Simon's mum helped him complete the form and he posted it back, with the two references requested, to the company, without much hope of getting a response. But that nice young lady telephoned Simon and arranged an appointment to see the boss, a certain Mr Carl Warringson.

Simon was ushered in to see Mr. Warringson by the same young lady introducing herself as Sharon. Carl Warringson was sitting at his mahogany desk with his feet up on the desk and a big fat cigar in his mouth. The first thing Simon noticed was Mr Warringsons' well-shod feet in expensive-looking black brogues.

'Sit down young man,' said the gruff voice, a mixture of New York Bronx and a broad London accent – his face hiding behind his feet and cigar. Not polite enough to stand up to welcome

Simon or to shake his hand, he continued with, 'Well sonny boy – what brings you here today?

 'Well, sir, I responded to the advert for a showroom assistant in the local paper and here I am.'

'And what do you know about the ladies clothing business?'

'Hmm, to be honest sir, I don't know anything about it, I just need a job to earn some money to help my mum, but it seems to me that it could be a very interesting trade to become involved with.'

Mr. Waringson took his cigar out of his mouth and his feet off the desk and stared at Simon – seeing him for the first time. He continued to stare for a couple of minutes, making Simon feel very uncomfortable. Finally, he said, 'I approve of a young lad trying to support his mother, and you look OK, you won't frighten off the customers in the showroom.'

 'Thank you, sir,' Simon muttered.

'You can start next Monday morning; the hours are eight till six – five days a week plus the occasional weekend morning. You will get two weeks' holiday a year plus Bank Holidays. The pay is three pounds a week minus tax and National Insurance, to be reviewed annually. Any serious misdemeanours and you'll be dismissed on the spot; any questions?'

 Simon was in a state of shock having not expected such a quick definite outcome and couldn't take it all in. 'Yes, sir, and thank you so much.'

'Good – and by the way, don't call me sir, it's not the bloody civil service here; we're in the clothing business which is an informal environment, so you can address me as Mr Carl – everything understood?'

'Yes, Mr Carl, and thank you again for giving me a chance.'

'OK sonny – off you go then.' Carl put the cigar back in his mouth and ushered Simon out of his office.

Simon slowly settled into his job, learning all about the ladies clothing business and trying to keep out of Mr. Carl's way. Sharon Welver, the girl who had been his first contact there, befriended and shielded him from the older senior staff that treated him more like a schoolboy than a work colleague. Sharon, although only eighteen years old, tended to touchingly mother Simon and ticked off anyone in the company who tried to bully him.

Simon spent his first year learning all about fabrics and carried big bales of cloth from the warehouse up to the design room on the second floor for the pattern cutters to do their work on them. He rarely saw an actual finished item of clothing – Mr Carl deciding that he was too young to be seen in the showroom with clients. Carrying heavy cloth worked up Simon's muscles as his body slowly changed from a boyish extremely slender figure to a young man's developing taut frame, although he remained on the slim side all through his twenties and thirties. He enjoyed his work and had a good eye for colour and matching fabrics together.

Socially, Simon was rather awkwardly placed, as most young people of his age were either still at school or at some sort of technical college. Although he was shedding his religious lifestyle and core religious beliefs, his mother suggested he join the local synagogue which was around the corner from their Chalk Farm flat. Simon wasn't keen; he felt he'd had enough synagogues to last a lifetime. But his mum explained that the local synagogue was modern in a nice airy building and, although religious-wise it was conservative, it was totally different from either his grandfather's hasidic chaotic shtiebel in Stamford Hill or the fanatically religious austere Greenshead set-up he had just escaped from. Besides, they had lots of singing with a choir and a proper cantor. The singing aspect sold it to Simon and he agreed to give it a try one Sabbath morning.

So sheepishly, Simon slipped into the back row of the ground floor men's section of the synagogue during the Sabbath service. (The women were congregated separately on the upper floor.) His mother had been right – it was a pleasant modern brick building – a bit like a small contemporary theatre, and it had none of that stale and depressing atmosphere of the ultra-orthodox synagogues. Opposite the upper floor women's section was a small choir gallery situated just above the ark where the Torah scrolls were held. There were about half a dozen teenage boys in the choir but they weren't very good, singing, the responses to the prayers out-of-tune and not singing together. But Simon liked some of the tunes and joined in with the choir and the congregation in the responses. Then it was the cantor's turn to sing solo in the most important prayer of the service. As soon as the cantor began singing Simon experienced a total transformation of body and mind – a feeling of contentment and happiness that he had never felt before. This man's singing was so beautiful – he did not want him to stop. When the solo ended Simon had to leave the synagogue as he was so shaken up with what he had just heard. He needed some fresh air and he wanted that sound to stay with him forever. Those five minutes or so of singing were a complete epiphany for Simon, and it was the start of a journey that would take him to new unknown worlds.

'You're back early,' Louise Feltstein, (Simon's mum having reverted to her maiden name after the death of her husband) was surprised to see Simon home far too early to have experienced the whole Sabbath service including the *kiddush* at the conclusion where drinks (whisky or soft drinks) with trays of smoked salmon and salted herring on biscuits would be available in the ante-room of the building.

'No, mum, it's not what you think – I quite enjoyed the service, although the choir left something to be desired. It consisted of a few lads – mainly larking around. But who is the cantor?'

'Oh, you mean Reverend Flackter, who is popular amongst the congregants with his sweet tenor voice as well as being a nice friendly man?'

'... Sweet tenor voice! No – no, mum – the voice I just heard in the synagogue was absolutely glorious. It gave me feelings I've never had before so I had to leave – with that man's voice still ringing in my ears. What's a man with such a voice doing in a small backwater synagogue like ours?'

'It seems that Flackter had some problems with the Italian authorities during the war due to being Jewish which impeded his opera studies, so when he and his wife fled to Britain, he switched from opera to becoming a *chazzan.* But the gossip amongst the synagogue ladies is that he's not particularly religious.'

'I couldn't care two hoots whether he's religious or not,' Simon responded – more belligerent in tone than he meant to be.

'Just join the choir and you'll get to know him,' said his mum, 'and you may even help them to sing better. After all, you have a nice budding tenor voice and they're desperate for new recruits.'

'OK' said Simon, 'at the end of the service next week I'll approach him and introduce myself.'

It so happened that Simon had to work on the following two Saturdays – as it was the time of year for showing the new fashion collections, and he was tasked with ensuring that the showroom and offices were kept in a tidy ship-shape order, ready for clients arriving on the Monday – when Simon was banished again to the warehouse, out of sight of the clients who turned up in over-dressed flashy outfits with lots of jewellery on their person and wearing very strong perfume. The last thing they wanted to see was a geeky adolescent boy hovering around the showroom, as they were expecting to see equally glamorous people presenting the collection. It was all part of the theatre of the fashion business.

Having been unable to keep Reverend Flackter's voice out of his head, Simon was impatient to get back to the synagogue and hear that voice again. But when his next free Saturday came around and he went to the synagogue Simon was nervous about approaching the *chazzan*. The voice got to him again and transported him into another world – it wasn't religious or even spiritual, but it brought out something in himself that he didn't even know he possessed. It was an inner sensation of feeling that he had become the music itself whilst listening to the exquisite voice.

'So you're Louise Felsteins' son,' said Reverend Flackter once Simon had backed up enough courage to introduce himself at the *Kiddush* following the conclusion of the service.

'Yes I am but my name is Simon Negrini, which was my late father's surname – my mother uses her maiden surname.'

Flackter creased his forehead – looking surprised and curious – suddenly taking a real interest in the young man standing before him with a glass of orange juice in his hand.

'Did you say Negrini? –'N-E-G-R-I-N-I?' said Flackter spelling out the name back to Simon.

'Yes Reverend Flackter – that's how my name is spelt.

'So you have an Italian background?'

'Well – my parents were born in England and my grandparents on my mother's side originate from Poland; however, my late father's family may have had Italian ancestry, but I don't know much about the Negrini side of the family.'

'My dear young man, I would love to have a longer chat with you, but now I need to say hello to other members of the congregation. Please come and visit me at home one evening – I only live around the corner in the Eton Rise block of flats – number ninety six. What about next Wednesday evening, say eight pm?'

 'We're in the adjoining block –Eton Place – so yes, I'll pop in to see you on Wednesday'. They shook hands with the standard greeting 'good *Shabbos*' as Flackter moved away to greet other congregants.

The following Wednesday evening Simon visited Reverend Flackter as arranged. He was greeted with a big smile as he was ushered into the living room.

'Please sit and make yourself comfortable.'

A lady, who looked somewhat older than Flackter, entered with a tray of tea and cakes and was introduced as his wife. Mrs Flackter, with a distinctive foreign accent and bright ginger hair, told Simon that his mother was a really nice woman and that she was delighted to meet her son. The two of them exuded friendliness and warmth in the manner of European *gemutlichkeit.* Simon liked them both and felt relaxed in their company.

'Your name is interesting' said Flackter, once tea and tasty honey cake had been taken with small talk about living in the area and how convenient it was being near the Chalk Farm underground station and a good selection of buses. 'I studied with a famous operatic tenor, Alessandro Bonci – who was a rival to the great Enrico Caruso, but with a sweeter voice. He was an exponent of the Italian singing style *bel canto*. Boncis' teacher was the operatic composer Carlo Pedrotti, whose best friend was one of Verdi's favourite tenors,' Carlo Negrini – yes Simon, your name-sake.'

Simon was all ears as Flackter continued. 'Verdi chose Negrini to create the role of Gabriele Adorno in the original version of *Simon Boccanegra* in 1857. Unfortunately, Negrini died at the age thirty-nine; we know he was married but don't know if the couple had any children.'

Simon was fascinated by all this information, especially about the tenor with the same surname, but the opera stuff went well over his head. Simon changed the conversation trying to explain to Flackter the extraordinary effect his singing in the synagogue had had on him. Flackter was of course flattered and invited Simon to audition for the synagogue choir. It was agreed that Simon would stay behind after the service on Saturday and Flackter would hear Simon sing something of his choosing to ascertain his suitability for the choir.

Simon said his goodnights and thanked Mrs. Flackter for the tea etc. He went back home with a thought at the back of his mind, feeling conscious of a whole new world opening for him. And unlike the strict religious world – this was a world he wished to learn about and fully embrace.

As Louise had implied, Simon had a pleasant young tenor voice and Flackter was delighted when he auditioned him and welcomed him into the synagogue choir with open arms. Flackter had seen something in Simon and sensed that he was hungry for knowledge about music in particular, but also about the arts in general. He suggested to Simon that he attend evening classes and highly recommended Morley College in south London.

Simon took to singing in the choir like a duck to water – learning all the songs and prayer responses with relish, and even in time becoming familiar with Flackters' own solo renditions, but never tiring of listening to the *chazzan's* exquisite sweet singing voice. Simon made friends with the other boys in the choir who were from the same neighbourhood around Chalk Farm and were all of a similar age. Of the eight boys he became especially close to, two of the boys both lived in Constable House – the block of flats directly opposite Eton Place.

The two boys were polar opposites. Frank Bamberg, who was tall with thick, wild, long dark brown hair and prominent facial features, was loud and full of jokes; not the brightest kid on the block – but great to be around. He never worried about embarrassing himself and got himself into various scrapes, especially with girls. Ian Monte, was a small thin boy with a dark swarthy complexion, and by contrast, was quiet and pensive with a terrific brain and doing brilliantly at school – always having a serious book on his person. In later life Frank made a career of being an Elvis Presley impersonator, whilst Ian became a professor of English literature and a specialist in the novels of James Joyce. Frank introduced Simon to Saturday night dance clubs in Finchley Road where one tried to meet girls, whilst Ian advised Simon on books to read, and the two of them attended Arsenal Football Club at Highbury on a Saturday afternoon, when the club was playing at home, and Lords Cricket Ground in St John's Wood, for Test Match cricket during the summer months. The three lads remained close friends throughout their teenage years and well beyond.

Chapter 6 – SCENE TWO

London and Paris 1954

Four years on from Simon starting work he was making great progress. As a nineteen-year old he had lost his geeky adolescent appearance; facial spots had disappeared and his body had filled out. And because of his history of asthma, he was ineligible for National Service. He had regular promotions at work and the boss, Carl Warringson, started to take a real almost fatherly interest in Simon's development in the company. Simon was now looking after clients in the showroom and the clients liked him, with his quiet sincere demeanour, ever smiling with good eye contact and being a good listener. He also became involved in developing a wholesale side to the business. So instead of manufacturing all the clothes, readymade collections were brought in from designers in Paris, Dusseldorf and Milan. And for High Street clothing ranges – small factories and showrooms were visited in Paris and the twice-yearly fashion exhibitions were attended in Dusseldorf.

Initially, Simon attended the various shows and factories as Carl Warringsons' assistant – basically his bag carrier. Simon's role was to listen and learn from Warringsons' ability to pick the most saleable garments and to negotiate the best prices. Simon admired his boss's professionalism and was determined to be allowed eventually to visit the shows himself as the buyer.

The evenings in the various cities were weird in the sense that Simon was left to his own devices, staying in a modest two-star hotel whilst Carl Warringson always booked himself into the most expensive hotel in town and dined in the best restaurants. Simon was given a small allowance for meals whilst his hotels were charged directly to the London office. Although Simon spent the evenings on his own, Mr Carl generally had company with him. For most foreign trips, his receptionist, Sharon Welver, who had been so helpful to Simon, accompanied Carl and stayed with him at the luxury hotels. Although Sharon was a twenty two year old unattached young lady, Carl was a forty four-year-old married man. To make matters worse, Sharon was friendly with Shelley, Carl's wife. Simon was unhappy about the situation, especially as he was fond of Sharon and thought she was making a bad mistake having an affair with her boss, old enough to be her father. But Simon had been sworn to secrecy and kept his thoughts about Carl and Sharon to himself.

One evening in Paris following a busy day visiting factories and wholesale showrooms, Mr. Carl invited Simon to join him for dinner at the famous Hotel Maurice as Sharon was feeling unwell and would not be joining Carl for dinner on that particular evening. Simon was delighted to be invited and was looking forward to experiencing haute cuisine which would be a real step-up from his usual cheap lonesome bistro dinner. In the glorious ornate restaurant with beautifully dressed waiters and formal service Carl ordered for Simon and they tucked into langoustine, duck al la orange and peach soufflé and shared a bottle of a 1945 vintage Chateau Petrus. Simon resisted the offer of a cigar and a large cognac, but Carl was in an expansive mood following his third cognac.

'Would you like to have children one day?' Carl suddenly asked Simon.

'I haven't really thought about it, Mr Carl.'

'Unfortunately, Shelley is unable to conceive as I would love to have another child'

'I wasn't aware that you had a child, Mr. Carl.'

'Oh yes' Simon. My daughter, Marie – let me think – is now age eleven, but we're estranged from each other.'

Simon nodded with interest at this revelation but remained shtum, not quite knowing how to respond, but it seemed that Carl didn't really want a conversation with Simon. The alcohol consumption had freed his inhibitions and he just wanted someone to listen to his stream of consciousness.

'Well, Simon, you know that I'm now a wealthy man, but I don't come from a rich family. My parents from The Bronx in New York were working-class people, who financially, suffered terribly during the 1930s great depression.

'Although as a young man I always wanted to go into business, the opportunities were just not there, so I joined the army. When the US entered the Second World War at the end of 1941, I was posted to London. As an older GI in his early thirties, I had a whale of a time dating young English girls who not only loved the American boys but who were particularly attracted to a mature man like me. I met Marie's mother in a London bar one Saturday night. Wendy Ritage, aged twenty-six at the time, was working as secretary in the Ministry of Defence and had moved up to London from a small village in Cornwall, where she was brought up; her parents and siblings remaining in Cornwall throughout the war years, and then beyond.

'Wendy, a lovely-looking and intelligent girl, became my regular date in London, and we had great fun together. London was an exciting place to be during the war years, even, or perhaps because of, the threat of being bombed. We were all full of adrenaline – not knowing if we would still be alive the next morning.

'Anyway, to cut a long story short, I got Wendy pregnant and I promised to marry her. But then I met Shelley at a tea dance at the Cafe de Paris in London's Piccadilly where I'd gone reluctantly with a friend – on a day that Wendy was meant to have off, but at the last minute she was told that due to an emergency officers' meeting she was needed in the Ministry.

'Shelley, as you know, Simon, was part of a very successful clothing manufacturing business, but during the war, was working as a nurse in a London hospital. Age twenty-four and single, Shelley was seeking a husband and I fell instantly in love with her. I knew straight away that my love life was going to get extremely complicated. Although I had agreed to marry Wendy because of the pregnancy, I was not seriously in love with her. She had been great company on nights out in Soho, but was basically a country girl, who, after the war, would wish to go back to her Cornish village. I was a city animal, and also eager to get into business, Shelley possibly being my passage into that world. Besides, the clothing business was my first choice of sectors that I wanted to get involved in as my dad worked in the industry as a pattern-cutter before losing his job in the depression.'

Simon, listening to Carl, was feeling uncomfortable with his boss trying to justify his behaviour towards Wendy and, although professing his love for Shelley, was here at this magnificent hotel with his young secretary in bed upstairs in his room.

Following a puff of his cigar and a large gulp of his cognac, he continued…'Wendy was devastated and I felt extremely guilty when I told her that I had fallen in love with someone else. Wendy would not contemplate an abortion and decided to have the baby. As it was wartime, she was not allowed to quit her job but negotiated a six-month leave – three months before the birth and three months after. Her family and friends in Cornwall supported her and she gave birth to Marie at her parents' home with the help of a local midwife. I was legally cut out of my daughter's life much to my devastation, but I understood why Wendy made that decision. I gave her a beautiful 18-carat white gold bracelet which I had inherited from my grandmother who came from a well-off family, but her life changed when she married my working class grandfather, but that's a whole other story for another day.

Financially, I did what I could at the time, but I was only on basic GI salary. However, as I started to make money, I increased the allowance substantially, which I kept paying even after Wendy married a local man. I would love to be able to have contact with Marie, but that's the price I've paid for treating Wendy so badly.'

Simon looked at his watch and saw that it was past midnight, and he had to get back to his hotel –which was about a twenty-minute walk away, so he thanked Carl profusely for an amazing dinner, stood up, shook Carl's hand and departed. Carl finished his cognac – called over the waiter to sign the bill and went up to his room. Sharon was fast asleep so he crept quietly into the king-size double bed. He wasn't tired as his head was full of what he had told Simon about himself, but deep in his thought process he knew that he had behaved disgracefully to both Wendy and Shelley. He had used both women for his own desires – sexual desire with Wendy and the desire to weave his way into Shelley's family and take over their business.

Back in London Simon resumed his life's routine – working during the day, and most evenings attending Morley College studying music. Since the original meeting with the Flackters' four years earlier, he had become close to the lovely, warm and friendly couple, visiting their flat most Sundays and learning from them, not only so much about music but also about theatre, art, history and literature – making up somewhat for his previous lack of a rounded secular education. On the Flackters' advice, Simon took several different courses at Morley which were: piano, music theory, singing, music history and later, when his piano playing improved, conducting. Simon's mum had played the piano as a youngster and there was an out-of-tune piano at his grandparent's house – which Simon used to tinker with during the period they lived there. Their current small flat was too small to house a piano, but Simon was given free rein to the Flackters' upright piano which was in their spare room that wasn't needed as a second bedroom.

Morley College was going through a golden period when Simon enrolled in 1950 as the composer, Michael Tippett was then in his final year as music director, having been appointed in 1940, following on from Gustav Holst. Other famous names associated with the college were the composers Ralph Vaughan Williams and the German soprano Ilse Wolf, who became Simon's singing teacher at the college. Ilse Wolf was a renowned *lieder* singer, who also was an expert in the baroque singing technique years before baroque operas rejoined the standard repertoire in the world's opera houses. Which was great for Simon, as Flackters' expertise and experience was exclusively in the nineteenth century Italian repertory.

Simon's budding tenor voice did wonders for the synagogue choir, and even the cheeky boys started to take the choir more seriously, taking their cue from Simon's enthusiasm for the singing of the sacred service whilst continuing to be totally enchanted by Flackters' sweet lyrical voice. And even more so having got to know him so well personally and realising that he actually was his voice; a sweet, kind and thoughtful man.

The third strand to Simon's then weekly routine was the Saturday night escapade to the local clubs – usually accompanied by Frank Bamberg. On one particular Saturday, Frank was busy dating his latest girlfriend, so Simon went out on his own to the El Toro club on Finchley Road. The club was in a basement with dark lighting, and the recorded music were the pop songs of the day, and because the attendees were mainly eighteen to twenty-year-olds and some as young as fifteen, no alcohol was served – the drink of choice was coke.

Simon was actually pleased to be on his own for a change because Frank could be a bit overwhelming – making inane stupid chat-up lines to the girls – which would make Simon cringe. Funnily enough, although lots of the girls ran a mile from Frank, there was always one girl who liked the tall, big haired and loud-mouth Frank who would disappear with him before the evening was over. Simon wasn't into chat-up lines and would just ask a girl to join him on the dance floor. The music in those days didn't burst one's ear drums so one could start a basic conversation whilst shuffling around the floor. In the slow songs in particular, all one had to do was to exchange names and then cuddle up to the girl. If one was really lucky, one could even get a kiss during a slow number and then politely part at the end of the song. However, when Simon danced a slow number with a girl called Barbara; she sort of stuck with him throughout various quick and slow numbers and even allowed him to buy her a coke. She told Simon that she was sixteen and a trainee hairdresser. She added that she lived just off Finchley Road and asked if he would like to visit her next Saturday night when her parents would be out. Although Simon didn't think Barbara was his type – she was sexy-looking with long blonde hair – and a terrific figure and smelt delicious. Before the end of the evening Barbara handed Simon her address and phone number and asked him to arrive at about 7.30 pm. Her full name was Barbara Conclave.

Simon was a bit nervous on the following Saturday when he rang Barbara's front door bell. What shocked Simon was that Barbara opened the door dressed only in a flimsy dressing gown.

'Were you expecting me?' Simon stuttered.

'Of course, Simon – come in,' said Barbara with a big smile on her face. 'Don't look so worried – Mum and Dad are out until late – so we're on our own and we can have some fun—OK?'

'Sure,' responded Simon, thinking how bold and shameless she was, but nevertheless, her direct approach excited him.

'Take your coat and jacket off and make yourself comfortable.' She led him into the living room, pointing to the settee to sit. The lights were dim and a Frank Sinatra romantic song was playing on the record player. 'I'll be back in a jiffy.' Barbara whispered in Simon's ear with a deep husky sexy voice. 'Why don't you get undressed whilst I get us a drink?'

Simon decided to stay dressed when Barbara left the room. She returned with two glasses of white wine.

'Too shy to undress...? 'Barbara remarked in a mocking tone and started to laugh.

'What do you want us to do?' Simon asked anxiously, but remained excited.

'Take your clothes off and let me see you naked.'

As Simon removed his clothes, Barbara slipped off her dressing gown. Seeing Barbara naked was too much for Simon and he made a lunge forward, grabbing her body and holding her tight.

'Kiss me, Simon.' They kissed and touched each other, both breathing heavily. 'Have you gone all the way before?' whispered Barbara.

'No—, have you?'

'No...but I would like to with you. Have you got any rubber with you?'

'No I never thought of that.'

'Well we better not then.' 'Maybe next time – bring some rubbers with you and we can go the whole way.'

'OK,' said Simon, feeling somewhat relieved as he thought that this was not the girl he wanted to have full sex with – she was far too forward for his taste. They played around with each other for a while before Simon made some excuse of needing to get home. He dressed and kissed Barbara goodbye, saying he would ring her to arrange another rendezvous.

'Goodnight Simon. Phone me soon.'

The following Saturday, Simon went to a different club with Frank and met Felicity Koskie, who two years later became his wife. He never saw Barbara again.

London and Paris 1959

Simon's personal life was in turmoil by 1959 – his marriage to Felicity was over, only having lasted barely two years, and whilst trying to find a suitable flat for himself, he was temporarily living back with his mother at Chalk Farm. However, his musical training was going from strength to strength. He had been attending evening classes at Morley College for nine years – becoming one of the best-known students at the college. His piano playing was now fairly decent – having bought a small upright piano at the Wembley home – now unavailable to him. But being back at his mum's and near to the Flackters' – they welcomed him back at their flat with open arms and gave him access to their piano once again as they had done before his marriage and his move to Wembley. He even rejoined the synagogue choir, having left when he moved away. Simon knew of course that he could never be anything but an amateur pianist, having started learning so late in life. Most professional pianists start piano lessons as small children. He was by then also aware that although he had a pleasant tenor voice and he had become a passionate opera lover, he wasn't good enough to be a professional singer. But what he was hugely attracted to was conducting. He was now in his second year in the conducting class at Morley College and loving every minute of it.

One evening when Simon was practising piano at the Flackters'... he heard a ring of the bell at the front door and when it opened he heard lots of loud greetings and laughter. At the end of his practice session he knocked at the door of the living room and Mrs Flackter shouted, 'Come in, Simon ...come in.'

Simon shyly opened the door gently and slowly moved forward into the room. The Flackters' were both sitting with large smiles on their faces. On the other side of the room sat a distinguished-looking youngish gentleman with stylish coiffure hair, dressed in a dark suit, white shirt and plain tie. All three had drinks in their hands and a plate of delicious looking canapés. The gentleman stood up and came towards Simon with Mrs Flackter doing the introductions.

'Simon, please meet my son, the conductor Sergiu Comissiona.'

The gentleman shook hands warmly with Simon and said in a European accent that Simon couldn't quite place – how pleased he was to meet him, as his mother had written to him about their talented young protégée.

'Please sit and join us for drink,' beamed Mrs Flackter. Simon did as he was asked and was given a small neat whisky, and he helped himself to a canapé. However, he felt he was intruding on a joyous family reunion and as soon as he felt able, he made excuses, thanking them for the drink – then making a hasty retreat back home.

'I didn't know Reverend Flackter had a son? 'Simon asked his mum.

'Well... actually he doesn't,' said Louise. 'The renowned conductor is Mrs. Flackters' son from a previous marriage in Romania. It's a bit of a mystery about her previous life – whether she was widowed or divorced. But she came to Britain as a single person – and met and married Flackter here in London. From what I understand from chatting to Valerie Flackter, Mr Comissiona was the principal conductor of the Romanian National Opera until recently but has now fled the Communist regime and is in the process of emigrating to Israel.

Maybe whilst he's in London you can take some lessons from him?'

'That would be fantastic, mum. I'll mention it to Flackter on Saturday in *shul* after the service.'

Unfortunately, it turned out that Mr. Comissiona was only staying in London for a very short time as he was off to Israel to become the musical director of the Ramat-Gan Chamber Orchestra. But he left a message with the Flackters' that Simon was welcome to contact him in Israel when he had settled down and maybe visit him there when he got around to putting on a master-class for budding conductors. Simon promised himself that he would take up that invitation when the opportunity arose.

At work the following Monday, Mr Carl called Simon into his office and informed him that he would be going on a buying trip to Paris without the boss and having full responsibility for the buying decisions.

'You OK with that Simon? '

'Yes, Mr Carl, I can do that as I've watched you negotiate with the factory owners often enough and I know the type of garments we need for the showroom.'

'Good – I'll give you two-thousand pounds to spend on the frocks. Spend the money over two days of buying – half the funds on day one and the rest on day two. Also, don't try any new factories – just stick to the ones you've been to with me so they will know who you are. On day two during the late afternoon, I've arranged for you to see the autumn range of our regular supplier *La Femme*. Maurice Blanc will bring the range to the Hotel Doree where you will be staying, and I've arranged with the management for you to see the range in one of their private function rooms. But only place orders for dresses you're absolutely sure are right for us and make sure you order a good range of sizes. I'm putting a lot of trust in you – so don't let me down. Oh, I forgot to mention. Sharon Welver will be accompanying you – but strictly no hanky-panky between the two of you,' said Mr Carl, with a wicked smile on his face and a cheeky wink of an eye.

What Mr Carl did not divulge to Simon was that one of their regular Parisian factory suppliers, Chofi Mode was in dispute with Carl Warringson over garments that were returned to the supplier for various faults. Chofi had refused to offer credits – not accepting that the garments were not up to standard. Meanwhile, Warringson, who had re-ordered various popular design lines for his customers, and which were then shipped to London on an invoice basis. Warringson was withholding payment, which was of a considerable amount of money, until a credit note had been received. Was this the reason that Warringson had decided to send Simon to Paris without him, as he didn't want to chance running into Jean Chofi around the wholesale clothing area of Paris?

Sharon, who was no longer having an affair with Carl Warringson, confirmed Simon's suspicions on the matter and concluded that Carl was a coward, but warned Simon not to go into the Chofi factory/showroom as Jean Chofi had a reputation for being somewhat hot- headed and one wouldn't know how he would react if Simon entered his business premises.

Simon and Sharon enjoyed a nice relaxing dinner together after checking into the Hotel Doree – in separate rooms of course. They dined at a fairly modest brassiere near the hotel and shared a rare joint of beef with sauté potatoes and a green salad which was excellent, and a decent bottle of burgundy pinot noir. The bill slightly exceeded their dinner allowance, which in typical Warringson fashion, was on the mean side for everyone except himself where only the very best would do. Simon paid the difference himself and wouldn't hear of Sharon chipping in. There was no romantic inclination between the two, but they were good friends and Simon had always appreciated how Sharon had looked after him when he first joined the company nine years earlier as a boy of just fifteen years of age.

They made an early start the next morning following a quick coffee and croissant breakfast, in the hotel. They went onto the Rue Saint Denis and into various wholesale showrooms that they had been to before with Mr Carl. They were well received by the owners who knew that they were cash buyers. With Sharon's help, Simon chose well. He bought several ranges, paying by cash that had been converted into French francs, and arranged for the goods to be shipped to London over the next few days.

By mid-morning they had bought from three different wholesalers all within a short walking distance from each other. As Mr Carl had instructed, he was not to spend more than £1,000 on the first day, the idea being that he could digest his first day's purchases overnight and be fresh for the next day – to be able to buy different styles and colours that would contrast nicely to his day one purchases. The money spent so far was the equivalent of £800.

'We will visit just one more wholesale showroom this morning looking to spend approx. two-hundred pound in French francs, ' Simon said to Sharon as they were crossing the road to Ettine Mode, another regular supplier in the area.

'That sounds good' said Sharon. 'We can then find a nice place for an early lunch.' I think you've done well so far; I'm sure Carl will be pleased with your purchases.'

'I hope so,' said Simon, not feeling that confident knowing how Mr Carl could be so critical. Etienne Mode was a big showroom comprising one central wide space with little warrens of corridors where the more specialist designs were hanging. Having bought a selection from the mainstream ranges in the centre, Simon asked to see some of the more unusual designs. They were let down a narrow path through a side door into a small room where the clothes were being displayed on long garment rails.

Simon, who wasn't good in small enclosed spaces – suddenly had a feeling of claustrophobic fear. Was he dreaming – or, more frightening – was he having a nightmare? He saw a vision of Jean Chofi lurking in the corner.

'I know you—,' Chofi barked in broken English – pointing a finger at Simon. 'I know that you're part of Warringsons' business and you owe me money,' shouting at Simon in a loud aggressive voice.

Simon tensed and his face was white, drained of blood. 'You need to speak to Mr Warringson, *Monsieur* Chofi,' said Simon in a quiet nervous voice.

'No – you should have visited my showroom with the money' Chofi came threateningly up to Simon, grabbing his lapels with his face almost touching Simon's.

Simon sensed that he was going to be physically assaulted and looked around to protect Sharon – but she had disappeared. As Simon was preparing for the worst outcome of the confrontation, Sharon rushed back into the room with the owner of Etienne Mode, and behind them was a *gendarme* who went towards Chofi, pulling him away from Simon.

The *gendarme* had a quick word with the showroom owner in French, which the owner translated to Simon and Sharon as. 'You two go with the *gendarme* – he will take you to the police station which is just around the corner; come back to do your buying here another time'

Simon and Sharon looked quizzically at each other, not knowing whether they were being arrested or being taken to the police station for their own protection.

'That was quick thinking, Sharon, to go for help.'

'I thought to get assistance when I saw the look on Chofi's face and realised that he meant business and was going to attack you.'

'You did well and I can't thank you enough.'

The exchange took place in the police station, the two of them sitting together on a bench in a corridor of the station. They were told to wait there and they had no idea what was going on. After sitting for about an hour – Chofi came into the police station with a big file under his arm, passing them by without looking in their direction and going into a *gendarme's* office, closing the door.

'Is Chofi, with a file under his arm, trying to pin Warringsons' business debt on us personally?' Simon whispered to Sharon – who shrugged and was beginning to look very glum indeed. It wasn't what she had bargained for accompanying Simon to Paris to help him with his first buying trip abroad without the boss.

'I can't see how a business financial dispute can be confused with any sort of personal theft situation.'

'I know Sharon – but this is France not Britain; Chofi is French after all, and the French authorities don't like the English. Besides....however preposterous it sounds, one can never be certain. We're unaware of what made-up story Chofi has given them.'

About an hour later, Chofi came out of the *gendarme's* office with his file and left the building swiftly – he did not look at all happy. The *gendarme* appeared and said he would escort them out to ensure that they would be safe and that nobody was waiting to attack us outside the station. This he duly did – he shook hands with them and off they went – highly relieved, back towards their hotel.

'Well, that's a relief.' Simon said to Sharon as they were both a bit shell shocked by the whole experience. 'So Chofi was wasting his time trying to get us into trouble with the police, but they realised that it was a corporate disagreement and nothing they needed to get involved with.'

'Yes Simon, that may be true but I was still frightened. Being in a foreign country with a different language, one felt totally out of control'

'I'm really sorry to have put you through this Sharon'– as Simon put his arm around her and gave her a comfort hug.

'I don't want to stay here any longer. I want to go back to London today.'

'Of course ... I understand, Sharon. I'll get onto the travel agent and change your flight. Perhaps it's best if you go straight home and don't go into the office tomorrow – I'll explain everything to Mr Carl when I'm back in London the following day.'

'I think that's a good idea...' said a subdued Sharon. They headed back to their hotel for Sharon to pack her bags, and for Simon to make all the revised travel arrangements.

Chapter 7

Paris and London, 1959

Simon duly arranged Sharon's premature departure from Paris –
apologising again for the trip turning out the way it did – but
thanking her for her quick response to the ugly situation
developing in the Etienne Mode showroom.

Simon felt very down in the dumps as he sat in the bar of the
hotel, but knew he had to sharpen up, as the salesperson from
La Femme was due to arrive at the hotel with his autumn range,
and he would have to be totally focused on picking the potential
winners from all the different samples. A few gin and tonics
would help lift Simon's dejected mood, but not too many to
lose concentration on the job in hand.

In fact, the appointment went as well as it could – the charming
young Frenchman, Maurice Blanc, who spoke perfect English
with his delicious French accent, was really helpful in pointing
out the features of each design, and his advice helped to make
Simon's order choice fairly straightforward.

Following Maurice's departure, Simon ordered another gin and
tonic and decided to have a meal in the hotel dining room
instead of going out to a restaurant.

Simon showered and changed in his room, and wondered what
to do with the £1,000 cash he had left to spend the following
day in various showrooms. The room did not have a deposit
safe – so he thought the most secure place to keep it would be
on his person. He put the cash in the breast pocket of his smart
black jacket, which he wore with a pair of grey slacks. He went
down to the restaurant and was shown to a nice corner table
with a good view of other tables – so he could indulge in a bit
of people watching. He ordered a *Pate Maison* followed by a
rare *Entrecôte* steak with French fries and green beans. He
chose a decent full-bodied bottle of red Bordeaux to accompany
the meal, which drank extremely well.

The food and the wine were having their effect on Simon, and he was beginning to unwind from the tenseness of the bizarre day he had experienced, as he perused the dining room. Glancing to his left, he noticed an attractive young woman eating on her own at the table; his thoughts immediately turned to the possibilities of a little romantic adventure – after all, he was alone in Paris, supposedly the most romantic city in the world. It would just take a bit of courage and cheek to approach the woman.

He got up from his seat and walked over to her table. 'Excuse me, *Mademoiselle* – do you speak English?'

The woman looked up with a smile on her face. 'Yes, I do,' she responded – as Simon took a good look at her. He thought that she was a little older than him. She had an open inquisitive face and long brown hair.

'Well, I'm sorry to disturb you, but I wondered whether you would like to share my wine, as a whole bottle is a little too much for me?'

'That would be very nice.' She looked Simon up and down; she must have approved of him; she immediately asked him to join her at her table, putting out her hand and introducing herself as Simone.

Simon bowed low, took her hand, kissed it, and said that her name was the female version of his – just without the e on the end, 'I'm Simon.'

'That's a good omen' laughed Simone as she gestured for him to bring the wine over and take a seat.

Simon sat and poured for Simone, wiping the glass that he had brought over from his table with a napkin, whilst the *Garson,* observing all of this, immediately appeared with a clean wine glass and a wry smile on his face. The thought went through Simon's head that maybe the *Garson* had sat Simone within sight of him, almost expecting him to make a move. Simon switched glasses and re-poured a glass of wine.

'I'm from Antwerp,' Simone explained 'and I've driven to Paris to spend a few days here to see the sights and maybe have some fun'. On the word fun – Simone gave Simon a flirty grin, looking straight into his eyes.

'Have you travelled here on your own and do you have friends or family in Paris?'

'Yes…to your first question, and no to the second one – I quite enjoy travelling on my own – having no one to please except myself. What about you Simon – what brings you to Paris?'

Without going into detail about the travails of the day, which was now looking decidedly up, he kept his explanation short and straightforward, just saying about it being a ladies' clothes-buying trip as he worked for a London fashion firm.

'And has the buying gone well for you, Simon?'

'Yes thank you, so far so good and with another day to go.'

Simon caught the eye of the *Garson* and indicated to bring another bottle of the wine to the table. Simone described herself to Simon as a lawyer specialising in commercial property – and a single woman living on her own in a nice apartment in the centre of Antwerp. She was originally from the Belgium coastal town of Knokke-Zoute where her family lived; they owned and ran a hotel on the seafront.

As the second bottle of wine was being polished off – Simone suggested that they should go to the Moulin Rouge, somewhere she said she had always wanted to experience and to see the cabaret there, but it was not the place for a woman to go to on her own. However, Simon had heard that the Moulin Rouge was generally an unsafe place to visit and said that he would prefer Lido de Paris on the Champs-Elysees, a much more upmarket nightclub, and that he had been told by his boss that the cabaret there was second-to-none.

'OK Simon - lets go to the Lido.' She put her hand on his and gave it a gentle squeeze.

Simon thought that he had definitely made the right choice as they entered the Lido and a handsome young man in a smart uniform escorted them to a plush banquette with a great view of the show floor. The show was called *Avec Plaisir* (with pleasure) and the girl dancers wore the most amazing costumes and headgear of beautiful flowers, each girl in a different coloured bright dress to suit the complexion of the particular dancer. The cabaret acts were certainly of a high standard and not at all tawdry. Simon ordered drinks – gin and tonics for them both – and he was beginning to feel very relaxed with a heightened sense of how the night might play out with Simone. He took off his jacket and folded it neatly on the banquette. He put his arm around Simone as they watched the cabaret, and as their lips met for a kiss. From the corner of his eye, Simon could see the young man who had served the drinks keeping his eyes on them, which made Simon feel a tad uncomfortable.

Once the cabaret acts had finished, Simon whispered to Simone, 'let's get out of here and go somewhere more intimate.' Simone nodded in agreement. As Simon had paid the entrance fee on the way in and the drinks as they were served, he picked his jacket up – slipped it in on and held hands with Simone as they headed towards the exit.

Neither of them had a clue where to go but instinctively they were both in the mood for somewhere more adventurous and *louche* than the Lido. 'Let's get a taxi,' said Simon, 'and ask him for a recommendation.' Getting into a taxi – Simone started to engage the driver in French. He seemed to know exactly where to take them. Simon leaned back in the seat and touched his jacket – unable to feel his wallet in the breast pocket.

Suddenly he felt a cold sweat breaking out as the realisation dawned that his wallet with all his cash had gone.

'What's wrong?' said Simone, looking at Simon, white-faced and in a distressed state.

'My wallet's been stolen and I had a hell of a lot of cash on me – and now I've no money at all.'

Simon explained to Simone that he did not want to leave his cash in his hotel room, and the reason that he had £1,000 in his wallet at the start of the evening – was for buying stock the following day. Simone's initial reaction was that Simon had been a fool carrying all that money, and even more of an idiot for taking his jacket off at the Lido. It dawned on them both that the waiter must have noticed Simon extracting his wallet from the breast pocket of his jacket whilst paying for the drinks and then taking his jacket off before cuddling up to Simone. He must have sneaked up to the banquette whilst the pair were kissing and slipped his hand quietly into the jacket and walked off with the wallet containing all his cash. They immediately understood that it would be a waste of time going back to the Lido – as the staff would only shrug and deny any accusation of theft. But of course they couldn't be sure it was the waiter – it could have been anyone there, maybe one of the customers, or a professional thief who visits this type of establishment to rob tourists. Alternatively, he could have just accidently dropped the wallet as he was putting his jacket back on. But no, he would have noticed that as it occurred and would have bent down to pick it up.

Simone paid the taxi fare, the driver having deposited them at a sleazy-looking basement club that offered live sex shows. She seemed quite excited at the prospect of watching people having sex, but Simon was too upset about the money to feel anything at all; certainly all his sexual ardour had evaporated. Simone took control and ordered a bottle of wine; Simon knew that he would be unable to settle the bill on leaving the premises and had visions of being physically attacked for the second time on the same day, but this time he would not have a friendly *Gendarme* to come to the rescue. Perhaps they should have gone to the Moulin Rouge after all.

The sex show was truly live with couples having sex right up there on the stage in front of them. The audience of about hundred people was predominantly men, mixed with couples, like the two of them. A few single women were also spotted amongst the watchers with everyone seemingly well behaved, steadily drinking, but nobody there seemed drunk. Following about half an hour of watching the show with everyone totally absorbed in the sexual activities on stage, Simone whispered to Simon that he should discreetly make his exit whilst all eyes were on the stage, and although she had very little money on her, and certainly not enough to pay for the wine as well as for the show, she would negotiate her way out later.

'Are you sure?'

 Simon looked at her with a mix of admiration and perhaps a little fear – as the thought went through his head that maybe she was part of a sting in cahoots with others. But Simon immediately rejected the premise as of course Simone wanted to go to the Moulin Rouge, so she would have had no pre-arranged accomplices at the Lido.

Simon slipped out of the darkened theatre auditorium and building without being noticed, and with some difficulty, he slowly found his way back to his hotel walking all the way. Unable to sleep, he thought about Simone and hoped she got out of the club without problems, and felt guilty leaving her there – but she had been so confident that she would be fine by herself – he had just followed her advice.

They met at breakfast in the morning and Simon noticed that she was wearing the same clothes as the previous night with the white cuffs on her blouse decidedly scruffy. Simone explained to Simon that she had told the club manager that her boyfriend walked out on her during the sex show with all their money and that she was unable to cover the bill. They were a bit sceptical but because she was a French speaker they gave her the benefit of the doubt and even showed her some sympathy that she had been stood up and said that she was better off without that stupid young man.

'I had just enough money on me to pay for a taxi to the hotel and I knew that if you had stayed, not being able to pay would have been really bad for you, as these night club guys could be really violent, but never to a woman.'

'Thank you so much, Simone. I'm in total debt to you for getting out of a mess of my own making.'

'No problem Simon. I just felt sorry for you losing all your money. What are your plans now'?

'Well, my work plans today are obviously cancelled; I will explain everything to the hotel – and phone the London travel agent to re-arrange my flight for today – and to take care of the hotel bill. I will of course have to let my boss know about the money. He will be furious with me.'

'If it helps, I could give you a lift to the airport?'

'That's so kind of you Simone and I'm really grateful for all your help.'

'That's fine, Simon. It was such a shame though that such a promising night turned out the way it did.'

The journey to the airport was uneventful and conversation between them sort of died, both realising that they were just 'ships in the night,' and that the chance meeting between them, that should have culminated in a night of passion, went terribly wrong – all because of Simon's carelessness. They were both honest enough not to exchange contact details, but Simon couldn't thank her enough for getting him out of trouble and for the lift to the airport. He kissed her on the cheek as he alighted from her car – and thanked her yet again. He marched swiftly towards the departure area of Paris-Orly airport without looking back.

The next day, back in London, Simon would have to see Mr Carl and face the music, which he was dreading. The phone call to him from Paris did not go well. Warringson shouted down the phone that Simon would have to pay back the £1,000 to the business from his own pocket and what a bloody fool Simon had been to lose the money.

'He's in a foul mood,' was Sharon's greeting to Simon in reception on his way into the showroom. 'I did try to explain that the Chofi attack was not our fault – and that he should not have sent us to Paris whilst he was in dispute with the Frenchman.'

'But I told you to stay away from Chofis' showroom,' he had screamed at Sharon.

'But we did as you said – and it was just bad luck that we were at Etienne Mode at the same time as he was.'

'Don't bother to sit down,' said Warringson, as Simon entered the boss's office. 'This won't take long. You're fired, and I want the money back. If you can't pay it straight away you can pay it in instalments but there will be interest charges. I want you gone from here today. Collect your personal belongings and get the hell out of my sight.'

Simon was lost for words as he left Warringsons' office, thinking that nine years of hard work and dedication counted for nothing in the boss's eyes – if one careless error was made. But Mr Carl had told him at his initial interview that he would not hesitate to sack him for any misdemeanour, large or small, and to be fair, losing all that money was definitely a major error.

Simon said his goodbyes to all his work colleagues including a special tearful parting and hugs with Sharon, who had been so supportive throughout his time there. They promised each other to keep in touch, but somehow Simon doubted that they would see each other again, and his instincts proved correct in that regard.

Chapter 8

New York 1983

Helene arrived home receiving a great welcome with hugs and kisses from her mum and dad. Uncle Carl was also there in the house and he received a special embrace from Helena. Mr Mentones opened a bottle of champagne to celebrate his daughter's return as Helena recalled many of her experiences in London, especially her unexpected debut at the Wigmore Hall and all the different people she'd met whilst there. She talked about her various trips to Dublin and finding a new boyfriend in Stephen – but she kept the Stephen thing fairly low key and did not divulge the extent, or details, of their newly found passionate physical relationship.

Dearest Stephen   *30 May 1983*

There are so many miles between us but my love for you grows stronger and more intense with each passing day, waiting until I see you next. The nights are very warm and moist, very sensual, and I lie awake at night listening to night sounds and thinking of our passion. How I desire you. My body aches for your touch and my lips want kissing. But my soul is satisfied. This is very unusual indeed. No matter how many miles or days separate us, I still feel as close to you as when we are together. Stephen, I love you so much and nothing can take that away. It's a fact, and love like this will last beyond eternity.

Helena xxx

My Darling,   *14 June 1983*

Last Saturday it was absolute heaven hearing your voice! I was so happy during those few minutes. It was like when we were together even though we were far away from each other. I miss you dreadfully but you are in my thoughts so much and the memory of our love making is as vivid as if you had made love to me last night. Stephen, I love you so much and my thoughts of you keep my heart light and happy.

Darling, I love remembering your caresses, your kisses. The thought of me lying next to you in bed, and feeling the warmth of your body next to mine. I love remembering the weight of your body on top of mine; the hardness of your body pushing the softness of my body apart; the gentle rocking together; the passion and our climaxes with the loveliness of being still afterwards. I never have to fantasise – only to remember.
Loving you always,

Helena x

Stephen was thrilled receiving the love letters from Helena but felt stymied in responding in kind, hence the telephone call to her last Saturday. Helena, steeped in American culture, was very open with her feelings and desires, although at times Stephen sensed innocence behind her full-on outpourings of love and lust. He felt responsible, being older and worldlier than her, for the deflowering of this beautiful young woman, who had given herself to him completely without reservation. Part of him wanted to respond in kind, but his reserved British background held him back and a sense of caution took hold, his head overruling his heart.

About visiting Helena in New York – his mind was made up; he would not go as he was not ready to be scrutinised by her parents as potential son-in-law material, however nice people he was sure they were. And there was this so-called Uncle Carl, hovering in the background, that she had spoken most lovingly of – he sounded a bit weird and wondered what Carl's real relationship with Helena really was. He was well aware that the

Mentones' were not her real parents, having adopted her as a baby.

As expected, Helena took Stephen's decision not to visit her in New York extremely badly, feeling foolish with her parents, as she had made a big issue to them about welcoming Stephen to their home – which they had heartedly acquiesced with.

The letters to Stephen stopped and Helena felt numb and emotionally shattered. She had assumed Stephen's feelings towards her were identical to hers about him, but maybe she had been mistaken and that for Stephen the whole experience had been a beautiful romantic interlude, but not a life-changing happening.

Chapter 9

Paris, 1862

The two young Italian artistic friends, Arrigo Boito and Franco Faccio, were having a whale of a time in Paris, cavorting around the city, making fools of themselves as young people are prone to do when they think that the world belonged to them and that the older generation were completely out of touch. They had been awarded scholarships from the Italian Ministry of Education as well as letters of introduction to famous composers such as Rossini, Berlioz, Gounod and Verdi. Boito was a budding poet who also had ambitions to compose operas, being both the composer and librettist. Faccio was exclusively a musician who was composing an opera with another Italian friend of theirs, Emilio Praga, as the librettist. Boito's feelings towards Verdi were sort of ambiguous. He respected the older man's contribution to Italian opera but thought his music not progressive enough. And Boito's older brother, the architect Camillo, had written a letter to Arrigo from Florence, writing that he had gone to a performance of Verdi's opera *Un ballo in maschera* (*A Masked Ball* –1859) and thought that it was a dreadful opera, written without thought, without knowledge and with no loftiness of concept or manner.

The two young men were presented to Constantino Nigra, ambassador to France. Nigra was tasked with commissioning a musical work for the London Exhibition. He had approached the seventy-four year-old world famous composer, Gioachino Rossini, who had long since retired from writing operas' and was in the last two years of his life. Rossini declined the offer, but suggested to the ambassador that Verdi might be interested, and added that the composer was currently visiting Paris. Verdi had been in St. Petersburg, Russia, for the premiere of his latest opera *La forza del destino (The Force of Destiny)*. Unfortunately, his visit there was unproductive as the premiere of the opera had been postponed for several months because of the soprano's indisposition. So the composer's mood in Paris was on the sour side when he and Nigra met, to discuss the London Exhibition commission. 'Absolutely no way' Verdi growled at Nigra, 'I never accept writing occasional pieces.'

This was not totally true, as Verdi had in 1848, set some patriotic verses by Goffredo Mameli, who had written the words of the Italian National Anthem and was a leading light of the Risorgimento (Rising Again). Mameli tragically died at the age of twenty-one, in 1849. Nigra did not have the courage to contradict the esteemed Verdi, and decided not to remind him of the 1848 musical setting. Taking a different route, Nigra mentioned to Verdi that he had been impressed with the artistic Italian young men currently in Paris, especially Arrigo Boito.

'Unusually, this impressive student is planning to be both a writer and a composer.'

'What a foolish young man.' Verdi sighed. 'Who does he think he is, Richard Wagner?'

'OK,' said Verdi. 'I will meet this young man and see what I make of him.'

When the two of them met, Verdi was impressed with Boito, who spoke to the older man with the utmost respect and showed him due reverence as the leading Italian operatic composer of the day. He made sure to keep his naughty fun side at bay and went all out to show Verdi that he was indeed a very serious young man. This seemed to work and Verdi asked Boito to write a text for a *cantata* suitable for the London Exhibition.

The cantata was *Inno delle nazioni (Hymn of the Nations)*, which was first performed at Her Majesty's Theatre, London, on 24 May 1862.

As a present to Boito for providing the text Verdi bought him a watch which the younger man cherished for many years.

The subsequent problem between Verdi and Boito arose through a *sapphic ode* that Boito had written in 1863, at a gathering of friends, to celebrate the success of his friend Faccio, whose opera, *I profughi fiamminghi,* had recently been premiered. Boito, perhaps having had one glass of wine too many – read out a stanza of the ode to the general gathering:

Forse giù nacque chi sovre l'altare
Rizzera l'arte, verecondo e puro
Su quell'altar bruttato com un muro

 (Perhaps the man is already born, modest and pure, who will set art erected once more on that altar, befouled like a brothel wall.)

This episode came to Verdi's attention through a figure, known to both the composer and Boito, Countess Clara Maffei, who was present at the gathering where the reading took place. It was unfortunate that Verdi had been made aware of the young guns over-confidence in their own abilities, as they, especially Boito, did not intend to launch a personal attack on the older composer, whom he very much admired, but had got carried away amongst friends on that particular evening, wounding Verdi, who was generally thin-skinned, and not someone to take an insult lightly.

Boito's own opera, *Mefistofele,* flopped at its premiere at La Scala Milan in 1868, and his publisher, Ricordi, was also Verdi's publisher. The older Ricordi, Tito, was a huge champion of Verdi; Tito's son, Giulio, although a supporter of Verdi, was a personal friend of Boito and was keen to promote the younger man. Giulio had this idea that Boito should collaborate with Verdi as a librettist. The problem being that Verdi was still holding a grudge against the younger man because of that *ode* reading, even though five years had passed.

It took a further eleven years for a reconciliation between Verdi and Boito to occur; much of the ground-work laid by the redoubtable Giulio Ricordi, who instinctively knew that the two artists were fated to work together to create two of the greatest Italian operas of the nineteenth century, *Otello* and *Falstaff.* Following Verdi's decision to bury the hatchet with Boito, the two men commenced writing to each other, and although they met together occasionally, their artistic collaboration was conducted by letters, and approximately three hundred letters were exchanged between them – up until Verdi's death in 1901.

Before they started to work together on *Otello*, Verdi decided, with Boito's assistance with the text, to revise his 1857 opera *Simon Boccangra.* The revised version premiered at La Scala Milan on 24 March 1881.

Chapter 10

London and Cornwall, 1959

Once Simon Negrini had got over the shock of being fired from his job, and had reassured his mum that he would soon find another one, he actually started to feel a sense of relief that he was now out of the London fashion trade, giving him an opportunity to find employment in a sector more conducive to his burgeoning musical ambitions. It was not that he hadn't enjoyed his nine years working for Carl Warringsons' clothing company, despite the man himself being a complete pain – for a lot of time. And he probably would not have resigned at any stage, because the steady income was crucial, what with paying his mum for his keep and having to pay a regular allowance to Felicity. He knew how important it was to earn money again as quickly as possible, as on top of everything else, he was saddled with the £1,000 debt he owed Warringson for the Paris debacle – and was sure that Mr Carl would insist on his pound of flesh – and expected to be reimbursed to the last penny.

It was Mrs Flackter who came to Simon's rescue, who, through her conductor son, Sergiu Comissiona, had got to know Mandy Lowes, who looked after and nurtured the contemporary composers, at the international music publishing house, Schoffs. Their London offices and musical scores shop was located in Great Marlborough Street, situated between Soho and Oxford Circus – not far from where Simon had worked for the past nine years – but this was a totally different world to the London rag trade area just north of Oxford Circus. Mandy, the daughter of Sir Charles Lowes, chief conductor of The Royal Liverpool Philharmonic Orchestra, was seeking an assistant. Mandy's most famous composer whom she worked with was Michael Tippett, who was becoming one of Britain's most successful composers, following the premiere of his magical opera, *A Midsummer Marriage,* at Covent Garden in 1955. Tippett was a lovely man but very demanding about his scores, writing both the words and the music for his operas, and unwilling to change anything – whatever Mandy or anyone else may suggest.

Mandy and Simon hit it off immediately, and she recommended him to her directors who offered Simon the job, which he was thrilled about – despite the salary being considerably less than what he was earning in the clothing trade.

His life now was totally involved in the musical world; working as an assistant at the publishing house during the day; attending evening classes at Morley College; singing in the Sabbath choir, and special times spent at the Flackters' flat.

Mandy assigned Simon to be useful to Michael Tippett, the composer aged forty-six. Tippett took the young man under his wing and he became exceptionally kind to Mandy's new assistant. Simon became a sort of bag man to the composer, making sure coffee was always on tap when requested – taxis' ordered as required – tables booked for lunch and, most important of all, keeping his manuscripts in good order and having the correct pages ready for Michael to peruse and correct as he, and only he, could deem what was necessary to correct.

Tippett was spending the summer in Cornwall, staying with friends in the tiny coastal village of Portscatho, on the beautiful Roseland Peninsula, and asked Mandy if she could send Simon down for a few days – to help the composer do some preliminary work on his second opera. It was to be based on Homer's *Iliad* and he'd planned to call the opera *King Priam*. Tippetts' friends would not be able to accommodate Simon, but had highly recommended The Rising Sun, a pub with rooms, at the nearby resort of St Mawes.

Mandy had to get authorisation from her directors to finance Simon's trip and, although they huffed and puffed about spending the money, they reluctantly agreed as they did not wish to do anything to jeopardise their relationship with Michael Tippett.

Simon caught the London to Penzance train, alighting at Truro station where Tippett, with another, somewhat younger man in tow, was there to meet him. Following a warm hug from Tippett, Simon was introduced to the other man. His name was John Amis, and he was doing the driving of the convertible Morris Minor car. Off they went for the fifteen mile journey to Portscatho; the two men in the front singing their heads off to some silly old Victorian ditty that Simon half recognised but could not place, whilst he sat in the back of the car admiring the Cornish scenery and loving the fresh air in his face and hair.

The house in Portscatho backed onto the lovely beach. It was an old Victorian house, not over large, with just three bedrooms, and as it was the owner's holiday home, sparsely furnished and plainly decorated. The owners were Mr and Mrs Smythe; Smythe, a stockbroker in the city by profession, was an old friend of Tippett's and considered himself a musical connoisseur. However, John Amis was the actual musical connoisseur, according to Tippett, and seemed quite close to the composer. Tippett let Simon know that John, nine years younger than Michael, was indispensable to him as a musical assistant as well as a dear friend. This information surprised Simon as Tippett had never mentioned the name of Amis in Schoffs' offices, and the thought went through his head – why was Tippett so keen to invite him down to Cornwall if his first-choice assistant was already there with him?

But over the following few days working with the composer at Portscatho, he came to realise that both he and John had plenty to do just keeping Tippett in line, as his brain was incredibly active and his interests were so wide and varied. It was a herculean task encouraging the composer to concentrate on the job in hand; researching the *Iliad* in preparation for writing his new opera. Whilst the work they were engaged with was predominately literary, Tippett let them know that the style of his music for this opera would be totally different from his previous successful opera, *The Midsummer Marriage.* 'Out with the lyricism – this one will be harsh and concise in keeping with the darkness of Homer's tale.' John and Simon looked at each other and rolled their eyes – both with the same thought; 'how will this go down with the conservative opera public?' But Tippett being Tippett, once his mind was made up – nothing on earth would persuade him to change it!

The Smythes' served drinks – gin and tonics – then a light meal of seafood salad – followed by strawberries and cream, with a dry Muscadet wine, before Simon headed off to St Mawes. He'd checked the local bus timetable, not wanting to miss the last bus, as they only ran during daytimes. The atmosphere around the room was light and jolly, until Morgan Smythe started quizzing Simon about his background and musical knowledge.

'You're Jewish...eh?' He sniffed. 'You don't look particularly of the Hebrew tribe.'

'Come on Morgan,' said Tippett. 'Let the young man be.' Ignoring Tippett, Morgan continued, 'So what did you do before working for Schoffs?'

'I worked for nine years in the clothing industry,' said Simon, who was beginning to feel a tad uncomfortable – with Smythes' questioning.

'Do you mean the rag trade?' Morgan retorted in a sarcastic tone of voice, continuing, 'I'm sure that gave you a great grounding for a successful musical career.'

Simon stood up and said he had to catch his bus, and he thanked the Smythes' for their hospitality, picking up his bag and making for the front door.

Michael followed Simon out the door and apologised for Morgan's rudeness. 'It's just his way – he likes to test out new

acquaintances to put them on their mettle; one needs to stand up
for oneself and tell him what's – what. He then won't do it
again. Will you come back tomorrow? I was looking forward to
John and you working together to keep me in good order,'
Michael said with a warm pleading smile on his face.

'Yes, of course Michael – I wouldn't let you down – see you in
the morning.'

On the bus to St. Mawes, Simon was deep in thought and
feeling angry towards Morgan Smythe, who had deliberately set
out to humiliate him, and wondered why Michael and John had
not immediately intervened to reprimand Morgan. But of course
Michael and John were guests of the Smythes' and supposedly
did not wish to cause any sort of fray with their friends and
hosts. Simon really liked Michael – and John seemed a decent
fellow – so he decided not to refer to the incident when back in
the house, but would be on his guard if Smythe picked on him
again and would defend himself strongly, as Michael had
advised.

Arriving at the pretty fishing village of St Mawes, with the sun
still shining, even though it was early evening, immediately
lifted Simon's mood, and he was looking forward to spending
time on his own in the hotel. The receptionist at The Rising
Sun, was nice and friendly, and allocated Simon a very pleasant
on-suite room with a harbour view. Although deemed a single
room, the bed was a large double – which pleased Simon as he
liked to shift around during his sleeping hours.

Simon was tired from the journey and all the goings-on at
Portscatho, so decided on an early night. Following a shower
and a change of clothing, he thought that a drink at the bar
would be a good idea to round off the day. He wasn't hungry as
the earlier repast at the Smythes' which had been a very late
lunch, was sufficient for his appetite. He'd heard that the food
was good at The Rising Sun and was looking forward to
enjoying a dinner in the restaurant the next day. Michael had
said that the plan was morning only for work and that after

lunch was fun time, and he would be welcome to join in with any plan of theirs or free to go off to do his own thing.

The bar was situated in a corridor with a view of the restaurant, which looked very busy, with mainly couples and families, and going by the noise level, everyone seemed to be enjoying themselves. 'A pint of bitter, please,' Simon ordered from the young barman.

'Certainly, sir, and will you be having dinner with us this evening?'

'No, not tonight as I had eaten earlier, but hopefully tomorrow.'

'Oh... So you're staying with us sir?'

'Yes... I've booked in for five nights.'

'Holiday?'

'Not really... I'm on a sort of work project, but I hope to have plenty of free time to enjoy the beauty of the area.'

'Good for you...sir. A combination of work and holiday sounds like the best of both worlds.'

As this small talk exchange was taking place, Simon couldn't help but notice through the restaurant – an extremely pretty girl waitress taking orders and carrying trays of food to diners. She seemed to have a way of serving guests that was poised and confident, but with a winning friendly manner. He was watching her perform her duties as he caught her eye and offered her a smile which, to Simon's surprise and delight, was returned.

As Simon was finishing his pint and thinking of heading off to bed, he noticed a small band setting up in the restaurant and a good number of people starting to enter the lobby heading for the bar. 'They come in for the music, sir,' said the barman to

Simon. 'We have music every night during the summer season and it brings a lot of people into the hotel. Great for bar business,' he added, giving Simon a cheeky wink.

Simon thought to have one more pint whilst listening to the band's opening numbers. They started playing well-known American show tunes and continued with some of the most popular hit numbers of the day. Hotel guests and bar customers started to sing along with the band – the general atmosphere was relaxed and convivial, and as the barman had said – drinks were being ordered in ever-increasing numbers.

'Excuse me – are you waiting to be served?' a man standing next to Simon at the bar inquired.

Simon turned to look at the man, whose accent he couldn't quite detect. It was a soft cultivated voice with a pleasant lyrical twang and pronounced diction. 'Sorry, I've been hogging the bar – but the bar was quiet earlier and I was the only one here. No, please go- ahead.'

'Thank you,' said the man with a smile. He then focused on the barman, ordering two gin and tonics. 'Did you enjoy the dinner?' the man inquired as he paid for his drinks and looked around for whoever the other drink was for.

'I didn't eat here tonight, although I'm staying in the hotel.'

'Oh' said the man, 'the food here is very good – excellent fresh fish'. 'So I heard,' responded Simon, 'and I'm looking forward to sampling the menu tomorrow.'

The man was tall and slim with an aquiline nose and high cheekbones, and around Simon's age, maybe a few years older. Just then a smartly dressed attractive blonde lady sauntered up to the bar and put her arm around the man's waist.

'Uh...You found me. Here's your gin and tonic.'

'Sorry, darling... but there was a queue for the ladies' loo.'

'I'm Harvey Donnell and this is my wife, May,' he said, addressing Simon.

'It's nice to meet you – my name is Simon Negrini.' The three shook hands and moved away from the bar itself to make way for others waiting to order drinks.

The bar area was now very crowded, with lots of people smoking as well as noise from everyone trying to be heard above the music and as it became difficult to engage in conversation. However, what Simon did establish was that Harvey and May were from the west of Ireland and were part of a family that owned a country hotel there. They had been married for four years and were holidaying in Cornwall before going back home to Ireland – to take over the reins from his parents of running the hotel.

'Good night, enjoy the rest of the evening and it was a pleasure meeting you both.' said Simon to his new friends as he left them in the bar area and sauntered off to his room. As he was passing reception, the lovely waitress whom he had exchanged smiles with earlier – was heading out of the hotel. They acknowledged each other with nods of the head as the girl went out of the main door and Simon went up to his room, hopefully, to enjoy a good night's sleep,

Simon slept well for part of the night, but with the window open on a warm summer's evening, he was woken by voices coming from outside the hotel. It sounded like a man and a woman chatting quite loudly and giggling. Simon assumed it was a courting couple who had consumed lots of alcohol, and had then decided to walk the beach to sober up – exchange kisses, and possibly even more. Were they staying in the hotel – as an established couple or as a casual holiday meet? Simon, now fully awake and thinking about the unknown couple and what they were or were not getting up to, turned his thoughts to the pretty young (maybe too young?) waitress and the eye contact they had made and felt aroused just thinking about her. After all, he was here in beautiful sunny Cornwall in high summer. The weather was dry and warm, and he was staying in a hotel on his own with a big double bed; how he would have loved to have someone share the bed with him, especially someone as gorgeous as that waitress. He just couldn't get her out of his mind.

At age twenty-four, Simon looked back on his love life, following his disastrous experience at the Greenshead boarding school. The sex in his short marriage to Felicity had been OK, but with both of them being inexperienced, it lacked any sort of erotic element and over time had become somewhat perfunctory. And just as they were beginning to learn about each other's needs and wants, Felicity became distracted and Simon was feeling that she was just going through the motions as a dutiful wife. Once he knew about her affair with Freddy, their sex life faded almost completely into the abyss, and the odd time sex was attempted between them – Simon felt he was being compared unfavourably with her lover, Freddy.

Looking further back before his marriage and before he met Felicity, there was that awkward encounter with Barbara Conclave in her Hampstead home – that he shunned and ran from. Sharon Weaver, his dear colleague from his ex-employers, who at odd times throughout the years in the company, he'd thought he'd get together with sexually, but they were such good friends and supporters of each other – that it just didn't develop in that way. And then he discovered that she was sleeping with Carl Warringson, which totally negated any possibility of him making any sort of sexual move towards her. And recently in Paris – the whole episode with Simone went totally wrong – due to his carelessness with losing the money.

The voices from outside the window had ceased and Simon was feeling sleepy again, tucking into the sheets and puffing up his two pillows – the night had by then turned a little chilly. He covered himself with the light blankets that he had earlier discarded and fell back into a deep sleep, dreaming of chasing the waitress along the beach – ending up swimming in the sea together.

He was awake early and feeling refreshed, Simon ran a high water warm bath – giving himself a lengthy relaxing soak, before dressing and heading down for breakfast. Enjoying a cooked full English of bacon, eggs, sausages, mushrooms, tomatoes and sauté potatoes – with tea and toast, he noticed Harvey and May making their way towards him. They exchanged pleasantries about their respective night time reposes – with Harvey asking Simon whether he would care to join them for dinner in the evening. Simon replied that he would be delighted to do so – wishing the couple a good day, as he topped up his pot of tea and buttered another slice of toast.

The bus to Portscatho was on time; Michael and John were pleased to see Simon arrive earlier than expected, so they got straight down to work, the three of them reading different chapters of the *Iliad* that Michael had selected for them. Mrs Smythe came in with coffee and Biscuits. John and Simon were each summing up to Michael the highlights of their particular chapter whilst Michael was furiously making notes that would help him construct the *libretto* for his proposed opera, *King Priam.*

Mr Smythe behaved himself during lunch – smoked salmon salad followed by raspberries and ice cream. Michael and John were off to play tennis for the afternoon, Simon declining the invitation to join them and taking an early afternoon bus back to St Mawes.

Marie, the waitress Simon had been drooling over, although only aged sixteen, could have easily been taken for a girl of eighteen. She was tallish with a fully developed woman's body, and straight-backed with piercing blue eyes. There was nothing of the adolescent about her physical appearance or her confident manner. She got the waitress job at The Rising Sun at St Mawes by lying about her age – giving them the false name of Margo Pento and a made-up address in Penzance. In any event, they were not inquiring into her background too much, as it was high season, and they were desperate for extra waiting staff.

Marie had left home in the village of Helford, situated on the beautiful Helford River – approximately thirty miles south of St Mawes, following a row with her mother and step-father. The plan was to go to London to study drama and acting. Meanwhile, she was spending the summer working to save the money for London. The job included board and lodgings, with a room share at the hotel's annexe, which she shared with her friend, Holly Fines, which was a few hundred yards from the main building.

Marie had got on well with her mother as a little girl, but as she got older she became curious about her father, whom she had no contact with at all, but knew that he had become a successful business-man in London, and that he was originally from America. Her mother, having worked in London during the Second World War, was consequently, open-minded and understood that there was a big wide world outside the villages of Cornwall. But Bob Tressant, her step-father, a fisherman, who had never been out of Cornwall, and although younger than her mum, had very traditional ideas about female roles in life. Marie's love for music and drama and her wish to go to London to study did not chime with Bob at all, and he thought that she was being pretentious; that her mother had spoiled her, giving her ideas unsuitable for a young Cornish lass from a modest home.

Marie had caught the eye of the nice-looking, tall and fair-haired man, staring at her from the bar area whilst serving in the restaurant, and she had flirtatiously responded with a smile; she saw him again as she was leaving the main entrance, on her way to her room in the annexe building. What was she doing? She reflected that he was a good few years older than her; he could be married, or at least have a steady girlfriend? Yet – she had taken an instant fancy to him, seemingly, so very different and more sophisticated than the gauche local lads she had gone out with in Helford. She knew she was young to have a full sexual relationship but if she was going to go all the way with anyone, it would be with an older experienced man – instead of someone her own age or even her fake age.

Before her shift, as it was a beautiful sunny afternoon, Marie went for a long walk by herself along the beach and thought about the strange man in the hotel. She decided that this was the man she was going to lose her virginity to. She would find out his room number and go through the back entrance fire-escape to go to his room – and then...? Who knew, maybe he'd reject her and call her a silly young thing and send her packing. But somewhere in her inner being, she knew that he would not do that – but respond to her overtures.

'Good evening Simon'... Simon received a tap on the shoulder from Harvey Donnell whilst he was nursing a pint of bitter at the bar. His thoughts were miles away, thinking of the lovely waitress from the previous evening. Turning around and shaking Harvey's hand, he offered his new friend a drink.

'I'll have what you're having, Simon, a good pint of local ale.'

'Is May not with you?'

'She's having a rest in the room – tired from all the walking we've done today. But she will be joining us for dinner.'

'Great'... said Simon. 'It's really kind of you to ask me to join the two of you at the table; I'm always self-conscious dining alone in a busy bustling restaurant, with everyone chatting away, and me reading my book.

'It's our pleasure. We've both enjoyed meeting you, and if you ever get over to Ireland and manage to travel to the west coast, please look us up at our hotel,' he said, whilst handing Simon a card with all the Irish hotel details.

The dining room at the hotel was as busy and as lively as it had been the previous evening 'You're our guest tonight, Simon, so please don't hold back. Order whatever you wish.'

'Thank you,' Simon said, as he looked around the room, but there was no sign of the waitress.

'May and I are having lobster, they do it grilled with garlic butter or as a cold dish with mayonnaise.'

Simon was just going to order the same as his hosts – lobster with garlic butter, when suddenly he caught sight of her. There she was, talking through the menu to a group of people at the far end of the dining room. 'No – sorry, I will have the lobster but the cold dish with mayonnaise.' Some instinctive thought in his head, silly as it was, warned him against eating garlic, something he may regret later – if by chance he managed to get close to the girl.

Cold or not, the lobster was delicious – served with an excellent mixed salad and a few new potatoes. Harvey and May had the grilled version and were raving about it – with butter dripping down Harvey's chin. Harvey and Simon had the smoked eel as a starter; May going for the potted crab – as the three of them set about polishing off two bottles of a fabulous Pouilly-Fuissé white burgundy. A top notch summer pudding with Cornish cream was the perfect desert that the three of them went for. They ordered coffee and cognac for the boys, whilst May enjoyed a Bailey's Irish liqueur with her coffee.

Unfortunately, the waitress was not serving their table. A very nice young man was looking after them, but Simon did manage to sneak a few glances in her direction; she looked harassed and was kept busy serving a whole load of tables.

The Donnells' were great company. The conversation flowed as the wine was being consumed – they certainly whetted Simon's appetite to visit Ireland one day. He did not know that it would be another twenty-six years before he would set foot on the Emerald Isle.

They moved into the bar area when the music started up – similar repertoire to the previous evening with a few variations – recent hits such as 'Mack the Knife' and' Dream Lover.' Both numbers were currently in the charts and sung by Bobby Darin. As Simon got up to order more drinks from the bar, he felt something touch his arm as someone pushed past him in the now very crowded bar area. He just saw the back of her as she looked back and pointed to the floor. Although it was dimly lit, he noticed a slip of paper, which he bent down to pick up. Although difficult to see in the dark, he could see it read: *write down your room number and hand it to me when I next pass by, Margo, aged 18 x*

Simon was shaking with fear and excitement, unable to take in what was happening. This gorgeous young girl whom he had yet to speak with was propositioning him. What should he do? Part of him thought to ignore the note completely, or write some excuse on it. But this girl had not been out of his mind over the past twenty-four hours; and anyway, which virile young man could turn down such a brazen approach from a beautiful girl? He wondered again about her age, but then thought the hotel would not employ her if she was too young. And she looked so confident and adult in her appearance.

He found a pencil, wrote down his room number and first name – putting the slip of paper into his trouser pocket whilst he went to the bar for the drinks.

'Are you OK Simon?' said Harvey, when he returned to the table.

'Yes…fine thanks, Harvey – I've probably had one drink too many today.'

Harvey laughed. 'The English don't have the capacity of us Irish!'

'I'll be alright. Better just to step outside for a minute to breathe a bit of air.'

'No problem, Simon. See you in a bit.'

Simon did in fact go outside to calm himself down, and on his way back, he spotted Marie carrying drinks from the bar. He nonchalantly passed her by and dropped the slip of paper onto the drinks tray she was carrying.

Guests spontaneously started to get up to dance and sing along to the music, and following Harvey and May shuffling around the crowded floor, Simon gallantly asked May to dance and, although Simon was a poor dancer, May sort of took control and led him around the floor with Simon conscious of trying not to step on May's toes.

More drinks were ordered, and although conversation was difficult because of the music and the loud voices of other guests, a warm rapport had established between the Donnell's and Simon; he particularly appreciated their Irish easy-going personalities and their close relationship – which was tension free, having love in their eyes for each other.

By the time they had decided to call it a night – when the music had finished, the bar had closed and guests had begun to drift off to bed. Hugs and eternal friendship were exchanged as the Donnell's, arm-in-arm, slowly climbed the stairs to their room.

A couple of hours had passed since Simon had last seen Margo, and although his ardour for a secret assignation with her had not cooled, his socialising with the Donnell's had given him time to reflect on what may possibly lie ahead during the night – if Margo did indeed come to his room. A sexual encounter with a beautiful young girl – who had herself instigated the whole affair, was a delicious prospect for a man, whose confidence had been at low ebb since his separation from Felicity; but this wasn't to be the beginning of a new relationship which Simon craved – it would be sexual liaison – nothing more. But would he be taking advantage of an impressionable young woman, probably living away from home for the first time?

On the other hand, maybe it was all a tease and she wouldn't come? Of course, she may have knocked on his bedroom door earlier, but with no response, had gone back to her own room in the annexe.

Simon went up to his room – showered and was reading in bed when there was a soft knock on the door. He put a towel around his naked body and answered the door. Margo entered and indicated to Simon to turn the lights off whilst putting two fingers to her lips, indicating that she didn't want to chat but just to get into bed. In the dark, Margo undressed – visited the bathroom – before slipping into bed with Simon. He kissed and caressed her, which led to gentle lovemaking. Simon at all times being aware of her inexperience and the fact this was probably her first time. However, Margo reciprocated to Simon's advances and intercourse took place, with Simon reaching a climax fairly soon after penetration – as he realised that Margo needed more time to achieve orgasm. Despite Simon's clumsy effort, she kissed and thanked him and the two of them cuddled up together and almost instantly fell asleep.

When the daylight woke Simon up – there was no sign of Margo or any of her things. But later, whilst tidying up his bed, he noticed a white-gold bracelet on the floor that Margo must have dropped and forgotten to pick-up, when she dressed in the dark and left the room.

Simon went straight to the reception area before going into breakfast and innocently handed in the bracelet to the young lady behind the desk.

'Where did you find this Mr Negrini?' she asked Simon with a quixotic look on her face.

'Well'... said Simon, feeling a bit sheepish, 'It was on the floor by the side of the bar late last night – the reception was closed for the night at that late hour so I thought it best to hang onto it until morning.' He added in a rather quiet conspiratorial voice –'It's a beautiful piece and I would imagine it being worth a great deal of money.'

The receptionist stared coldly at Simon. 'Well yes... it's a valuable piece. I'm surprised Margo hadn't noticed it missing?

Simon reddened and felt uneasy. He said...'Oh – you know who the piece belongs to...Margo? Is she a staff member at the hotel?'

'One of our waitresses – she always wears the bracelet when on duty.'

Before Simon could add another word, the receptionist informed Simon that Margo had to dash off home early that morning, as there had been, unfortunately, a family problem that needed her urgent attention. I'll make sure Margo gets her bracelet back. Thank you, Mr Negrini.' She dismissed Simon – as he guessed that she had not believed him – thinking that she wasn't getting the whole story from the gentleman guest.

For some unknown reason, Simon had made a note of the hallmark number of the bracelet – before handing it over to the reception.

Chapter 11

Cornwall, 1959

Carl Warringson was enjoying a coffee and a cigar in his London office – thinking about the success of his autumn fashion collection that had gone down extremely well with the buyers visiting his showroom over the previous couple of weeks. It was always crazy that in the fashion world, winter clothes collections were sold in high summer and summer collections were shown during the depths of winter.

Carl turned his mind to the young man who he had ceremoniously sacked earlier in the year – which, in retrospect, was a bit harsh, considering his excellent record working for him for over nine years – up until the Paris incident. On the other hand, since Simon left the company, Carl had done a bit of investigating about what actually had happened that night in Paris, and, through quizzing Sharon, whom Simon had confided in, understood that the young man had been really stupid going to a night-club with so much cash on his person.

His private phone began to ring and he wondered who that could be, as very few people had his private number. 'Hello?' Carl answered rather gruffly. 'Who's that?'

A voice with a strong south west accent replied. 'It's Bob speaking.'

'Bob who?'

'Bob Tressant, your daughter's step-father.'

'Why are you calling me on my private number Bob?' said Carl, with a touch of impatience in his voice.'

'Carl, I'm sorry but Wendy's dead'.

'Dead...Wendy? What? How? When? '

Carl, now fully alert, felt a painful knot in his stomach and he immediately formed a picture in his head of Wendy and himself enjoying nights out in London during the war – mixed with a profound sense of guilt in the way he had abandoned her following her pregnancy. Thinking about Wendy's pregnancy, Carl almost screamed down the phone *'Marie – Marie.'* His voice changed almost to a whisper – he asked, 'is she OK?'

'Yes, Carl, Marie's fine and she's here with me – having run away, but we managed to find her and give her the news about her mum and she immediately came home.'

'What's happened, Bob?'

Bob explained everything to Carl, starting with the rows Wendy and himself had had with Marie, who'd left home without telling them where she was going.

Bob continued... 'Wendy was devastated at Marie walking out as the two of them had been close. Consequently, she fell into a depression. The night she died I was out at a fisherman's convention, but when I left the house, Wendy seemed fine and almost in a happy mood, so I had no qualms leaving her alone. When I got home about midnight, I went up to the bedroom and everything was so quiet that I was alerted to something being wrong – Wendy being such a light sleeper, that normally she would wake up as soon as I entered the room. I spoke to her but no answer came. Then I saw a box of pills opened and lying on the bedside table. I tried to wake her but to no avail and suddenly I realised that she was dead, having taken an overdose of pills. I called 999 and medics came, confirming that Wendy was indeed dead. I had no idea where Marie was and was desperate to try to find her. I knew how friendly she was with Holly Fine and I also knew that Holly had gone off to work during the summer at a hotel in St Mawes. Perhaps Marie had followed her friend to work at the same hotel – but which hotel? I telephoned the various hotels in St. Mawes until finally I spoke with a receptionist at The Rising Sun, who had no record of Marie Ritage – but did say that Holly Fine was a member of staff. They put me through to Holly, who was very cautious of giving me any information – but eventually admitted that Marie had been working at the hotel, under a pseudonym, and was in fact her roommate. Marie had sworn Holly to secrecy, but when I told her that Wendy had died, she said that of course she would tell Marie, who was away from her room – but she would convey the message to Marie as soon as she saw her. She gave me her condolences before hanging up the telephone.'

Carl did not utter a word as Bob talked through the sequence of events, starting with Marie leaving home, Wendy's suicide and Bob's endeavours to trace Marie and get her back home. Carl was in a state of shock. The conversation finished with Bob saying that he would keep in touch with Carl and let him know the funeral arrangements for Wendy.

Carl travelled down to Cornwall for the funeral but felt out of place amongst the local villagers – who had turned out in full to give Wendy a proper Cornish send off.

Marie would have nothing to do with Carl, despite having previously been curious about him, and she totally rejected his approach at the funeral – turning her back as he tried to greet her. She decided that she was not prepared to acknowledge him as her father and reverted to the way her mother had brought her up; to hate him for the way he had abandoned her – having made her pregnant, and despite his promise of marriage, went off to marry another woman who would open the door for him in his business ambitions.

During a drink with Carl at the local pub the day after the funeral, Bob had tried to explain to Carl the state of his relationship with Wendy and Marie that led to the tragedy of Wendy's death. Marie resented Bob, and as she got older she became quite hostile to him, believing that he'd made Wendy unhappy, which, according to Bob, was completely untrue. Their marriage hadn't been perfect by any means, but they sort of rubbed along reasonably well. However, Bob realised that there was a frustration in Wendy and that she had missed the exciting life she had enjoyed in London during the war years.

'What was the row about with Marie?'

'She wanted to invite one of the local lads she was hanging around with, to stay the night with her in her room at home. Both Wendy and I were really shocked at this request and we both absolutely refused – after all, Marie was only aged sixteen – although she looked older – being grown-up for her age; a very bright and confident girl. Besides, she kept going on about moving to London to study music and drama, but again we thought she was too young and we told her that she should wait until she was eighteen before leaving home. The problem was that she was influenced by her friend Holly Fine, who was three years older than Marie and had persuaded her younger friend to go to St. Mawes with her and had evidently recommended her to the 'Rising Sun' management for a summer job at the hotel.'

Carl listened to Bob trying to justify all that had happened, but he suspected that Bob was giving him a sanitised version of events and relationships – when things in the Tressant household were actually a lot worse than was being explained to him. A wife doesn't commit suicide and a daughter doesn't run away from home, giving a false surname and address to a new employer, unless things were really desperately bad. He suddenly felt weary and wanted to get away from Cornwall, feeling he was not wanted there, and decided to leave that evening.

At the Rising Sun, Holly Fine was called to the reception desk.

'Holly, we're really sorry to hear about the tragedy with Margo's family,' said Georgina, the head receptionist. Holly noticed that Georgina skirted around saying what had actually happened – her mum committing suicide. 'Don't get me wrong, Holly, we really liked Margo and she was good at waitressing. The guests really took to her,' continued Georgina, 'but we won't have her back'

'That's harsh, Georgina, considering what she's going through at home.' Holly was looking uncomfortable and couldn't wait for the conversation to end.

Georgina added … 'We can't employ someone dishonest.'

'Oh god, give her a break,' snapped Holly. 'The poor girl has just lost her mother, and she had good reason to keep her real identity and address secret. Margo needed to get away from a bad atmosphere at home and she needed to feel secure here – without continuously looking over her shoulder to see if her step-father showed up at the hotel looking for her.'

'Look, Holly, we know that you're being loyal to your friend but I've liaised with our general manager, and he made a firm decision that we would not have Margo back working at the hotel.' But before you go Holly, could you please confirm Margo's correct name and address?'

'Sorry Georgina, I gave my word to Margo to keep her details secret.'

'Right then'... said Georgina, in a sharp tone of voice – 'This is Margo's bracelet which was handed in to us by one of the guests, who had found it on the floor by the bar, on the night before she left the hotel; could you please return it to Margo when you next see her? '

'Yes, of course I will.'

Holly wondered how in gods' name could Marie have dropped her precious bracelet and left the hotel – without noticing it was missing. She must have been in a dreadful state of mind when travelling home by bus early that morning...poor Marie.

'And we also have an envelope of money owed to Margo from wages and tips,' added Georgina, handing everything over to Holly.

When Holly travelled back to Helford on her next day off, she visited Marie with the envelope of money from the hotel, but forgot to give her back the bracelet.

As part of the divorce settlement with his wife, Shelley, Carl Warringson sold his majority holding in the clothing business back to the Lambit family, thereby cutting all his ties with London. He remained however a very wealthy man but an extremely lonely one – feeling terrible about the sad death of Wendy. It was obvious that his daughter Marie, wanted nothing to do with him and he reluctantly accepted that state of affairs.

He decided to move back to the US, but thought to try his luck on the west coast, in the State of California, and maybe get himself involved in politics there, being a big admirer of the Republican Party and the current president, Dwight D Eisenhower, then in his final year of his two-terms presidency. Carl detested the Kennedy family, and any thoughts of the young senator Jack Kennedy, becoming the next Democratic president, were absolutely anathema to him.

He had no actual family left in New York except the Mentones', who were like family. He would make a point of keeping in touch with them and visiting them once or twice a year. Before emigrating to California, he would settle a lump sum of money with Marie, making sure that the money went to her personally and not to Bob Tressant, whom frankly he didn't trust and he assumed that Bob would leave Marie to her own devices – now that Wendy was dead, and would move on with his life elsewhere.

Marie had been in a daze since her mum had died and actually hadn't noticed her missing bracelet. Prior to working at the Rising Sun, she only very occasionally wore it and kept it in a locked drawer in her bedroom at home. She took it with her to St Mawes and wore it there in the restaurant to look more grown-up. With everything that had happened, she somehow thought that she had brought the bracelet back with her and that it was lodged safely in its usual place in her bedroom.

Within a few months of Wendy's death, Bob had decided not only to leave Cornwall for the first time but to emigrate all the way to Australia, having applied for a visa, which had become less cumbersome following the 1958 Australian Immigration Act. Bob realised that Marie had only tolerated him because he was her mum's husband, but since her death, Marie had made it very clear that she didn't want anything more to do with him. Financially, Bob had become aware of Carl having given a substantial lump sum to Marie, and also, her mother had left a little amount for Marie in her will. The house in Helford was rented accommodation and that left Bob with very little money, except some personal savings and what was left of Wendy's estate once Marie had had her share. He had just enough funds to qualify for an Australian visa and was determined to start a new life there. He had old friends from the village who had settled in Australia – and from various letters received from friends – it seemed there were great opportunities for fit men who were willing to work hard and stay out of trouble.

Marie had broken up with both her father and her step-father, and she had enough funds to move to London and apply to colleges to study music and drama.

Simon had stayed on in the Rising Sun for a couple of more days hoping to see Margo again, but there was no further sign of her. He spent the days with his musical colleagues at Portscatho going through the motions, but his heart wasn't in it. His new friends, the Donnells', had left the hotel and had gone home to Ireland, so he spent the evenings at the bar, chatting to the barman and eating bar snacks, as he couldn't face sitting in the restaurant on his own thinking of Margo. He felt guilty about his sexual encounter, despite the fact that she had made all of the moves that had led to the encounter. But he suspected that Margo was actually younger than she had told him, and the fact that he had not used any protection bothered him hugely.

Chapter 12

Sant' Agata, Busseto, Italy
1880

'My dear maestro, our task here is arduous as the drama that concerns us is skewed, like an unsteady table, and we don't know which leg is too short, and however we try to adjust the table, it still wobbles.'

'Yes... my friend Boito. I admit that the table is shaky, but by putting a leg or two in order, I think it can be made to stand upright.'

The exchange between the thirty-eight year old writer/composer, Arrigo Boito, and the sixty-seven year old famous Italian operatic composer, Giuseppe Verdi, took place at Verdi's home in Busseto, during a rare personal meeting between the two men, whose working relationship were generally conducted by regular correspondence. The shaky table in question was Verdi's 1857 opera, *Simon Boccanegra*, and Boito and Verdi were discussing various ideas on how to revise and improve that problem and unloved opera.

Verdi was still an imposing figure in his late sixties; upright in bearing and looking taller than his five feet eight inches height. His sharp features, aquiline nose and piercing eyes were offset by a full grey beard turning white and a thick head of hair covering the top of his ears – curled to the back of his neck. Dressed all in black, rarely smiling, he cut a figure of some severity. But behind that severity was a man of the people, loved by the people and who possessed not only musical genius but deep intelligence, understanding and sensitivity.

Boito, when he first met Verdi, eighteen years previously, had been in total awe of the senior composer, but also because he, Boito, represented a new generation of artists and thought that Verdi's operatic style was somewhat old fashioned. As over the years he had himself experienced the failure of his opera, *Mefistofele,* he developed a lasting admiration for Verdi, acknowledging that trying to move opera composition forward to a more realistic dramatic form had to go hand-in-hand with keeping audiences onside, who still expected lots of *bel canto* singing with *coloratura* arias and high note *cabalettas'* – the drama being secondary to the singing.

Boito was a much more sober character than he had been in his youth and was now approaching middle-age. He had a thick moustache – wore rimmed spectacles – a wing collar shirt – and a three piece suit finished with tie, watch chain and tie pin. He looked more the banker, lawyer or senator than a leading poet.

Villa Verdi was originally farmland that the composer acquired in 1844, and he started to build his villa in 1848. He lived there from that year until the end of his life. When Boito visited the composer in 1880, the villa had only just been fully completed to Verdi's satisfaction. The village of Sant'Agata was situated near the town of Busetto, which in itself was close to the village of Le Roncole, where Verdi was born.

'Maestro'... said Boito, 'I have made changes to the first act as you had suggested, compressing the first two scenes into one, respectively the Grimaldis' family garden scene and the Palazzo Grimaldi scene. The third scene which was set in the vast piazza of Genoa, I've eliminated and created a brand new scene – set in the Council Chamber, which was your idea, maestro, and I think that it was a brilliant idea, combining high political drama interwoven with the developing personal machinations of individual relationships, kidnapping accusations and horrific curses. I have also expanded the role of the villain Paolo, taking my cue from the character of Iago in the opera *Otello* that I've started to do some preliminary work on for you.'

'Dear Boito, that sounds absolutely excellent and I especially appreciate the work you've done on the new scene; a political earthquake taking place in the Council Chamber with Boccanega showing his stature as a great leader and statesman. I see this scene lifting the whole opera onto a higher plane, and some of the music for this scene is already swirling around in my head.'

'Thank you, maestro, and we are always so happy to work with you and to help rescue this opera. But I have had some different thoughts about revising *Simon Boccanegra.*' Verdi looked at Boito somewhat sceptically. 'I think we have enough new text, thanks to you, and I will do my job in making the necessary changes and additions to the music.'

Boito, seeing Verdi's reaction, decided to keep his counsel, keeping his thoughts to himself and not wishing to annoy the maestro. He did not pursue the matter further and changed the conversation to inquiring about the building work involved in completing Verdi's villa and his plans for the attached farmland. The composer's demeanour relaxed immediately with Boito turning the discussion to domestic matters and away from the tough world of opera.

Boito spent a few more days at Sant' Agata, enjoying the warm hospitality of Verdi and his wife, the retired soprano Giuseppina Strepponi, before returning to Milan.

*An enclosed garden surrounded the villa. Verdi himself designed the park in every detail. He ordered the construction of a lemon house and the planting of towering *Ginkgo Biloba*. He instructed masons to craft an array of neo-classical statues and drew plans for an artificial lake in the shape of a treble clef. With its construction of roses and milk – leaved magnolias, the garden was intended to mesmerise its occupants no matter the season. It was, and still is, an Eden. But for Strepponi, it must have felt more like a very elaborate cage. Here, she was practically invisible, living more as a nun than the wife of a famous composer.

*(*Far Out* magazine – Sam Kemp)

Chapter 13

Counties Mayo and Galway
1985

Simon's friend from his teenage years, Ian Monte, had met a lovely Irish girl at university in London who became his steady girlfriend and then his long standing partner for many years – that eventually led to the pair deciding to get married. Ruby Finglas was Irish and her family home was in County Mayo, in the west of Ireland, just outside the town of Castlebar, and that's where they had decided to tie the knot. Simon was delighted to have been invited to the wedding of his old friend and was looking forward to making his first visit to the Emerald Isle. He had kept the details of the delightful couple he had met in Cornwall during the summer of 1959 and, whilst perusing the map of Ireland, realised that Lough Corrib in County Galway, was a drivable distance from Castlebar, and he was determined to visit Harvey and May Donnell at their country house hotel, whilst visiting Ireland.

Simon flew to Dublin, hiring a car at the airport – and spending one day in Dublin City exploring some of the famous sites and monuments before driving west to Castlebar. The wedding was in the family's garden adjacent to their house, where they had erected a huge canopy tent with black and white check mock square plastic flooring in the centre of the newly laid tiles that covered the complete tented area. The long tables for the wedding breakfast were placed at the sides of the tent in a square formation with the top table at the back of the tent placed across the space for all to be able to view the speeches without impediment. The centre floor area was free for dancing following the meal and all of the official proceedings.

The actual ceremony was outside of the tent in the garden itself with the guests placed in rows of seats; ten rows in depth. The date was 23 June which was the eve of St John's Day on the 24th. St. John's Day was celebrated mainly in the west of Ireland – and in the County of Mayo in particular. The origins of the day were associated with John the Baptist of biblical fame. One of the traditions of the eve of St John's Day was having a bonfire night. This duly happened late in the evening at the wedding in the garden behind the tent with hand-held hot fried food served around the fire, which had a real sense of communal togetherness about it.

Having quietly visited the local registry office the previous day for the legal proceedings and signing of the relevant documents, the happy couple had decided on a pagan wedding with not a religious officiate in sight. The couple's hands were tied together whilst making love pledges to each other, whilst a close friend of Ruby's recited a selection of secular romantic poetry, which had the guests in tears with the sensitivity of the occasion. For Simon, the midsummer sunny afternoon in Ruby's family garden had strong reminisces of Michael Tippetts' great summer solstice 1952 opera, *The Midsummer Marriage.*

Lough Corrib is the largest lake in the Republic of Ireland; it connects the lake to the sea at Galway. The 176 km lake traverses both the counties of Galway and Mayo. Harvey and May Donnell owned a Victorian country house hotel by the lake near the town of Oughterard. Their house, which had been in Harvey's family for six generations and had been a hotel for 100 years – was always run by a member of the Donnell family. The house stood in 180 acres of parkland and woodland. The current family custodians of the hotel Harvey and May had been in charge since 1959, and were hoping that one of their three children would eventually take over the reins when the time came. The hotel was called 'Lough Corrib House'.

When Simon entered the hotel – the first thing he noticed was the skin of a tiger spread-eagled across the landing. Other family bric-à-brac he noticed were fish in glass cases, Victorian clocks, framed maps and paintings, books, bibelots and a vintage bagatelle machine. There was no reception area as such but a little cupboard of a bar which doubled as the reception. Simon pressed the bell by the bar/reception and Harvey appeared almost immediately – all smiles and welcoming.

'Simon, you haven't aged at all. It's great to see you – welcome to Lough Corrib!'

'You too Harvey...you look fit and well and I'm thrilled to see you again after twenty-six years.' The two men hugged each other. 'What a wonderful place you have here on the lake; how's May and the family?'

'May's fine... thanks, and the family are all well. May is busy in the kitchen at present but she's looking forward to seeing you. So, what have you been up to Simon? Are you still in the music publishing business? I remember you were some sort of an assistant to a composer who was holidaying in Cornwall – at the time we met in St Mawes?'

'Yes Harvey, my dear mentor, the now great composer Sir Michael Tippett, had been working on ideas for his second opera, *King Priam,* at that time, and I had been invited down to help with some of the text. Although, looking back I don't think I contributed much at all. I think Michael just wanted a few pals with him in Cornwall to play tennis and have some fun. I stayed in music publishing for some years but now I'm a jobbing orchestral and operatic conductor.'

'That's fantastic, Simon, and you couldn't have visited us at a more opportune time, as we have the artistic director of Glyndehurst Opera Festival staying with us – a Mr Stephen Zandors. I'll introduce you to him later. Meanwhile, you must be tired from your journey, so let me show you to your room.

'He grabbed Simon's bag and led him upstairs to his lake view spacious bedroom.

Dinner, being a fixed no-choice four-course menu – May being the head chef – was served at 8.pm sharp with a large Victorian gong being struck to denote that dinner was served. Simon ordered a gin and tonic in the drawing room before dinner and was briefly greeted by May – who had popped out of the kitchen to warmly welcome Simon to Lough Corrib. As he was hugging May, telling her how she looked as gorgeous as she had twenty-six years previously in Cornwall, from the corner of his eye he noticed a clean cut quite handsome man enter the room. Simon knew Stephen Zandors from his picture only, as Zandors had been featured in the musical press, at his recent appointment as artistic director of Glyndehurst Festival Opera, based in East Sussex, near the English south coast. May immediately withdrew from Simon's arms and addressed the newcomer to the room. 'Good evening Mr Zandors…how was your day?'

'Excellent – thank you, May, and I am looking forward to another of your fabulous dinners.'

'Well – I must get back to the kitchen otherwise there won't be any dinner! Oh... let me introduce you to Mr Simon Negrini. Mr Negrini, please meet Mr Stephen Zandors. And now I really must fly back to the stove.'

The two gentlemen shook hands but before they had a chance to exchange any words between them, besides the cursory 'pleased to meet you' routine, the gong went off and everyone headed out towards the dining room.

The dinner was as superb as had been anticipated, as May's culinary skills were widely known in the restaurant and travel press. The breads were wild garlic focaccia and pumpkin seed soda bread. The first course consisted of smoked chipotle and gin, cured hake, fennel, orange, and labneh; followed by Castlemine farm rump of organic lamb, mint, apricot and lamb rissole muhammara, carrot and wild garlic. The pudding was baked custard, strawberries, and strawberry granita elderflower. Finally the Irish cheese course; Kylemore – young buck blue, creeny sheep – served with quince, parmesan sables, oat cake and sourdough cracker. Simon washed it all down with a full-bodied intense bottle of Italian wine from Puglia – *Poggio Passano Primitivo.*

Simon, feeling replete, relaxed with a sense of well being, retired back to the drawing room for coffee and liquors. Not finding a free table, he noticed Stephen Zandors sitting at a table on his own and asked whether he could join him at his table.'

'Of course, Mr Negrini, please take a seat.'

'Thank you, but please call me Simon.'

'And I'm Stephen,' Zandors responded.

Coffees and cognacs were served and the two men spoke about the wonderful meal they had just enjoyed and what a beautiful spot Lough Corrib was.

'Are you on holiday here?' inquired Stephen.

'Well, sort of,' responded Simon, going on to explain how he had originally met the Donnells' all those years ago in Cornwall and promised to visit them in Ireland one day; and as an old friend of his had invited him to his wedding in Castlebar, County Mayo – it seemed a perfect opportunity to look up these old acquaintances.

'And what about you, Stephen – what brings you here?'

Stephen briefly explained that he was a professional opera administrator, recently appointed artistic director of the Glyndehurst Festival. The reason he was staying at the Donnells' country house hotel was for an exploratory idea to build an opera house in the grounds of Lough Corrib House, as a west of Ireland summer opera festival.

Stephen continued. 'A wealthy benefactor from America was prepared to fund the venture, and because I previously had working experience with the Dublin Grand Opera Society, and, had been approached by the Donnells' whilst still working in Ireland, the benefactor's agent had asked me to do feasibility studies about the general opera situation in Ireland – and whether a festival based here could be practical and attract an international opera audience.'

Simon's reaction was immediately positive, and, although he didn't know much about the Irish arts scene, he could envisage an opera house by the lakeside. 'What do Harvey and May think about the idea?'

'Well... actually they are very keen on the idea in principle; provided the finances are all in place and local planning authorities get onboard.'

Simon disclosed to Stephen that he too was in the music profession as a conductor. 'Yes – I think I know the name…Negrini. Were you an associate conductor of the Halle in Manchester a few years back?'

'Yes, I was, and thoroughly enjoyed my time there; it was towards the end James Loughrans' twelve-year stint as music director, who had had the unenvied task of following on from the great Sir John Barbirolli – who had been there for the previous twenty-seven years.'

'So – what are you doing now?'

'I'm mainly conducting opera – in small provincial houses around West Germany, on a freelance basis.'

'We must talk some more, Simon, 'Stephen said in a slightly abrupt manner, as Simon was just about to elaborate on his conducting career, 'and it's been a pleasure meeting you.'

'It was my pleasure to meet you too…Stephen.'

Stephen rose immediately from his chair, wished Simon goodnight and went off to his room.

Simon was not ready to go up to his room, so he ordered another drink and chewed over in his head the events of the day. The visit to the country house was mainly to keep a promise made to Harvey and May back in 1959, to look the couple up if he ever travelled to Ireland, never thinking at that time that it would be twenty-six years before he set foot in the Emerald Isle. If he had realised how fabulous Ireland was in every aspect – the historic city of Dublin being hugely impressive; the scenic west of the country which was stunningly beautiful, the Donnells' estate – which was much bigger than he had ever imagined – gloriously set on Lough Corrib, he would have visited years earlier, but the modest-minded Donnells,' had totally played down where they came from and the sort of country house their family owned. But that was so typical of the Irish that Simon had come across in his short time in the country. The people were extremely friendly, and always happy to chat to strangers, but they weren't 'show-offs,' as some people in England were; Simon was unexpectedly falling in love with Ireland and its people and hoped he would be able to return soon.

As those thoughts were swirling around in his mind – Harvey and May entered the drawing room with a tray of drinks. 'Sorry that we haven't had a chance to chat properly so far, Simon, but we've been rushed off our feet since you arrived.' Harvey, with a big grin on his face, offered Simon another cognac. 'This one is on the house.'

The drawing room had by then emptied out, with all the other guests retiring for the night – as the couple sat down and joined

Simon. The three of them spent the following hour or so catching up and reminiscing about their meeting in Cornwall all those years ago and what they'd all been up to since then. The atmosphere was full of bonhomie and good cheer with the three of them delighted to be together again.

With a break in the conversation and Harvey going to get more drinks, Simon turned the conversation to the opera festival proposal, hoping to find out about Stephen Zandors, who he was most curious about. Harvey, coming back with top-up drinks and fresh coffee, picked up on the change of conversation and started to talk about the background to the project.

'We had a very wealthy American elderly gentleman as a guest here a couple of years ago, who had become an opera lover late in life – spending the summer months touring Europe visiting all the major opera festivals. He loved it here and saw the possibilities of building a theatre by the lake and putting on an annual summer opera festival, thinking that he would emulate John Listie, the founder of the Glyndehurst Festival in England during the 1930s.'

Harvey continued… 'To be honest, I initially thought it a mad idea by an eccentric American, but I made some inquiries into the opera world in Ireland and contacted the Dublin Grand Opera Society. I spoke to Stephen Zandors, an Englishman, who was then working for the society in an administrative role. Stephen was very helpful and filled me in with opera performances in Ireland, something I knew nothing about, not having any previous interest or knowledge of that particular art form. Stephen was immediately enthusiastic and explained to me that compared to the UK and Europe, opera in Ireland was under-represented. The crown jewel was the Wexford Opera Festival, founded in 1951, specialising in unknown or forgotten works, producing three different works on a nightly basis annually, over a two-week period, during late autumn. Wexford attracted an international audience as well as involving the whole population of the small market town based in the south east of Ireland in the enterprise. Stephen was a bit reticent to criticise the society he was employed by, but I got the gist that it was on the old-fashioned side – not really keeping up with modern production styles or hiring the best international singers. And of course they did not even have an opera house, instead performing in the unsatisfactory Gaiety Theatre. Stephen explained that he was leaving Dublin to take up the appointment of artistic director of Glyndehurst Festival Opera, but he asked us to keep in touch with him, and that he would be happy to help move the project forward.'

Simon listened intently to Harvey's exposition of how the opera plan got started, but was keen to know a little more about Stephen Zandors, as his first impression of him was mixed. Stephen was polite enough – very much the English gentleman, but he sensed a touch of arrogance about him, or maybe it was just Simon, with a chip on his shoulder about his unusual background for someone making his way as a conductor in the classical music business.

Chapter 14

London, October 1959

'Where did you put the coffee pot, Margo?' shouted Holly, as she searched the kitchen – still half asleep following a late night. She sniffed the stale air and opened the windows. The flat needed airing following all the smoking they had indulged in the previous evening whilst also drinking too much wine and brandy. Margo could not stop yawning as she entered the kitchen, too tired to even speak to her friend. She just pointed to the left shelf. Once the coffee was made, the two friends sat at the kitchen table and started to wake up and chat through the previous evening's shenanigans.

Marie Ridge had kept her pseudonym of Margo Pento and a fake address in Penzance, not wanting any further contact with either her father, who had moved to California, or her step-father, recently emigrated to Australia. Following her mother's death and receiving a small inheritance plus a reasonable lump sum settlement from her father, she had the confidence to move to London and enrol in one of the colleges for music and drama.

Holly Fine had decided to move to London with Margo and they agreed to share a flat together. Back in Cornwall, Margo had not become aware of her missing bracelet until Holly, who had guiltily held onto the bracelet a lot longer than she should have, sheepishly returned it to her. Holly had explained that she was given the bracelet together with the wages envelope by The Rising Sun Hotel but had forgotten to bring it with the money when first visiting Margo following her mother's funeral. Margo was sceptical at Holly's explanation and suspected that her friend had thought of keeping the bracelet. But nevertheless, she banished those thoughts and planned to move to London with Holly.

They found a small flat in Kentish Town – a cheaper option than nearby Hampstead, and which was not too far from Central London, where Margo hoped to study. As Margo was too young to negotiate with landlords and sign rental agreement forms, they thought it best to have the agreement in Holly's name as she was now aged twenty. The rent, however, was paid by Margo, as Holly was short of money and looking for a job, either as a receptionist or in retail sales.

The so-called shenanigans had been an evening at home. The two girls were entertaining Holly's new boyfriend – whom she had met at a well-known jazz club in London's Oxford Street. His name was Freddy Wakeson. He was about ten years older than Holly and a successful sports journalist, writing a regular column for one of the popular dailies. Holly seemed smitten with Freddy; the only problem was that he was a married man and had no intention of leaving his wife. Margo had certain basic cooking skills, and she knew a pasta recipe which she could knock-up quite effectively. She had prepared a prawn cocktail for starters and bought in a chocolate cake and ice cream for dessert. She had also purchased several bottles of cheap red wine, bottles of beer and packets of cigarettes. Holly, who had absolutely no cooking skills, did the dusting, vacuum cleaning and general tidying up as well as setting the table for dinner.

Holly was mature for her age and a fiery redhead; her strong facial features and green eyes denoted a very attractive woman, especially when she smiled, but some men were intimidated by her forthright manner. Unlike her younger friend Margo, Holly had enjoyed many sexual encounters in Cornwall, both with boys of her own age and with several older men. Now living in London she was keen to meet a more sophisticated type of man than she had previously experienced. Freddy fitted the bill to perfection. He was tall and rugged with many previous conquests, and the fact that he was a married man did not bother

her at all. He had admitted that besides his wife, he was also having an affair with a neighbour's wife, who was mad about him. This particular friend had actually left his wife when Freddy confessed about the affair. Being a sports reporter, he was away from home a lot, which gave him the freedom to enjoy the company of a variety of women. Holly admired Freddy's openness and had no problem with him being with other women. In fact, she found the idea quite exciting.

Margo had recently found out that she was pregnant but had not told Holly. She knew that the father would be the man she had seduced in the St Mawes hotel. Other than that his name was Simon, she knew nothing about him – as they did not chat at all when she went up to his bedroom. And then of course she left the hotel early the following morning when she received the message about her mum. And even if he had tried to find her, he would have gotten nowhere, as the reception only knew her as Margo Pento from Penzance, and not by her real name, Marie Ridge from Helford River. The only person who had known her real identity was Holly, and she swore to Marie that she had not divulged anything to reception. Besides, Simon and Holly were unaware of each other and Margo had never confided in Holly about her hotel encounter.

Margo enrolled at Covent Garden's Music and Drama College, having passed the entrance exam with distinction. She told the authorities in confidence about her pregnancy, so they did not push her too hard physically. The students were from all different countries and a few years older than her. Margo enjoyed the cosmopolitan atmosphere of the place, and in the early weeks of her time there a young Israeli man befriended her. His name was Dov Katz. Dovs' background was orthodox Jewish – he had been a pupil at Greenshead Jewish Boarding School from 1948 to1951. He'd turned away from religion as an older teenager, which had estranged him from his family and eventually he left Israel to live in London. Dov had coal-black hair – a friendly expressive face with a warm smile and a winning English accent, Hebrew being his first language. Dov was studying singing at the college; his lyrical baritone voice was perfect for the Verdi operatic repertoire which was full of wonderful baritone roles.

The dinner for Freddy had been planned by Holly, whose first thoughts were that Margo could make herself scarce for the evening, but then she realised her hopeless cooking skills and asked Margo to stay in for the evening and take care of the cooking. The day before the allotted evening, Margo was chatting to Dov at college and without thinking, she invited him to dinner for the following evening. Holly was none too pleased when Margo told her that she had invited her new friend, having envisaged Margo acting more like hired-help than host and leaving the two lovebirds to naughtily flirt at the table. As it turned out it was a traditional dinner for four, with adult small talk at the start – but morphing into something more raucous as the dinner progressed and the wine flowed.

Freddy and Dov took an instant dislike to each other. Dov was a homosexual man – sensitive about other people's feelings and had a deep love for the arts. Freddy, on the other hand, was full of himself – rather bombastic in manner and very anti-queers, as he called homosexuals. Dov had not announced himself as queer, but Freddy had an inkling that Dov was of that persuasion. Freddy held court about all his travels and the major sporting events he had attended, which Holly lapped up – looking into Freddy's eyes whilst her man was showing off. The girls mainly talked about how much they were enjoying living in London and how different it was from rural Cornwall, however beautiful the scenery was there.

'So Dov – what are you studying at college?' asked Freddy.

'Opera and singing – I'm a baritone.'

'Oh!' Freddy exclaimed. 'I used to have a friend who was mad about opera – but we fell out because I had an affair with his wife.'

Holly started giggling at that remark and Freddy joined her in a giggling fit. When the laughing stopped, Freddy continued 'I went to an opera once in Milan – it was by Verdi, but I can't for the life of me remember the title. I think it was Simon something?'

'You mean *Simon Boccanegra,*' chipped in Dov.'

'That's the one – and what a boring piece it was. It was a mixed-up plot with dreary music.'

'Sorry to disagree,' piped up Dov – but I love *Simon Boccanegra* and would love one day to sing the great title role.'

Freddy got the giggles again. 'I should introduce you to my one-time friend who also was a fan of that particular opera, but he's disappeared and I have no idea where he's living; however, I'm sure he would not wish to be friends with me again.' he added with a smirk and a wink to Holly.

Dov was feeling uncomfortable with the conversation and thought that Freddy was being disrespectful to his ex-friend, but Holly was enamoured and kept rubbing Freddy's arm whilst looking into his eyes. Margo, who was saying very little, busied herself serving the food, pouring the wine and distributing cigarettes to the others, but not smoking or drinking much herself, which was only noticed by Dov. Her pasta dish was delicious, but again, it was only Dov who congratulated Margo on her cooking. Holly and Freddy were more interested in each other than Margo's food.

Things around the table got even trickier when the conversation turned to politics. Margo excused herself to plate up the dessert and Holly was just hanging on to Freddy's every word, totally ignoring Dov as if he wasn't at the table. Dov... expressed his left-wing views but was unable to vote in UK elections being a foreign national. Freddy explained that although he came from a left-wing family and until very recently held similar views – he was now in the process of moving to the right and thinking of voting Conservative at the upcoming election taking place the following week on 8 October. He said that he liked the cut of the Prime Minister, Harold Macmillan, who had told the British people that 'they had never had it so good.' Although Labour was ahead in the polls, the Tories were closing the gap.

'Why have you changed allegiances?' asked Dov, his opinion of Freddy becoming increasingly negative as the evening progressed.

'Well... although Macmillan was a toff and would have no conception of the ordinary person and how they managed their lives, Gaitskell, the Labour leader, was not from the working class either; in fact, his background was rather privileged – private school, Winchester College and New College Oxford. Besides, the Tories stand for aspiration, whilst Labour attracts the scroungers in society.'

'I don't follow UK politics that closely,' Dov responded, 'but I believe you exaggerate regarding so-called "scroungers," as I know a lot of young people at college who support Labour and none of those are "scroungers." In fact, they are as aspirational as you are. And what about the previous Labour leader – Clement Attlee, who himself was not working class, but his government created the National Health Service and was generally very progressive.'

'Maybe... but with the way my career is developing – the Tories are a better bet for my future.'

Dov did not respond but changed the subject to sport. Freddy then started boasting about his superior knowledge of sport in general and football in particular. Dov enjoyed football and had attended a few matches at Highbury to see Arsenal play at their home ground. Freddy, being an Arsenal supporter, gave Dov a history lesson of Arsenal as the atmosphere around the table became a bit more collegiate. Freddy had brought a bottle of brandy to the dinner party and when Margo served coffee, he opened the bottle and the three of them switched from the wine to the brandy – Margo again holding back on the alcohol. The evening ended with a game of scrabble with raucous laughter whilst polishing off the bottle of brandy.

Dov helped Margo with the washing up whilst Freddy and Holly disappeared into Holly's bedroom. Dov talked openly with Margo about his sexual orientation as he was drying up the dishes, and Margo told him about her pregnancy. She confessed about her boldness in seducing a strange man in his hotel bedroom and how stupid she had been in not insisting that the man used protection.

'He was very irresponsible' remarked Dov.

'No,' it was my fault. I led him on and forbade any conversation with him. I was just looking for the sensation of having sex with a mature man without the complications of getting to know one other. I thought that would be so exciting, and it was in a way, except that the man finished too quickly.'

'Didn't you even know his name?'

'Yes, his name was Simon, but that's all I knew about him.'

'How old was he?'

'I would guess about mid-twenties – and to be honest – I sensed that he was a really nice man.'

'Have you thought about what you will do about the baby, Margo?'

'I don't know, Dov, it's too early to say – but my instincts are to have the baby. I couldn't face an illegal dangerous abortion. And then I would put the baby up for adoption.'

'Let me help you any way I can, Margo.'

'You're so kind, Dov, a real friend.' They hugged and held hands together.

Holly and Freddy eventually emerged from her bedroom, both looking somewhat dishevelled.

'Where do you live, Dov?'

'I share a flat in Kilburn.'

'That's on my way to Wembley, so I'll give you a lift.'

'Thanks Freddy.' Goodbyes were said, the boys heading off into Freddy's car and the girls feeling sleepy, being ready to hit the sack for what few hours were left of the night.

Chapter 15

Milan 1880

My Dear Maestro Verdi

I hope this letter finds you and your wife well. I must thank you for your kind hospitality when I visited your beautiful villa recently. Having communicated with each other so much by post it was wonderful to see you in person looking so healthy and being able to actually hear your wise words in person.

Forgive me Maestro, for my boldness, but can I remind you that during our discussions I mentioned that I had a different idea about the revision of the opera "Simon Boccanegra," but I did not get the opportunity of expressing the idea to you.

I have taken the liberty of writing an alternative libretto for you to read through, and to decide whether this idea is something you wish to work with me on, or if you prefer to revert to the previously agreed revised libretto.

I know my idea is controversial, but you, my dear Verdi, have endured many controversial situations in some of your greatest operas and you were always courageous in dealing with the censors, even if you had to make changes of location to the opera, "Ballo in Maschera," as it was too dangerous to write about the assignation of the King of Sweden, moving it to Boston, with the lead role being the colonial Governor. You also experienced trouble with the censor with regard to "Rigoletto," and everyone damned "La Traviata" for highlighting prostitution. But the biggest risk you took was with "Stiffelio," about a religious leader having to deal with his unfaithful wife. Maestro, you are a brave artist, not shying away from difficult subjects, even courting unpopularity if need be.

The idea I had for the revision of the opera, Simon Boccanegra, *the alternative libretto enclosed with the letter, is to give Simon a new love interest later in the opera, but the love interest is for a man. I know this would create a scandal and the censors would have something to say about that! The man is Pietro, a long-standing colleague and supporter of the Doge, who had a secret relationship with Simon in their young days. Simon, being what's known as 'bisexual, 'later fell in love with Maria, Fiesco's daughter. (This would extend the role of Pietro, who in the original and revised libretto has only a tiny part, with very little to sing.)*

The other change is to make the opera purely a story of reconciliation and forgiveness, (as Mozart did in his opera, La Clemenza di Tito,*) so Paulo, although still the villain, doesn't poison the Doge, but only thinks about doing the dastardly deed. He is not executed in the final act but Simon forgives his treachery – which gives the opera a generally happy ending; Simon lives but abdicates in favour of Gabriele Adorno.*

Maestro, I know my ideas are bold and perhaps even dangerous in our political climate, but I know you like to challenge the establishment, and this libretto would certainly cause a stir. But if any artist alive today is prepared to challenge the accepted norm of behaviour in matters of love and intimate relationships, that artist is my esteemed maestro, Guiseppe Verdi.

With kindest regards to you and your wife,

    Arrigo Boito.

Verdi's response to Boito's letter was short and to the point. No way was he prepared to change the revised libretto at this stage as he had already composed most of the new music required, especially the Council Chamber Scene, and had touched up other bits of the original 1857 score.

He expressed shock that Boito, a colleague that he was beginning to trust, should come up with nonsense such as a man's love for another man. Besides, the idea was not only distasteful to his own personal beliefs, but also it would never ever be able to reach the stage – the censors and opera managements' would run a mile from tackling the subject. He finished by telling Boito to bury the idea and never ever mention it to him again.

Boito was chastened with Verdi's response but not totally surprised. He realised that his proposal had overstepped the mark. But another part of him thought that Verdi, a canny operator, perhaps would have been more open to discuss the concept if it had been the composer's own idea. He was used to being the boss with his various librettists and expected them to carry out his ideas, and obviously Boito still had work to do, for Verdi to accept him as an equal colleague and a joint collaborator on the operas.

When the revised *Simon Boccanegra* opened at La Scala Milan in 1881, Boito's special guest was the widow of the tenor Carlo Negrini, who had sung the part of Gabrielle Adorno at the 1857 premier of the original version of the opera. Boito presented the widow, Clelia Bonola, with a copy of the defunct libretto, as a personal gift, on the condition that it should remain private and not be shown to anyone in the opera business.

PART TWO

Chapter 16

Helena Mentones

Following the breakdown of the relationship with Stephen Zandors, Helena put all her energies into her music. She had fallen head over heels in love with Stephen – it was love at first sight when they'd met at the National Gallery in Dublin – and in her mind, she was planning for a joint life together either in Europe or in New York. But as she began to get over the pain of rejection, she examined herself in greater depth with regard to her state of mind when she visited Dublin for the first time. Perhaps it wasn't Stephen she had fallen in love with, but love itself? Away from home, without her parents fussing around her and being over protective, she had a desire for freedom and adventure and Stephen had been the conduit for such an adventure. Perhaps it could even have been someone else? It was just that Stephen presented himself to her at the gallery and he seemed to fit exactly what she was seeking. And yet, despite Stephen being everything she had been looking for in a man – very attractive – mature – kind and thoughtful as well as being part of her musical world – she realised that she had to move on; to put the whole affair down to experience however delicious it had been, especially the passionate sex, which had felt so perfect between them.

Meanwhile, Helena had applied to compete in ARD (International Music Competition) for their 1984 event in Munich, and if she was successful in passing the audition and preliminary rounds, which could be conducted in New York, she would be going to Europe again.

Helena loved her parents deeply – but as she matured into adulthood she felt that they overprotected her and wanted to be involved in every aspect of her life. Helena certainly did not want to share details of her love life with them. Hence that sense of freedom when she had been in Europe. As well as her parents, her uncle Carl also fretted over her and wanted to know all about her activities – friends and boyfriends. Helena often wondered about Carl and his background and, despite him having been a tough businessman – he was always loving and very generous with her. Consequently, she had a real feeling for him, which was hard for her to rationalise. She knew from her parents that Carl had served in the US army during the Second World War and was posted to London. Helena was also aware that Carl had been briefly married in London and had become involved in his wife's family business – taking the business over and making a lot of money, but the details were all very vague and Carl was always reluctant to discuss his past, especially his time in London. Her parents were protective of Carl because he had evidently been hugely helpful to them, with his knowledge of how things worked in Britain, facilitating them in Helena's adoption process.

Over the years Helena realised that her mum and dad did not wish to gossip about Carl, so Helena stopped pushing the issue. What was strange though – was that Carl had re-married a divorcee – who was, evidently, a very wealthy lady, with two children from a previous marriage, but both Helena and her parents had never over the years met this lady or her children and Carl never spoke about them when visiting New York from his home in California. Although Carl was now a man into his early seventies, he was still fit, well and active, having retired from ownership of a chain of very popular restaurants in California.

He had become a patron of the arts and was on the board of several famous orchestras and leading opera houses. However, when chatting to Carl, Helena realised that he knew very little about music in general – but had become, surprisingly enough, an opera *aficionado* in Los Angeles. Helena was unsure whether Carl actually liked music very much, but the prestige of being on boards of arts organisations gave him the respectability in his late years that he had always craved.

Helena had been aware from a young age that she had been adopted, but when she asked about her natural parents her mum and dad admitted that they knew very little about the details of her natural mum's life. Her natural father was unknown and her mum had died during childbirth. The adoption agency also knew very little other than her name, her age and that she had been living in London, sharing a flat with a male friend who was not the father of her child, and that her family were from Britain's West Country. The adoption agency at the time had made inquiries in the West Country but found no trace of her family background. The man friend she shared a flat with – only knew that they had met at the music and drama college that they had both attended and that they were good friends only and not a couple in a relationship. Nevertheless, the friend evidently had been hugely shocked and distressed that her mother had not survived giving birth. The young man had left London and gone back to his home country in the Middle East soon after the tragedy and became non-contactable. He had mentioned that she had a female friend when they first met; the two girls had shared a flat when they had moved to London together, but evidently had had a bad fall out and lost touch.

The only evidence Helena possessed about her real mother was a cryptic note found amongst her belongings that mentioned a family heirloom – a bracelet that she had given to a friend to look after whilst she was in hospital giving birth, and the hallmark number had been written down in the note. As a sentimental gesture to her birth mother, Helena carried the note with the hallmark number at all times and never travelled anywhere without the note in her possession.

Helena hadn't pursued the matter further with her mum and dad as she grew into an adult, and the fact that she loved her parents deeply kept her curiosity about her personal history buried in the back of her mind, and she did not dwell on the matter. Instinctively though, she felt that one day more information about her natural parents would emerge.

At school, Helena was a star pupil, excelling in a variety of subjects, but music became an obsession very early on in her school life. The school took music seriously with a passionate teacher, Hilda Frender, a Holocaust survivor, encouraging the pupils to take up a musical instrument at the youngest age possible. The school had a decent piano and Helena initially wanted to be a pianist, but having discovered the cello, her love for the instrument became absolute. Hilda Frender's sister Bertha was a private teacher of the cello in New York, and Hilda arranged an audition for Helena with her sister. Bertha immediately saw the potential in Helena and took her on. Helena's parents were happy to pay the fees. Bertha, two years older than Hilda, was also a Holocaust survivor and Bertha escaped the gas chambers in Auschwitz by playing the cello in the camp orchestra whilst Hilda stayed alive by conducting the orchestra. Bertha never spoke about her war experiences to Helena during her lessons with her and certainly Hilda did not divulge anything about herself to the pupils at school; Helena only found out about their background through her parents – as they attended regular parent evenings at the school and the teachers were more open about themselves with the adults. Bertha was more austere than Hilda and less forgiving with Helena – if her cello playing was anything less than perfect, which kept Helena on her toes. Hilda was a warmer personality and they spent more time talking about various great pianists of the past than ticking Helena off about any mistakes she made on the piano. The contrast between the sisters suited Helena's ambitions well, as she wanted to be a professional cellist, so Bertha's 100 per cent focus on technique was the right approach. Piano lessons with Hilda at school were more relaxed – as Helena had turned away from wanting to be a solo pianist, but piano was essential to be able to develop into a creative musician and not just into an instrumental machine.

By the time Helena went to music college – she had become a very good cellist, but despite Hilda's and Bertha's lessons, Helena realised that her general musical knowledge was quite limited. Why was that? Partly this was to do with her family having no real interest in music, so not attending concerts or listening to recordings at home gave Helena a distinct disadvantage amongst her new colleagues at college. Her fellow musicians mainly came from homes and families that were steeped in music – either having parents who were practising musicians or coming from families where music played a central part in their lives, by attending concerts and listening to records at home. The Mentones' gave Helena every encouragement in her musical ambitions but she did not hold it against them that her parents' interests were in lighter entertainment and sporting events.

Helena joined the college orchestra and played in the cello section which gave her an excellent grounding of the orchestral repertoire. The leader of the cello section, Andrew Storrgod, became her first boyfriend. Andrew came from a Finnish family who had moved to the US when his father, the conductor Benjamin Storrgod, became the musical director of the New York Symphony Orchestra.

Helena and Andrew were both aged eighteen when they met at college. As the two of them were both dedicated to music study and practice, they were rather gauche and naive when it came to the machinations of the art of young love and completely inexperienced sexually. Andrew brought Helena into his world and took her home, introducing her to his parents, who became fond of her, although she was rather intimidated by his famous father, whose musical knowledge was out of this world. He'd conducted a huge repertoire, from the baroque period to the moderns, and was known in the musical world as a specialist in the music of the high Romantic nineteenth century composer Anton Bruckner. Storrgod was offered the musical directorship of the New York Symphony, when he conducted, to great acclaim, a complete cycle of Bruckner's nine numbered symphonies, plus the two earlier symphonies, known as No.0 and No. 00.

Andrew was extremely tall and had – light brown wispy hair with strands of hair covering his forehead. He was thin and pale, with thick spectacles, which gave him a sort of nerdy look. Helena, however, had grown into a beautiful young woman but was quite shy, not really appreciating how many boys, much better looking than Andrew, would have loved to date her, but Helena did not, at that young age, possess a flirtatious nature and boys were a bit wary to approach her. With Andrew, it was the cello that brought them together as he helped her settle into the cello section of the orchestra. Helena's best girl friends, who she had known since childhood – Katie Longstock and Sandra Farham, both feigned surprise at Helena's boyfriend choice, but Helena saw in Andrew a highly intelligent, kind and thoughtful young man, who was very respectful to his family despite his father's being a strict disciplinarian who had high expectations for his son. In fact, Helena did not find Andrew unattractive – she saw his sparkling eyes (once he had taken off his spectacles) and sensual mouth that she thought would be nice to kiss.

Helena and Andrew spent most of their time together practising the cello and Andrew taught Helena a lot about various composers – many she had never heard of. They kissed in private and held hands in public but in the early months of their relationship, it went no further than that. One of the composers that Andrew spoke to Helena about was the Swiss -American Ernest Bloch, whose most famous musical work was, *Schelomo* (Solomon), the Hebrew Rhapsody for cello and orchestra premiered in 1917. The college orchestra's conductor, Henry Wanderson, had chosen to programme *Schelomo* as part of the programme for the college's end of term concert. Andrew, being the leader of the cello section of the orchestra, was given the solo cello part, a hugely difficult piece to learn and to play.

Helena sat with Andrew for many hours whilst he practised the part, whilst Helena, unconsciously, learned the part with him.

When the scheduled performance date was just a few days away, Andrew caught the flu and took to his bed. Panic ensued amongst the concert organisers and the conductor, as *Schelomo* wasn't in most cellists' repertoire, even if they wanted to bring in an established professional soloist. Helena, having worked so closely with Andrew learning the piece, boldly went to see the conductor and offered her services in playing the solo part. The conductor, Henry Wanderson, was very sceptical about whether this eighteen year old girl, only in her first year at college, would be able to undertake such a challenge. But when the conductor went through the piece with Helena, he was impressed how much she knew the part. There were a few passages she needed to work on but on the whole Mr Wanderson was satisfied that she could do it. However, when the rehearsal with the orchestra took place a day before the concert, Helena moved from the back of the cello section to centre stage, which caused nerves to bother her. Besides, being unused to playing solo with an orchestra generated several mistakes, and the conductor giving her worrying looks didn't help matters.

The Bloch piece is unlike a conventional concerto, which sets the solo instrument apart from the orchestra, sometimes in dialogue and other times in opposition. A cello concerto is especially difficult as the instrument is deep sounding and needs careful balancing by the conductor for the solo cello to be heard. As *Schelomo* was a rhapsody, the soloist is more integrated with the orchestra than the standard concerto – balancing becomes even more tricky than usual. Consequently, Helena became confused during the orchestral rehearsal as she couldn't hear herself play. The conductor became increasingly frustrated and began to wonder whether he was wise to offer such a difficult solo part to the musical novice Helena.

Helena felt dispirited after the rehearsal and almost threw the towel in, cancelling her performance, which would at that late hour cause chaos to the whole programme. She controlled her nerves and telephoned Andrew's father, Mr Storrgod – hoping he was at home in New York and not guest conducting somewhere else in the world. Luckily, Benjamin Storrgod answered the telephone, and after inquiring about Andrew and wishing the patient well, Helena, stumbling over her words, asked if he could spare her a few minutes to help with certain difficulties with her playing of the solo cello part of Bloch's *Schelomo*, and said she would bring her cello with her. Storrgod said that he was willing to help but she should leave the cello at home as they arranged to have a short chat about the piece early the following morning – literally hours before the concert. Helena arrived at the Storrgod home at the agreed time; popped upstairs to see Andrew, who was still in bed but beginning to feel a lot better, and then sat down with his father in Storrgod's study, both nursing a large mug of fresh coffee.

'Forget about any playing difficulties; my sources have informed me that you know the part backwards and you have a good technique for someone with limited opportunities so far to play much in public, especially with orchestra. *Schelomo* for sure is a difficult piece but I'm confident that you have the measure of it. But, my dear Helena, what do you know about the character of King Solomon? What do you know about the composer Ernest Bloch? And most importantly, what do you know about Judaism?'

Helena repeatedly shook her head at the questions – feeling embarrassed about her lack of insight of the background to the piece she was about to play to an audience.

'Yes – I thought so. Please don't take this personally – but that's the trouble with music education these days – it's all about the technique of the playing, but music is so much more than that. Andrew mocks me for doing too much research into every piece I conduct and never forgets to remind me that I turned to conducting when I realised that my piano playing was not quite good enough to make a career as a concert pianist. He's right, of course, about my abortive piano career, but he misses the point about the wider aspects of music. How much time did Andrew or Wanderson spend talking to you about the background to the piece?'

Again, Helena shook her head.

'Look, Helena, I have a very busy day ahead and I can't spare much time with you this morning, but I've left three books for you to take away and I've marked the passages you should try to read before the concert, and try to think about what you've read whilst playing the piece tonight. Trust me, your playing won't let you down, but have a polite word with your conductor Wanderson – that he should not drown out your playing – by letting the orchestra rip. Now, off you go and good luck for tonight.'

Helena went back home with the books Andrew's dad had given her and instead of picking up her cello for a final practice of her solo part in the Bloch Rhapsody, she grabbed a sandwich and a cold drink whilst checking out the books and where they had been marked. The first book was a biography of Bloch, and Storrgod had highlighted a few paragraphs that referred to *Schelomo* and how the composer had originally wanted the character of Solomon to be a singing part for a deep bass voice, but although Bloch was Jewish, he had felt that his Hebrew wasn't sufficiently proficient enough to go down that route. From a chance meeting with the cellist, Hans Kindler, whose wife had sculpted a wax figurine of Solomon – the idea grew that Solomon would be represented by a solo cello as a substitute for the human voice. The piece represents King Solomon, not in all his pomp, but as a sad old man with despairing thoughts that with worldly wisdom there was grief and sorrow.

But Bloch was not so much interested in the actual character of Solomon but in the meaning of some of the darkest passages of the *Book of Ecclesiastes,* supposedly written by Solomon in his old age. The deep growl of the cello perfectly mirrored the state of mind of the king, but orchestral passages in the work contained music of oriental perfumed exoticism and lyrical sensuality which suggested concubines dancing erotically.

Time was running out for Helena, as she was due at college for a final run through, but she still managed to read a paragraph or two about King Solomon. Other than knowing the name, she had virtually no idea about him. His dates are thought to be 970 – 931 BCE. The son of King David, Solomon was responsible for building the First Temple in Jerusalem and was the penultimate king who had ruled over both the Kingdom of Israel and the Kingdom of Judea. He was an extremely wise king as well as being fabulously wealthy and hugely powerful.

What Helena managed to read about Ernest Bloch (1880 –1959) surprised her, as she had thought him to be a composer exclusively writing Jewish-inspired music. *Schelomo* was the culmination of a series of works that explored Bloch's Jewish heritage. But his range of musical styles was wide and varied with an overall impressively large output. He composed a body of work in the neoclassical style and was also influenced by American native music, as well as an early foray into writing opera, composing a *Macbeth* opera which was highly considered at the time. Helena had not even heard of the composer before *Schelomo* was chosen to be performed by the college orchestra. Thinking he was a minor musical figure whilst learning the piece, Helena realised that Bloch was a significant twentieth-century composer, and she was determined to pay him the greatest respects.

New York was a city highly populated by Jews, but Helena, although coming across Jews in her everyday life – in particular her two music teacher sisters, Hilda and Bertha Frender, did not have specifically any Jewish friends, and as far as she knew, her parents' social circle did not include Jews. They certainly were in no way antisemitic and she had never heard any racist comments at home, but her parents were socially conservative and generally mixed with people from similar backgrounds to themselves.

The paragraphs in the book about Judaism that Storrgod had marked for her to read – were not about the Holocaust or about any type of Jewish victimhood, but rather stressed the long incredible history of the Jewish people and what a proud people they were, excelling themselves in so many different aspects of cultural, social, professional and commercial activities. This description of Jews spoke to young Helena, and for the first time since learning to play *'Schelomo,'* she felt deeply about what Bloch was trying to convey in the music: *'I am proud of my Jewish heritage; we are a people full of world weariness but also a people who are able to express incredible joy.'*

'Schelomo' was the second item on the programme, which was an all American one. The concert opened with Leonard Bernstein's effervescent overture to his operetta, *Candide*, and the concert closed with Aaron Copland's majestic third symphony, which included the famous 'Fanfare for the Common Man.' Helena felt very nervous during the overture, but thankfully, the piece only lasted a few minutes so she had no time to dwell on her nerves. The audience gave her warm applause as she took her place, carrying her cello, in front of the orchestra and taking a seat on the stall provided. Shaking hands with the conductor and the orchestra leader, Helena started to play – a sort of cello solo to open the piece, with light orchestral accompaniment – so no time to think about anything as the cello has to set up the whole opening structure of the work. As the music proceeds the orchestra begins to take a more prominent part in the proceedings culminating in the most amazing lyrical climax full of emotional intensity. Later on in the piece, the same beautiful melody is played solo on the cello. By this point which was about halfway through the twenty odd minute score, Helena forgot about her nerves and as someone who previously had no knowledge of Jewish history, felt through the music the whole Jewish experience in her soul, through the music and a real connection to the composer and to what he was trying to express. In other words, she gave herself up to the piece and the cello almost played itself. The big theme comes back once more for the full orchestra, but the cello has the last word with an almost abrupt finish.

Silence in the auditorium – Helena was in a state of shock that she had actually finished playing – then the clapping started with many people cheering. Coming out of her daze, she smiled and bowed to the audience – shook hands again with the conductor and leader – acknowledging the orchestra with a large wave of her arm. Conductor and soloist were hand in hand – both bowing deeply – the conductor whispering in her ear how marvellously she had played.

In the front row she spotted Andrew with his father clapping madly and stamping their feet. Andrew must have made a miraculous recovery to have managed to be well enough to attend. Next to them sat her mum and dad looking so proud of their daughter, although she imagined that the music had gone over their heads somewhat. After several more calls for Helena to take a bow, the clapping slowly subsided and the orchestra left the stage for the interval. Her parents, Andrew and his dad went backstage to congratulate Helena, and as she was hugging her mum and dad Hilda and Bertha Frender entered the room, smiling from ear to ear and feeling just a little smug that they had contributed so much to Helena's musical emergence as a wonderful cellist. Benjamin Storrgod was gracious and could not have been more complimentary to Helena and told her that she had not only played the part brilliantly, but she had captured the essence of the piece especially in her soft playing. Helena admitted to him that the last-minute reading she had done on the composer etc. had been invaluable as she immersed herself in the rhapsodic nature of the work and the soulfulness of its message.

She thanked him profusely for his help and for his understanding of what she needed in her head to be able to convey the world of King Solomon in all its sorrow, whilst the magnificent contribution of the orchestra was overwhelming in its many colours of showing the splendour of the Hebrew Temple and Court. The conductor, Wanderson, popped into the room briefly with his congratulations, before returning to the stage for the Copland symphony. Andrew was very quiet but was obviously a bit shaky coming straight from his bed. He told Helena that she was fantastic and that he could not have played it any better. But Helena noted an element of regret in his voice and manner, which of course was understandable in the circumstances for as much as he was thrilled for Helena – he had been looking forward so much to playing *Schelomo* in the concert.

The second half of the concert was ready to commence as they all made their way back into the auditorium – her parents having saved a seat for her next to them. The Copland was beautifully played and even her parents smiled at the recognition of 'Fanfare for the Common Man,' which introduced the final fourth movement of the symphony.

If Helena thought she was now a musical star she would have been greatly mistaken. Once the euphoria of the concert died down and Andrew was back as leader of the cello section, Helena was back to being the junior cellist in the college orchestra. And she could forget about Benjamin Storrgod engaging her for any of his concerts – in fact, he tended to ignore her when she was in his house visiting Andrew. She gave the odd recital at her old school with Hilda Frender at the piano. She entered a few local competitions and always came first or second, but those competitions had no real significance in the wider musical world.

Helena spent the following few years being a conscientious student; learning lots of cello repertoire – solo, chamber and concerto pieces – and again, Andrew being hugely supportive in her endeavours.

The problem was that once she had graduated in 1981 there were almost no engagements offered to her, except some fringe events that paid very poorly. She was still living at home with her parents, who had no issues with that, as they were comfortably off from her dad's pharmacy business. But Helena did not wish to be dependent on her parents and even thought of giving up her ambition for a musical career. Andrew had been successful in getting a post with an orchestra in Philadelphia; not the famous Philadelphia orchestra, the orchestra of famous conductors such as Leopold Stokowski followed by Eugene Ormandy. His appointment was with the city's second orchestra, with a position in the cello section of the East Coast Symphony Orchestra.

As Philadelphia was only eighty miles away from New York, Andrew came back to his parents' home whenever he had a few days off and spent time with Helena. Whilst in Philadelphia he shared a house with three other fellow male musicians from the orchestra. It certainly helped Andrew that he was the son of the conductor Benjamin Storrgod in getting the post.

As Helena was spending less time with Andrew she spent many hours in the local library, and she eventually managed to get a part time job as a librarian. Having spent so much time practising the cello, her general education had been limited. The library was a great source of knowledge in wide-ranging subjects, especially history and literature. She became an avid reader of both the classic novels and quality contemporary fiction. Helena had more time to see her old friends, Katie Longstock and Sandra Farnham. Unfortunately, she was becoming distant from them as their focus was in fashion and exploring the nightlife of New York – something Helena had no interest in at all. What Helena was discovering from reading was that the world was a big place with so many different types of peoples and cultures.

Helena was beginning to explore – through reading books by such figures as D H Lawrence and female writers including Daphne Du Maurier, Colette, Anais Nin, Erica Jong and the French writer, Simone de Beauvoir – intimate subjects such as sensuality, eroticism and female sexuality. Helena was maturing as a woman and felt that as much as she was very fond of Andrew, she saw him more as a good friend or even as a brother that she didn't have, but had doubts about their sexual relationship. Helena wished to experience uninhibited sexual passion and amazing orgasms – that was lacking with Andrew.

She realised that she needed to travel – to see new places and meet new people and hopefully enjoy a passionate love affair. Her life was too narrowly based living at home in New York, with a routine existence between home, practising and learning new repertoire for cello, the library and seeing Andrew when he was in town.

Helena's rather dull life continued more or less the same for another couple of years except for the odd forays with her friends, Katie and Sandra, to a Manhattan bar and even once to a louche night club which she hated, finding the type of people there superficial and pretentious, so she never repeated the experience. With Andrew they went to the New York Met opera as often as they could afford the tickets, and Andrew's father gave them free concert tickets whenever he was conducting his New York symphony orchestra.

Helene's big opportunity to travel came in 1983, when, at that time, Benjamin Storrgod, was away from New York, guest conducting in London, with the Royal Symphony Orchestra. The London's orchestra's manager just happened to mention to Storrgod during a break in rehearsals, that they were looking for a cellist and if he could recommend someone, he would set up an audition for that person. The maestro didn't think much about it but when back in New York and hearing Helene practising with Andrew one day in the house, it made him sit up and listen to her playing and remembering how well she had performed the Bloch Hebrew Rhapsody some years previously at her college concert. He thought – why not? He was also worldly enough to know that the romance between Helene and his son was puppy love and did not have real longevity. His instincts guessed that Andrew could actually be gay, but those thoughts were something he would very much keep to himself. He would give the Mentones' a call and get their thoughts on the matter, before approaching Helene with the idea – knowing how protective they were of their only child.

The Mentones' had mixed feelings about Helena going to Europe. They were savvy enough to realise that a career in music meant constant travel, if Helena was going to have any kind of a successful career. But in any event, they would not stand in their daughter's way. Besides, they were a bit in awe of Benjamin Storrgod, he being a famous conductor. Classical music was not really their thing, but they also respected any famous person, in whatever sphere their fame had occurred. It would have been an unwise move to refuse career help from Storrgod – who was a great contact for Helena to have onside. Perhaps they were a bit naive to even think about making decisions for their twenty-three year old daughter. Helena was way past the age of having to get permission from her parents to do anything or to go anywhere at any time.

Helena of course was absolutely thrilled with the prospect of going to London, making new musical contacts, and hopefully, new personal contacts. In the back of her mind she hoped that she might also have the opportunity to visit Dublin for a few days as she had become fascinated with Ireland from books she had picked up in the library. She had read books by the historian, J C Beckett and the historian/politician, Connor Cruise O'Brien. For a more republican viewpoint she had read books by Tim Pat Coogan. She had tried James Joyce's *Ulysses* but found it difficult; she loved reading W B Yeats, which portrayed the Celtic and Romantic Ireland.

Helena broke the news to Andrew that she was going to London for an audition and he was thrilled for her on that issue, but much less thrilled when she told him that although she would always consider him a wonderful friend, she wanted to end being his girlfriend. Andrew took it badly and became very sulky with her. He even complained to his father about her, but surprisingly, his dad would not hear a critical word about Helena and told him to man-up and move on with his life.

Helena did not unfortunately pass the orchestra audition in London, but she met and fell in love with Stephen in Dublin – which ended in heartbreak.

Helena passed all the preliminary rounds for the 1984 ARD competition in Munich and left home and New York again for destination Munich in Germany. She won first prize in the cello section and became the overall winner in all the categories for that year. Besides a cash sum, a solo recording with the Decca label was part of the prize, which she recorded whilst still in Munich – a mixed programme of Bach's cello suites and Kodaly's sonata for solo cello, which was a major work for the instrument.

The agent, Keith Foes, whom she had met in London the year before, contacted Helena by telephone, sounding very puffed up and full of self praise when speaking with Helena. To be fair to him though, he had originally given Helena the idea of entering the ARDS competition. He proposed to represent her and that if she signed up with him, he would arrange immediately for an audition for her in London with the British Philharmonic Orchestra, which was not only considered at the time, the leading London orchestra, but as well as their London and international touring season, they were the resident orchestra throughout the summer months at the country's famous opera festival on the south coast of England – the Glyndehurst Opera Festival.

Helena had originally thought, and still did, that Foes was overbearing and annoyingly, too self-confident for his own good, but she signed up with him nevertheless, as she assumed that that was what agents were like – being part of a very competitive business – in making sure one signed up the best artists before the competition did. Besides recommending ARDS to her, he had also been instrumental in getting the engagement at London's Wigmore Hall in 1983, playing with the renowned Bocca String Quartet – standing in for the cellist Janet Shall following her unfortunate car accident.

Helena flew to London for the audition. She tried to erase any thoughts of Stephen from her mind. When she arrived in London, she checked into a hotel that Keith Foes had booked for her, a large non-personal hotel in the Russell Square area.

Although being nervous attending the audition, she was confident that she had acquitted herself to the very best of her ability. Keith Foes rang her at her hotel the following morning to give her the good news – she had passed the audition and she would be offered a place in the cello section of the orchestra from the beginning of the 1984/5 season.

Helena flew back to New York and gave her parents the news that she had got a job in London, playing for one of the great orchestras of the world. Her parents were delighted for her but sad for themselves, as they realised that Helena would develop a life of her own in England, and that she might become estranged from them – by not only being thousands of miles apart from each other, but also by becoming culturally too sophisticated for them – losing the closeness they had always had since the day they adopted her nearly a quarter of a century earlier.

Helena telephoned Benjamin Storrgod – sharing her good news with him and thanking him profusely for all his help he had given her over the previous few years. She inquired after Andrew but did not speak with him or arrange for them to meet each other.

Helena spent the following few months preparing to leave for London, this time on a more permanent basis. Keith Foes arranged temporary accommodation for when she was due to arrive back in London and advised her that she might wish to share a flat with one or two of her orchestra colleagues, once she had settled in and made a few friends.

Chapter 17

Stephen Zandors

Stephen had loved living in Dublin at his bohemian flat in Leeson Street, but that period of his life was coming to an end. He was surprised but thrilled and excited to have managed to clinch the artistic directorship position at the prestigious opera festival at Glyndehurst, on the south coast of England – a position that was sought after by much bigger names than his in the music industry.

Acting as a consultant to the proposed new opera festival on Lake Corrib, on the border between Counties Galway and Mayo, would keep a link for him in Ireland, but even if that project ever saw the light of day, it would be some years before the opera house was built and performances ready to be staged. However, he was keen on the idea and thought it could be something special, attracting an international audience and doing wonders for the local economy of the area.

Stephen missed Helena hugely, especially whilst he was still living in the flat where they had enjoyed so much fun and pleasure together. He had genuinely fallen in love with her but was reluctant to commit. Refusing to visit Helena in New York freaked her out and she took the view that Stephen was only looking for a casual affair. That was partly true, especially that first weekend, after they had got together at the National Gallery of Ireland. But when Stephen met up with Helena in London, he became aware of the way she conducted herself in dealing with aspects of the music business, and her playing with the Bocco String Quartet at the Wigmore Hall, was nothing less than a triumph, and he saw something in her that was not so much visible in Dublin, where she had come for a few days purely as a tourist. But seeing this beautiful talented young woman in real life situations made him realise that he had met someone really special who he could spend the rest of his life with.

So why did he mess it up? Perhaps subconsciously he thought that she was going to be a big star on the classical music circuit, and was nervous about his own status in a relationship pecking order. Of course, if he had known then about his winning the Glyndehurst artistic directorship at the time, he would have felt more comfortable, but with no disrespect to the Dublin Grand Opera Society, the company was a backwater in the operatic world, and at the time he didn't see any prestigious jobs coming his way.

Stephen also worried about what his parents' attitude would be if he had taken Helena home to meet his parents in Suffolk, England, and in particular, if he had hinted at a possible marriage. His parents, being such British snobs, would quiz the poor girl about her background and would wish to know who her real parents were etc. Even as a man in his mid- thirties, his parents still had an unhealthy influence on him, however much he had tried to break away from their sterile attitude to anything that didn't fit in with their ultra- conservative narrow view of the world.

Actually, it wasn't even his professional status or his parents' disapproval that was holding him back from committing to Helena. It was a more cultural thing between them. Helena, although born in England, was an American through and through and gushed like Americans do, whilst Stephen, the son of the most traditional British family imaginable, had been trained not to show emotions over many generations – stiff upper lip and all that. Helena's love letters to Stephen were wonderful and sincere but they scared him – all emotions out there, nothing held back – so American and so non- British. To make it worse, he was rubbish at writing any sort of personal correspondence, let alone love letters. Receiving her heartfelt words froze him and made him feel exposed.

On reflection, he knew all that was absolute rubbish and he had probably let the love of his life slip away – the complete fool that he was.

Stephen had rebelled, to a certain extent, against his parents right-wing political views, but it was a limited rebellion. He still voted for the Tory Party, but supported the one-nation Conservatives and was only a half-hearted supporter of Margaret Thatcher.

Stephen had a local friend from nearby Orford, Peter Allcote, the son of the local butcher, who would eventually take over from his dad and run the shop. They got to know each other in the local pub, The Kings Head, where Pete was doing part-time bar work to supplement his meagre wages his dad paid him for working in the butcher shop. Stephen often popped into the King's Head for a pint when mooching around Orford after walking the coastal path from Chillesford, which was close to his family estate.

The year was 1967 and both Stephen and Pete were aged nineteen. They were total opposites in so many ways, but they saw something in each other that led to a mutual curiosity which developed into a friendship between the two young men – both Suffolk born and bred but they could have come from different planets.

1967 was a gap year for Stephen between Eton College and Cambridge University. A lot of his school friends who had places mainly at Oxbridge (shorthand for Oxford and Cambridge universities) travelled to far-flung places as a right-of-passage before university life. Stephen, as a boarder at Eton, decided to spend the year at home in Suffolk, as he loved their particular landscape with the North Sea, the rivers' Alde and Ore as well as Butley Creek, to explore; in fact, the whole of the Suffolk coastal area was one of the most beautiful areas in the whole of England. As well as coast and rivers, the area was rich farming country and it also contained some magnificent forests.

Stephen loved both cycling and walking, but the terrain of the coastal paths, farmlands and forests, made it more suitable for walking than cycling, and once he got to know Pete Allcote better, he suggested that they did some serious walking together in their beautiful Suffolk coastal area.

Walking the Suffolk coastal paths together, the two lads bonded; walking side by side stimulated chat that was more than the casual banter one generally engaged in whilst drinking pints in the pub. Pete was very much rooted to the local area – being educated in the local school and having never ventured very far from Suffolk – except for the occasional family holiday on the Essex coast and a couple of school trips, once to London and once to the city of York. Whereas Stephen had been on many family vacations to various European holiday hot spots in France, Italy and Switzerland and regular trips to the North Norfolk coast and Cornwall. And going to London was a regular occurrence for Stephen, either with his Eton College mates on a pub crawl, or with his family for cultural fare – catching up with opera, concerts, theatre and eating at the best restaurants. Despite Pete's limited worldly experience and local education – leaving school at age sixteen and immediately starting to work for his dad in the butcher shop, he was a thoughtful and curious young man. The local library was a great outlet for Pete, who borrowed books on all sorts of subjects including history and politics. So, despite Stephen's perceived superiority of knowledge, education and worldly experience, the truth was that, because of Pete's natural intelligence and curiosity, they were actually two equals.

During the summer months, the boys cycled to Aldeburgh or Walberswick for swimming and picnics on the beach. Once the weather got a little cooler, they attempted longer walks – deciding to walk the whole of the Suffolk coast which was sixty odd miles long from Felixstowe to Lowestoft. The plan was that they would walk the path in two tranches, both times starting from Aldeburgh which was exactly half-way of the full path – two thirty mile walks. They tackled the Aldeburgh to Lowestoft first on a warm early autumn day, starting out at dawn cycling to Aldeburgh, and having checked the tides beforehand, walked the whole way on the beach with a short ferry ride between Walsberwick and Southwold.

A couple of weeks later they walked the other thirty mile track – again starting from Aldeburgh beach. This was a more varied walk than the previous all-beach one, as the coast was not a straight line between Aldeburgh and Felixstowe. From Aldeburgh to Snape, through what's known as the Sailors Path, which in times past, was a well-known smugglers' rat run, then onto Blaxhall forest leading to Chillesford on the way to Butley River, where they stopped for an early picnic lunch. Then they followed the Butley River path, where they met a man repairing the local ferry boat that, when in usage, crossed the short strip of river as if one was walking back to Orford. They got into a chat with the man, and when they told him that they had started off walking from Aldeburgh early that morning, he looked at them as if they were mad, unable to contemplate covering such a distance in a morning. Then when they told the man that they were off to Felixstowe, the man just shook his head, totally perplexed at the energies of youth!

Staying on the same side of the river where the path winds its way down to Shingle Street, there was an eerie landscape of a layered beach that felt that one could be on the moon whilst being on the beach. On they walked to Bawdsey, which eventually led, via another more standard beach, but a rocky one, which is hard on the feet for walkers, down to the ferry that crosses over to Felixstowe. At the end of a long tiring day, they had to negotiate a longish walk from the ferry to Felixstowe railway station. They caught a train back to Ipswich where one of Stephen's brothers picked them up and drove them back to Aldeburgh to collect their bicycles.

What did the boys talk about during their walking marathons where a deep feeling of camaraderie between them had established itself? In the misty early morning when starting off from Aldeburgh – both of them were conscious of the long day of walking ahead of them, so the conversation wouldn't exactly flow at that stage. They'd just talk small talk about what food goodies were in their respective rucksacks to tuck into during the picnic. Once they reached Snape and made a short pit stop for some coffee from their flasks, the boys feeling less tense as the walk was then well on its planned trajectory, and with the sun coming through the clouds, conversation started to open up between them.

Pete was telling Stephen about his girlfriend, Nancy, who was the same age as Pete, whom he had known since his schooldays, and they'd become boy and girlfriend in their final year at school – having remained so ever since. Nancy was a pretty girl with a friendly disposition and a lovely smile. Like Pete, she was from an Orford family going back many generations and had no desire to move away from her home village. Going out to town for Nancy was a trip to nearby Aldeburgh – just across the river but a good half an hour's drive by car, or three quarters of an hour's journey by bus. She would occasionally visit Aldeburgh during daytime for shopping or go with Pete on a Saturday night for a dance at the Jubilee Hall. Nancy worked at the local post office, and as well as being very efficient on the counter, all the local customers loved her for her interest in everyone's personal problems and health issues. She always asked after their children and even remembered all the kids' names.

'Do you love her?' Stephen asked Pete as he turned around towards his friend on the wrought iron bench as they were just finishing off their flasks of tea before setting off on the next trance of their walk.

'Of course I do,' Pete responded too quickly for Stephen to be sure that he meant it, or perhaps he was still trying to work out for himself exactly what 'love' was. 'To be honest, Stephen, I've nothing to compare it with – Nancy being my only girlfriend I've ever had, and we plan to marry in a few years' time. She's great to be with as well as being intelligent, caring and practical. She'll make a really good wife.'

Stephen, listening to Pete, had no intentions of putting doubts in his friend's mind, and having met Nancy on several occasions he appreciated that she was a lovely girl, and they seemed devoted to each other, but how did they know at aged nineteen, that they would wish to spend the rest of their lives together? Maybe Pete was more mature than he was as Stephen couldn't imagine having a steady girlfriend with marriage in mind at that stage of his life.

'Following a few moments of silence between them and as they re-started walking again, Pete broke the silence. 'What about you Stephen?'

'To be honest, Pete, I haven't actually met that many girls, as my friends have always been boys, but yes, it would be nice to have a girlfriend.'

'Why don't you come with me and Nance to one of the Saturday night dances at the Jubilec Hall in Aldeburgh? They always get a good few single girls there and you might see someone you fancy.'

'Sure, Pete, that's kind of you to ask. I would love to go there with you two sometime.'

Pete had always been reserved about the nature of his relationship with Nancy – not discussing any detail about their physical love life. Were they having sex or not? Although the couple held hands and he had seen them kissing and cuddling – Stephen's instincts were that they were saving up full sex for marriage and not before, which was very much the nature of things in small country villages, such as Orford, where everyone seemed to know everyone else's business.

As the two boys walked through Blaxhall Forest towards Chillesford, Stephen decided that he had no intentions of confiding in Pete about his sexual awakening with his mother's friend in Wales, but clarified his earlier remark. 'We didn't really have much opportunity at Eton College to meet girls and to be honest some of my friends were more interested in looking for boyfriends than girlfriends.'

'That's disgusting, Stephen. I can't understand why a boy would fancy a boy, and in any case, in Orford that sort of behaviour would be totally frowned upon, even though I read in the papers the other day that the government had decriminalised homosexuality between consenting adults in private. Maybe you could find a nice girl at the Aldeburgh dance, and then we could hang out as a foursome.'

Stephen was feeling a little uncomfortable with the conversation about girlfriends as, although he would be happy to join his friends at an Aldeburgh dance, and maybe flirt with some of the local girls, he couldn't envisage taking a local girl home and introducing her to his parents as his girlfriend. They would only welcome a girl from the same class background as them and viewed the locals as of a lower order – needed of course for trade and service, and although they were polite to the locals, they would never socialise with them or consider them their equals.

Although Stephen was a Tory – he had liberal ideas, unlike his parents who had very reactionary views about social and moral behaviour, and they especially hated the Home Secretary, Roy Jenkins, who had been the minister responsible for the legalisation of queer behaviour, and who was also lining up Parliament to vote on legalising abortion.

However, Stephen admired Jenkins but kept this to himself, especially when discussing politics with his father at home.

To change tack from talking about girlfriends with Pete on their marathon walk, Stephen turned to politics, although he thought Pete would have little interest in the subject, but he was wrong as Pete showed a real enthusiasm for it.

'You know, Stephen, that this constituency has always voted Conservative, and my dad, being a shop owner, had always voted that way – but now they've reduced the voting age from twenty-one to eighteen and I was eligible for my first vote at the 1966 election last year, I voted Labour and was thrilled that they got back in with a decent majority. My dad was disgusted and thinks the Labour Party are in hock to the unions – but in my opinion, people like us, lower middle-class country folk, should be natural Labour Party people instead of voting like a *toff* – for the Tories. What do you think…Stephen?'

'To be honest Pete, with my background I feel I'm naturally a Tory, and my father would disown me if I ever admitted to him that I had voted Labour; although I don't like or trust the prime minister Harold Wilson, I do admire certain Labour cabinet ministers, such as Roy Jenkins and Anthony Crossland.'

'Good for you Stephen – but Wilson's alright too; you should follow my example and vote Labour next time and just don't tell your father.' The two boys chuckled at Pete's remark – and on they went – trekking towards their destination of Felixstowe.

On a subsequent walk with Pete in November of that year, politics came up again in their chat together. At this time they just stuck to a beach walk from Aldeburgh to Walberswick – a decent fifteen mile hike, keeping away from the country paths which had become extremely soggy following a very wet autumn. They'd checked the tides beforehand to make sure they walked during low tide, making walking a lot easier, as they avoided walking on stony ground but had nice soft sand to tread into with their boots. The boys talked about the economic woes of the Labour government. Harold Wilson and his Chancellor of the Exchequer, James Callaghan had just devalued the pound. Wilson had broadcast to the nation and made a remark about the 'pound in your pocket' which his opponents considered a rather scurrilous statement that tried to cover up the seriousness of the situation.

Stephen had cut out Wilson's statement from *The Times* newspaper. It read: '*From now on, the pound abroad is worth 14% or so less in terms of other currencies. That doesn't mean, of course, that the pound here in Britain, in your pocket or purse, or in your bank, has been devalued.'* Stephen tried to hide his sarcasm as he read out the *The Times* quote, as he knew how keen his friend Pete was on the Labour government and didn't wish to enter into an argument with him.

Pete's brow was furrowed and he looked serious. 'The problem with the Labour Party was that they were not in government for enough time to create a fairer society. The 1945 Labour government was a great reforming one but then they were out of office for thirteen years – time enough for the Tories to roll back Labour's achievements in favour of people with inherited wealth. Wilson's been trying his best but it's an uphill struggle.'

Although Stephen disagreed with Pete's analysis and thought Wilson was a charlatan, he was quietly impressed with his friend's seriousness and his real interest in politics. The chat then drifted off from politics to other more frivolous subjects such as pop music and gossip about swinging London.

They arrived at the Anchor Inn at Walberswick with aching legs and hungry stomachs. They knocked back a few pints of local beer and a large plate each of a slap-up Ploughman's lunch, including ham, cheese and pickles, as they waited for Stephen's mum to arrive by car to give the boys a lift back to Aldeburgh where their bikes had been left.

Stephen reflected on his friend Pete Allcote and how different they were. In many ways Pete was the more mature of the two for their nineteen years, which Stephen acknowledged to himself. Pete knew and accepted his future trajectory – eventually taking over his father's butcher's shop, settling down, marrying and starting a family with Nancy, and living a productive good citizen's life in his home village of Orford. But Pete wasn't just a robotic carbon copy of his dad – as demonstrated by supporting the Labour Party which went against his family's solid conservative values.

During the boys thirty mile walk from Aldeburgh to Felixstowe in the summer of 1967 when Pete was talking about his girlfriend Nancy Feathering, Stephen was tempted at the time to tell Pete about his sexual adventure, in a suburb of Cardiff, Wales, with his mother's attractive friend, Laura Elling. He had felt uncomfortable unburdening himself to his friend, not wanting Pete to be judgemental about his having sex with a married woman, especially with Laura's husband Ben and Stephen's mother Susan, asleep in the house when the liaison occurred.

Laura and Susan had been friends for many years – having been at boarding school together during the pre-war years of the 1930s'. They were inseparable and hugely supportive of each other when one of them got into trouble with a teacher or was bullied by one of the other girls.

They stayed close friends during their teenage years but their paths diverged on marriage. Susan married the wealthy upper-class gentleman Kenneth Zandors, whilst Laura married a middle-class Welsh Jewish chemist, Ben Elling, who was ten years older than her. Although their lives went in different directions, the two women kept in touch through the years of bearing children and bringing up families. As the years went on and their respective children had grown-up, Susan and Laura started meeting up again – just the two of them without spouses as Kenneth was rather snobbish about Ben Elling – thinking of him as just a tradesperson, despite Ben having achieved major medical qualifications and his chemist shop being very successful. Stephen had heard a lot about Laura from his mum over the years but had never actually met her. Kenneth was spending the weekend at his club in London, The Carlton Club in St James, a bastion of the Tory party; the club was hosting a special weekend to bolster support for their beleaguered leader, Ted Heath, who had lost the general election to Harold Wilson's Labour.

Stephen's older brothers were also away so it was just Stephen at home the weekend his mother invited Laura to stay. Stephen, at age eighteen, was curious to meet this long-standing friend of his mother – not for a minute thinking that he could be attracted to a woman about the same age as his parents, mid-forties, which seemed quite old to an eighteen year youth. However, he was struck by how different in style Laura was to his mother, who wore sensible clothes, classically designed outfits bought from O & C Butcher Outfitters in Aldeburgh – the establishment that women of her class shopped at. Laura, however, was dressed in her name-sake, Laura Ashley, a Victorian-inspired long floral frock, and was sporting a large straw hat – the look the girls in their twenties were wearing along the Kings Road in London. This gave her a look much younger than her actual age. Her hair was long and blonde – naturally set and nothing like the perm hair style his mother preferred. Laura, tallish, had a longish face, a slightly bigger nose than was ideal, sparkling blue eyes and a good set of teeth – not a conventional beauty by any means, but she had a lovely smile and conveyed a sense of living for the moment – being interested in everything and everyone.

Stephen immediately felt a connection with Laura but became shy and withdrawn in her presence, not being conscious that he found Laura physically alluring and that he became aroused in her company. Whilst his mum was in the kitchen, Laura slowly drew Stephen out of his reticence and the conversation turned to music. It transpired that they both loved the music of George Gershwin, and Laura mentioned that she had heard Gershwin's opera *Porgy and Bess* recently and was totally smitten with the music and the story, which was so different from any other opera that she had heard. Laura, saying this to Stephen, was looking at him straight in the eyes, which although it made Stephen a little uncomfortable, also added to his arousal.

Just as the conversation was getting interesting, his mother came back into the room and Stephen noticed that Laura immediately changed her facial expression from a sort of 'come-on' stare of the eyes to a more matronly serious look, and gave a full concentration on her friend's mention of the lunch she had been preparing.

The rest of the weekend passed by without Laura and Stephen having an opportunity to continue their chat about Gershwin – Stephen mainly kept out of the way as not wanting to come between the two old friends who were mainly reminiscing about their boarding school days. He did overhear though, when the ladies thought Stephen wasn't about, both being critical of their respective husbands – Susan complaining about Kenneth's right-wing views which she worried about and considered his political rhetoric was becoming even too extreme for the Conservative Party. Besides, his arrogance and snobbishness upset her, as although she herself was a staunch Tory – she liked to be considerate of others less fortunate than themselves. And because of Ken's attitude, they were unable to keep staff for long and even their cook walked out on them the previous week – hence Susan having to do all the cooking for the weekend. Laura listened and nodded sympathetically throughout the tirade, but did not comment – maybe thinking that her friend was living in a different world to her with domestic staff etc. But what Stephen then heard was Laura complaining about Ben's dullness and that despite loving her husband, the spark had gone out of their marriage and that made her feel frustrated. At that point Stephen entered the room and noticed that the conversation straight away changed from personal matters to more domestic chit-chat.

'So what do you think of my friend Laura?' Susan asked Stephen once Laura had left to drive back to Cardiff after lunch on the Sunday.

'She's not very happy with her husband who's older than her and is now in his fifties.'

Stephen took in what his mother was saying but deliberately feigned a lack of interest in the subject and just mumbled. 'That's a shame for her as she seemed a very nice woman.'

Stephen left the room in a state of arousal, but maybe it was all in his imagination, as why would a sophisticated woman of the world be interested in an inexperienced young man? And besides, she was his mother's oldest friend and surely she wouldn't do anything to cause an upset between them?

A couple months later Susan told Stephen that Laura had reciprocated the invitation and not only had invited her to Cardiff for the weekend, but had also inquired as to whether Stephen would like to come along 'I didn't realise that the two of you had much in common when Laura stayed with us?

'Well, we did have some musical interests that we shared.' Stephen sheepishly responded.

'Oh I see,' said his mother with a quixotic look furrowing her brow.

'It was nice of her to invite you, but you don't have to come with me and be bored out of your mind for a weekend that will mainly consist of mainly female chit-chat.'

'No – 'I'll come with you,' replied Stephen with more enthusiasm than he meant to show to his mother, and added, 'I'm sure you'll be pleased with the company for the journey – and now that I've passed my driving test, we could also share the driving.' His mother was surprised that Stephen had offered to accompany her but made it absolutely clear that she would do all the driving – not wanting a novice driver to take the wheel as that would be too nerve-racking.

Stephen telephoned the record shop in Aldeburgh and inquired about a recording of the opera, *Porgy and Bess*. The helpful assistant recommended a complete recording taken from a live performance in Berlin of the opera in 1952 – an all black cast with the soprano, Leontyne Price, as Bess ,and the bass, William Warfield, as Porgy. They didn't have it in stock but would order it for him and telephone when it arrived. A week later, following a call from the shop, Stephen cycled to Aldeburgh to collect the recording which the assistant kindly wrapped up for him in gift paper.

The drive down to Cardiff was uneventful. His father and brothers were left on their own for the weekend, but new domestic staff and a cook had been employed so the men could amuse themselves in any way they wished without worrying about cleaning the house or cooking meals etc.

Arriving at the solid suburban house in a quiet tree-lined street, they received a warm greeting from Laura, who was thrilled with the present Stephen had bought her. His mother was surprised that Stephen would have gone to such trouble for her friend. The first evening was convivial enough with Ben joining them for dinner following a very busy day at his chemist shop. Their children had gone to stay with friends for the weekend so it was just the four of them. Ben was friendly, polite and welcoming, but Stephen could gauge that he was stolid and a bit boring compared to Laura's love of life and vivacious personality.

Wine was served during dinner which consisted of homemade chicken liver pate' – roast duck with red cabbage and sherry trifle for dessert. Laura was an excellent cook and, although she had some domestic help, she did all the cooking herself. Board games were played after dinner with some jazz music playing softly on the record player. At about 11pm both Ben and Susan started to yawn and decided to head off to bed.

 Stephen and Laura stayed put and Laura offered Stephen a can of beer whilst she poured herself another glass of red wine, suggesting that she put the *Porgy and Bess* record on the turntable. Stephen nodded in assent whilst opening the can and sipping the beer. Laura took off her top and, as she was wearing an almost see-through dress, Stephen could look at the contours of Laura's mature but still shapely figure with a growing sense of a flirtation happening between them.

'So tell me Stephen – what are your plans for the future?'

'This is a gap year for me and I have a place at Cambridge University starting in September 1968 – so it's a long gap year – more like a two-year gap than the usual one.'

'And will you be leaving a local girlfriend behind when you head off to Cambridge?'

Stephen, blushing said that no, he did not have a girlfriend.

'Ah well – you'll have plenty of opportunities to meet girls at university. I hear that some youngsters' main reason for applying to universities would be to meet people of the opposite sex.'

'Yes, Laura, it would be nice to have a girlfriend.'

'As you're such a handsome-looking chap – you should have no problem finding one.'

Blushing again, Stephen thanked her for the compliment.

'I know I'm the same age as your mum, Stephen, but do you find me attractive?'

That arousal feeling that Stephen felt when they were together back home in Orford stirred his loins again as he replied, 'I do think you're very attractive, Laura, and the age gap is no problem for me – it's just that you're married to Ben and my mother is your oldest friends.'

'Let me worry about the two of them as this would be our little secret and nobody in the world would know about us' Laura stared at Stephen with lust in her eyes, and her body felt hot with desire.

Just when Stephen wondered what would happen next, Laura rose from her chair and announced that it was time for bed. She showed him to his room, with a cursory kiss on his cheek; Laura said she was off to bed herself.

Finding the bathroom and cleaning his teeth – Stephen couldn't help feeling a sense of disappointment that nothing had happened between them downstairs, but then he thought that it would have been mad, with both Ben and his mum upstairs in their respective bedrooms; what if they heard something and came down and found them in a clinch or even in a state of undress? It would not be worth even thinking about.

Just as he was coming to terms with the madness of his thoughts of unrealistic expectations happening between him and Laura – he heard the bathroom handle quietly turn. He jumped out of his skin and wondered who was there and why he hadn't locked the bathroom door. But before he got to the lock, the door opened and there was Laura in a skimpy and sexy – looking nightdress. Stephen's mouth opened in astonishment whilst Laura closed the door and locked it – putting her hand to her lips, uttering 'shush' in the quietest of voices. She lunged at Stephen and they started to kiss. The situation was so dangerous in the bathroom, even more so than downstairs, but that added to the excitement. Full sexual intercourse was followed by lying together in an empty bath – a bit awkward physically but just manageable. A first for Stephen, which Laura guessed, and she'd very much taken charge of the proceedings as they both climaxed together. One at a time, they stealthily crept out of the bathroom and to their bedrooms – thankfully unnoticed.

Stephen couldn't sleep and found it hard to believe what had just happened in the bathroom. Laura had guided him into her and it felt so natural; an act he had thought and dreamed about so often for a number of years had finally occurred. He could never have guessed how he would come to lose his sexual innocence, but he was thrilled it was with such an experienced and lovely woman as Laura.

The next morning everyone sat around the kitchen table at breakfast and there was no indication that anything had been remiss the previous night. Laura almost ignored Stephen and only spoke to him about breakfast matters. 'Would you prefer tea or coffee, Stephen?' And, 'how do you like your eggs?'

Nothing happened on the second night there as Laura and Ben had invited friends around to join the party for dinner and Laura concentrated on the social side of the evening – making sure the conversation flowed, and all in all she was the perfect host.

Back home, Stephen telephoned Laura when nobody was around the house and spoke to her in terms of endearment. Laura's response was tender and loving – thanking him for giving her a wonderful time and for not 'spilling the beans' to anyone about the bathroom liaison. But she made it clear that it was a one-off and that she wanted to protect her marriage and her friendship with his mother. However, she didn't regret anything and he shouldn't either as it was all part of life's rich tapestry. Besides, once at university he would be spoiled for choice to find a girlfriend or girlfriends. But just as they were saying their goodbyes, Laura, almost in a whisper, added, 'Despite what I've just said – if you're ever by chance anywhere near Cardiff in the future – please look me up.'

Stephen managed to arrange a couple of trips back to Cardiff, telling his parents that he was visiting an old school friend from Eton College. Laura and Stephen met up and had sex in a hotel that Laura had booked, and this time they had more time and room space to explore each other's bodies fully and only slowly reach orgasm. The second time it was even better as they were less self-conscious of having sex together – Laura showed Stephen lots of different ways to enjoy sex before actual intercourse, and when finally their lovemaking included intercourse, it was even more sexy and beautiful – having built up to it nice and slowly.

Laura was correct in one respect – when Stephen finally got to Cambridge he did meet lots of girls his own age and enjoyed several sexual liaisons, but for some reason, he never established a relationship that could be considered boy and girlfriend. However, he never forgot Laura and was grateful to her for showing him the path towards successful sexual experiences. He knew that any future with Laura was absolutely hopeless for so many obvious reasons, and consequently they lost touch with each other. But over the years he occasionally asked after her when chatting with his mother and Laura seemed to be fine and still married to Ben. Thank goodness that neither he nor Laura had ever divulged their secret to anyone about what had happened between them, firstly at her home or subsequently in a hotel.

Chapter 18

Dov Katz

Dov was born in 1935. The Katz family had emigrated from Germany in 1930, a few years before the Nazis' came to power. The family followed the orthodox tradition of the Jewish religion and Dov showed a strong aptitude for Hebrew study at a young age, culminating in his parents' decision to send him to England to study at the Greenshead Jewish Boarding School in the north of England. Dov arrived at the school in 1948 and was shocked at the lack of basic facilities as well as the horrible food, which one was forced to eat. But above all, he hated the cold weather which he never adjusted to in his three years at the school. The studies were OK, and he made some good friends there, including a boy from London, whose name was Simon Negrini. Simon was a lovely sensitive boy whom he quite fancied; Dov already had the understanding that he was a homosexual, but he was too scared to approach Simon as he was sure that Simon was a straight boy and was still very innocent about sexual matters.

Back in Israel, after leaving Greenshead Boarding School – Dov got himself into trouble with some local Rabbi, after being caught having relations with another boy, and he decided to leave the religious life completely. His parents were devastated, but he was adamant that he wished to live a secular life. He enrolled at a local school to catch up on his secular education which had been badly neglected at Greenshead, and though he had an uneasy relationship   with his parents, he continued to live in the family home. When he turned eighteen he did his two years and eight months National Service in the Israeli army, and, on being demobbed, he left to go back to England, but this time to London, and he auditioned for a place at Covent Garden's Music and Drama College.

Dov was always aware that he possessed a good voice but never thought much about it, but when he stopped going to the synagogue he started to attend opera performances – mostly small professional companies that toured around the country of Israel, and Dov would travel to wherever these companies were performing. Sometimes they would perform at a Kibbutz or at a town hall. Dov not only got to know the standard repertoire of opera but also became friends with some of the singers and the musicians. A singer friend recommended Dov to his teacher and the teacher was so impressed with Dov's budding baritone voice, that he gave him lessons without charging fees.

In London, Dov started to attend opera performances at both Covent Garden and Sadlers Wells opera – always opting for the cheapest standing place, and was amazed at the superior standard of performance compared to what he had been used to in Israel. Hearing some of the world's greatest singers at Covent Garden was such joy for Dov – which gave him the determination that one day he would sing on that iconic stage.

Dov was accepted as an opera student at the college and with his open and personable manner, he quickly made friends with fellow students. He had been awarded a small grant from the Israeli Cultural Department – on condition that he returned to Israel at the conclusion of his studies and use his knowledge in helping to develop the art form in the new young state.

Besides Dov's grant – he beefed up his income by working in a bar several evenings a week. The bar was located in the area of Kilburn, where he also shared a flat with a friend he had met at college. Kilburn was an inexpensive area of north London and its inhabitants included many Irish people. Dov got on really well with the Irish population – who were friendly, full of humour and loved all types of music, especially traditional Irish.

Dov and Marie became good friends at college – Dov feeling protective towards his younger colleague in whom he sensed vulnerability.

The dinner evening at Margo's flat, where he'd met Margo's flatmate Holly and her 'full of himself' married boyfriend, Freddy Wakeson, whom he had clashed with, was the night Margo confided in him that she was pregnant.

Margo's so-called friend, Holly Fine, wanted Freddy to move in with her at the flat she shared with Margo in London's Kentish Town – thinking that Freddy would leave his wife Susanna, and that they would start a new life together. As Holly had signed the tenancy agreement – she felt she could just ask Margo to leave the flat. In fairness to Freddy, he was so disgusted at Holly's suggestion to throw Margo out of the flat, that he ditched Holly and refused to see her again. At the same time, Holly lost her job and decided to go back home to Cornwall. The two girls who had been best friends growing up, ceased speaking to each other and Holly left London during a day that Margo was at college – so goodbyes were not exchanged and Holly travelled back to Cornwall completely unaware of Margo's pregnancy.

Margo did not wish to stay in the flat she had shared with her now ex-friend, and moved in with Dov at his Kilburn flat, as Dov's friend who had previously shared the flat had moved out to live with his girlfriend.

Dov and Margo's relationship was purely platonic, but he was a marvellous friend to her – accompanying her to the hospital for the routine pregnancy tests and updates. Unfortunately, as it got nearer her time to give birth, Dov received an urgent call from his parents in Israel that his older brother had been killed in action – fighting in the Israeli army, and he had to leave London immediately to attend his brother's funeral. Before he left London – Margo asked Dov to keep her beloved mother's bracelet with him and return it to her when he got back, as if she went into labour she just might mislay it in the hurly burly of the hospital. She did not want to leave the bracelet at the flat whilst it was uninhabited, as the area was notorious for break-ins.

Although Dov was not close to his brother – he was shocked and devastated with the news, and felt he needed to spend time back at home in Israel to comfort his parents. He was so taken up with his own family tragedy that he didn't give much thought to Margo in London and to the expected birth of her child. Some weeks passed and Dov thought to telephone the hospital in London to inquire about Margo, and hopefully, receive some good news about the baby. Unfortunately, he got through to a junior nurse who had not been involved in Margo's case, and who had picked up the information about Margo from a more senior colleague – but being a busy hospital with the nurses under pressure, she hadn't listened attentively to what the senior colleague was saying.

'What was your relationship with Margo Pento, – Mr Katz?' asked the nurse.

'We were very close friends, but we were not lovers – and I'm not the father.'

'I see, sir, and I'm so sorry to tell you that your friend, Miss Pento, died in childbirth, and we were unable to save the baby.'

Dov thought that he was in bed asleep and experiencing a nightmare, being unable to take-in what the nurse was saying. Finally, following a long pause, he screamed down the telephone – 'Oh my god' – what actually happened?'

'I'm really sorry, sir – but I don't have any further details – you'll need to speak to a more senior colleague. That's all the information I have. So sorry for your loss, Mr Katz'

Dov – was just starting to come to terms with his brother's death, and he was so broken in spirit with the news about Margo that he just blocked it out of his mind and went into a severe depression. He didn't contact the hospital again as he couldn't face listening to explanations and regrets from the professionals. Nothing they could tell him would bring Margo and her baby back to life.

What Dov didn't know was that, although Margo did indeed die in childbirth – the baby had survived.

Chapter 19

Freddy Wakeson
1960

Susanna Wakeson was threatening to divorce her husband Freddy. She was aware of Freddy's infidelities, but as long as she wasn't confronted with them, she chose to ignore the facts. It was hard to pretend his affair with their neighbour and family friend, Felicity Negrini, wasn't happening as she saw with her own eyes how much they casually brushed up against each other when they thought they were on their own, but Susanna noticed – even if Felicity's trusting husband, Simon Negrini, was totally unaware of anything going on between them. When Simon left Felicity in 1958, which put paid to any more socialising between the two couples, Felicity kept her distance from Susanna. The affair continued for some time but the cheating pair only got together away from their home area, so for Susanna it was 'out of sight – out of mind.'

But the following year, it was a different story. A young woman called Holly Fine, who was furious for having been ditched by Freddy, found their home telephone number – called Susanna and told her all about her relationship with her husband.

Freddy, having already been divorced once, did not want to lose Susanna, and despite his womanising, he loved his wife. Holly had been very spiteful when he'd split from her, mainly in the way she had treated her friend Margo – in trying to oust her from the Kentish Town flat, when his understanding was that it was Margo who not only had paid the deposit initially but was also covering Holly's share of the rent, as Holly's earnings were erratic, and whatever money she earned she spent it on herself.

But besides her bad behaviour, he was getting tired of her anyway – as she always wanted to go to clubs in Soho and stay out until all hours of the night. Whilst Freddy, although enjoying clubbing, needed to be fresh for work in the morning, and getting home at all hours was really upsetting Susanna; besides, he was running out of excuses for arriving home the time he did. Surely…he could only have had so many nights out with the boys from the newspaper? However, for Holly to phone Susanna was a dastardly thing to do, and he considered himself well clear of her.

Freddy pleaded with Susanna that he would turn over a new leaf and he sort of meant it, although he was still meeting up with Felicity when he travelled away from home to cover sports events. He decided he wouldn't chase any more women, but would stay faithful to both Susanna, his wife, and Felicity, his mistress.

For some months, Freddy's life did indeed settle down. When he wasn't travelling to cover a sports tournament for his newspaper, he curtailed his evening drinking sessions with his pals from the office and got home for dinner with Susanna on time. However, when Freddy's newspaper sent him to Badminton, near Bristol and Bath, about a hundred miles away from London, to cover the horse trials, he invited Felicity to join him there and they stayed together for several nights at his hotel.

For their next rendezvous, Freddy and Felicity had planned to spend the night together in Manchester, at the famous Midland Hotel. Freddy would be there covering a late November Football Association cup tie, between Manchester United and Arsenal. Although Freddy, being an Arsenal supporter, was desperate for an Arsenal win, and for his team to knock out United – journalistic etiquette obliged him to remain neutral. Freddy had driven up from London to Manchester the night before the game and spent a boozy evening with his football writers and commentator pals. Felicity, who wasn't interested in football, had planned to take the train to Manchester the morning of the game and meet Freddy at the hotel post-match tea- time. Unfortunately, Felicity's mother caught the flu and her dad had phoned his daughter – imploring her to drop any plans she may have had for the weekend and travel down to Sussex, to nurse her mum and cook for him, as he was hopeless in the kitchen. Felicity was torn between doing daughter duties – going to Manchester to be with Freddy, or, despite looking forward to Manchester she felt she had no choice but to be a dutiful daughter. She telephoned the Midland and left a message at reception for Freddy – that she wouldn't be coming, and changed her overnight bag from sexy underwear and nightdress, to more basic clothing, and headed off to Sussex.

Freddy had been looking forward to Felicity joining him at the Midland Hotel, Manchester – being disappointed to receive the message that she wasn't coming after all. His disappointment was even more painful – as Manchester United had beaten Arsenal in the football match; his newspaper report had to remain neutral as he dared not show any Arsenal bias – but his own private thoughts were that Arsenal were robbed – as he considered the penalty awarded to United spurious and that the referee showed favourable bias to the home side.

Freddy was feeling sorry for himself, so he decided to cancel his room at the hotel for Saturday night and planned to set off for London sometime during the evening. With his bag packed – he thought to grab a coffee and a sandwich in the hotel lounge. Being late afternoon, following a Manchester United home match at Old Trafford, the lounge was busy with a lot of post-match banter at various tables.

'Would you mind if I joined you?' Freddy asked the woman – sitting solo on a corner table.

Without looking up from her book, the woman waved her arm towards the seat opposite.

A waiter arrived at the table – Freddy ordering a coffee and a ham and pickle sandwich – whilst the woman requested another coffee. Freddy surreptitiously eyed the woman sitting opposite him. She was dressed casually in a dark loose-fitting top with faded charcoal grey jeans – a student-type look, but she seemed older than a typical student – more late…than early twenties. Freddy noticed a rucksack by the side of her chair, which added to her casual style. Despite not wearing any make-up, she had a beautiful face with lovely long loose dark-blonde hair and hazel eyes. She was obviously someone who had no interest in drawing attention to herself – fully engrossed in her book and not making any eye contact with Freddy. Being an imposing-looking man, Freddy was used to women flirting with him, or at least giving him the once-over, and he started to become fascinated with the woman sitting opposite, especially as the fascination was completely one-sided.

'Have you been to the match today?' Freddy asked the woman, who seemed rather irritated at being disturbed from reading her book.

'Sorry – what match?'

'Oh – you're not a football fan then?'

'Absolutely not,' came the retort; 'I can't stand football, or any other sport as a matter of fact.'

Freddy, feeling rather chastened, did not pursue the conversation and the woman went back to her book. After about ten minutes, the waiter appeared and the woman requested her bill. When the bill arrived – cash and change were exchanged.

'Excuse me,' the woman said to the waiter, 'do you by any chance know what time the last train leaves from Manchester's London Road Station – to London, Euston?'

'You mean Manchester Piccadilly, madam – the name of the station was changed from "London" to "Piccadilly" earlier this year – but I believe the last train is at nine pm.'

'Yes, sorry, I had forgotten about the station name change – but thanks for the information.'

'You're very welcome madam.'

Freddy, listening to the exchange, was wondering about the woman's accent; a Commonwealth country – maybe New Zealand? Canada? 'I'm trying to detect the accent?'

'South African,' the woman replied, taking her eyes away from her book and actually looking at Freddy.

'Oh yes, of course, I should have known that – having been to South Africa several times.

The woman responded 'Really?' Do you have family there or just go for holidays?'

'Neither,' – said Freddy – the trips were work oriented. I'm a sports reporter for a London newspaper.'

'I see'

'My name is Freddy Wakeson,' he said – as he stood up to shake the woman's hand.

'I'm pleased to meet you' she said – as she returned the hand shake but remained seated. 'I'm Carol Verblunnen.'

'And what brings you to Manchester…Carol?'

'I was here for a job interview – being a BBC trainee based in London. So far, I'm not really sure which end of the media I wish to specialise in. My accent is probably wrong for presenting, but maybe producing or editing programmes? The interview was for an editing job at BBC Manchester – but the interview did not go well.... I don't think I'm qualified enough for what they wanted – but never mind, it's all good experience doing various interviews.' Carol shrugged as she said that – but there was no hiding her disappointment at the outcome of the interview.

Carol explained to Freddy that she had got a lift from a BBC colleague up to Manchester, but as the colleague was staying on in the city, she would have to catch a train back to London. Freddy said that he was driving back to London that evening and she would be very welcome to accompany him in the car. Carol hesitated for a moment and wondered about the prudence of accepting a lift from a complete stranger – but she was physically strong and could look after herself – so she accepted the offer. Carol grabbed her rucksack, and Freddy collected his bag from the reception – and off the two of them went to the car park to alight into Freddy's car.

A November fog descended as Freddy started to drive out of Manchester, but being an experienced driver, he thought he could cope fine with a bit of fog. Carol was quiet in the car so Freddy asked if he could put the radio on. He switched to the *Third Programme* thinking it may impress Carol. Being Saturday evening, it was opera night on the station and the opera that was being broadcast was Verdi's *Simon Boccanegra.*

'Are you OK with opera, Carol?'

'Yes, I like opera but know very little about it. The only opera I've seen is *La Boheme,* back in South Africa, and I thought it was absolutely terrific.'

'Well,' responded Freddy, 'I never go to the opera but I did see *Simon Boccanegra* once in Milan, and, to be honest, I was bored stiff – but perhaps just listening to the music on the radio is a better option. What do you think, Carol?'

'Sure, I'll give it a listen. If I'm going to get on at the BBC, a bit of high cultural knowledge won't do me any harm at all.' Carol chuckled and pulled a down-the-chin face, giving Freddy a semi tragic-comedy look.

The broadcast was of a fairly new recording of the opera from 1958, starring the great Italian baritone, Tito Gobbi, and his real-life brother-in-law, the imposing Bulgarian bass, Boris Christoff, plus the lovely Spanish soprano, Victoria De Los Ángelis. Fairly near the beginning of the opera's prologue there is a beautiful short aria for the bass, *Il lacerato spirito,* and Christoff's deeply expressive voice came over really well in the car. Carol and Freddy glanced at each other and nodded in admiration of the singing. Freddy was thinking of his old friend Simon Negrini, who loved this particular opera and a feeling of guilt came over him – not only had he fallen out with his friend because of his affair with Simon's wife, but now he was considering cheating on Felicity yet again, maybe with Carol?

But then…he thought that he was running away with himself, as far as Carol was concerned, as all he was doing was giving her a lift to London, and so far nothing Carol had said, or intimated, had offered any sort of flirtatious signals – that should make him think that it was anything but just a drive to London, and nothing else.

As Freddy and Carol approached the market town of Chesterfield in Derbyshire, the fog had got worse, and as they drove through the town, they came across the Georgian ivy-clad hotel in the High Street that looked inviting – so Freddy suggested that they stop for a break and maybe have a bite to eat there. Carol thought that was a good idea – they parked the car and walked into the lobby of the hotel. The receptionist said they were serving dinner and had only one table left as it was a busy Saturday night. The pair looked at each other and shrugged – as if to say 'why not?' Freddy said. 'Yes, we'll take the table, and the receptionist escorted them to the dining room – introduced them to the maitre d,' who showed them to the table. Realising that they were both hungry as they studied the menu – both decided to go for *table d'hote* – a three-course meal of wholesome comfort food of the traditional English variety – leek and potato soup and roast Rib of beef with Yorkshire pudding, served with roast potatoes, carrots, gravy and horseradish sauce. Desert was an apple crumble served with ice cream.

'Shall we get a bottle of wine, Carol?'

'Sure – why not.' Carol was beginning to enjoy herself. Freddy caught a waiter's eye and ordered a bottle of red pinot noir.

Whilst they were enjoying the comforting food and the very acceptable wine, Carol asked, 'Are you married, Freddy?'

'Yes, I am.' Freddy's initial thoughts were. 'Here we go – *I will now get a lecture about married men picking up single women.*' But surprisingly – Carol's response was not what Freddy expected.

'To be honest, I don't believe in marriage, or monogamy, for that matter. It's mad that in 1960, when people are living longer, one marries in their twenties and has that one sexual partner for the next fifty years. Religion has had a lot to do with that constraint; and besides, marriage is a way of keeping women down – under the control of their husbands.'

Freddy…was seeing Carol in a very different light to what he had imagined about her. She was a bit of a free spirit – so different from both Felicity and Susanna who were both basically conventional-type women – who accepted all the cultural norms of the day without too much questioning. Holly of course was a total airhead and just did whatever she felt like doing – without any consideration for anyone else. Carol seemed to him to be a thinker – and not one to accept the norm that others have inflicted on society.

'Are you OK to drive on to London tonight, Freddy?'

'Well, Carol – I'm a bit tired to be honest; do you have to be back in London tonight? '

'Not really.'

'Shall I go to the reception and see whether they have a room for tonight?'

'OK,' said Carol, smiling at Freddy. Having booked a double room, he collected his overnight bag and Carol's rucksack from the car, which was parked just outside the hotel's entrance.

The double room that Freddy had booked was on the first floor of the hotel. Finishing off the bottle of wine, they ordered coffee – a reflective mood settled in at the table.

'Carol...I hope you realise that none of this was premeditated. I really did plan to drive straight to London tonight and did not have any ulterior motive in mind.'

'Look...Freddy. As far as I'm concerned it doesn't matter whether you planned this or not. We're both too tired and full of food and wine to even think about any sexual activity tonight.'

Freddy felt as if Carol had just poured a glass of cold water over him – and any lustful thoughts he may have had towards Carol evaporated immediately.

The bedroom was a decent size with a high ceiling, but it lacked colour – the walls were dull beige without any artwork on display. The bed was a large king size and the bathroom spacious with a big bath-tub, but the lighting was rather dim. He took the lead from Carol's pronouncement in the dining room, and they each separately took a bath – cleaned their teeth and got into the bed well apart from each other – Carol in a light blue cotton night shift and Freddy in a T-shirt and boxer shorts. Having switched off the lights they turned aside and were back-to-back, drifting off to sleep.

Sleep came quickly to them both, but after a couple of hours, they awoke, and without turning on the lights, the pair started chatting together.

Carol said. 'The problem with men – especially young men, is that they get too excited having sex, and finish things off far too quickly – whilst us women are just getting going – as we like it nice and slow – needing lots of touching with plenty of foreplay.'

 They had put the side bedroom light back on – so Freddy could see Carol's expression clearly, and she had spoken without any embarrassment or coyness. Freddy thought about his wife and his various lovers and their reluctance to talk about sex – just wanting to get it over with, usually in the dark, and yes, he was guilty of quick sex – not being considerate enough to their needs.

Listening to Carol talking so openly about sex – got him feeling lustful for her – wanting to touch her for the first time. He moved his hand towards her arm and she clasped his hand into hers – squeezing it hard. 'I know you said "no sex tonight," Carol, but could we?'

Squeezing his hand even harder and looking at him with a wry smile, she said, 'I said "tonight" – it's now the early hours of the morning!'

Freddy, realising that she was gently mocking him, moved closer to Carol and, removing his hand from hers, snuggled up – putting his arm around her waist. Carol reciprocated by putting down her head onto his shoulder. Freddy gently stroked her hair – saying in a quiet voice, 'I'll hold off as long as I possibly can.'

'Thank you, Freddy, but don't fret about it – just be passionate and bear in mind that I'm not particularly fragile.'

They started to kiss each other – slowly, just lips brushing at first but with ever-increasing intensity. The passion was heightened for both of them. Freddy, conscious of what Carol had said earlier about men's sexual performance – prolonged foreplay for much longer than he had been used to with others, but then Carol whispered in his ear. 'Please enter me now Freddy.' Not used to women saying anything at all during sex – Carol's request overwhelmed him and he found it increasingly difficult to hold things back – but he did concentrate on restraint – not wishing to disappoint Carol, and managed to keep going until he heard orgasm purring coming from her and miracle of miracles – they climaxed together and they were a happy contented pair of lovers when they cuddled up together – turned the side bed lights off, and almost instantly, both fell asleep.

Waking up to the morning light – the late autumn sun shining through the curtains, they both felt hungry and no wonder why – it was 10.30 am and they were supposed to check out of the hotel by 11.00 am. 'Shall we stay another night, Carol, if we can keep the room?'

'Yes please…Freddy – I would love to stay on.'

Freddy phoned reception and, it being a Sunday, the room was available but it was booked for Monday. So Freddy confirmed over the phone that they would like to keep the room for another night – ordering tea and toast to be brought up – it being too late for a full breakfast.

Whilst Carol was in the bathroom, Freddy phoned Susanna from the bedroom telephone – explaining that due to the fog he was staying on another night and would be back home sometime on Monday. A knock on the door brought in the tea, toast with butter and jam. Having enjoyed their tea and toast, they went straight back to bed and stayed there all day – ordering room service for coffee and sandwiches at lunchtime, and again in the evening – fish and chips with a bottle of champagne.

They had sex many times during the day and the following night – with Carol taking more and more the dominant role – telling Freddy what she wanted him to do – engaging in different aspects of sex that were new to Freddy. He was totally smitten with Carol. He'd believed that at the age of thirty, it took having sex with a woman of his own age, instead of his usual lovers, who were generally considerably younger, to really understand his own sexuality. He realised that he wasn't the macho dominant man he thought he was – but took the greatest pleasure and sexual satisfaction in being the more submissive partner. And as the day went on – he learnt to hold back longer and longer to ensure that when he climaxed – Carol was ready to climax with him.

Freddy and Carol drove back to London on Monday. He dropped her off at the BBC headquarters at Portland Place in the west end of London, just off Regent Street North, before heading home to Susanna in Wembley. The two of them promised to stay in touch and meet up as often as possible, and for once Freddy was more enthusiastic than Carol to develop the relationship. For Freddy, the liaison with Carol was sort of an epiphany, whilst for Carol, who was determined to maintain her independence, was happy to see Freddy again, but didn't want him to break up his marriage because of her, as the last thing she wanted, was a full-time relationship with Freddy, or with anyone else for that matter.

The two of them did in fact get together several times over the following few months and the sex was fantastic – even better than in Chesterfield, but Carol eventually broke it off as being a free spirit – she did not want any commitments, whilst Freddy was becoming too insistent on trying to arrange new meetings with her, so Carol thought it best to move on. Though she had enjoyed her time with Freddy, all good things must come to an end.

Freddy was devastated and his pride was hurt, as he had always been the one to end affairs – as he had done with Holly, and was to do so a few years later, with Felicity. Carol was different to the others and he would have left Susanna if Carol had asked him. Without a lover, Freddy started getting home at reasonable hours and paying more attention to his wife. And then Susanna became pregnant and that changed everything for Freddy, as he really wanted to be a father. His first wife had been unable to conceive. It seemed that the same was the case with Susanna, but happily, it was not so. Nine months later, a little girl was born and they named her 'Lizette' after Susanna's grandmother. Freddy was mad about his little girl, and for some years, he stayed faithful to Susanna, but a Leopard doesn't change its spots – as Freddy's roving eye emerged again some years later.

1962

Freddy had been at Highbury to watch his beloved Arsenal play Everton – not on football reporting business but purely as a fan. After the match, that Arsenal had won 3–1, he popped into the Duck and Drake pub, where a lot of fans and pundits repaired to after the match. He met a few of his journalistic friends there and shared a couple of pints with his colleagues. Two guys sitting at the bar caught his eye as one of them looked ever so familiar, but he couldn't for the life of him remember where he'd seen this chap before. Then it came to him...and he made his way to the bar and tapped the man on his shoulder.

'Sorry to disturb you – but I know you.'

The man turned around and looked a bit puzzled...but then he realised who the chap was. Yes, I believe we have met before. Your name is Freddy...but I can't think of your surname.'

'Freddy Wakeson... is me,' he said with his outstretched arm to shake the hand of Dov Katz.

'Freddy... what a surprise, and let me introduce you to my friend, Brian Montague. Brian, this is an acquaintance of mine, Freddy Wakeson.'

The two men shook hands, politely greeting each other. Dov said...'Brian is the real "Gooner" as he goes to the entire home games at Highbury; I'm more of an armchair supporter, but Brian dragged me along today – pleased that I came. It was a good game with a great win for Arsenal.' he added with a winning smile.

'How are you, Freddy, and what have you been up to?'

'I'm fine thanks, and how are you?'

'Yes... I'm good, thanks.'

'Dov...I owe you an apology.'

Dov furrowed his brow. 'Please Freddy – if it's about the evening we met at the Kentish Town flat with Margo and Holly – there's nothing to apologise for and you were kind enough to give me a lift home.'

'No Dov – I acted poorly that evening and I was quite rude to you. You have every right not to talk to me.'

'Freddy... your behaviour that night was the least of things I've dwelt on these past three years – as great tragedies ensued later that year.'

'What do you mean Dov?'

'Well, that night at the flat, whilst you and Holly disappeared into one of the bedrooms. I was helping Margo with the washing up and she confided in me that she was pregnant but was not in touch with the father. It was a passing one-night affair whilst Margo was working in a hotel in Cornwall, and the next day she had to dash back to her home village, as her mother had committed suicide by taking an overdose of drugs. Anyway, Margo and I became close during her pregnancy months and she came to live with me after giving up the Kentish Town flat – when Holly went back to Cornwall.'

'Yes' said Freddy. 'Holly turned out to be quite the bitch. I sent her packing and would have nothing more to do with her after she told me of her plan to cheat Margo out of the flat's rental agreement.'

'Holly treated Margo abominably, and you were right to ditch her, but she never found out about Margo's pregnancy.'

Brian was listening intently to the exchange between his friend Dov and this Freddy chap, but he probably knew the whole story from Dov anyway. Brian was a nice-looking young man with dark long hair, which was becoming fashionable, and a good physique, although not very tall. He was wearing an Arsenal sweater and tight jeans. Brian was a fellow student at the music college, and shared a flat with Dov, in the Swiss Cottage area of north London.

'Look...Freddy, there's no easy way to say this but it was tragedy upon tragedy.' Freddy was looking startled and open-mouthed as Dov continued. 'Just before the baby was due, I got called back to Israel for a funeral – as my older brother had been killed serving in the Israeli army. I ended up staying there for two years – my family being inconsolable. I felt obliged to help them with the grieving process – to be there whilst they tried to rebuild their lives. I came back to London last year, whilst the college kindly kept my place open for me.

'But I'm sorry to have to tell you... that tragedy followed tragedy. Margo died in childbirth and the baby did not survive.'

'Oh my god,' said Freddy, shocked to the core hearing this ghastly sequence of events – feeling an awful rotten so and so, thinking back to that evening in the flat, where he almost ignored Margo and was rude to Dov.

'Dov... if only I could re-run that evening in the flat and behave as I should have done, as a *mensch* instead of the idiot that I was.'

Dov, seeing how distressed Freddy was, put an arm around him, saying, 'Freddy...please forget about that evening. We can all behave badly at times, but you had nothing to do with the four tragedies.

Starting with Margo's mother's suicide which happened before you met her, but she never mentioned it during that evening. My brother's death was not only a huge family loss – but the timing was so unfortunate – as I had to leave London suddenly just when Margo had needed my support at the most critical moment of her pregnancy, and at that period of her life – she only had me – and I had promised to look after her before and after giving birth. So ever since the awful event I've been beating myself up about not being there for her.

Brian ...seeing how distressed Dov was becoming – put an arm around his friend and gave him a sympathetic look –full of concern and love.

The three of them moved to a table at a quiet corner of the pub and ordered drinks.

'To be honest, Dov, I didn't know anything about Margo or her background, as Holly spoke very little about her friend when we were together – other than they had been childhood friends. Holly had helped Margo to get the job in the Cornish hotel before coming to London together, following her mother's death. But what about Margo's family – surely they would have given her support when she became pregnant?'

'Good question, Freddy, but it was complicated. However close Margo and I became, she spoke very little about her life in Cornwall, and when I probed the issue, she clammed up. All I got from her was that the Pento family's hometown had been Penzance – but when I tried to trace her family, I came up with a total blank. Holly had emigrated to West Germany and was non-contactable.'

'So how did you find out about Margo's death?'

'Well, when I got to Israel I became fully immersed in mourning for my brother – not inquiring about Margo for a couple of weeks. And when I did telephone the hospital to inquire – a nurse gave me the sad news about Margo and the baby. As I said – I tried to find a family member of Margo's, but being in Israel, I was relying on long-distance phoning which was difficult. I even tried the hotel that she had worked in, as I had remembered Margo telling me that the name of the hotel was "The Rising Sun" in the holiday resort of St Mawes. But when I contacted the hotel – they were very polite but point blank refused to give me any information, not even confirming that she had worked there. I got the feeling though...that they did know her and that Margo had told me the truth about her work at that particular hotel. But I suspected that her name wasn't Pento at all and that, although she was from Cornwall – her home-town wasn't Penzance either.'

'That was all very odd, Dov. Why would Margo have been so secretive about her real name and background?'

'I did ask her once about her father or step-father – but she would not talk about them; so I did not pursue the issue – not wishing to upset her during her pregnancy.'

'I could ask my newspaper to dig around.'

'No...Freddy, there's no point in stirring things up publicly. My only concern was for Margo and her baby's well-being, but as they are dead – let things be.'

Freddy left Dov and Brian in the pub, having exchanged telephone numbers, and promised to keep in touch. He wanted to be home in time for dinner, and after hearing such tragic stories, he couldn't wait to hug his daughter Lizette and be thankful for the joy he had in being a dad.

Chapter 20

Carl Warringson

Carl knew that it was hopeless to try and form a relationship with his daughter Marie following her mother's suicide. She just did not want to know him and have anything to do with him. He could not blame her as she must have felt bitter knowing the history of his relationship with his one-time girlfriend, Wendy Ritage, and how he had abandoned her when she was pregnant with Marie. At least his daughter accepted the money he had settled on her – enabling Marie to afford to study and live in London. He had known that Marie had given a false name and address at the St Mawes hotel she was working in just before the tragedy – so that she could be independent of her family and without anyone visiting there unexpectedly, or either telephoning or contacting her by post. Even when she had to return home when her mother died, she did not divulge her secret identity. Her friend, Holly Fines, who was also working at the hotel at the same time, must have known Marie's pseudonym, but she was obviously sworn to secrecy.

Purely for nostalgic reasons, Carl had kept a note of the hallmark number of the bracelet that originated from his grandmother – which he had given to Wendy at the time of their parting.

Living back in America, he decided not to dwell on his years in London – not even trying to make contact with Marie. He had done well in London, business and money wise, but in personal terms he had totally screwed up; he had hurt people. Besides ditching Wendy, the consequence being that he was not able to ever have a relationship with his daughter. He had also been unfaithful to his wife Shelley, which had led to divorce. And in business he had not always played by the rules. For instance, he cheated his supplier Jean Chofi in Paris – which had led to his young apprentice, Simon Negrini, to being physically attacked in Chofi's showroom. It was only the quick thinking of his assistant Sharon Welver, who had accompanied Simon on the trip to Paris – that stopped a potential serious assault. And then he sacked the young man for being careless with the money he gave him to buy stock. Poor lad; he must have been in a state of shock that evening following the incident in the Paris showroom and then spending hours in a police station – not knowing what would happen to him. And another thing to feel bad about – was that he had taken sexual advantage of Sharon and then casually dumped her, even though she carried on working for him in the company.

Carl met Angela Holbine at a reception for the Republican candidate Barry Goldwater, during the 1964 US election. Carl had disliked President Jack Kennedy – having supported Richard Nixon in 1960, but like all Americans, was shocked when Kennedy was assassinated in Dallas during 1963. The vice president, Lyndon Johnson, who had taken over from Kennedy, was now running on his own ticket and was expected to win the election. Although Carl had preferred Johnson to Kennedy – he was a loyal Republican and would vote for Goldwater, even though he expected him to lose and probably lose quite heavily. Angela, a wealthy divorcee with two adult boys, was a fundraiser for the Republicans, and was still a good looking woman for someone in their fifties. Angela and Carl hit it off together immediately – soon becoming a recognised couple at Los Angeles social gatherings for the well-off conservative-minded community – coming from the worlds of business and the arts. Angela was more refined than Carl, who still retained aspects of his Bronx background, despite his business success in London. He was on the way to repeating that success with building a chain of medium-priced Italian restaurants, specialising in pizzas, which had become popular with the younger crowd that patronised eating establishments, and with much more frequency than their parents' generation had.

Angela invested heavily in Carl's business, which helped the rapid expansion, without relying too much on bank loans with their greedy interest charges. Angela was intuitive enough to know that Carl had a great knack for business and she had every confidence that the restaurant chain would be a huge success. However, Angela, being a great patron of the arts and a regular at the opera – knew that Carl needed educating in all aspects of the arts.

Carl had given Angela a slightly sanitised version of his personal life, during his London years, and she had no desire to know all the gory details, but she made him promise, as a condition to marrying him, that he would not try to make contact with his estranged daughter, or even try to inquire about her whereabouts. She expected him to draw a line on his London years but she was OK with his occasional visit to New York to see his friends, the Mentones'... and his goddaughter, Helena Mentones, but Angela did not ever visit New York with Carl as she detested travelling and preferred to stay in her own patch where she was known and respected.

As much as she tried to encourage him – Carl didn't really get the arts. He understood business, worshipped money and was especially interested in social status – something he could ride on Angela's back to achieve. But he was savvy enough to know that he would need to be able to hold a conversation, at least about some aspect of the arts world, when they mixed with Angela's circle of friends and fellow benefactors. Paintings, theatre, literature and classical music concerts left him cold, but there was one area of the arts that began to appeal to him. That was 'opera' and for all the wrong reasons; initially anyway. Firstly, it was expensive to attend – attracting the wealthy people he was eager to fraternise with, and everyone dressed in their finest at the opera. Secondly, he recognised some of the arias from his childhood that his parents played on their wind-up gramophone –78 rpm – especially the tenor, Enrico Caruso, singing, with tears in his voice, *vesti la giubba,* from the opera, *Pagliacci* by Ruggero Leoncavallo.

Angela, noticing Carl's burgeoning interest in opera, made sure that she booked tickets only for the popular titles – *La Traviata* – *La Boheme* – *Tosca* – *Carmen* – *The Barber of Seville* – *Faust,* and the operetta, *The Merry Widow.* She avoided booking anything out of the standard repertoire, especially the long music dramas of Wagner. But when the new planned production of Gounod's *Faust* was postponed, at short notice, because of the soprano's indisposition, and not having a suitable understudy, the opera that replaced it was Verdi's *Simon Boccanegra,* in a traditional production that had been revived several times since it was first seen at the Los Angeles opera in 1950. Angela had been confident in Carl's reaction to *Faust* because, although it was not the banker it had been earlier in the century, when it had been one of the most famous operas in the world, it still attracted many traditional opera lovers. The opera, by the 1960s, had faded somewhat from its glory days but it contained arias, duets, ensembles and choruses that had a life of their own, and anyone of a certain age with record collection, would have had something from *Faust* in that collection, even if it was just the famous 'Soldiers Chorus'.

Simon Boccanegra? The opera had never been popular, even the revised version of 1881, and did not contain any famous tenor Verdi arias, such a *La Donna e mobile* from the popular *Rigoletto.* Angela was concerned that Carl would be bored stiff with no numbers to remind him of his parents' record collection. Besides, the plot was hard to comprehend; following a short prologue, Act One opens twenty-five years later. Carl and Angela attended the first night of the revival, but despite Angela's unease about Carl's reaction to this connoisseur's opera – her husband actually loved the piece. Whereas at previous operatic performances of well-known repertoire, Carl had no interest in the plot but eagerly awaited the familiar arias that brought back family memories – with *Simon Boccanegra* he related to the dramatic elements, firstly in a political way; especially the part known as 'The Council Chamber Scene'. He was mesmerised by Simon, the Doge of Genoa, taking control of all the different factions in the chamber, trying to preach peace –then controlling a baying mob, and finally forcing his long term colleague, Paulo, who had become the enemy, to curse himself. However, it was the earlier scene in Act One that had hit him in the gut – the Doge, Simon Boccanegra, finding his long-lost daughter, making the drama become synonymous to Carl's own personal history – thinking of what could have been with his own daughter, Marie, which brought tears to his eyes.

From a reluctant opera-goer – Carl had become an enthusiast and he joined the opera's fundraising scheme, as well as making a generous contribution himself, which endeared him greatly to the committee hierarchy. Although he also joined the board of the Philharmonic Orchestra with Angela – concerts bored Carl and he never took the trouble to read up on the great composers or try to understand anything about basic musical form and how music history had developed over the centuries. He got 'opera' – but it was more about the drama than the music for him, other than the famous arias and ensembles. Angela did not push him to appreciate concert music – she was just pleased that he liked opera. And as far as chamber music was concerned, once bitten – twice shy. She took him to a Beethoven string quartet concert and he fell asleep for the whole programme...So never again!

1984 -1986

Glyndehurst Festival Opera, from Sussex in England, had toured the USA in 1984 and gave several performances of two Mozart operas' in Los Angeles: *Le Nozze di Figaro* and *Cosi fan tutte*. Glyndehurst was famous for programming the Mozart operas' as the works were perfect for a company like Glyndehurst, which specialised in ensemble singing with long rehearsal periods – eschewing the star system – when the bigger the star's name, the less rehearsal time the star was prepared to give. This type of ensemble opera performance was revolutionary to the Los Angeles patrons who had always worked on the 'star' system.

The opera *aficionados'* loved the way Glyndehurst presented the operas, giving the performers standing ovations every night, but the more traditional patrons, which included Carl and Angela, preferred cheering their favourite star singers and did not appreciate the subtle performing style of ensemble opera. In any case, Carl was not a Mozart opera fan – too much *recitative* for his liking. But when the artistic director of the company did a presentation for the benefactors, setting out Glyndehurst's future programme plans – he announced that they were to produce Verdi's *Simon Boccanegra* in 1986, which was unusual repertoire for them – more a Grand opera than an ensemble piece – but they needed funding for the production, so Carl immediately offered to give the company a large donation, as long his name was boldly featured in the programme book. The artistic director was thrilled and told Carl that if he attended the opening night on 28 May 1986, not only would his name be listed in the programme book, but he could take a bow on stage with the performers at the conclusion of the performance, and they would say a few words thanking him for his generous donation. Carl was thrilled with the invitation and arranged the transfer of funds to the company. He put 28 May 1986 in his diary and he couldn't wait for that day to come.

The musical director of Glyndehurst at that time was the Dutch maestro, Bernard Haitink. Haitink had made a name for himself during the 1960s and 1970s conducting the big symphonic works of Anton Bruckner and Gustav Mahler – having been music director of the famous Concertgebouw Orchestra of Amsterdam. Opera did not feature much in Haitink's early career, perhaps because the Netherlands was more famous for concert music than for opera. Glyndehursts' appointment of Haitink to succeed John Pritchard in 1978 was somewhat of a surprise in the opera world, but they hit gold, as Haitink took to conducting opera like a duck to water, and the ten years he remained as music director there, were golden years for the Glyndehurst Festival Opera. And from Glyndehurst, Haitink went on to be music director of The Royal Opera House, Covent Garden, where he remained in post for fifteen years.

Verdi operas were never a major feature at Glyndehurst and Haitink himself was not particularly attuned to the popular nineteenth century Italian repertoire. However, middle-period Verdi operas, which *Simon Boccanegra* belonged to, shook off their *bel-canto* style predecessors and were in effect, Italian music dramas' – which suited Haitinks' musical sensibility to perfection.

The producer was the great theatre director, Sir Peter Hall, and the cast for the opera were British and American singers of the highest quality – who were chosen by the casting director, with input from Haitink and the new artistic director, Stephen Zandors. Stephen's appointment commenced for the 1985 season but he had no input to that season, as the choice of repertory and casting were well advanced by the time Stephen arrived at Glyndehurst – so the 1986 season was his first season proper.

Stephen was still working in Dublin when the decision to programme *Simon Boccanegra* was made, and Stephen contacted his soon-to-be new Glyndehurst colleagues, suggesting that perhaps they would consider performing the original version of the opera dating from 1857, instead of the revised 1881 version. This idea was firmly rejected out of hand by the board, as they reasoned that *Simon Boccanegra* was a hard enough sale to the public as it was – not being one of Verdi's bankable operas – but the attempt to revive the original version would be commercial suicide. Stephen did not wish to cause any waves with the board or his colleagues before he had even got his feet under the table as artistic director, but he was determined to put on a production of the original version of the opera someday – if not at Glyndehurst – then at another opera theatre.

During the rehearsal period, the American baritone who had been cast to sing the role of villain 'Paulo', the character who is a Boccanegra supporter at the outset of the opera, but turns into the villain of the drama as the opera unfolds – had to pull out due to illness and his replacement was the Israeli born, British baritone, Dov Katz.

Helena Mentones was by 1986, an established member of the cello section of the British Philharmonic Orchestra, based in London, but decamped to East Suffolk for the Glyndehurst Festival Opera season during the summer months. Stephen and Helena had not been in touch for a couple of years but she had become aware that Stephen had been appointed artistic director of Glyndehurst. She did not wish to spend the summer having awkward encounters with the man she had been madly in love with three years earlier. She had explained her dilemma to the orchestra's management – asking to be excused from the orchestra for the summer season. The management were none too pleased, but, thinking very highly of her playing and not wishing to lose her completely from the orchestra, they reluctantly agreed. Being self-employed, she would not be paid for the three months, so she asked her agent, Keith Foes, to see if he could find her some recital or chamber music engagements for the summer months. He told Helena that he would do his best, but the summer months were not the time of year for small-scale events, as the summer in London was dominated by the BBC Proms, performed at the gigantic concert hall, the Royal Albert Hall, in Kensington.

Helena's godfather, Carl Warringson, her Uncle Carl, now an elderly gentleman of seventy-five, had been in touch with Helena with the news that he was sponsoring one of the Glyndehurst productions during the summer. He had been invited to the opening night by the Glyndehurst management and was intending to travel. Carl, having no real interest in orchestras, was totally ignorant of the fact that the regular orchestra at Glyndehurst, was the same one that Helena was a member of, and she presumed correctly, that Carl had been unaware of any past connection between Stephen and her. Also, Stephen had no realisation that the 'Carl' Helena had spoken to him about in Dublin, was actually the same gentleman that was sponsoring the opera.

Carl had promised that he would spend a few days in London when in England and that he would take Helena out to dinner at a restaurant of her choosing.

Freddy Wakeson's daughter, Lizette, was a beautiful young woman of twenty-five, who had followed in her father's footsteps and become a journalist – not a sports writer like Freddy, but an arts journalist, writing features about well known musicians, artists and writers. Her expensive private school education and becoming an Oxford graduate, had given her the opportunity to mix in the 'arts' world which she loved enormously. Being part of that crowd, together with her father's contacts in the publishing industry, opened the door for Lizette and she wrote for several leading magazines; occasionally for the more upmarket Sundays' and was starting to write a biography of the once famous, but now almost totally neglected, of the nineteenth-century operatic composer, Giacomo Meyerbeer.

Lizette went regularly to the opera in London, usually in cheap seats or sometimes even standing, but had never yet attended a live performance of Verdi's *Simon Boccanegra* – so she requested it as a birthday present from her dad. Her mum was not keen at all on opera and although her dad was hardly a fan either, he would do anything for his daughter, so he bought two top-priced tickets for the opening night of the *Simon Boccanegra* new production at Glyndehurst.

SIMON BOCCANEGRA

Opera composed by Giuseppe Verdi.
Librettist: Francesco Maria Piave
First performance: Venice 1857.
Opera revised by Verdi and the librettist, Arrigo Boito.
First performance of the revised version: La Scala Milan 1881

Simon Boccanegra had fallen in love with Maria, daughter of a nobleman Jacobo Fiesco. Maria had given birth to a daughter with Simon but the daughter had disappeared and Maria died. Boccanegra was proclaimed Doge by the crowd, helped by the plebeian Paolo Albiani.

Twenty-five years later Boccanegra discovered that an orphan named Amelia Grimaldi was in fact his long-lost daughter. Genoese aristocrats including Gabriel Adorno, who was Amelia's lover, was planning a rebellion against the Doge and Paolo had turned against his old comrade. When Boccanegra informed Paolo that he could not marry Amelia, Paolo arranged to have Amelia kidnapped. The plot was foiled and whilst Boccanegra addressed the council chamber, he demanded that Paolo cursed the criminal who had kidnapped Amelia, suspecting that Paolo was in fact the culprit.

Paolo poisoned Boccanegra, and Adorno thought Amelia was the Doge's lover, as father and daughter had kept the discovery of the truth of the matter secret. But when eventually Boccanegra admitted that Amelia was his daughter, Adorno changed sides and pledged his allegiances to Boccanegra. Adorno puts down a rebellion against the Doge that had been led by Paolo.

Paolo is condemned to death whilst the poison was beginning to work on Boccanegra. Fiesco met again with Boccanegra and learnt that Amelia was his granddaughter, which led to reconciliation between the two previously sworn enemies. Adorno married Amelia and Boccanegra died. Fiesco announced to the crowd that the new Doge was Gabriele Adorno – whilst the people shouted that 'no', they wanted Boccanegra. Fiesco responded that Boccanegra was dead.

Flipping through the programme book whilst enjoying pre – performance drinks, Freddy had a real jolt when he saw the name, Dov Katz – who was singing the role of 'Paulo' in the opera. He and Dov had not been in touch with each other for many years – although he remembered that Dov had been studying singing at a London music college.

Freddy never really imagined that he would see his name listed for performing at such a prestigious opera festival, such as Glyndehurst.

'Have you heard of the baritone Dov Katz – Lizette?'

'No, dad, he's not a singer I've come across before. Why?'

'Look here in the programme – he's singing here tonight as 'Paulo' and he's an old acquaintance of mine.'

'That's strange dad – because I had looked up the cast when you booked the tickets and I didn't see his name listed?'

'No – you wouldn't have – because look here at the note at the end of the page, stating that Richard Dale-Sharre was indisposed and that Dov Katz had stepped in to sing the role of 'Paulo' at short notice.'

'You must say hello to him after the performance, dad,' Lizette said, feeling pleased that her dad had known one of the singers, and that maybe, it would stop him being bored with the opera. Lizette was aware that dad had seen *Simon Boccanegra* many years ago in Milan – he had hated it!

The premiere performance was a huge success with the cast, conductor, chorus master and stage director, all receiving standing ovations. The new artistic director, Stephen Zandors, came onto the stage when the applause started to die down – holding the arm of an elderly gentleman. Stephen took a microphone and firstly thanked the audience and all the performers for a hugely successful evening. He then turned to and introduced Carl Warringson to the auditorium, announcing that, 'Without the generous financial support of Mr Warringson, we would not have been able to produce *Simon Boccanegra* – so would you please show your appreciation.'

The audience rose again as one and vigorously applauded. Carl did not speak but took a low bow whilst the emotion in him welled up – feeling so much pride in what he had been able to achieve, in helping to programme this wonderful opera, at such a beautiful opera festival.

Freddy sought out Dov Katz at the conclusion of the opera. Lizette had gone off to join the queue to pay homage to the conductor, Bernard Haitink. Father and daughter planned to meet up in the bar later.

Dov and Freddy embraced – Freddy congratulating Dov on his performance in the opera.

'Well,' said Dov, it's an important dramatic role in the opera and its' fun playing the villain. But to be honest Freddy – Paulo doesn't get to sing much and I would love to tackle the title role one day, and now that I've reached the age of fifty – it's the perfect age to be a Simon Boccanegra.

'Listen... Freddy – it's so good to see you and I would like to have a chat – but now's not the time. I'm off to the first night dinner party celebration with all the cast – so can I give you a call and perhaps we could meet up in London?'

'Yes...of course, Dov – don't let me keep you – and of course I would love to get together in London soon.' Freddy congratulated Dov again and having both checked their respective telephone numbers with each other – they embraced once more with a promise to meet again soon.

Freddy and Lizette met up again in the bar as arranged – with Lizette excited about having managed a few words with the great conductor – who had signed her programme book.

'So – did you see your old friend, Dad? – I thought he was excellent as the villain, by the way.'

'Yes... it was good to see him and we've planned to see each other in London.'

'That's great... Dad, it's always good to catch up with old friends again.'

Freddy was wondering though – what it was that Dov wanted to chat with him about.

He didn't have to wait long – Dov called him a couple of days later.

They met up in a quiet bar just off Bond Street in Central London. Ordering pints, they chatted about the opera – Dov asking after Lizette and saying how sorry he was that he hadn't met her at the opera. Freddy explained that Lizette was desperate to chat to Haitink but she knew they were meeting this evening – and sent her best regards. When they were on to their second pint – Freddy asked Dov what it was he wanted to chat with him about.

'Well, Freddy... I've established my singing career mainly in West Germany, so I spend a lot of time there. Compared to the UK the opportunities for a non-famous opera singer like me in West Germany are so much greater.'

'Why's that...?'

'It's simple, Freddy. West Germany has about fifty opera houses compared to just a handful here and to get a gig at our leading house, the Royal Opera House – one must be a big name, and even the supporting roles go to the artists who have graduated through their own training programme. So my bread and butter is West Germany. Anyway... that's all by and by.

'The reason I'm telling you this is that recently when I was in the Hanover opera – not singing on that particular night, but in the audience, eying up the competition on stage in the role of Count de Luna, in Verdi's *Il Trovatore,* I bumped into Holly

206

Fines, who is a resident of Hanover, having settled there after her marriage to an American military man broke down. Not being an opera fan, Holly was there because a friend of hers was singing the small of 'Ines' in *Il Trovatore.* Anyway, we got chatting about the old days, in the bar at the interval, and reminisced about the night of the infamous dinner party in Kentish Town – about a quarter of a century ago with Marie and co.'

 "Marie" I said to Holly..." you mean Margo?"

"No"... Dov – Margo Pento was a pseudonym. Her real name was Marie Ridge.

"But why use a pseudonym?" I asked her.

"Well... Dov, that's a long story. The important thing I want to tell you is that although Marie died in childbirth, her baby survived"

'I was shocked and told Holly briefly about my role in the lead-up to Marie giving birth and my unfortunate absence at the crucial time.'

"But Holly, I said... I spoke to the hospital"

 "Then... you must have been given incorrect information."

'Anyway'... Dov continued to explain the conversation to Freddy.

'By that time the interval was over and Holly gave me her phone number – asking me to call her and she'd explain things in more detail. I couldn't concentrate on the second half of the opera at all – thinking about what Holly had just told me. But where did Holly receive this information?

'A few days later we had a long chat on the phone and Holly tried to fill in the gaps. She gave me details about Marie's background and her difficult relationship with her step-father and why she had left home, giving herself a false name and address. Holly also confirmed that she did not know about Marie's pregnancy and she said that she still felt awful at the way she treated her friend at the time.'

'Well'... interjected Freddy – that makes two of us with deep regrets about our behaviour on that fateful night.'

'Anyway... Holly explained that after years of being estranged from her own family she travelled back to Cornwall and made peace with her elderly parents.'

'Holly continued her monologue...'

"I asked my parents if they knew where Marie was as she owed her a huge apology. They were surprised that I didn't know about her death in childbirth. I asked them how they knew and they told me that a nurse working at the maternity hospital in London actually was a local girl from our village"

"The nurse told my parents that although Marie had registered in the hospital as Margo Pento, from Penzance, she had found an old school note in the young woman's bag, with the name of Marie Ridge, and an address in Helford. Unfortunately, there were no surviving members of the Ridge family there. A neighbour, who knew about the friendship between Holly and Marie, pointed them to my parents' house, and having invited the nurse in, she told them about Marie. But when I asked my parents about the baby – they said that there had been some confusion – as a young trainee nurse had informed an inquiring gentleman that both mother and baby had died. The nurse continued to explain to my parents' that the gentleman concerned was a Mr Katz, who had telephoned all the way from Israel, saying he was a close friend of Margo's. The trainee nurse had been severely reprimanded for giving Mr Katz incorrect information, but Mr Katz did not leave a contact number – so the hospital was unable to correct the information about the baby – who had survived – and was soon adopted by a wealthy American couple from New York."

Freddy was all ears as Dov explained.

'I was speechless at the other end of the telephone – trying to take in this bombshell news, when Holly said how sorry she was that she'd lived with the secret for many years – knowing that Dov was under the impression that the baby had also died. When I didn't respond, Holly added – that she had thought over the years about trying to make contact with me, and, if she had known that I was singing at opera houses in West Germany, she may have done so – but knowing how I must have felt about her – she was too much of a coward to even try to contact me. But, she continued to say, meeting me by chance at the opera made her realise that she had to come clean – and relate all the facts that she knew.'

'After twenty-four years, Freddy', said Dov, 'all the personal devastation of that time came flooding back to me and I felt sick in the stomach. I thought that Holly, who had behaved so badly towards Margo – I mean Marie – continued to do so by not trying to make contact with me or even with you, Freddy, as you could have passed the information back to me. But when I calmed down a bit – I realised that the important thing was that the baby had survived. And even if I had known the truth at the time – what could I have done? I was in no position to adopt a baby. I would have just liked to know who the father was – I would certainly have had a few choice words to say to him. But despite the silly nurse that I spoke to at the time, who informed me of the baby's death – the outcome was for sure the best for the baby – to be adopted by a good established well-off family.'

Freddy said very little during this long explanation from Dov except at the end when he remarked with a half-smile on his face.

'What's up with you and me? We don't meet for years on end, but every time we do, you have a massive tragic tale to tell!'

Putting an arm around Dov, Freddy said, 'Let me buy some more drinks and you can tell me all about your opera career and why an opera that I don't care much about seems to follow me around forever!'

With a guffaw laugh, Freddy went up to the bar and ordered two more pints with two whisky chasers on the side – and spent the rest of evening talking and laughing together without mentioning past sad events again.

PART THREE

Chapter 21

The Lough Corrib Festival, 1993

Sunday 5 September 1993

The Opening Production of the Festival

First Performance

SIMON BOCCANEGRA (original version – 1857)

Music: Giuseppe Verdi

Libretto: Francesco Maria Piave – with additions by Giuseppe Montanelli after the play by Antonio Garcia Gutierrez

Conductor: **Simon Negrini**

Director: **Lizette Wakeson**

Sets   John Tern

Costumes   Deirdre Lance

Lighting   Nigel Ings

Choreography Lindsay Dole

The Lakeside Opera Chorus: *Chorus Director* Terry Wardes

The Orchestra of the Lakeside Opera Orchestra – *Leader Vasko Silev*

Paulo Aiden M'kay

Pietro Brendan Cocaran

Simon Boccanegra **Dov Katz**

Fiesco Forbes Bineson

Amelia Grimaldi Karen Perian

Gabriele Adordo Riccardo Forz

Maid Eithne Frele

'I can't believe it's actually happening' Stephen Zandors announced to the crowd of colleagues and well wishers gathered in the Lough Corrib Opera Bar, a couple of hours before the opening performance.

'When we started talking about building an opera house on Lough Corrib in the 1980s and starting a festival – it was a dream that I never thought would come to fruition, and yet – here we are and an opera performance will commence shortly.'

Everyone within hearing of Stephen's words... stood to raise their glasses and toast the opening night and to the ongoing success of the Lough Corrib Opera Festival.

Just under two hours later, the conductor, Simon Negrini, walked into the orchestra pit – bowed to the audience who applauded loudly – turned to Vasko Silev, the orchestra leader, who made a downbeat gesture with his baton – *Simon Boccanegra* was under way – the festival having begun.

Simon Negrini had renewed his boyhood friendship with Dov Katz – the boy he'd had a crush on during their respective time at the Greenshead Jewish boarding school in the late 1940s'. Years later, they'd then come across each other at various West German opera houses during the 1970s and 1980s. By that time in their respective lives, Simon and Dov had abandoned all aspects of their religion but still remained proud of their Jewish heritage and culture, and Simon was a supporter of the State of Israel, the country of Dov's birth. Who would have thought that two orthodox thirteen year old Jewish boys who had met at boarding school and then lost touch with each other for many years, would meet again as professional musicians, both being involved in opera performances in West Germany with Simon as a conductor and Dov as baritone soloist?

Dov had slowly made progress with his career during the latter years of the 1960s – picking up small parts with fringe opera groups, mainly around London and occasionally in other UK cities. London's leading opera houses, Covent Garden and Sadler's Wells, were closed doors for him, so to supplement his meagre income – he took on work singing at weddings and bar - mitzvahs. When Dov's agent recommended a new singing teacher, the renowned Italian baritone, Toto Motti, his technique and interpretive skills improved dramatically.

Motti took very few pupils and his fees were high. But Dov won a scholarship from his ex-music college as he'd been a student that had been voted by the college principal as the most promising music student of his final year at the college in 1964. Having Motti named as his teacher on his CV, helped Dov's agent to find work for his client in West Germany, and, for the following two decades, Dov's engagements were almost exclusively in German opera houses.

Verdi operas were Dov's speciality and taking small supporting baritone roles, he could study the senior singers first-hand, who were singing the starring baritone roles in the Verdi cannon of operas such as *Macbeth, Ernani , Luisa Miller, Rigoletto, La Traviata, Il Trovatore, La Forza Del Destino, Ballo in Maschera, Don Carlos, Aida, Otello, Falstaff* and of course *Simon Bogganegra.*

Dov, who'd moved to West Germany, sadly parted from his flat mate, and discreet boyfriend, Brian Montague, and they went their separate ways. The catalyst for the parting was Brian, who wanted to stay in London – having no desire to live anywhere abroad, especially West Germany, with the horrors of the Second World War still fresh in people's minds during the 1960s.

Dov Katz was first reunited with his old friend Simon Negrini, when they were both engaged by Cologne opera for a series of performances of Verdi's popular opera, *Rigoletto,* during the autumn season of 1981; Simon as the conductor and Dov singing the supporting baritone role of Marullo, one of the duke's courtiers. This was a step-up for them both, as Cologne was a major West German opera house, compared to the small provincial houses they had been performing with during the previous decade. Opera careers were slow burners both for conductors and singers. However, a conducting career had longevity and although singers much less so, the baritone voice was ideal for singers in their forties and fifties. Dov had been working his way towards the major Verdi baritone leads, which were ideal for the mature artists who would be able to convey the multi-faceted characters Verdi and his librettists had created, such as, Nabucco, Macbeth, Rigoletto and Simon Boccanegra.

For the final performance of the run, the baritone singing the title role of Rigoletto, had lost his voice and was unable to perform. Dov, who had sung Rigoletto with a fringe company in London many years before, also as a last minute substitute, had continued to study the role with his coach, and heroically offered to sing the role, whilst the management were able to find a young singer to take over Dov's contracted small role of Marullo. Dov spent the whole day of the performance going over everything with Simon, who was a great help in advising him where to hold his voice back and where to go full throttle – in conjunction with Simon's own interpretation of the opera in matters of *tempi* and orchestral balance.

The performance was successful, with Dov receiving a huge ovation from the audience and winning massive brownie points from Cologne Opera House management. However, Dov still continued to be engaged for supporting roles, but at least he was regularly performing at a West German leading opera house and was able to turn down offers from the small provincial companies. Following his debut at the Glyndehurst Opera during the 1986 festival in *Simon Boccanegra,* and even though the debut was in a minor role, Germany began to offer Dov major roles, specifically the great roles of the Verdi cannon that Dov aspired to and which he considered masterpieces of Italian opera repertoire.

'Congratulations Dov.' Simon said, patting him on the back in the bar after the performance.

'Thanks, Simon, but I couldn't have done it without you nursing me along and miming the words – as well as making sure that the orchestra didn't overwhelm my voice.'

'No problem Dov. I would do the same for any singer; it's important for an opera conductor to understand voices and adapt the orchestral volume accordingly, depending on the individual voice size.'

They both left the bar and went to the restaurant to join the full cast, stage director and designer, with the backstage staff and senior management, for a celebration dinner, to thank everyone for a successful run of *Rigoletto.* It was a joyous but raucous affair, with much back slapping and lots of praise for Dov in saving the final performance.

It was the early hours of the morning when the dinner party broke up with everyone feeling a bit worse for wear, having consumed too much champagne and wine. Luckily, both Dov and Simon were staying at the aptly named Opera Hotel, located next door to the opera house. The momentary breath of fresh air between the two buildings sobered them up a bit as they headed for the hotel bar for a final night cap. Large Remy Martin cognacs were ordered as they both sat back and following the noisy chat at the dinner, the two of them suddenly felt emotionally drained and quietness developed between the two old friends.

For some reason, Dov, in a stream of consciousness, started talking about Margo/Marie. He was almost chatting to himself about something that had affected him deeply over the years. Dov was thinking about the drip-drip information regarding the sequence of events leading to the tragedy of Marie's death and the mystery of her baby – with him believing that the baby had died at birth and then the recent bombshell far-fetched story from Holly Fine about the Cornish nurse. The fact that the baby hadn't died but had survived and was subsequently adopted – brought back to Dov all the memories of that time in his life and his beautiful friendship with Marie. He realised that Holly was an unreliable witness and not to be trusted – but why would she make up such a story?

Dov started to talk to Simon about Marie and his time at college where the two of them had met and he'd become close to this lovely but lonely girl who was calling herself Margo, although her real name was Marie. She was very talented with the ambition to become a dancer and an actress. Now perceiving Simon's interest – Dov continued to talk about the night he had been invited to Marie's flat for dinner and meeting her flatmate, Holly Fine, who was there with an obnoxious new boyfriend named Freddy. This Freddy, whom he had continued to meet by chance intermittently over the years, had in fact matured into a more decent human being and had become chastised regarding his behaviour at that infamous dinner party evening back in 1959.

'Sorry, Simon, to bore you with all this stuff from long ago and I'll shut up now.'

'No...No...Dov – you're not boring me at all,' Simon said – as certain distant memories began to stir in his head. 'You said her name was...?'

Dov looked at Simon, feeling rather perplexed. Why was he showing interest in Dov's convoluted past life? 'She was known as Margo Pento but her real name was Marie Ritage.'

'Did you say the girl was from Cornwall? Which part of the County?'

Giving Simon a weird look, Dov responded that she was from the small village of Helford, on the Helford River – but posing as Margo Pento, she had made the much larger town of Penzance her hometown.

'Carry on your story Dov.' Simon, now fully alert, was thinking hard. – It couldn't be – could it? No....much too much of a coincidence. But strange pathways can merge occasionally in real life and not just in literature, drama and opera.

Dov began to feel tense – sensing Simon's serious intent in hearing Dov's tale, and gave Simon a shortened version of his initial knowledge of Marie's and the baby's supposed death – and then years later hearing that in fact he had been given incorrect information from a hospital nurse – that incredibly, the baby had survived.

The more Dov spoke the more Simon began to have an eerie feeling about the beautiful young girl he had met at The Rising Sun Hotel, St. Mawes, during the summer of 1959. He had enjoyed a sexual liaison with her in his bedroom and then she disappeared – never to be found. She had given her name as

Margo but remained completely mysterious; not wishing to engage in any conversation with him. If she had died in childbirth, that baby could have been his. *I killed her...oh god, please no. – These thoughts are* ridiculous. *– This Margo that Dov is talking about could have been anyone. This is just an old guilt feeling coming back about that night at The Rising Sun... The guilt of taking advantage of an innocent girl and specifically that I hadn't used protection.* And Dov mentioned the name of Freddy – was that the same Freddy who had caused him so much grief with his ex-wife, Felicity?

Simon and Dov did not get together again for some time; they were both flitting around West Germany on different assignments and were never in the same place at the same time.

But in 1982, they were both engaged in Munich, for Verdi's *Nabucco,* with Simon conducting and Dov singing the title role for the first time. In fact, it was Dov's first major Verdi role anywhere that he had been engaged for, and not just as a replacement for an indisposed artist. (Although this turned out to be a one-off major role for Dov until later in the decade) The opera was about the Babylonian king Nebuchadnezzar, who destroyed the Temple of Jerusalem and held the Jewish people captive in Babylon. The piece was an apt opera for Simon Negrini and Dov Katz to perform – both men with traditional Jewish backgrounds.

Dov had knocked Simon off course with the tale of his friendship with Marie, or was it Margo? The sad death of his college friend followed by the convoluted sequence of events – left a question mark as to whether the baby had survived or not. He had reasoned that it would have been too much of a coincidence for the poor girl to have been the same person he had enjoyed a brief sexual encounter with – in a St Mawes hotel bedroom all those years before. Simon convinced himself that the conducting of such a dramatic and emotionally charged opera as *Rigoletto,* had had an effect on him that had clouded his judgement – when Dov was relating his story. The fact that the opera featured a father and daughter relationship which ended tragically for the daughter – had turned Simon's thoughts to what joy it would have been to actually have had a daughter. He dismissed from his mind the possibility of Dov's tale having any personal significance, although deep down the names of Margo and Freddy still troubled him – was it about Margo, and his old nemesis Freddy, that Dov was relating to him? He thought again about the note the girl had dropped for him in the bar of the hotel setting up the assignment, and he remembered clearly the signature in the note. It was most definitely …'Margo.'

Dov and Simon met in a quiet bar during a rest day from a performance and Dov immediately mentioned a gold bracelet – which had been a family heirloom that Marie had requested Dov kept safe for her whilst she was giving birth in the hospital. Simon went pale and started shivering as he remembered that he had found a gold bracelet on the floor of his hotel bedroom and had handed it over to the reception – with the receptionist recognising the bracelet as belonging to Margo Pento. Could this be the very same bracelet?

'Do you have the bracelet here in Germany?'

'Yes, I do Simon, I keep it in a locked safe wherever I'm living as it's the only link I still have with my dear friend and I consider the bracelet a holy relic.'

'Could I see it please?'

Dov responded with a furrowed brow. 'Why do you wish to see the bracelet?'

'There's a possibility that I may have had a brief encounter with your friend in Cornwall a short time before you met her in London.'

'Dov was absolutely gobsmacked to think that his old school friend and his current musical mentor may have been the villain that he had carried murderous thoughts about for so long and was sitting right next to him.

Simon added. 'If I see the bracelet I'll know for sure whether it was the same girl or not that I met in Cornwall twenty-two years ago. I took a note at the time of the bracelet's hallmark number – I still have the note, and like you, I have always taken it with me on my travels and kept it with my papers...a sort of talisman.'

Simon said to a stunned Dov, 'Let's leave things until the end of the opera run, as there are only two more performances to go and we must stay professional throughout. None of our colleagues or the opera management should be made aware of there being any strain in our relationship.'

The two final performances of *Nabucco* went without a hitch with nobody becoming aware of any tension between the two artists. However, neither artist showed up for the party following the final performance.

They met the following day for lunch in downtown Munich; both were nervous and kept the conversation to small talk and general chit-chat whilst consuming omelettes and salad – keeping off the alcohol. Whilst they were finishing off the meal and sipping coffees, Dov lent into the pocket of his bag and brought out the bracelet, handing it to Simon. Simon knew immediately it was the same one he had found on the floor of his bedroom in the hotel – without having to check the hallmark number. But he had the number with him anyway and, yes, the numbers matched and his instincts had been proven right. He was the man who had probably made Marie pregnant, and that made him indirectly responsible for her death. He said nothing to Dov – gave him back the bracelet – and asked a waiter for the bill, which he promptly paid. Then he rose from his seat and left the restaurant without a glance at Dov.

Dov sat there for ages in a trance, unable to digest what had happened between them. He put the bracelet carefully back into his bag whilst his thoughts turned to Marie who had died so very young.

When Dov went back to the opera theatre a few days later to collect his pay cheque and his personal belongings he had left there during the opera run, from the manager's office – he was handed a letter marked 'Private and Confidential'.

Dear Dov,

I would like to apologise for explaining myself in a letter and by taking the cowards option of writing instead of facing you again face to face. Margo and I had caught the eye of each other around the bar area and later in the restaurant. She dropped me a cryptic note when I was back in the bar area, sitting and drinking with new Irish friends I had met at the hotel. I was relaxing and listening to live music when I saw the note. It just stated that her name was Margo and that she was aged 18 and she requested my room number. I believed that I felt a mixture of sexual excitement and fear of the unknown, and I was a bit sceptical about her age as I thought she looked younger than 18. Anyway, I managed to get a note back to her with my room number. I'd thought she wouldn't come to my room, but she did. It was a first-time experience for her and the secrecy of the whole escapade made me finish quickly which had been too early for Margo to get maximum pleasure. Nevertheless, she seemed happy and content, cuddling up to me as we both slept. Then she vanished as if it had been a beautiful dream. The bracelet was the only evidence that it wasn't a dream and that it had really happened. I'd tried to look for her around the hotel but the receptionist told me that she'd had to dash home due to a family problem, so I had no way of finding her. Of course, now I know that she had given me a false name and I actually knew nothing about her, as part of our encounter pact that she'd concocted was that there was to be no talking. Her instructions were 'just make love and I'll go'. I went along with that stricture, and to be honest, the 'no talking' idea was for me an exciting aspect about the whole encounter as we focused entirely on the sex act.

I have related the events of that strange evening and night as best as my memory allows me to do, and being a conductor, I do professionally rely on memorising scores. The information you have gathered about the events and related to me has given enormous grief and much guilt, and that guilt will remain with me forever. The only thing that will relieve the guilt is to find Marie's baby, who of course is now an adult.

I apologise again to you, Dov, for causing you such heartache, especially for you to discover that your old school friend and musical colleague is the man that you have hated for many years.

Please forgive a stupid young man that had acted impulsively and taken advantage of a young innocent girl who was seeking adventure, and I, Simon, am the one who just happened to have been in the right place at the appropriate time.

Simon Negrini

Chapter 22

Dov Katz refused all operatic engagements that Simon Negrini was conducting following the revelations that Simon, of all people, had had sexual relationship with his dear friend Margo Pento – now known to have been Marie Ritage, during the summer before Marie's pregnancy, making him in all probability the man who'd caused the pregnancy. What was he thinking at the time – having unprotected sex with a young innocent girl aged sixteen. He accepted Simon's word that she had written in her note that she was aged eighteen, but Simon admitted that he thought her to be younger. Also, what was he doing playing sexual games with such a young person who had been working out her own fantasy – by not conversing together to get to know one another, even superficially, before engaging physically. Simon should have been more responsible, even if Marie had instigated the whole encounter; Simon should have had the moral courage not to have gone along with it. Of course, there was the possibility that Marie could have had sex with another man after her escapade with Simon, but Dov thought that unlikely – as Marie would have admitted to that when she told him about her pregnancy that night in her Kentish Town flat. She had been very open about the escapade with Simon, so there would have been no reason to keep a secret about an association with another man. No, it was Simon who was responsible, and for that he would never forgive him.

Simon hadn't forgotten about the Margo/Marie he had met in Cornwall back in 1959 but had put it down to youthful indulgence and had always hoped that it would have been the same for her and that she'd developed into a mature adult with a full and successful life ahead. The shocking disclosures by Dov Katz had changed everything – Simon realising that a young man's indiscretion had possibly cost a girl her life and that he had a son or a daughter somewhere in the world. But the sad thing was that Simon had accepted that at the age of forty-seven, and without a wife or regular girlfriend, he would never be a father, but if Dov's information was correct and the baby had survived, he or she would be aged twenty-two. But the chances of him ever finding his offspring would be almost zero, which made Simon doubly sad.

Simon spent five years during the 1960s in Israel studying conducting with Sergei Comissiona, who had established a long-term relationship with the Ramat-Gan Chamber Orchestra, and had become a sought-after conducting teacher and mentor. Comissiona had originally invited Simon to attend a series of master-classes, when he had first met the conductor at the north London flat, where the conductor's mother, Mrs Flackter, lived and was a neighbour of Simon's own mother, residing at a nearby flat. The master-classes were so successful for Simon, as Comissiona had seen something musically special in Simon and had offered him free private tuition on the basis that Simon would pay back the tuition fees only when he became a fee-earning conductor, which he did in due course. Meanwhile, Simon worked at the Ramat-Gan Kibbutz to earn his keep doing whatever was required – a mixture of farm labour – handy work around the buildings and helping in the kitchens. Simon became very fit and broadened out physically over the years spent at the Kibbutz.

Back in London and living again with his mother, Simon was desperate to find work in the musical world, but was unsure how to go about it. Mr Flackter, Comissiona's step-father, friend to Simon and residential neighbour, came once again to the rescue by putting Simon in touch with a young up-and-coming artist manager, Keith Foes. When Simon met Foes at his London office, the first thing he asked Simon was about his piano playing. Simon made it clear to Foes that he was intent on becoming a conductor not a concert pianist. Foes, rather patronisingly, explained to Simon that the concert world had plenty of conductors and being in his thirties, Simon was still young for a conducting post with a decent orchestra, but what he should do is would be to hone his piano technique and look for work as a piano accompanist to well-known singers or instrumentalist. That way, working with musicians more established than he was, his name would slowly become better known and then they could start looking at conducting posts – either as an assistant conductor or as a *repetiteur*. Simon asked what a *repetiteur* was. Foes explained, with a decree of irritation in his voice, that Simon had a lot to learn on how the musical world worked. A *repetiteur* was an opera coach – helping singers to learn their roles in opera and accompanying them in rehearsal before the full orchestra became involved with the conductor. Many famous conductors in the past had begun their career as *repetiteurs.*

Simon once again started to visit the Flackters' flat almost on a daily basis to spend hours on the piano – working on his technique. He had no intention of ever performing piano solo, but having taken advice from Keith Foes he was hoping to become an accompanist, mainly as a route to conducting, which ultimately was his great ambition and for which he had spent five long years studying hard in Israel with Mrs Flackter's son, Sergei Comissiona, to help him achieve that ambition.

Keith Foes was as good as his word and despite Simon having taken a dislike to the young artist agent, thinking him to be rather arrogant, he couldn't fault him on his professional ability, and before long the musical gig offers started to come through. This was a great relief to Simon, as the savings he had bought back from his Kibbutz work in Israel were beginning to run out and he needed to contribute to his mother's household budget.

The 1960s was a great time for music in London. The drab 1950s had morphed into the Swinging sixties and the pop/rock world of the Beatles and The Rolling Stones were conquering the world. And in classical music, young exciting new talent was emerging, cellist Jacqueline Du Pre, pianists Daniel Barenboim and Vladimir Ashkenazy, violinists' Yitzhak Perlman, Pinches Zuckerman and the conductor, Zubin Mehta. The young fashionable musicians brought new audiences to concert halls and opera houses and suddenly it became quite hip to be a classical music enthusiast. Politically, the tired old

Tories with their aristocratic associates had been swept aside for the egalitarian Labour government – whose ambition was to create a more equal society as well as being supporters of the arts.

Simon began his musical career accompanying young artists straight from Music College, mainly violinists and a few cellists. The cello sonata repertoire contained far fewer works than the violin offered, but Simon, although enjoying working with young violinists, absolutely adored the cello repertory and was always asking Keith Foes to find cello talent for him to work with. Accompanying singers took longer to find for engagements, as singers, being generally more temperamental than instrumentalists, tended to stick with the known accompanist and were reluctant to change to an unknown pianist.

In the late 1960s Simon got a fantastic lucky break. He was offered a junior *repetiteur* job at the Covent Garden Opera House – whose musical director during that period was the great Hungarian conductor Georg Solti. Solti took a few years to win critics and audiences over when he first arrived at the Garden, but Solti was in his pomp later in his decade in charge there and the opera house was in a golden period with sold out performances and hugely enthusiastic audiences. A Solti night at the opera was much sought after with his brilliant incisive conducting and for his choice of singers – mixing world-class stars with home-grown British artists that Solti had nurtured during his time at the Garden. Initially, Simon had very little association with the great conductor but over time, Solti got word from some of his singers that Simon was doing great work with them – above all, he slowly built a reputation of being patient and understanding with singers and they started to ask especially for Simon to coach them in their various roles – bypassing the more senior *repetiteurs* in the opera house.

By the 1970s – Solti had left the opera house to be replaced by Colin Davis. Simon by then had had several promotions in the house to become a senior *repetiteur,* and, although having great respect for Davis – the overall performance temperature had dropped a notch or two and Simon was beginning to look elsewhere for conducting opportunities. However, other than a few fringe opera performances at St Pancras Town Hall, for which he had been engaged to conduct several Handel operas – which at that time were totally neglected repertoire – no other conducting engagements had come his way.

Simon stayed several years at Covent Garden, gaining huge experience of opera and singers, but was keen to learn the symphonic repertoire. With Solti's influence he was appointed an associate conductor of The Halle in Manchester whose principal conductor was James Loughran. The position was for a two-year engagement. Simon was ecstatic and considered it his first real breakthrough in a full-time conducting career.

Before leaving Covent Garden, he was engaged to conduct his first and only opera performance there – perhaps as a leaving present. The opera was Verdi's *Ill Trovatore* – the final performance of a very successful run that Davis himself had been conducting. The cast was a first-rate international one; the production was rather dark and dreary but the audience were there for the singers and cheered them to the rafters. Simon didn't try anything too individual – he just followed Davis's conducting performances and supported the singers the best way he could, by not letting the orchestra overwhelm them. *Trovatore* was, after all, a singer's opera with beautiful melodies throughout the piece. He received enthusiastic applause and the few critics that attended were reasonably sympathetic in their reviews.

During the period from leaving Covent Garden and beginning at The Halle, his agent, Keith Foes managed to get a number of guest conducting engagements for Simon with various orchestras, mostly ones of the second rank around Europe in out-of-the-way locations, but they were perfect for Simon to learn orchestral repertory.

Simon's two years at The Halle were everything he had hoped they would be. He got on well with the principal conductor and formed many friendships with various orchestral members. He conducted much standard repertory – Beethoven, Brahms –Tchaikovsky etc. and also got stuck into a number of knotty contemporary works. He had a special affinity for concerto soloist, be it pianists – violinists or cellists, and had a particular success conducting Ernest Bloch's Hebrew rhapsody *Schelomo* with the famous Hungarian – American cellist Janos Starker. Starker told Simon after the concert that he felt that Simon had a natural feeling for the piece and that he was an excellent accompanist.

At the end of Simon's two successful years at The Halle, he had hoped that other conducting positions with orchestras, in either Britain or Europe, might come his way, but that was not to be. However, various inquiries from West German opera houses were sent via his agent Keith Foes and Focs advised Simon that a good conducting career could be had with opera in West Germany as so much opera was being performed there. His ten years working at Covent Garden had done wonders for his CV and he would have no trouble receiving continuous engagements as a guest conductor in West Germany.

Dov Katz's terrible disclosures, and his own discovery, that the girl he had slept with for one night in Cornwall, and who had most probably carried his baby – tragically died within a year of their meeting. It had shaken Simon's previous belief that his life and career were on an upward trajectory – following the hurdles of his earlier life and having, against all the odds, become a conductor. Dov's rejection of Simon, both personally and professionally, hurt him enormously. After all, the two men had a shared boyhood past and had both, against all the odds, developed successful careers in the classical music world, which was generally closed to men of their respective backgrounds.

Despite the great emotional hole in his heart Simon's opera conducting career in Germany continued to flourish, but purely as a freelance guest conductor as he was unable to secure a musical directorship at any of the German opera houses, big or small. At times he had dark thoughts that perhaps Dov, whom he hadn't seen or heard from since that fateful day of when he'd seen the bracelet, was spreading poison about him to opera house managements, but he dismissed those thoughts from his mind – knowing that Dov would never do such a thing. He was not that sort of person, however much he personally despised Simon. The reason for not securing a musical directorship was probably more prosaic – that too many foreign conductors were ploughing their trade in Germany, and as a musical director could stay at an opera house for many years, fewer opportunities arose than conductors vying to fill them. He did occasionally get offered engagements to conduct various British orchestras, again as a one-off guest gig, but they were great opportunities for him to renew his acquaintance with the orchestral repertory as well as being able to spend time with his now elderly mother and visit the Flackters. Simon rented a small apartment in Munich but spent more time in hotels than his apartment – the life of a travelling musician.

'How's your piano playing these days, Simon?' asked Keith Foes on the phone to Munich one morning in the 1980s.

'Well Keith, I don't play as often as I did when I was a *repetiteur* at Covent Garden. These days when I arrive at an opera house for rehearsals the coaching of singers has already occurred with the opera's own *repetiteurs'* and I concentrate on rehearsing with the singers and orchestra. Sometimes though, when I'm not happy with a particular singer, I would give them one-to-one extra coaching with piano accompaniment.'

'Yes Simon, I do know what a conductor does and how opera rehearsals work.'

'Well, Keith, I was only responding to your question.' Simon, not for the first time, was thinking what a plonker his agent was, and wondered why he had stuck with him for so many years.

'The reason I'm ringing is that, knowing how much you love the cello, I have a female client who's a terrific cellist and currently is the first chair of the cello section in the British Philharmonic Orchestra and is keen to further her solo career. She had a great success recently playing the Bach cello suites for solo cello at the Wigmore Hall and they've booked her for a couple of cello and piano recital programmes, but she needs a pianist partner. If the concerts go well there could be a recording contract with Decca to follow. I thought of you as it gives you a break from opera and it may lead to greater things together as a duo – concertos with you conducting and recordings.'

'Sounds interesting, Keith. So what dates are we looking at?' Keith's dates were fine for Simon as they came between two different opera engagements. 'Look, Keith… let me think about it, and please send me a list of the sonatas for which I need to look at the piano parts.

'Incidentally, Keith, – what's this lady's name?'

'Sure Simon I'll send you all the suggested programme details. Oh yes, sorry, I forgot to mention her name. The name is Helena Mentones, who is originally from New York.'

Chapter 23

'How slowly shall we play the adagio movement of the Beethoven?' Helena looked up from her cello and smiled at Simon.

'Well, Helena, let's look at the composers marking for the movement – bearing in mind that of all Beethoven's five cello sonatas, this final one – No.5 in D major Op.102 No. 2 – is the only one of the five with a proper slow movement. The marking is *adagio con molto sentimento d'affection,* meaning; very slow indeed and to be played with much affection, so let's give it what Beethoven intended.'

'Yes, Professor Negrini,' said Helena in a jocular voice, and with a big grin on her face,' adding... 'You've certainly been doing your homework on the cello sonata repertory...maestro.

The Beethoven was the second piece of the programme Helena had devised and sent to Simon, via Keith Foes, for his agreement. Simon had been more than delighted with her choice of piece – the opening Beethoven sonata was to be followed by Brahms cello sonata No. 2 and the programme would be completed after an interval, with the great Romantic cello sonata by Rachmaninov. This was a beautifully designed programme which was a journey from the late classical period (Beethoven) to late ripe Romantic Rachmaninov, via the Romantic period's high point of Brahms. When Simon first saw Helena's choice of works – he immediately realised that this cellist was someone with an understanding of musical history.

Once Simon had agreed to a cello/piano partnership with Helena Mentones, signed the contract with Keith Foes, and agreed to Helena's suggested programme, he made arrangements to fly to London and to meet with Helena. When Simon agreed to take the engagement his focus was primarily on the three cello sonatas that had been proposed and he hadn't really given Helena herself as a personality much thought. Keith Foes had described her as a charming and friendly young lady, as well as being a fantastic cellist. Once in London with the arrangement to meet and be introduced to each other at Keith Foes' offices, Simon began to wonder about Helena. After all, in a duo programme, the chemistry between the two artists was all important and Simon was hoping that the two of them could form a personal friendship as well as an artistic one.

Helena was already sitting in Foes' office, having arrived early when Simon arrived. Helena stood to greet Simon and he gave her a peck on both cheeks – then shook hands with Keith Foes.

'Well, the two of you meet at last' said Foes as he looked at the pair with an initial impression of an uncanny likeness between them. Coffees were brought in by Foes' secretary and the three of them engaged in small talk for a while before Foes asked them both if they were happy with the programme.

Simon and Helena smiled at each other as both answered almost in unison 'Yes absolutely happy.' They both gave a nervous laugh to the way that they had answered at the same time.

'Look – why don't you go off and get to know one another. There are some good places for lunch around here. I would especially recommend Andrew Edmunds in Lexington Street. In fact, Andrew is a friend of mine; he's an art dealer as well as a restaurateur. I'll tell you what, my secretary Joan will book a table for you, and I'm sure Andrew will give you a table in a quiet corner so you can chat away without disturbances.'

Helena and Simon looked at each other and nodded in agreement.

'Sounds like a lovely idea,' said Simon… 'Thank you, Keith.'

'You're welcome, but don't forget that you should start rehearsing tomorrow – as the concert is only ten days away!'

As they said goodbye to Keith, thanking him for the coffees, Simon thought that for once Foes hadn't made a facetious comment or annoyed him in any way.

Lexington Street was situated in a quiet, slightly off-the-beaten track part of London's famous and once notorious area of Soho.

The restaurant that Keith Foes recommended was named after the name of the owner Andrew Edmunds and the building was an eighteenth century town house. The restaurant itself was a small dark and cramped room with a few cubby-hole areas tucked around several corners. The place seemed to have a sort of raffish atmosphere.

As they announced their arrival, they were shown to one of the cubby-hole tables set with a wine bottle as a candle stick holder, which meant they had nobody else sitting close to them.

'Hello... I'm Andrew Edmunds,' announced this gentleman who came over to their table and shook hands with them both. Mr Edmunds was a pleasant looking forty something gentleman, casually dressed with a slightly receding hairline and of medium height with a mischievous glint in his eyes.

'Thanks for choosing my restaurant for your lunch and as you have been recommended by my good friend Keith Foes – please accept with my compliments a nice bottle of Beaujolais to enjoy with lunch.' He put the wine on the table and opened the bottle.

'That's very generous of you, Mr Edmunds,' said Simon.

'Please call me Andrew and I'll leave you to it. Someone will be with you shortly with the menus and I hope you enjoy your lunch.' Edmunds sauntered off to chat with people at another table around the corner.

The menus' duly arrived and Simon poured the wine as they toasted each other. 'Well, unless you're one of those strange people who drink red wine with fish, Mr Edmunds has helped us with the choice of food. We're to ignore the fish options and go for the meat dishes.'

Helena laughed and nodded in agreement. The menu, which changed every day, was hand written on cardboard in a sort of a scrawl which, in the dark room, was hard to read. Simon put his spectacles on and read the menu out to Helena. They both chose buttered asparagus for starters – Helena ordering the breast of pigeon salad and Simon going for the pot roast rabbit. Once the food ordering was out of the way with the starters arriving fairly quickly, the two of them started, tentatively at first, to sound out each other.

Helena told Simon about her musical background, how the breakthrough came from winning first prize at the Munich ARDS competition in 1984 and her moving to London to take up a cello chair with the British Philharmonic Orchestra. Simon gave a potted version of his surprising rise to conducting opera and concerts – given that his early employment had been in the clothing business and that his dreadfully unsympathetic boss had done him a favour by sacking him, which had opened the door for him to pursue a musical career.

'Tell me, Helena... how did you meet Keith Foes?' Simon asked.

'I was in London during 1983 for an orchestral audition which was unsuccessful, but whilst there, I signed up for a master-class with the great cellist, Paul Tortelier, and Keith Foes happened to be there scouting for new talent.'

'That sounds like Keith.' Simon chuckled.

'He heard me play the Elgar cello concerto for Tortelier and was impressed, and to be fair to Keith, he did suggest that I enter the ARD's competition which was great advice at the time. Anyway, due to a cellist's indisposition, Keith got me an engagement with the Boca string quartet, playing the second cello part of the Schubert string quintet. So unexpectedly I made an unscheduled Wigmore Hall debut.'

'That's great,' Simon commented.

They both ordered chocolate tart with prunes and ice cream for dessert as well pushing the boat out with another bottle of the delicious Beaujolais, justifying it by returning the compliment to Mr Edmunds by buying the same complimentary bottle of wine.

'I've spent too much time talking about myself. It's your turn now, Helena. Please tell me about your family background.'

'No…Simon, I loved your story. You have had such an interesting and diverse life. You should be proud of your achievements.'

'You're so kind, Helena, and I'm all ears.'

'Remember, Simon, I'm a lot younger than you so my experiences are more limited compared to yours. On the other hand, my background is far from straightforward. My mother died giving birth to me in London during the year of 1960 and my father is unknown. I was so lucky to have been adopted by a marvellous couple from New York who've been wonderful loving parents to me. I am so grateful to them but when I became an adult, they, with the best intentions, stifled my development somewhat and were reluctant to give me my independence – so I'm so pleased to have had the opportunity to work here as a musician in London, the city of my birth, which I really love. Like you, I'm single and wary of men having been badly hurt by someone I met in Dublin.'

'Have you tried to trace your birth parents, Helena?'

Simon was beginning to feel uneasy listening to Helena's personal story.

'Father, no, but would love to know about my mother; the problem being that my guess is that she had a complicated family situation – coming from somewhere well away from London and trying to build her own life away from home. Again it's just a hunch, but I think my mother was very young when she died. The main problem was that the name she was known by at the hospital was untraceable, so it's a cold trail when one tries to investigate.

'Do you know the name your mother went by?' 'Well, the only evidence I have is a crumpled note the hospital found with my mother's belongings, signed by what looked like the name of Margo – which they gave to my adopted parents.

'Are you OK Simon? You've suddenly gone white and you look as if your brain is whirling around.'

Simon's brain was indeed whirling around when Helena mentioned the name Margo. It couldn't be; it just couldn't be?

After all, Margo was not such a rare name. So... no – no – it would be too much of a coincidence – but he could see some facial features in Helena that resembled him.

'No, sorry, Helena, I'm fine, but just feeling that your story is so very moving. Tell me, this crumpled note that you inherited – what else did it say other than "Margo"?'

'It was difficult to read as the writing was very faint, but the word "bracelet" was written with some numbers beside it. That was all the text on the note – very little to go on – but I've kept the note as a memento and always have it with me.'

'Do you have it on you now?'

'Not actually here but I do have it in my London flat.'

Helena was rather startled that Simon was taking such a keen interest in her parentage, as after all, the two of them were only getting together for a professional musical engagement – but she was appreciating his kind curiosity.

Changing tack slightly, Simon asked 'How did your parents from New York know about adopting a baby in London?'

'What my parents told me was that it was near impossible to adopt in New York, so they asked a friend of theirs, who had been living in London during the 1940s and 50s to inquire about adopting a British baby. This friend, who has remained to this day a close family friend, arranged everything for them, and all they had to do was to travel to London – go through an interview process with the hospital authorities – fill in some paperwork, and that was that.'

Maybe twenty years earlier, Simon would have lost control of his feelings at that stage and upset Helena's emotional equilibrium, by sharing his suspicion that this moment was possibly the most amazing coincidence one could dream of – Helena finding her birth father and Simon meeting a daughter he never thought he had or if he did never imagined to find. But Simon, at age fifty-three, with his experience of dealing with various orchestras and their diverse personnel, had the maturity to curtail his excitement and seal his lips just as he was on the verge of asking her whether she could check the numbers on the note she kept in her possession. What reason would he give on asking her for the numbers? She would know that something was afoot and that would seriously unsettle her.

After all the chatting and personal disclosures, both Helena and Simon became thoughtful and the flow of conversation dried up, as they felt that enough had been said and that they should pay the bill and leave the restaurant – being the last lunch customers still there.

Simon decided to do nothing more until after the concert – so they could concentrate totally on rehearsing. They spent quite a lot of time together over the ten days of rehearsal – enjoying a few more meals together and discovering much common ground between them on their views about many subjects, as well as musical tastes and interpretive ideas, and consequently, a real friendship developed between them, but the serious chat about their personal history they'd engaged in during the lunch at Andrew Edmunds, was not repeated.

The concert was a great success in a full Wigmore Hall. The musical partnership between Helena on the cello and Simon as pianist was a natural collaboration, as if they had been playing sonatas together for years. The emotional intensity of the Rachmaninov and the passion they put into their respective playing had some of the audience in tears. The enthusiastic applause demanded an encore and Helena obliged by playing a *sarabande* from one of Bach's cello suites as an emotional cooler after the heated Rachmaninov. And then Helena bought Simon back again and together they played Dvorak Gypsy Melodies for cello and piano, which brought the house down.

In the artists room Simon and Helena embraced and said how much they enjoyed playing together. Keith Foes was there and congratulated them both – promising more engagements for them as a duo and talking again about recordings with Decca. Some members of the audience made their way to the Artists Room – thanking them for a beautiful concert, and amongst the throng of people, a familiar face appeared all smiles with his arms out to hug Simon – who introduced him to Helena.

The totally unexpected arrival was Dov Katz.

Chapter 24

'What a wonderful surprise to see you here Dov – it's the cherry on top at the end of, what I hope was, a successful concert and what a delight it was to make music with Helena.'

Dov, with a big smile on his face, gave Simon another hug, telling him how much he had missed his friend and musical mentor and how he had regretted their fallout which led to non-communication between them for a long six years. Helena, standing aside whilst the two men became absorbed with each other, was curious about what had gone on between the two men that had resulted in such a long estrangement.

'So Dov – what brought you to the Wigmore Hall this evening?' Simon said.

'It had nothing to do with you, Simon.' Dov pronounced with a wicked grin on his face. 'I had heard about the wonderful cellist Helena Mentones and as I was in London with a free evening I thought to pop along to the Wigmore Hall. To be honest, I hadn't even noticed who the pianist was!'

This remark Dov uttered with a completely straight face but winked at Simon whilst saying it.

Simon laughed but was familiar with Dov's dry humour from old times. 'Well, I hope the pianist didn't disappoint.'

'To be honest, Simon, keep with the day job of conducting!'

The banter between the two old friends continued for a while when Simon announced, 'Helena and I are off to dinner at the Ivy restaurant – please join us, Dov – I'm sure the *maitre-d'*, who I know well, will oblige me with an extra guest on our table.'

He took Helena's arm and nodded to Dov, 'C'mon folks – let's go and enjoy a celebration dinner together!'

The Ivy restaurant in West Street, located between Leicester Square and Covent Garden, was packed with theatre and opera types, for which it was famous, and the atmosphere around the table was high octane. They received a warm welcome from the maitre d' who showed them to a table for three instead of two to accommodate Mr Negrini's extra guest. Champagne was ordered and glasses clicked as they celebrated the successful concert and the reunion of Simon and Dov. Looking around the restaurant, they recognised many familiar faces from the opera and the musical world in general, which resulted in nods – arm waves and air toasting of champagne glasses. The three of them all ordered the same food: crab cocktail followed by Tournedos Rossini steaks and a large bowl of green salad between them. Polishing off the champagne, they went on to drink a Pomerol red wine to accompany the steaks.

'So what are you doing in London, Dov, and how long will you be here for?' Simon was addressing his old friend.

'I've got an audition at Covent Garden where I've yet to make my debut.'

'That's great, Dov – it's about time the Garden heard the great Katz strutting his stuff.' So what's the opera you're auditioning for?'

'Well – they're reviving *Simon Boccanegra* again and my agent had suggested me for the villain Paulo – which I did at Glyndehurst a few years ago.'

'Oh...' interjected Simon – 'not the great title role, Dov? I would have thought you would be just right for singing Simon Boccanegra himself at this stage of your career?'

'I would love to sing the title role, Simon, but the opera house's reserve the part for big-name stars only – but maybe one day?

I'm staying in London for a few more days to catch up with some old friends.'

Turning to Helena, Dov asked with a winning smile. 'So tell me about the wonderful cellist, Miss Mentones – how did you and our beloved maestro here get together professionally?'

'Well, our joint agent Keith Floes introduced us and suggested we could make a successful musical partnership.'

'To be honest Helena, I thought the two of you blended together beautifully as if there was a magic connection between you,' Dov added, guffawing heartily. 'But seriously, Helena, the uncanny thing is that you and Simon look a bit alike.'

Helena laughed at Dov's remark but Simon felt queasy, knowing that he had to continue with his investigations into the possibility that he and Helena were father and daughter, and now with Dov in London all the three actors involved were in a position for the truth to out – or was it all a figment of his imagination and the bracelet with hallmark numbers sheer coincidence?

We would soon find out!

At the conclusion of the evening after much drink, laughter and general bonhomie, Simon took Dov aside and asked him if the two of them could meet for a chat – preferably the following day.

Although they had consumed much alcohol, Dov saw a tense, worried expression on his friend's face. 'Is everything OK Simon?'

'Yes...yes, Dov, but we need to talk.'

'Sure, Simon – let's meet tomorrow.'

There were big hugs between the three of them before they went their separate ways in taxis' that lined up outside the Ivy restaurant; Helena home to her flat and the men to their respective hotels.

Simon and Dov met up the following morning for coffee in Soho. In a quiet corner of the coffee bar, they reminisce about the concert, the fabulous post-performance dinner and above all, about Helena, who Dov was hugely impressed by both musically and personally.

'Dov... that's what I need to talk to you about. I'll come straight to the point – it's just possible that I'm Helena's father!

Dov nearly fell off his chair as he knocked his coffee cup – spilling the remainder of his coffee on the floor.

'Why? How? What's happened? Please tell me everything Simon.'

Simon explained as best as he could the sequence of the conversation he and Helena had had over a recent lunch. Helena had spoken at length about her tragic early life and had said that she knew nothing at all about her father and only very rudimentary aspects of her mother. She had been adopted by a well-off very decent couple from New York. But the key thing was that Helena mentioned an antique bracelet as a family heirloom that she had never seen, but amazingly, she actually had the hallmark number, and even more amazing, was, that she kept the note with the number written on with her, as that's the only souvenir originating from her birth family and she'd said she kept the note in her London flat.

'Before you ask me, Dov, no, I didn't ask her if she knew the number by heart or if she could let me see the note – as I could see that she was becoming anxious about my physical reaction to her story. I made an immediate decision there and then, to drop the issue entirely until after the concert – and then to contact you to pursue it further. But of course I didn't have to get in touch; you just showed up at the Wigmore Hall, which seems to be telling me something. And the other thing is that, although I've only known Helena for a couple of weeks, I feel that we've known each other for years. OK... I do understand that a successful partnership between two musicians can become personally close in a very short time. Simon put his arm around Dov, saying with feeling. 'What if it's true? Wouldn't it be the most wonderful thing? On the other hand, I would have a lot of explaining to do about my behaviour with her mother and she might not want to have anything to do with me.'

'Don't be silly Simon. If indeed this all stacks up – Helena wouldn't exist without your so-called young man's poor judgement all those years ago.'

Simon... you talked about various coincidences – and I have a further one for you. The bracelet is here in London.'

Simon looked at Dov with incredulity.

'Let me explain, Simon, I had noticed a small chip on the bracelet and as I was visiting London, I took the decision to take it with me and find a good London antique jeweller for it to be fixed – taking the view that London would be the best place for antique jewellery repairs. So the bracelet is being fixed right now but I memorised the hallmark number – which is: KLS852269305.'

'Dov...this is all leading us in one direction. We have to sit down with Helena and tell her what we suspect, but the proof of the pudding is, do the hallmark numbers match?

'What do you mean "we" Simon? You have to do this yourself – you're the potential father – not me!'

'I understand what you're saying, Dov, but other than the original physical act – you're more part of the story than I am, as well as the fact you have the bracelet, when of course the repairs are done.'

'OK... Simon – I know what you're saying, so if I suggest the following. Firstly, without going into detail, you must speak to Helena to arrange a meeting, but this is the tricky bit –you'll have to ask Helena to bring her mother's note with her, or if not, she should memorise the hallmark numbers. If you wish, I could be there – but will only come into the room if the numbers match and you've had a few moments to acquaint yourselves with each other as father and daughter. I can then add my part of the story – especially everything I knew about her mother, my dear friend Margo/Marie and how I managed to have possession of the bracelet. So hold off until I get the bracelet back and then Simon – it'll be up to you to set things in motion.'

A few days later, Dov telephoned Simon to say that the bracelet had been perfectly repaired and he should make his move. The nerves then hit Simon and he hesitated to contact Helena, knowing that the meeting could change both their lives forever. A timely call from Keith Foes, with the good news, that the Decca Record Company were interested in making a cello and piano recording with Helena and Simon. They particularly wished to record Cesar Franck's famous violin sonata, transcribed for cello and piano.

Foes continued to tell Simon that he had contacted Helena and that she would be looking at the score of the Franck, liaising with Simon about performing the work and discussing with him what other sonata they should perform as the filler to the disc. Simon was only half - listening as Foes was rattling on about how he was going to promote the new musical partnership of Helena Mentones and Simon Negrini – following some excellent reviews for their Wigmore Hall concert. He continued by saying that he also wanted to book Helena to perform concertos' with Simon conducting the Halle – an orchestra Simon had previous history with.

'Yes...yes, Keith – I really appreciate all your efforts and I will talk to Helena and get back to you.'

Following the conversation with Foes, Simon thought that at least he had good reason to contact Helena and that she would probably be expecting his call. When Simon rang Helena, she was hugely excited about the proposed record deal and spoke at length about the Franck piece which she hadn't realised there was a cello version of the great violin sonata which had actually been approved of by the composer.

'We must get together soon Simon.'

'Yes, we must, Helena but as well as the music there is something else I need to talk to you about; a more personal subject.'

'Oh... Simon – what on earth would that be about?'

'Don't worry, Helena, it's all good news. 'Simon could hear a touch of anxiety in Helena's voice.

'Give me a clue?'

'Well, Helena – you remember the chat we had during lunch at the Andrew Edmunds restaurant some weeks ago, and you mentioned a keepsake note from your birth mother that you had always kept close to you? I would like to see the note if that's OK with you?

'Why, Simon? I don't understand?

'I won't say any more on the phone but I may have some information about your birth father.'

'What do you mean, Simon? What could you know about that?

'Maybe nothing at all or maybe everything – that's why I need to see your mother's note.'

'Simon – I have the note in my safe at the flat. When can you come over?'

'Whenever is good for you, Helena.'

'I'm free later today after orchestral rehearsals – could you come over to my flat at 4 pm?'

'Yes Helena... That's fine – I'll see you later, and please don't fret – all will be good.' Simon uttered those words without much conviction in his voice.

Simon grabbed a taxi from his Covent Garden hotel to Maida Vale, West London, where Helena was living and arrived just after 4 pm. Helena opened the door and they hugged each other tightly as Simon could see the worry on Helena's face.

'Come in, Simon, and I'll get some tea.'

With tea and cake served and whilst indulging in general chit chat - Helena said. 'What's all this about then?'

'Do you have the note, Helena?' Helena had the note under a book on the table and handed it to Simon.

Simon's eyes went straight to the number written on the note, which he'd memorised, and there it was – the identical number staring him in the face: – KLS852269305. Helena was looking at him intently as he uttered the words he'd never have thought he would ever say.

'Helena – give me your hand.'

Helena held out her hand, which was shaking as Simon gripped it firmly. 'Helena – I know this is absolutely unbelievable but I think I'm your natural birth father!'

Helena removed her hand from Simon's and jumped up from her chair and screamed, 'Is this some kind of joke? Am I missing something that goes on in the higher echelons of the classical music world? Now that I'm establishing myself as a soloist I have to go through a cruel initiation ceremony?'

'No...No – of course not. Please sit down and I'll tell you what I know – which to be honest isn't much – but the man you met after our concert and who was with us for dinner at the Ivy, Dov Katz, has much more information about it all.'

'So what are you now telling me, Simon, that Dov Katz is also my father?'

'...Not at all. If the information we have is correct I'm your father, but Dov had once known your birth mother and he also has the bracelet that belongs to you.'

At the mention of the bracelet – Simon noticed a change of demeanour in Helena. She was now listening seriously to Simon and moving away from the cynicism of her initial reaction – thinking that the whole thing was just an escapade to test her toughness to survive in the music business.

'No…Helena…we would never be as cruel as to play a practical joke on you – especially on such a sensitive matter. I'll tell you everything I know, but I want Dov to relate his story and give you the bracelet. Can I call him and ask him to join us?'

'OK… Simon… Dov can join us – if you can get hold of him.'

Simon used his new mobile phone which he'd recently purchased and was just getting accustomed to using. He spoke to Dov – gave him the address and told him to bring the bracelet.

Meanwhile, Simon tentatively spoke quietly and slowly to Helena – telling her the story of his time in St Mawes, Cornwall, during the summer of 1959. How he'd met, and then lost touch with, the young girl calling herself Margo, aged sixteen, but who'd said she was eighteen, at the hotel he had been staying at. Margo was doing a summer holiday job there as a waitress. Without going into too much detail, he explained that the two of them had only known each other briefly, but they did consummate their fleeting relationship.

The next morning Margo Pento had vanished from the hotel – the reception informed him that she had been called home to Penzance on an urgent family matter. They were very cagey with him – unwilling to divulge any more information about her and certainly would not give an address, or any other contact information. He said that he did travel to Penzance and made some enquiries, but came up with a blank – nobody in Penzance knew anything about a family called Pento.

There was one thing though. Margo had left a gold bracelet behind at the time they were together. He took it to reception and they said that they would make sure that the bracelet would be returned to Margo.

A few years later, he went to Israel as a conducting student, living and working on a Kibbutz. It was only years after he had returned to London, that he met his old school friend, Dov Katz, who was working as an opera singer in Germany. The link between, Dov, Simon and Margo – whose real name was Marie Ritage, slowly and shockingly unravelled – which led to a serious fall out between the two men.

If this had been a plot of a novel one would think it too farfetched, but this was real life, and the strange coincidences that linked them were completely off the scale in terms of believable credibility.

Dov arrived at Helena's flat – immediately noticing the awkwardness in the atmosphere between Simon and Helena. Politely refusing refreshments – he took out a small packet from his pocket and carefully laid it down on the table. Helena stared at the beautiful gold bracelet in amazement. Neither Dov nor Simon said a word as Helena picked it up and put it on her wrist – which fitted perfectly. Slowly taking the bracelet off, she looked for the hallmark number which was faintly engraved by the side of the clasp which read: KLS152269305. Helena, without checking her mother's note, knew immediately that the numbers matched, but she checked it nevertheless just to be sure.

Dov related his story – explaining how he had befriended Margo at the Covent Garden music college they had both attended, but was never a boyfriend, as he had been, and still was, a homosexual. Margo was a beautiful girl and a lovely thoughtful person, but very secretive about her past and her family. Margo had a friend called Holly Fines and the girls shared a flat in Kentish Town. Holly was very different from Margo – an opportunist who was not fully to be trusted. Dov then spoke about the night Margo invited him to dinner at the flat – Holly was there with a new boyfriend – an older married man, whose name was Freddy Wakeson. Freddy and Holly had behaved badly throughout the evening, and when the two of them disappeared into Holly's bedroom – Dov helped Margo with the washing up. Margo secretly confided in Dov that she was pregnant, and although she knew who the man was – the fact was that they knew absolutely nothing about each other and she had no wish to even attempt to trace him.

Helena was looking sharply at Simon at this point of the story – Dov noticing her expression and quickly added that Margo held no animosity towards the man concerned – admitting that actually she had made all the running towards the hook-up and that her impression was that he was a kind and thoughtful man.

Helena was finding it difficult to absorb all Dov's information. Dov thought that he had said enough for now and that all the follow-up information that slowly emerged which linked Helena and Simon together, should be saved for later or for another day. He finished the first part of the saga by explaining to Helena how he had come by the bracelet – Margo asking him to keep it safe for her whilst she was in hospital giving birth.

A distressed Helena put her arms up in the air and shouted, 'Stop! ... I can't take any more of this and I don't care if I'm your daughter, Simon, or if the whole thing is one big hoax; you've both freaked me out today and I want you to leave me right now.'

The two men got up to go, muttering apologies for upsetting Helena, and as they were heading to the front door, Helena looked at them both.

'You may be my father, Simon, but as you said earlier – Dov has more information about my mother that you have, so I would like to talk again to Dov another day, so please telephone me, Dov – but the way I feel at the moment I don't want to see or hear from you Simon, until I've filtered the sudden shock of it all which has completely disturbed my mental equilibrium.'

Simon and Dov left the flat and they went their separate ways without mulling over what had just happened, as they were both emotionally drained. Except, that as they parted – Dov put his arm around Simon attempting to reassure his friend. 'It'll all be fine in the end.'

Later in the evening, Simon was going over in his mind the events of the day – his thoughts being that it wasn't meant to be like that. He had expectations of it being a huge emotional experience for both of them – kissing and hugging each other – celebrating finding each other instead of being sent packing like a naughty schoolboy.

Helena spent ages that evening examining the bracelet and thinking that if it was all true, this beautiful gold antique bracelet belonging to her mother had come down through generations, and by touching it, she had this vision of touching not only her mother but also her grandmother and possibly her great grandmother.

But her feelings towards Simon were very mixed. He had been a thoughtless young man, but his thoughtlessness had led to her existence. He should have tried harder to find the young girl, and if he had found her, he could have been with her during her pregnancy and perhaps she would have survived childbirth.

On the other hand – Dov had tried to exonerate Simon from blame, saying that it was Margo/Marie who had led the affair and it wasn't his fault that she had given him a false name. Dov seemed to have behaved exemplary throughout and she needed to know more from him about his friendship with Margo/Marie. How he'd subsequently found out about her family and the link to Simon?

Helena had never been overly curious about her birth parents as her background was totally secure. She couldn't have had better adopted parents than the Mentone'-s. And of course, her uncle Carl – had been a sort of grandfather to her. But now the can-of-worms had opened up – she felt it her duty to find out as much as she possibly could.

She had liked Simon very much from the moment they met and they had immediately developed not only a musical partnership but a real friendship. But this father thing had changed everything between them and she felt something more akin to hate than love for him. She certainly couldn't think of him as her father as she already had a father who she was very happy to have. And how would the Mentones' feel about all this development? Perhaps she wouldn't tell them, at least until Simon and she had a DNA test to verify the paternity. One immediate decision was that she didn't wish to carry on making music with him – although that would probably dash her recording debut.

She met Dov again a few days later in a local coffee bar, filling her in with everything he knew about his Margo/Marie, from sharing a flat together to escorting her to the hospital for check-ups. He told Helena about the sudden death of his brother, and how he'd had to go back to his family in Israel – leaving Margo at the worst possible time, as the baby's birth was imminent. He further explained to Helena about the phone call to the hospital from Israel – how the junior nurse had given him incorrect information that neither mother nor baby had survived the birth.

It was only years' later, meeting Holly Fines by chance at the opera in Germany, that he'd discovered that Margo's baby had survived and that Margo's real name was Marie Ridge. Holly had discovered the truth from the Ridges' neighbours, who had been briefed by a local nurse that had worked in the London maternity hospital and assured them that the baby had survived.

The only clue they had was the bracelet they had kept and cherished over the years. And then he'd checked numbers with Simon who'd had the foresight at the time to write the numbers down and keep them. He also mentioned to Helena that he had bumped into that Freddy character several times over the years who, to be fair to him, felt bad about his boorish behaviour that night in Kentish Town, when he had been smitten with Holly. But Holly had tried to cheat Margo/Marie out of her lease of the flat, because, as she was three years Margo's senior, Holly had signed the lease on Margo's behalf but then tried to take advantage of the situation. Freddy was so disgusted with Holly's behaviour that he ditched her. But again, to be fair to Holly, she redeemed herself by finding out the truth of Helena's existence and had given him that vital piece of information.

Helena was trying to digest the sequence of events that had led to where they were now and still found it all absolutely incredible. But one thing she was sure of was that Dov Katz was genuinely a lovely man – with a kind heart and totally loyal to his friends. Her mother had been blessed by having such a caring friend.

The next day Helena telephoned Keith Foes – informing him that she would be thrilled to record the cello version of Cesar Franck's violin sonata for Decca, but no way would she record it with Simon Negrini, and that he should forget about concerto recordings with Negrini and the Halle Orchestra. Foes, ever the commercial agent, assured Helena that the record company was interested mainly in her. He would find her another pianist accompanist.

'After all'... he added, 'Negrini is known mainly as a conductor who had lots of ongoing opera projects on the go – so he won't be too upset about missing out on the cello/piano recording.'

When Helena was off the phone, Foes wondered what had happened between Helena and Simon as they had seemed such a natural musical partnership.

Foes arranged for Helen to meet with the established Russian pianist Nicholas Luganeski. Together, they rehearsed the Franck sonata in A major many times, as if their lives depended on it. They decided to couple the disc with Chopin's cello sonata. Not having previously heard a performance of the Franck, not even in its original violin form, Helena did some research on the composer of the genesis of the piece. Amongst many texts on the sonata, she was particularly taken with a concert programme note, written by someone called David Mintz. It was Mintz's description of the final fourth movement that stood out and motivated her to get behind the notes and to express to the audience via her playing the romantic essence of the music.

The sun comes out at the start of the finale. Listening to this movement is what converts a casual concert-goer into a life-long music lover. It's a superb finale, culminating in a magnificent apotheosis. However, the movement passes through various phases – quiet music in different remote keys interrupting the journey and trying to halt the inevitable reach of the summit. But the triumphant conclusion wins out as indeed it must in Franck's glorious creation.

The Decca recording was a huge success – Helena's name spreading throughout the classical musical world – with people starting to talk about her as a worthy successor to the great and much-loved Jacqueline du Pre´ – who had sadly died the year before at the young age of forty-two.

Foes, conscious of not upsetting Negrini, who after all was also a client, had finally managed to get him a conducting engagement in Italy, at the opera house in Venice. The opera was *Simon Boccanegra*; not the usual 1881 revised version but the original 1857 Verdi score which had its world premiere in Venice.

Chapter 25

La Fenice Opera House
Venice, 1989

Simon Boccanegra – opera in a prologue and three acts. The original version – first performed in 1857.

Prologue

Paulo and Pietro are seeking a candidate from the Plebeian power group to stand for election as Doge of Genoa. They decide that the famous Corsair, Simon Boccanegra, who led various raids on the enemies of Genoa, should be their choice for the nomination. Paulo assures Simon that as Doge, his great political opponent, the patrician Fiesco, whose daughter Maria Simon had been in love with and who he'd had a child with, would no longer be able to stop the couple from marrying. Meanwhile Pietro canvases support for Boccanegra amongst the citizens.

Unknown to Simon, Maria had died and the baby had vanished with a nurse – causing Fiesco to turn from political rival to sheer hatred for the man, Boccanegra, and swearing vengeance, once he had discovered his daughter's death in his palace. Having seen Simon hovering around the palace gates – Fiesco confronts him, but not telling him about Maria's death. Boccanegra tries to befriend Fiesco but is spurned to any form of reconciliation unless Simon can let him have his granddaughter. Simon tries to explain that he had no idea where the child was. Fiesco storms off in anger. Boccanegra finds a way into Fiesco's palace and to his horror discovers Maria's body. As he staggers out of the palace – a large crowd has gathered and, seeing Boccanegra, proclaiming him as the new Doge.

Twenty-five years later, The Doge had sent many of his political opponents into exile and had their properties confiscated. Amongst these opponents is Fiesco who had been living under a pseudonym, Andrea Grimaldi, and plotting with other nobles to overthrow Boccanegra. Years earlier, an unidentified orphan had been discovered in a convent; in fact she was the lost daughter of Maria and Boccanegra. The Grimaldi family adopted her. The girl became a substitute for the Grimaldis' daughter, Amelia, who had died. This orphan took on the name of Amelia and would now be the heir to the Grimaldi family fortune, as the sons' had been exiled.

Act 1 Scene 1

A nobleman, Gabriele Adorno, has come to visit his lover, Amelia Grimaldi. Adorno's father was killed by Boccanegra and consequently his son had become involved in a political conspiracy against the Doge. The Doge pays a visit to the Grimaldi's and Amelia is petrified that the Doge has come to force her to marry Paolo, his political henchman. Before the arrival of the Doge, Fiesco arrives and Adorno asks his permission to marry Amelia. Fiesco gives Adorno his blessing but lets him know that Amelia is not actually a Grimaldi but rather an adopted orphan. Adorno is not put off by the information – he just loves Amelia whatever her background. Adorno and Fiesco leave Amelia to greet the Doge.

Scene 2

Boccanegra enters. To Amelia's pleasant surprise he announces that he was granting a pardon to her brothers. She tells the Doge that she loves Adorno and will not marry Paolo. She admits that she had been adopted and was not born a Grimaldi. She tells the Doge of what she knows about her early life as it dawns on Boccanegra that Amelia is his missing daughter. They are both overwhelmed with happiness as to have found each other.

Paolo is told in no uncertain terms to forget about marrying Amelia. Devastated and angry Paolo arranges for Amelia to be kidnapped.

Scene 3

There are festivities by the harbour; present amongst the crowd is the Doge who is confronted by Fiesco and Adorno accusing him of abducting Amelia. Amelia enters, protesting the Doge's innocence. She explains that yes, she had been abducted but does not reveal who had carried out the act. The crowd shouts out for justice.

Act 2

Adorno and Fiesco had been arrested by Paolo and Pietro. Paolo tries to persuade Fiesco to murder Boccanegra; Fiesco refuses. Paolo then suggests to Adorno that Amelia is the Doge's mistress – and with that information Adorno would be prepared to murder Boccanegra. When Amelia enters – Adorno confronts her with the accusation of being unfaithful. Amelia tries to reassure him but does not reveal that she is Boccanegra's daughter. Adorno hides as Boccanegra approaches; Amelia admits how much she loves Adorno, and in response to her pleading, Boccanegra agrees to pardon him even though he believes that Adorno was part of the conspiracy against him. Boccanegra, alone and tired – falls asleep. Adorno enters and is prepared to stab him when Amelia returns to stop him. When Boccanegra wakes, he tells Adorno that Amelia was in fact not his mistress but his daughter. Adorno, amazed at the revelation, drops to his knees and begs forgiveness from both Amelia and Boccanegra. A crowd has gathered and the rebellion has commenced. Boccanegra tells Adorno to go and join his rebellious comrades – but Adorno, in a complete about-turn, swears allegiance to the Doge.Boccanegra instructs

256

Adorno to quell the riot and if he's successful, Amelia would be his reward.

Act 3

Adorno had succeeded in stopping the fighting and had all-round distinguished himself in the service of the Doge. Meanwhile, Pietro informs Paolo that he had prepared everything as instructed as Paolo gives the order for the murder of Boccanegra by poisoning. Outside the palace, a wedding chorus can be heard. Paolo informs Fiesco that the Doge had been poisoned and that he should flee, otherwise Fiesco himself might be implicated in the murder. The noble Fiesco – although a sworn enemy of Boccanegra, would never resort to cold-blooded murder and he stands his ground and refuses to leave.

The poison is beginning to take its effect. Fiesco emerges from the shadows as Boccanegra recognises the voice of his ancient adversary. Boccanegra is full of joy that at long last the two men could be reconciled as he informs Fiesco that Amelia is his long lost granddaughter. Fiesco shows humility and remorse for his stubborn nature whilst pointing the finger at Paolo and reveals his treacherous act of poisoning Boccanegra. The happy couple of Amelia and Adorno arrive for their wedding; Boccanegra, now dying from the effects of the poison, summons the strength to tell his beloved daughter that Fiesco was not her guardian but was in fact her grandfather. The dying Boccangra names Gabrielle Adorno his successor as the new Doge.

When Keith Foes offered the Venice *Simon Boccanegra* conducting engagement to Simon Negrini, his first reaction was of ecstatic joy as he had never conducted anywhere in Italy; Venice's opera house, La Fenice, was a jewel of a theatre. He had been to the opera in Venice several times whilst visiting as a tourist, but had only dreamt of actually conducting an opera at La Fenice. But when Foes informed him that it was the earlier original 1857 version that was being produced there – his joyful initial reaction was somewhat muted. He had never heard a performance or a recording of the 1857 version and everything

257

that he'd read about the original *Simon Boccanegra* had damned the opera with faint praise. It was very rarely ever performed anywhere in the world. But, the fact that a performance was so rare meant that the production planned for Venice would attract critics, opera house bosses and opera connoisseurs from here, there and everywhere – a bit like the Wexford Opera Festival, in Ireland, that only ever produced rarely performed operas. Of course…looking at the engagement from a career trajectory point of view – it would put him in the international operatic spotlight.

When Simon eventually managed to get hold of the 1857 *Simon Boccanegra* score, he was pleasantly surprised how good the piece was. Other than the loss of the famous dramatic Council Chamber scene, which the librettist Boito had added, and Verdi's music, for it was one of his greatest big ensemble scenes in all of his operas, the two versions were almost identical with tweaks here and there that only musical experts would recognise. In one way though, the earlier version was musically more consistent than the revised version. 1857 was very much Verdi in his prime middle period, whilst the later 1881 version was a mix between middle and late period Verdi, which musically could seem disjointed in parts. But one did miss the Council Chamber scene in the first version.

There was something else that Simon had discovered whilst researching the background of the original *Simon Boccanegra*. The tenor who sang the role of Gabriele Adorno, at the very first performance, shared a surname with Simon; the tenor was Carlo Negrini.

When Simon inquired about who had been engaged to sing the title role – the management of La Fenice proudly told Simon that the world's leading exponent of the title role of *Simon Boccanegra*, Piero Capudizo, had been persuaded to learn the original version of the opera specifically for the Venice production – although the famous baritone was in his sixties. That in itself would attract many opera lovers who were fans of Capudizo. Simon had managed to convince the management to engage Dov Katz to sing the part of Paolo – a part Katz had sung all over Germany, as well as at the Glyndehurst Opera Festival in 1986.

It was great that the two old friends, Dov Katz and Simon Negrini, were reunited in Venice, especially as they had been through such trauma regarding the discovery of Simon being Helena's father. Springtime in Venice – the weather was glorious, warm but not yet hot, and the city was not yet full of tourists.

The following day, serious rehearsals would commence at the opera, but they had a free day and they walked their feet off all around the spider web of canals that made up the city; they talked and laughed as they thoroughly enjoyed exploring Venice and each other's company.

'It will eventually be good between you and Helena – but be patient, Simon, and give her time,' Dov said as he put his arms around Simon's shoulder. 'Although Helena is becoming a star musician, her background was very stable and you've unsettled her. But in time and once you've been through the DNA process, she will embrace you – accepting the reality of your newly found relationship. And besides everything else, the two of you play like angels together…'

'I hope you're right, Dov, but Helena lost all respect for me by my behaviour towards her mother and blame me for her death.'

'Look, Simon, Helena is an intelligent, thoughtful person and knows that despite everything it was you and Marie who created her – she just has to work things through in her head and then she'll be fine. Of course, she also has concerns about how her adopted parents would feel about the revelations; she is very close to them, despite her protests about them smothering her, and feels hugely grateful for everything they've done. Come on, Simon, let's stop for a drink – my legs are beginning to ache.'

They found a nice little bar – drank several Campari's and sodas and talked about the differences between the two versions of *Simon Boccanegra.*

The rehearsals went splendidly – with the great baritone, Capudizo, in terrific form – being very collegiate with all his colleagues who were a bit star truck by him, especially Dov Katz, who studied every gesture of Capudizo – the way he husbanded his voice during rehearsals, saving his big baritone sound for the actual performances. Dov was hoping some opera company would offer him the title role instead of the smaller role of Paolo, and he didn't mind which version it was – either he would grab at, given the opportunity.

The first night went splendidly, with the who's who in the opera world, as well leading Italian politicians in the audience. His agent, Keith Foes, the artistic director of Glyndehurst Stephen Zandors, the critic Lizette Wakeson, daughter of Freddy Wakeson, were all there for the performance, which received very enthusiastic applause – with Capudizo awarded a standing ovation.

Back in his dressing room, Simon received Zandors, who was hugely complimentary, and it was a reunion between the two men since Glyndehurst in 1986, and previously in Connemara, during their respective visits to that beauty spot during 1985. Simon remembered their conversation at the Donnells' hotel – talking about the opera house they were planning to build there. Stephen proudly told Simon that the building was under way and the plan was to start the first festival in September 1993.

As Stephen left the dressing room, an elderly, smartly dressed gentleman with a walking stick and a thick folder under his arm, knocked on Simon's door – entering and introducing himself as Ricardo Negrini.

'Please take a seat, *Signor* Negrini.'

Thank you... and many congratulations on your fine conducting of Verdi's wonderful score.'

The gentleman had a thick Italian accent but his English was most credible. 'Maestro Negrini, did you know that you are a direct descendant of the great tenor Carlo Negrini, who had premiered the role of Gabriele Adorno in *Simon Boccanegra* right here at La Fenice in 1857?'

Simon looked at this dapper gentleman in astonishment.

'Please let me explain, maestro – firstly, who I am. Carlo Negrini, who came from a Jewish family, had a younger brother, Vincenzo, who also changed his name from Villa to Negrini, in honour of his older brother whom he had worshipped – I'm Vincenzo's great grandson. Carlo Negrini and his wife Clelia had one son, Claudio. Claudio had no interest in opera or music in general – becoming a successful diplomat. Claudio abandoned his father's stage name of Negrini and became known as Claudio Villa, which of course was his genuine legitimate Jewish family heritage name.'

The gentleman continued … 'Claudio Villa never spoke about his father's fame as an opera singer – in fact, he became a bit snobbish about the opera business and thought it rather a shabby career compared to the diplomatic service. So because of Claudio's change of name and his dismissive attitude to opera, the consensus took hold over time that Carlo and Clelia had been childless. You must remember, my dear maestro – that Claudio was only ten years old when his father died and communications in the nineteenth century were not what we're used to today – and sometimes incorrect information about one-time star singers became general currency to a later generation. Anyway, Claudio also had a son, Roberto, who unlike his father reverted back to the name of Negrini in honour of his famous grandfather, whom he had a fascination for, and Roberto became an opera enthusiast, perhaps partly as a rebellion against his father with his haughty anti -opera attitude. Unfortunately, things became tough for Roberto in Italy and he emigrated to London, and when he had a son, he gave him the English name of Arnold, and that, my dear cousin, was your late father.

'I've spoken enough and I'm sorry to have taken up so much of your time as you must be tired after your energetic conducting.'

'Ricardo, if I may call you that, you have not taken up my time at all, but I'm lost for words at my family revelations. I've experienced other personal revelations lately and my head is spinning with all you have just told me.

'Can I take you out for dinner'?

'Thank you my dear Simon, but I'm a very old man and it's already past my bedtime. But another time whilst you're still here in Venice I would be delighted to enjoy a lunch or dinner with you– perhaps, if I may suggest, a day that the opera is not scheduled so that we can spend a relaxed time together.'

'Yes... of course, Ricardo, I would love that and to think that I conducted tonight the same opera here at the same theatre, that my great, great grandfather Carlo Negrini sang at the premier performance of the tenor role of Gabriele Adorno in 1857.'

Ricardo Negrini stood up to leave and the two men embraced. He gave Simon his card and then handed the folder he had been carrying to Simon, saying, 'This document will be of great interest to you.'

Ricardo left the room leaving Simon with so many varying emotions swirling around in his mind—.

Simon Negrini's Italian was reasonably proficient due to him being engrossed in the world of Italian opera, but he found the old document Ricardo Negrini had left with him, difficult to read. He could see that the document was signed by Arrigo Boito, Verdi's famous librettist, who had written the revised text for the opera, *Simon Boccanegra,* and who had then gone on to write the libretto for Verdi's *Otello* and *Falstaff.* Simon reasoned not to struggle with the text but to take it with him when he met Ricardo again.

As Ricardo had suggested they arranged for lunch on a free day at the opera house. They met at Harry's Bar at Calle Vallaresso, overlooking the Grand Canal. They embraced as newly found relatives and as Ricardo was well known there by the management, they were given one of the best seats in the restaurant. The manager immediately came to the table with two Bellinis' – compliments of the house. They ate a fabulous *fegato a la Venezia* – washed down with an excellent bottle of Barolo.

At the conclusion of the meal, Simon took the Boito document out – Ricardo where he had come by this important text.

'Well Simon – it's a family heirloom as Boito gave the text to Clelia Negrini, the widow of Carlo Negrini', at the premiere of the revised version of *Simon Boccanegra,* when it was performed at La Scala Milan in 1881. Remember, that Boito was about thirty years younger than maestro Verdi and was a bit of a revolutionary in his young day, being a leading member of the *Scapigliatura* artistic movement.'

Simon asked about this *Scapigliatura* movement and Ricardo responded that the movement was similar to the French bohemian; the literal meaning *Scapigliatura* was 'dishevelled'. Anyway, Ricardo continued,

'Boito suggested to Verdi that they add a late love interest for Boccanegra with Pietro, a colleague who was with the Corsair back in his sea-faring days. Yes, a homosexual love – really shocking for its time, and that Paulo is forgiven for his treachery; makes the opera all about reconciliation and not about revenge. Verdi would have none of it and almost had another serious fall out with Boito.'

'Has anyone else seen these texts —?'

'No…when Boito gave the texts to Clelia – he made her promise not to show them to anyone. Before she died, she gave them to Carlo's brother Vincenzo, who in turn gave them to his son and so forth through the generations, until they came into my hands. I always thought I should show them to someone in the opera world – despite Clelia's original promise to Boito to keep them hidden. But that was a long time ago – nowadays an opera plot featuring two gentlemen in love with each other would not be so shocking – hey—? And ignoring the homosexual aspect, Verdi would have really appreciated that the opera's conclusion would be all about reconciliation, not only between Fiesco and Boccanegra, but also between Paolo and Boccanegra.'

'Ricardo…this is a hugely historic document, so why give it to me—?'

'Because you are a family member as well as an opera conductor – being here in Venice, conducting the original version of *Simon Boccanegra,* in which your ancestor Carlo Negrini sang the role of Gabriele Adorno. You, my dear cousin, are the obvious person to hand this libretto over to, and maybe, one day, find a composer who would set the text to music?'

The two men parted with promises to keep in touch and Simon went back to his hotel thinking about the incredible document he now had in his hands.

Chapter 26 –

Renvyle House Hotel, Connemara, Ireland, 1990

'Good morning, Stephen, how's the head this morning?'

Ken Moyle nudged Stephen with a cheeky chuckle in his voice.

'To be honest Ken – I'm suffering – as too much of the demon drink was consumed last night – staying up far too late enjoying your impresario musical act in the lounge until the early hours.'

'Ha ha,' retorted the irrepressible Ken Moyle, who'd spent the night drinking like a fish, playing and singing – switching between piano and guitar – belting out song after song in his distinct County Cork accent, and still being fresh as a daisy at breakfast time.

'The trouble with you "West Brits" is that you don't have the staying power of us Irish, and as you'll be spending more time with us in the future we're going to have to get you into training.' Ken said, laughing his head off – giving Stephen a hard pat on the back which was meant to be in camaraderie but made Stephen, the well-behaved Englishman, wince.

Ken Moyle, the current general manager and a relative of the family that owned the hotel, had brought a whole new dimension to the entertainment side of the place by adding what was known as 'Irish Craic' to the proceedings – attracting not only the family holiday crowd but a fair smattering of the Dublin louche set, as well as various Irish politicians who wished to replicate Dublin's traditional night life in the depths of Connemara.

Ken was best friends with each and every guest in the hotel and took a personal interest in everyone's story – wanting to make sure that for whatever reason one had chosen Renvyle House for a holiday, one left there with a sense that it had been a magical experience.

But for the reprobates, who kept the bar going all night, and the loungers, who took part in the music and singing, Ken Moyes was a legend and an addiction; this group of fans never missed a summer at Renvyle. Ken would start off quietly playing his guitar – singing a few Irish ballads whilst the night got going. As the drinks flowed, and one never saw Ken without a pint of Guinness in his hand, he switched to the piano – the singing becoming more animated, with requests for well-known standards and show-tunes – everybody then joining in with the choruses. Some of the regulars who knew the ropes started making requests, and that's when the banter started, with Ken daring the person making the request to solo the song themselves with him accompanying on the piano. But of course that was all an act, as the soloist had rehearsed the song beforehand and was eager to show off his or her (although it was mainly men who came forward) singing – as well as remembering all the words.

Ken contrasted the singing with reciting funny stories, poems and all sorts of nonsense stuff that the guests loved and they kept egging him on for more outrageous stuff, but Ken's humour, although absolutely hilarious, was never tasteless or sexually oriented; just good clean fun with everyone having the opportunity to be a star for the night. Ken orchestrated everything with his energy, humour, musical expertise and above all, making sure that all were having the time of their life.

The banter between the two men continued for a few more minutes when Stephen, with a more serious expression on his face, asked Ken about the advert at the reception regarding land for sale. Ken responded that the advert was for a small half-acre of land down the road at Tully Cross with views to die for.

'Give Annie McVay a call, Stephen. I believe her phone number is on the advert. It would be a great spot for you to build a house in the area.' Ken whispered in Stephen's ear, 'I believe what Annie's looking for is a steal – so don't let anyone get in there before you. Call Annie this morning. He gave Stephen a big wink as he moved off to greet another guest.

The 150-acre estate contained Renvyle House Hotel – the country house hotel in wild glorious Connemara, situated by the Atlantic Way – an expansive coastal route that takes in some of the most outstanding landscapes in the whole of Ireland. Renvyle House was once the home of the chieftain and one of the oldest and most powerful Gaelic clans in Connacht, that of Donal O'Flaherty who had a house on the site from the twelve century.

Renvyle House became a hotel in 1883 and the guest list over the years had included luminaries such as the poet and statesman, Oliver St John Gogarty (James Joyce's inspiration for the character of Buck Milligan in *Ulysses,* as well as W B Yeats, (who spent his honeymoon there), Lady Gregory, Augustus John and Winston Churchill. Now in the late twentieth century, Renvyle House was a popular family holiday resort welcoming guests from all over Ireland and from around the world.

Annie McVay's house was one of a row of a terrace of stone cottages, in the tiny village of Tully Cross, about half a mile down the road from Renvyle, accessible by climbing very steep wrought iron steps. A neat late-middle-aged lady opened the door and invited Stephen into the cottage. She introduced him to Mr McVay, who was a tall, bald and bespectacled man, late sixties on first impression. The gentleman was conservatively dressed in a three- piece suit and tie – more suitable for a morning in Dublin city than one in the wildness of Connemara.

Tea was served with Annie quizzing Stephen about his life and his interest in the area. Stephen explained about his role at the new planned opera festival an hour's drive away on Lake Corrib which was due to open in early September 1993, and how it would be great to have a holiday base there. Her husband kept quiet and remained standing whilst Annie was interrogating Stephen, and it seemed that the land was very much the concern of Mrs McVay, Mr McVay being a disinterested party, only in attendance to be supportive to his wife's endeavours. The seller of the land was not the couple but Annie McVay herself.

Leaving her husband behind, Annie and Stephen left the house to view the land which was situated just beyond the village on the opposite side of the road on the way back to Renvyle. Annie gave Stephen a small map with the outlines of the land clearly marked off in red ink. 'There you are, Mr Zandors, what do you think?'

'Mrs McVay – it's a magnificent spot.'

Stephen was trying to keep his excitement under control. Stephen's upbringing had been in a most beautiful area of Suffolk, England, but it was mostly flat and rather tame with big open skies. This was of a different order; an untamed mixture of sea and mountains as a backdrop and what a view to wake-up to in the morning if he built a house there. The pair made their way back to the house, Stephen with his thoughts and Annie, realising that Zandors was weighing up his options, left Stephen with those thoughts and did not intrude.

Once back in the house both parties adopted a more business-like pose.

'What is the sort of money you are seeking, Mrs McVay, and does the land come with planning permission?'

'Yes Mr Zandors, I have the planning permission here.'

She took out an official-looking document from the folder sitting on the coffee table. Annie explained that the only permission available at that stage was 'outline' but full planning permission would be a straightforward matter as no view would be affected by a building in that spot – so there would be no objections, provided his building plans were tasteful and would be a natural fit with the unique Connemara landscape.

'I am asking for a very reasonable price of £5,000 Irish pounds for the land, and to secure it; I need a £2,000 deposit.'

Stephen, not usually that impulsive, agreed the deal immediately and took out a chequebook from his pocket and wrote Mrs McVay a cheque for £2,000, saying that he would instruct his solicitor to arrange the balance of the fee once contracts had been drawn-up between the lawyers. Annie McVay seemed delighted with the outcome and shook hands warmly with Stephen as he stood up to leave. There was no sign of Mr McVay, who had slipped out of the house whilst they were viewing the land.

Stephen walked back to Renvyle House with great excitement and couldn't wait to tell Ken Moyle what he had done and that they would be neighbours once he had the house built. Moyle seemed most amused by the news but in typical fashion remarked. 'You better get your song repertoire increased; I don't want to hear 'If I Was a Rich Man' from *Fiddler on the Roof* every bloody time you join us for our nightly sing-song!'

Stephen had been invited to Renvyle House for a long weekend by Ken Moyle, on a complimentary basis. Ken, as well as being the entertainer was also a canny operator – he had heard about the new opera festival being planned at Lough Corrib. Ken knew all the competition in the area, including Harvey and May Donnell, who were friendly rivals; the two establishments actually offered very different concepts of a Connemara holiday. The Lough Corrib Hotel was all about tranquillity set by a huge lake – a restaurant that served world-class food and hospitality that came from another era. It was more like a retreat than a holiday hotel. Renvyle, on the other hand, was an expression of the full Connemara experience, sea, mountains, wild scenery and the full Irish Craic in the evenings.

Ken Moyle realised that Harvey and May's place would only be able to accommodate the people involved in putting on the operas, but the punters attending the opera might like something else other than a B-&-B near the venue. A nightly coach service during the festival from the opera to Renvyle would work, allowing the opera patrons to arrive at Renvyle in time for the sing-song, letting their hair down following a night at the opera. Ireland enjoyed both high and low culture without the class differentials that could be so stifling sometimes in England.

Stephen Zandors' life was changing. Having spent five years as artistic director of Glyndehurst Opera Festival in the south of England, his attention was turning to a future life in Ireland. He had loved his time there in the early 1980s working with the Dublin Grand Opera Society but had thought that his life and career had moved back permanently to his home country, as the Glyndehurst role had been a huge step-up in career terms, and he'd never thought that he would turn back to Ireland for the next stage in his career.

But the Lough Corrib project came out of the blue. Firstly, as a consultant at the time he had been still working in Dublin, and then as the guiding light of the whole enterprise. Stephen became totally absorbed in making the new opera house actually happen, and other than a few hitches along the way, the opera house on-the-lake was built on time and on budget, culminating in the decision to open the festival in early September 1993 – which was following the end of the Glyndehurst festival that closed at the end of August, and the Wexford opera, which commenced in late October.

Stephen's title would be Chief Executive and Artistic Director – chosen unanimously by the board of trustees – co-chaired by the owners of the Lake Corrib hotel and estate, Harvey and May

Donnell. Initially, Stephen thought that he could do both jobs –
staying on for another five-year term at Glyndehurst together
with running the Lough Corrib festival. But the Glyndehurst
board rejected Stephen's suggestion and said that he would
have to choose between the two opera festivals and Stephen
didn't hesitate in choosing the exciting brand new Lough Corrib
Opera Festival.

The wealthy elderly American gentleman, who had agreed to
fund the building of the opera house, was as good as his word
and the funds came through without any problems.
Unfortunately, the gentleman had died and his estate refused to
promise any more funding for the project but in honour of the
late benefactor, the new building was named after him: the
Andrew J Carbenton Opera House. So the full title of the
festival was: The Lough Corrib Festival at the Andrew J
Carbenton Opera House.

The problem was how to find funding for the opening of the
opera house, scheduled for September 1993. His board of
trustees were beginning to get edgy as, having miraculously
built an opera house by a lake in the middle of nowhere they did
not want to be left with a white elephant. The trustees, led by
his friends Harvey and May Donnell, had no connections in the
opera world nor in the arts world in general, were leaving it to
Stephen to sort out the funding to get the festival opened and
hopefully, established as an annual event.

The saviour turned out to be Carl Warringson, the gentleman
who'd financed the production of *Simon Boccanegra* at
Glyndehurst in 1986. He had agreed to fund the first season of
two mainstream operas' plus a short contemporary piece. The
one stipulation Warringson insisted on, besides having his
names splashed in bold on all the literature associated with the
festival, was that they programmed the opera *Simon
Boccanegra* in the festival, as he had become obsessed with that
particular Verdi opera. Stephen had been reluctant to agree to
that demand, as the opera wouldn't be novel enough to draw the
movers and shakers of the opera world to such a remote

location in the west of Ireland. Besides, the resources needed for *Simon Boccanegra* were too ambitious for Lough Corrib, as a huge chorus was required for the famous Council Chamber scene. On the other hand, if they programmed the earlier 1857 version of the opera, they would overcome the various obstacles. Firstly, without the big Council Chamber scene, the chorus required would be substantially reduced. Secondly, it ticked the box of kicking off the festival with a novelty; and thirdly, it would satisfy the festival's benefactor, Carl Warringson, who had insisted on *Boccanegra*.

How did Stephen manage to reel-in Warringson to agree to fund the festival? Stephen had realised that he needed a third-party interlocutor to persuade the egotistical gentleman to become involved.

Stephen had been seeing the musical journalist, Lizette Wakeson, as an on/off girlfriend for a couple of years. They had originally met at Glyndehurst in 1986, when Lizette had attended the opening night of *Simon Boccanegra*, accompanied by her father, Freddy Wakeson, who was treating his daughter to a visit to Glyndehurst as a birthday present. Recently, Freddy, having reached the age of sixty, was retiring from his long-time position as a sports journalist for *The Planet* daily newspaper. He was planning a long holiday, with his wife Susanna, in California, and Lizette suggested to Stephen that her dad would be an ideal person to befriend Carl Warringson. Like Carl, Freddy was not in any way an airy-fairy precious man of the arts. He was a hard-boiled newspaper man from the east end of London, who had developed in a tough environment both as a kid and as a sports journalist, specialising in football, boxing and equestrian events. Lizette had broached the idea to her dad, who was highly amused at the idea of selling opera funding to a grumpy old man, but Freddy was always up for a challenge. Freddy had been briefly introduced to Stephen at Glyndehurst and he'd become aware that his daughter was seeing Stephen romantically, and as he would do anything for his daughter, he agreed to contact Carl Warringson, on the opera festival's behalf, whilst in California.

It was an act of genius to involve Freddy Wakeson in befriending Carl Warringson with a view to extracting a promise to fund the Lough Corrib Opera Festival. The two men, the elderly Warringson on the cusp of his eightieth birthday and the sixty year old Wakeson, got along like a house-on-fire, as they were both from working-class backgrounds with a deeply held scepticism towards figures from the arts world. In their different ways both got involved in arts funding to please the women in their lives. Warringson, to keep on the right side of his society wife, and Wakeson to please his daughter, whose career was wrapped up in the arts and who was personally a massive opera enthusiast – dating a leader in that field.

Over dinner, the two men talked about their personal history, with Carl showing great interest in Freddy's long career as a sports journalist. Carl spoke about his time in London during and after the Second World War and his time in the fashion industry. He mentioned a wartime girlfriend, who he had treated badly who'd given birth to a daughter who he had been completely estranged from. The girlfriend from Cornwall had died tragically in 1959. He had attended the funeral and met up with his teenage daughter, who didn't want to know him. He settled a decent sum of money on her, but had never heard from her again once he had moved to California.

'What was your daughter's name Carl?'

'Her name's Marie.' Carl recited her name with a far-away look in his eyes.

Freddy thought about the teenage Marie, known to him at the time as Margo, who he had briefly met all those years before, and had sadly died in childbirth. For a moment he wondered whether this had any connection to Carl's Marie, but immediately dismissed the thought as it would be too much of a coincidence; after all, Marie was not an unusual name. Whilst deep in thought, Carl changed tack and started to boast to Freddy about the successful restaurant chain he had built up and sold for a substantial profit. The moment to quiz Carl further about Marie had passed, as Carl was back to his show-off egotistical self.

Chapter 27

Stephen Zandors was delighted with the outcome of Freddy Wakeson's visit to California and his ability to persuade Carl Warringson to cover the costs of funding the inaugural season of the Lough Corrib Opera Festival. Freddy and his family would have complimentary tickets to all the festival operas for life. Carl Warringson would have his name splashed on all the festival's publicity material, as well as in the programme book. The champagne bar of the opera house would be named: The Carl Warringson Bar.

Once Stephen had assured his board of trustees that they had funding for the first season, he started to think seriously about the programme in detail and what artists to engage for the festival. The first version of *Simon Boccanegra* (1857) ticked all the boxes of a festival rarity as the opening production. He immediately thought of the recent production in Venice which he had attended that was conducted admirably by Simon Negrini. Stephen had met Simon on several occasions – the first time actually at the Lough Corrib Hotel, but somehow they were a bit wary of each other, each making assumptions about the other that were based more on perception than fact. Stephen thought that Simon had a chip on his shoulder, as his journey towards conducting had been far from orthodox routes, whilst Simon assumed that Stephen had a gold-plated background walking into opera's top administrative positions whether he deserved them or not. Of course, both men's assumptions were totally exaggerated; nevertheless, they still contained a grain of truth.

Leaving personalities aside, Stephen made contact with Negrini via Simon's agent, Keith Floes. The two men had a brief telephone conversation and agreed to meet at Floes' London office. The meeting got off to a good start as both men put their best foot forward – trying to put aside any prejudices they may have had about the other, and conducted the meeting in a professional manner.

'Simon, I would like to invite you, on behalf of the Lough Corrib Opera Festival, to open the festival conducting *Simon Boccanegra* – the 1857 version.'

'That would be a pleasure and an honour Stephen and do you have someone in mind to sing the title role?'

'Well…to be honest I would love to be able to engage Piero Capudizo, who sang the role so brilliantly at the Venice production that you conducted, but his fee would blow our complete budget for the festival.'

'…Stephen – may I suggest a dear colleague of mine, Dov Katz, a wonderful Verdi baritone. Dov, for some unknown reason, has yet to sing the title role on the stage, but knows the part of both versions extremely well, having sung the role of Paulo Albiani countless times all over Germany, sharing the stage with all the great Boccanegras' of the day. In fact, he sang the role of Paulo both at Glyndehurst in the standard 1881 version and at the Venice performances of the 1857 original.'

'Yes Simon, I did note his performances at both those productions, but to be fair there's not a lot of singing for Paulo and we need a big personality for Boccanegra.'

'Trust me, I know Dov's talent and capabilities and he'll be a great Boccanegra. He'll be in demand to sing the role all over the world once he gets his chance.'

Stephen reluctantly agreed to Simons' choice, but would have preferred someone who had experience in the role.

'Simon… have you ever conducted one of Michael Tippett's operas'?'

'Well...no actually. My conducting career has been mainly in Germany and Tippett rarely gets performed there. Interestingly though, I know Michael, who's a lovely man, now very elderly. I was a publishing assistant to him when I was working at Schoffs over thirty years ago – in fact I spent time with him in Cornwall, whilst he was working on his second opera, *King Priam*, when both John Amis and I were helping Michael with some of the literary sources for the opera.

'Why ask about Tippett?'

'Well... for our second production I was thinking about Tippett's *The Knot Garden* as a real contrast to the Verdi. The opera, in English of course, is on the small scale, without a chorus, so good for our budget and the opera's been relatively neglected since its premiere at Covent Garden in 1970.'

The two men, Stephen and Simon left the agent's office and went off to Langan's restaurant, just off Green Park for lunch. As the wine flowed, Simon talked about his background and gave Stephen a brief account about how he'd had found, by some kind of miracle, a lost daughter he'd never thought he had. But the daughter was in a state of shock and did not wish to acknowledge him as her father – despite a DNA test confirming the paternity.

Stephen listened with interest and thought that Simon must have huge willpower to have become a successful conductor despite a personal chequered past, and that knowledge about his colleague softened his previous dislike for the conductor. Meanwhile, Stephen confided to Simon that he was currently dating Lizzete Wakeson, but he had foolishly let the love of his life slip through his fingers some years before, because at that period of his life, he wasn't sure where his career was leading him, if anywhere at all. He added that also he had been concerned about his parents' reaction to his choice of wife. His father in particular was a die-hard old-fashioned English conservative snob, who would have been horrified at him marrying an adopted American girl whose birth parents were unknown. As well as that, the girl was a musician, a budding cellist, and that would have been an anathema for his parents, who had no respect for musicians and hated the music business that had been his own career choice.

Simon couldn't believe what he was hearing, as Stephen's love-life confession sounded so much that the girlfriend was Helena, his daughter; thinking about it, Helena had mentioned about a previous lover who had caused her so much heartache, but she hadn't given him any details about who that man was. Simon had not quizzed her about the episode – seeing how upset she had become talking about it.

Simon decided to keep his powder dry – just nodding in sympathy with Stephen's tale whilst changing the subject, turning the conversation back to professional matters. He talked to Stephen about the composer Michael Tippett – and their time together all those years before in Cornwall.

Simon told Stephen that he would not commit to conducting the Tippett opera, *The Knot Garden,* for the festival, but he would study the piece, which he'd never seen or heard, and try, if possible, to contact Tippett himself, seeking his advice on the matter and would let Stephen know if felt able to tackle the opera, as well as the Verdi piece, for the festival.

Whilst on their third bottle of a lovely Haut-Medoc wine, Simon related to Stephen about his meeting with a gentleman named Ricardo Negrini in Venice. The gentleman had introduced himself to Simon as a distant relative and took him through the family tree of the tenor, Carlo Negrini, who Stephen might or might not have known, was the tenor Verdi had chosen for the premiere of the original 1857 version of *Simon Boccanegra,* in the role of Gabriel Adorno, and who'd had a great success in the role, although the opera itself flopped badly. Anyway, the great revelation was that he was a direct descendant of the great tenor.

'That's amazing Simon. I knew I had picked the right man to conduct the Verdi opera to open our festival!'

'But there's more, Stephen. Ricardo Negrini handed me a precious document which was completely unknown to the public. Evidently, when the great librettist, Arrigo Boito, who had been responsible for the revision of *Simon Boccanegra*, and had also written an alternative libretto for the opera. Verdi hated it and it nearly scuppered their friendship which had taken years to cultivate after a shaky start many years' previously.

The alternative text had a happy ending with a general reconciliation at the end of the opera. Paulo Albiani does not suffer execution and Simon does not die of poisoning, instead forgiving Paulo for his treacherous plotting. But the real controversial aspect of that secret text, is that Boito gave Simon a love interest, that's not in the original play or libretto. The love interest is with Pietro, a minor character in the opera and a henchman of Paulo. Boccanegra and Pietro had been long-time comrades-in-arms and lovers going back to when Boccanegra was a Corsair – carrying out dangerous raids on the high seas on behalf of the Genoa State. When Boccanegra was elected Doge, the two men continued their relationship but in utmost secrecy. At the opera's conclusion, their secret had become public and although shocking to the traditionalist such as Fiesco, the public accepted the situation as they adored their heroic Doge, Simon Boccanegra.'

'How did your elderly relative come by this libretto?'

'When the revised 1881 premiere of *Simon Boccangra* was performed at La Scala Milan, Boito invited Clelia Negrini to attend the performance as his guest. Clelia was Carlo's widow – the tenor sadly having died before his fortieth birthday in 1865. At a private meeting following the performance, Boito gave the libretto to Clelia as a gift, but made her promise to keep the text a secret, which she did, and consequently, the libretto was handed down through the Negrini family generations when Ricardo Negrini decided to gift it to me, when we met in Venice during the run of the 1857 version of *Boccanegra,* that I was conducting at La Fenice Opera House.'

Stephen was absolutely fascinated by Simon's revelations, realising that he had completely underestimated the man and that any doubts in his head about him – dating back to their first meeting at the Lough Corrib Hotel, had been a gross misjudgement. To say that Stephen and Simon had bonded over lunch was an understatement, as they both staggered out of Langhams in the late afternoon sunshine, as newly discovered firm friends.

Simon thought long and hard about what Stephen had revealed about his regrets in losing who he'd referred to as 'the love of his life'.' Of course the woman concerned may not be Helena, but instinct told him that indeed it was as he suspected; it all sort of fitted. Stephen was living and working in Dublin at the time Helena had visited the city and in a strange sort of way one could see them together as a couple. They would make a striking pair, and heads would turn in admiration.

Could he become the repairman matchmaker? If he facilitated the getting back together of the two of them, would he earn sufficient brownie points from his newly found daughter? Helena had remained in a state of denial, since the discovery of their father/daughter status. But first, he needed to be sure that Stephen Zandors was actually the boyfriend Helena had spoken of during their long lunch at the restaurant Andrew Edmunds.

During Simon's next meeting with his agent Keith Foes, to catch up on current and subsequent conducting engagements, as well as discussing Simon's invitation to conduct the opening season at the Lough Corrib Opera Festival in 1993, Keith mentioned Helena Mentones and how well her career was developing.

'I don't know what happened between you two and I don't wish to intrude on private grief,' said Keith with a total lack of sincerity. 'But…you're missing out Simon, by not accompanying Helena at her recitals and for her recordings. It so happens that the Russian pianist, Nicholas Luganeski, has had to pull out of Helena's next Wigmore Hall recital, due to some visa issues. I was wondering whether you and Helena could patch up your differences and perform together again? After all you were such a natural partnership when you were a duo.'

Not wanting to get into any details about the issue with his relationship with Helena, Simon asked, 'out of curiosity, Keith, do you know what Helena's programme is?'

Keith fumbled around with a stack of papers on his desk and eventually found what he was looking for and put on his spectacles. 'Ah yes... here we are.'

Keith looked closely at the paper in front of him. 'Beethoven Op 5 No. 2 – Janacek's *Pohadka* – subtitled – *A Fairy Tale*, and Grieg, Cello Sonata in A minor.'

'Intriguing programme Keith - let me think about it.'

'OK, Simon, but let me know soon, as I need to see who else would be available if you don't take the engagement.'

Simon left the office in deep thought. Again he was full of admiration for Helena's choice of programme. The Beethoven was an early lively work – very different from the late Beethoven sonata they played together at their previous Wigmore Hall concert. The Janacek was a total novelty that he didn't know but he was in awe of Janacek's music and would love to get an opportunity to play the piece. The Grieg sonata was also rarely performed, but again, he was rather fond of the composer and knew that Grieg's melodies would be delicious and would sit well under a pianist's fingers. Yes... it was definitely a programme to get excited about, but he had to have the courage to contact Helena and persuade her to agree to play together, despite the strain in their relationship.

In the end, it was a joint effort to ease the strain between them. Helena had been thinking that she had been rather harsh to Simon and she had given herself time to come to terms with the situation. It had been confirmed by a DNA test that he was definitely her birth father, but that fact didn't actually change anything about her life, except adding another dimension to it. They agreed to perform together again but decided that, for the time being anyway, their father/daughter relationship would be a secret between them.

Simon asked Helena if her old boyfriend was Stephen Zandors?

'Why do you ask and how do you know Stephen?'

'Well...I had known Stephen casually for some years, but recently we formed a close friendship and I have been invited to conduct *Simon Boccanegra* at the opening of the new Lough Corrib Opera Festival in 1993.'

Helena went quiet and mumbled something about that she didn't really want to talk about that person – but admitted that Stephen Zandors was indeed the man who'd professed undying love and then unceremoniously dropped her. Simon decided not to pursue the matter on the telephone to Helena but would leave it until they met to rehearse for the concert – and then try to put Stephen' case forward, as best as he possibly could.

The rehearsals went extremely well and the concert was everything they'd hoped it would be. The Wigmore Hall was packed, as Helena was so much better known now than she had been at their previous concert at the venue. The critics were out in full and generally gave the artists ecstatic reviews – although one or two of them were a bit scathing about the Grieg. Not about the performance but criticising the piece itself – rating it not quite on par with other late Romantic cello sonatas.

Following the concert they revisited the Ivy restaurant where they had dined after their previous Wigmore Hall concert. As they enjoyed a delicious seafood dinner with a bottle of

Taittinger champagne, Simon gingerly put Stephen's case to Helena.

'You know Helena – Stephen started to tell me about how he had screwed up with the love of his life, and at that stage I had no idea who the woman was. It was as he continued to talk about her that it occurred to me that it could be you. I divulged nothing to Stephen who hadn't mentioned a name, but he seemed so sincere and put it down to his lack of self-confidence at that period of his life. Would you ever think about giving him another chance?'

Helena stared at Simon for a full minute without uttering a word. When finally she started to speak in a quiet voice, Simon had to lean into Helena to hear what she was saying as it was a noisy restaurant.

'Look, Simon...I opened up emotionally to Stephen as I had never had with anyone else and that's why his subsequent indifference was so hurtful. I wrote him such intimate and loving letters and then he made a feeble excuse that he wasn't any good at writing letters. I mean, someone with his educational background not being able to write letters? That was just absurd.'

Simon didn't intervene and let Helena get all the hurt out of her system. But he could see Helena's expression beginning to soften.

'But before it all went wrong – it was such a beautiful romance and I was genuinely in love and thought Stephen was too.'

'Maybe he was,' said Simon, but the practicalities of putting the relationship on a more permanent footing was just too much for him.'

He continued...making his first intervention. 'Would you consider giving him another chance?'

'I just don't want to be hurt again…Simon.'

'I completely understand,' Simon said and he left the matter there – not resolving or reviving the affair, but perhaps just opening the door to a possible reconciliation between the pair.

Keith Foes was delighted with the reviews Helena and Simon received for their Wigmore Hall concert and booked the pair to play the same programme at different venues all over the UK and Europe. They recorded the Grieg sonata which they both loved to play together and the audiences always gave it a rapturous response.They managed to convince the record company to have the Janacek *Pohadka* as filler, despite the executive's doubts about the saleability of Janacek, especially the unknown and unusual short fairy tale. The other major cello piece which the pair learnt especially for the disc, having not played it in public, was the Tchaikovsky Rococo Variations, (a cello/piano version).

Simon himself wrote a little note on the sleeve about the Janacek piece. It became a best selling classical record with a lovely picture of Helena with her shoulder-length hair sporting the cover.

Pohadka is based on an epic poem by the Russian author Vasily Zhukovsky entitled 'The Tale of Tsar Berendey.' The work presents scenes from the story rather than being a complete description of the tale. The story is about the Tsar's son Prince Ivan's love for the beautiful Princess Maria. The problem is that the princess's father is the King of the Underworld, Kaschel, and Kaschel wants to own Ivan's soul. The first movement is a duet for the lovers, followed by Kaschel chasing the couple on horseback. The second movement begins in an atmosphere of magic. The palace the lovers reach belongs to another Tsar and Tsarina who put a spell on Ivan, whom they wish their daughter to marry. This causes Maria to turn into a blue flower. A magician is on hand to sort things out , and Maria, now turned back into a beautiful princess, together with Ivan, escapes again, this time to Ivan's parents' palace where they tell the story of their adventures, celebrate and live happily ever after.

Making music together and travelling to venues for performances solidified the growing affection for one another, and the strangeness of how it was discovered that they were father and daughter – faded somewhat into the background.

They began to build a beautiful loving friendship that would sustain them in the years ahead.

Chapter 28

During 1991, the great conductor, Sir Georg Solti, returned to the Royal Opera House to conduct a new production of *Simon Boccanagra*, the revised 1881 version. Solti wanted the foremost Boccanegra of the day, Piero Capudizo, to sing the title role, and he was booked for the six performances of the initial run. Capudizo, who had attended all the rehearsals in London, returned home to Italy for a family wedding, a couple of days before the dress rehearsal but planned to return to London in time for that final run through, as a full performance with an invited audience. Unfortunately, Capudizo was involved in a serious car accident whilst in Italy and had to cancel his London performances. In fact the accident finished the famous baritone's career and although he recovered from the crash, he never sang on stage again.

Solti was hugely upset at the news of the accident, as Capudizo was a treasured colleague of his, and he'd only agreed to conduct the production on the understanding that Capudizio would sing the title role. Solti was on the telephone every day to Italy and had initially hoped that perhaps the accident wasn't as bad as initially thought – hoping that Capudizo would recover enough to sing the latter performances. But when it dawned on Solti and his colleagues that they had to rule out any chance of the baritone's return for any part of the run of performances, they had to quickly find a replacement baritone. But none who could sing the part were available; the production and musical team started to get frantic.

Dov Katz, the best known interpreter of the role of Paolo on European stages, and who had been engaged for the Covent Garden production, was quietly following the panic setting in amongst his colleagues. Dov sensed his opportunity and went, with trepidation, to see Solti in his private room.

'I can take over the title role, maestro. Although I've never sung it on stage, I've studied all the great Boccanegras' whilst performing Paolo in so many different productions.'

'No my dear Dov – we need a star performer. After all, this is Covent Garden, one of the leading opera houses in the world, and we need you to sing Paolo.'

Dov left the room without persuading the maestro.

He then went to see the director of the new production, Elijah Moshinsky, who was a friend as well as a colleague, and asked him whether he could intervene on his behalf with Solti and whether he had any suggestions as to who could take over the role of Paolo if he sang Boccanegra.

Moshinsky was brilliant as he'd not only found a young singer who he had worked with as Paolo on another production of *Simon Boccanegra* in Paris, but this young man was also able to travel immediately to London, if required. Moshinsky also suggested, in the most deferential manner to Solti, his renowned senior colleague, that they together audition Katz for the role.

'You'll know if he's up to the role musically and I will test his ability to have the force of personality and command of the stage needed for this great role. And if we're not happy with him we should postpone the production until we find a suitable candidate. '

Solti nodded at Moshinsky's suggestion, adding that the board of management would be very unhappy if the show was postponed; as it would mean refunds for ticket holders and compensation for all the other cast members.

In the end they needn't have worried. Not only did Katz know the role fluently, but he was also the right sort of age for the mature Doge. Dov Katz was magnificent in the title role, which fitted him like a glove; but Dov had always known, deep inside himself, that he was born to sing Simon Boccanegra, and here he was making his debut at the prestigious Royal Opera House Covent Garden, in a brand new production by Elijah Moshinsky, with beautiful atmospheric designs, conducted by maestro Sir Georg Solti. The audience initially were hugely disappointed that their favourite Verdi baritone was indisposed but they warmed to Dov Katz as the opera progressed. There was only lukewarm applause for the prologue but the temperature warmed up for the first act recognition scene for father and daughter.

But what followed – known as the Council Chamber Scene, was sensational. Katz showed himself to be a great singer/actor as he dominated the stage in one of Verdi's greatest dramatic inventions. When at the conclusion of the scene Boccanegra demands that Paolo curses himself, Katz opened up his voice in a magnificent fashion and had the audience in his hands. The audience went wild at the close of the act.

The second and third acts were equally superb – Solti keeping the intensity of the drama with fabulous playing from the orchestra, and Katz just continuing to grow in stature as the opera progressed. He was not just singing the role of *Simon Boccanegra* – he *was* the Doge. The final scene, as Boccanegra and his old foe Fiesco are reconciled – the Doge dying from the poison that Paulo had administered, had the audience in tears as it was so beautifully performed by the two magnificent artists.

The audience gave the cast, chorus, conductor and the directorial team a standing ovation and stamped their feet when Dov Katz came onto the stage for his solo bow. Not only had he saved the show, but he'd also presented himself to be one of the great Boccanegras of the day, if not indeed *the* greatest. The critics were massively enthusiastic about the whole performance and production, rating Dov Katz, notwithstanding the popular Capudizo, to have inherited the mantle of the Verdi baritone god, Tito Gobbi.

Once Dov Katz's triumph had reached the opera world, friends and colleagues made a point of going to London to catch one of the performances. They included Simon Negrini, Stephen Zandors, Helena Mentones, Freddy Wakeson and his daughter Lizette, who wrote a glowing review of Dov's performance and the production in general for her opera magazine. Stephen Zandors was thrilled to bits, having originally only reluctantly agreed to engage Katz for Lough Corrib – now his festival was going to open in 1993 with a world opera star singing the title role of their opening production – the original 1857 version of *Simon Boccanegra.*

Simon Negrini invited Dov Katz out for dinner to celebrate Dov's Covent Garden triumph and booked a table at one of London's finest – Wiltons located in Jermyn Street, St. James's. They ate oysters and Dover soles' and drank champagne. They finished with traditional British bread and butter pudding and coffee'-s accompanied with cognacs.

All through the meal they talked about Dov's fabulous performance of the title role of *Simon Boccanegra,* and how they were both looking forward to working together in Ireland, on the original version of the opera, at the opening of the Lake Corrib in 1993.

Once they had talked enough about opera and the music business, the conversation turned to more personal matters.

'You know, Dov, during the period when we were estranged, I thought a lot about you and our friendship all those years ago at the Greenshead boarding school. We were so young and innocent and the school was a disaster. It's amazing we came through all that religious extremism and we both have enjoyed successful musical careers, despite such an unpromising start.'

'Simon, I remember you being more innocent than I was, as even at that age I knew that I preferred boys to girls – not that there any girls around us in Greenshead' chuckled Dov.'

He looked straight into Simon's eyes. 'You didn't know anything about sex, let alone where your orientation lay. I was also aware that you had a soft spot for me.' Dov laughed whilst Simon had a serious thoughtful look on his face.

'Yes, Dov, I did have a thing about you back then. When Ronnie Don, the housemaster at Greenshead, subtly morphed from treating me like a young friend to touching me sexually, I was horrified at his actions. But in bed at night I thought of you and how much I wished it was you touching me. To be honest, Dov, I was very confused about the whole sexual machinations and thought that you and the other boys were much more knowledgeable about it all than I was, but I felt too timid to ask questions. Do you remember the boy from Amsterdam – I think his name was Pinchas; he was a bit older than us and seemed to know an awful lot about sex.'

'I remember him, Simon. He was all bluff and bluster having picked up some tidbits about sex from his older brother, but believe me, he was as innocent as the rest of us. 'You know though, Simon – Ronnie Don shouldn't have gotten away with sexually abusing you; he should have been reported to the police.'

'You're right, Dov, and I had thought about it many times over the years but it's only in recent times that stuff like that has started to come out into the open, with the media taking an interest, and it seemed that so many young boys in all sorts of establishments had been abused. To be honest, so many years had passed and I didn't wish to revisit that period of my life.'

'I quite understand, Simon, but have you ever had any homosexual experiences or desires since your boyhood?'

'Absolutely not...' Simon said, with more vehemence than he meant to convey.

Simon continued...'Once I left Greenshead I wanted to bury that part of my life and start over again. I couldn't wait to meet and date girls, and that I did with a vengeance and never looked back. On the other hand, I haven't exactly made a success of my love life; a failed young marriage and then getting a young girl pregnant. She died tragically – giving birth to a daughter, who was lost to me for so many years.'

'Don't be so hard on yourself Simon' said Dov quietly – lightly touching his friend's hand.

'It's such a shame that you're exclusively heterosexual, as we'd make a perfect couple.' laughed Dov – as he kept his hand on Simon's hand.

Dov continued...'We are of similar middle age, known each other from boyhood, both successful musicians who occasionally work together and most importantly, we're both currently single.'

'All I can say, Dov, is that if I was going to have a gay affair, the only person I could ever contemplate it occurring with, would be with you.'

'That's very touching, Simon, and just in case you were never aware of it, I fancied you too, during our time together at school, but kept my desire for you secret as I didn't think you were ready for any type of sexual engagement. Then that rogue, the housemaster, complicated things by trying to seduce you. Our little group of boys guessed what was going on and to be honest one or two of them were rather jealous that you had been the chosen one, but I realised how confused you must have been and thought that it was your sexual innocence that made you so attractive to the housemaster.

'Simon was listening intently to Dov, trying to remember how he had felt during those distant times, but it all felt like something from another world that he had left behind so long ago.

'Let's get out of here, Dov, but I don't want the evening to finish; maybe we can go to a late night bar somewhere?'

'Would it be presumptuous of me to suggest a gay bar in Soho that I frequent sometimes when visiting London?'

With a mischievous smile on his face, Simon said. 'Why not, Dov, it will certainly be a first for me!'

The bar in question was more a male-only night club than a gay pub. There was an admission cost to entry, the cash taken by an unsmiling man sitting behind a grill barrier and looking at them both up and down as if he was deciding whether they were suitable customers for the club. Dov paid the correct amount – and the man pressed a button to release the lock on a door that they pushed open, and they were immediately into the main bar area of the club.

The room was quite dark and pop music was softly playing in the background. Seeing men exclusively in the bar area felt strange to Simon but it was quite normal for Dov. At first glance it seemed a varied age group from men in their twenties to others much older. Nationalities seemed mixed with a number of Asian men, a few black guys with some of the white men looking European, possibly Italian or Polish, and some typical British-looking chaps. There were signs in large print plastered all over the walls warning about the HIV/Aids pandemic and urging all men to have safe sex and save their lives. Another thing that Simon observed was all the men seemed ordinary – not camp in any way – just the same as guys one would see in a mixed-gender bar or pub.

Simon and Dov ordered gin and tonics and sat on the bar stools taking in the atmosphere around them. There were groups of three or four men together and a good number of solo guys, perhaps cruising around the club and hoping to get lucky?

As they finished their drinks, Dov nudged Simon to look around the rest of the club. Away from the bar area, the lighting was even more dimmed – with a maze of narrow corridors where solo guys were lurking – eying up other men. They emerged into another open area where groups of men were congregated –

laughing and joking amongst themselves. That led onto via another warren of narrow passageways to an even darker area where men, coupled up, were kissing and touching each other. Dov watched Simon, who was clearly fascinated by seeing men entwined, and signalled Simon to follow him into a private alcove where they began to kiss each other tenderly, gradually turning more passionate – an action that was forty-two years overdue. The first man Simon had ever voluntarily kissed was the same person he had wanted to kiss all those years before and now it felt like the most natural thing in the world – his only thoughts were why it had taken so long; they should not have wasted so many years to express their love for each other.

Dov whispered into Simon's ear, 'Come back to my hotel tonight.' Simon nodded his assent and with arms around each other they left the club.

The pair became gay lovers that night and swore undying love for one another.

After a full English breakfast with endless cups of tea, they talked over what happened to them and how they would handle the situation publicly; after all, they were both public figures in the classical music world – deciding that for the time being anyway, they would keep their new found relationship a secret. They were particularly aware that both were going to be involved in the new Lough Corrib festival, and Ireland had yet to decriminalise homosexual relationships between consenting adults.

As both men had a music-free day, they talked and talked about their future life as a couple. Simon told Dov all about his meeting with his distant Italian Negrini relative and how he had discovered that he, Simon, was a direct descendant of Carlo Negrini, the tenor who had premiered the role of Gabriele Adorno in 1857 at La Fenice Opera in Venice.

Dov was open-mouthed, gobsmacked at the revelation, and even more so when Simon told him about the secret Boito libretto that Riccardo Negrini had bequeathed to him. When Simon explained that this version of *Simon Boccanegra* that Verdi had rejected – considering it absolutely shocking, contained a homosexual element to it; Boccanegra and the character known as Pietro, a minor part in the two established operatic versions, were long time lovers. Dov couldn't contain himself.

'But that's amazing Simon – considering what's just happened between us. It's as if we're following in real life here and now; the trajectory of the whole *Simon Boccanegra* opera creation saga.'

'Yes... and it's us getting together that completes' the jigsaw puzzle of our lives following elements of the opera. A relatively humble man, a Corsair fighting for Genoa – unexpectedly becomes the head of state, but his female lover dies and their daughter is missing.

Does that sound familiar, Dov?'

Dov had become speechless listening to his friend and newly found male lover – lay out the parallel lives of the operatic characters and their own life journey.

Simon continues…'Twenty-five years later, Boccanegra discovers his long-lost daughter, and the daughter had fallen in love with Gabriele Adorno, who was in cahoots with Fiesco, a sworn enemy of Boccanegra and the secret grandfather of Boccanegra's daughter.'

'So we still have a missing part of the jigsaw puzzle, Simon,' Dov said... finding his voice again.

'Yes' said a thoughtful Simon; 'If Stephen Zandors is our Gabriele Adorno and Helena, my daughter, is the Amelia, it means that the pair of ex- lovers are destined to get back together and I must play my part in that endeavour,'...added Simon, his thoughtfulness turning more to mirth as he started to see the amusing side to all the parallels shaping up between art and life.

'To complete the circle of the opera characters, we still have to find our Fiesco' Simon said, seeing the connections as a bit of divertissement. He nudged Dov with a grin on his face.

Dov... picking up on Simon's less than serious expression, added, 'At least with Boito's secret libretto you don't need to be poisoned in the last act of the opera!'

'Well... that's a relief, Dov, and as you've sung the role of Paulo umpteen times before the recent promotion to the title role, you'd be the one to administer the deadly poison. Perhaps I should keep well away from you and be careful what I drink!' Both men burst out laughing at the same time, realising the surreal nature of their less-than serious turn of the conversation.

Chapter 29

Lough Corrib, Galway, Ireland, January 1993

Stephen Zandors had left his position at Glyndehurst Opera Festival and was now full-time engaged in planning the opening of the Lough Corrib Opera Festival scheduled to open in September. He had bought the land at Tully Cross from Annie McVay and following tricky negotiations with the County Galway planning department, he had received full planning permission with certain restrictions on the height and the general size of the building, so not to be interfering in any way with anyone's view of the magnificent scenic wonders surrounding the land. He was thrilled with the plans of his Dublin architect he had commissioned. The house was scheduled to be ready to move into in time for the opening of the festival. His plan was to live there from Easter until after the festival and spend the winter months at his London flat.

Stephen had given up on the idea of three opera productions for the initial festival – settling for two in the first year, building to three for subsequent years. The amazing secret 'Boito' libretto that he had received from the conductor Simon Negrini would be the contemporary work pencilled in for 1994. He had received permission from both the 'Boito' estate and the Negrini family to perform the work. He had commissioned the music from one of the leading contemporary opera composers of the day, Timothy Seda, who would also conduct the piece. For the 1993 festival, the opening would be the 1857 first version of *Simon Boccanegra* with Dov Katz repeating his triumph in the title role he had enjoyed at the Royal Opera House Covent Garden during their 1991 season. The conductor would be Simon Negrini, who would also conduct the second production of the festival – Michael Tippett's *The Knot Garden* (1970).

Negrini had been reluctant to take on the Tippett as well as the Verdi, but after studying the opera and speaking with Tippett himself, who was full of encouragement, he decided to bite the bullet and conduct both operas. Tippett had said that he would try to attend the opening performances of his opera, but as he was elderly and quite frail, he was unsure as to whether he would be able to make the journey to the west of Ireland. There would be three performances of each opera and the festival would conclude with a gala performance of popular arias and choruses' from various operas' which hopefully would raise money for future festivals.

Stephen was aware that Helena Mentones had been touring the UK and Europe, performing a cello and piano recital with Simon Negrini, and as Negrini would be at Lough Corrib for the duration of the festival, perhaps, with the help of Simon, he could persuade Helena to perform their recital programme at the festival on one of the nights that did not have an opera performance scheduled. As Stephen was settling into his new role and feeling that Ireland, especially Connemara, was a place he wanted to take roots, he couldn't get Helena out of his mind and imagined the two of them in his Tully Cross home, looking out in awe of their surroundings – rekindling the love they had established in Dublin ten years ago.

Helena Mentones and Simon Negrini were engaged to give their recital of Beethoven, Janacek and Grieg at the 1993 Aldeburgh Festival in Suffolk, England, during the month of June before finally retiring that particular programme at the Lough Corrib festival in September. When Stephen Zandors became aware that Helena was performing at Aldeburgh, which neighboured his family home village of Orford, it was too tempting to resist getting over to Aldeburgh to hear the programme live... and it was a great excuse to meet up with Helena again. Simon had told Helena that Stephen's visit to the Aldeburgh Festival was strictly professional as he had every right to hear the programme that he had booked for his Lough Corrib festival. Helena was no fool and guessed that the main reason for Stephen to attend Aldeburgh was to see Helena as Simon had been busy quietly pushing Stephen's case at every opportunity during their time together at rehearsal breaks or at dinners following a performance.

Actually, Simon had been pushing at an open door, because despite Helena still feeling sore towards Stephen, part of her wanted to see him again and maybe revive their original love affair. However, she was too proud to admit it to Simon and she told him that she couldn't stop Stephen's professional duties and that she had only agreed to perform at Lough Corrib as a favour to Simon; it had nothing at all to do with Stephen. They were all professionals and it was their duty to act accordingly, but any chance of a relationship revival with Stephen was preposterous; that had happened ten years before and they'd all moved on in their private lives. Equally, Simon thought she was protesting too much and knew Helena wasn't being honest with him, but he kept his counsel – instinctively knowing that once they met each other again – all past hurt feelings would dissipate.

The Aldeburgh Festival was started in 1948 by the composer Benjamin Britten and his life- long partner, the tenor Peter Pears, as the couple had set up home in the town of Aldeburgh. The festival originally performed at the Jubilee Hall in the town and in local churches in Aldeburgh, Orford and Blythburgh. As the festival grew, Britten and Pears set about converting an old malt house in Snape, seven miles from Aldeburgh, into a state-of-the- art concert hall. The hall opened originally in 1967 but unfortunately it burnt down the following year – reopening again in 1969, and it became a world-famous venue both for performances and recordings, with its superb acoustics.

The Aldeburgh Festival audience were very enthusiastic about the performance of Helena and Simon's cello and piano recital. Simon said a few words to the audience after the Beethoven and before they played the Janacek. With the Janacek work being a rarity, Simon explained the background to the piece with a brief description of the fairy tale that it is based on. After the interval, the Grieg cello sonata, which the two of them had played together so many times by then, just sang with its lyrical melodies soaring through the superb Snape Maltings concert hall. The love for the piece shone out by the playing of the two artists—, the sophisticated audience of Aldeburgh knew a great performance when they heard one—, they cheered and stamped at the conclusion of the sonata. Simon left the first encore for Helena alone as she played a movement from one of Bach's cello suites, and they came back together for a second encore of the 'The Swan' from Saint-Saëns *Carnival of the Animals*.

Stephen Zandors had slipped into his centre stalls seat just before the start of the concert and he had felt apprehensive at seeing Helena again – hearing her playing the cello after a ten-year gap. She looked even more beautiful than he had remembered from their Dublin and London days together – but more poised and confident. After all, she was now a world-famous classical music cellist with a number of best selling recordings to her name. But he still noticed certain vulnerabilities about her expression that had originally attracted him to her. He again thought how mad he had been to let her go, and was determined to win her back.

One thing bothered Stephen though. He knew he had work to do to persuade Helena to trust him that he wouldn't let her down as he had before, but he couldn't hold back an 'Othello' syndrome in his head. He knew he was being ridiculous because he hadn't even got to first base yet with Helena, but the green-eyed jealousy monster was working on him, and however much he tried, it just wouldn't let him be.

He saw the communication between Helena and Simon – realising immediately that the two artists on the stage were more than a musical duo – it was a relationship. The look in their eyes for each other was palpable to anyone who cared to see—.

He felt a sudden hatred towards Simon, and the friendship they had recently established dissipated instantly; an insane jealousy and anger consumed him. What the hell was a man in his late fifties doing with a young woman of thirty-three? But as a man in the musical business, he knew that it was not uncommon in his world that older men, conductors especially, got together with younger female musicians, perhaps starting off as a mentor which led to them becoming lovers.

He decided not to go backstage to greet the pair; he was almost in tears at the frustration he felt. He also realised that there was only one person to blame – himself and him alone. He'd brought it all on himself by his own fears of not being worthy of Helena back in 1983.

Backstage... a lot of well-wishers crowded out the artists' room, but there was no sign of Stephen Zandors.

'Perhaps he didn't come; he could have been held up somewhere? '

'I'm sorry Helena – but he was definitely in the audience as I saw him clearly in the centre stalls,' said Simon, putting his arm around Helena, sensing the hurt she felt – that despite her protestations she had been looking forward to seeing Stephen again and had expected him to join them after the concert.

Chapter 30

London, June 1993

Helena Mentones was back in her London flat following her triumph at the Aldeburgh Festival. She was still upset at Stephen Zandors' strange behaviour at Snape Maltings and couldn't really understand why he had failed to join the throng in the artists' room following the performance. After all, she had agreed to perform at the Lough Corrib festival purely as a favour to Simon, and Stephen would hardly have been able to ignore her during her stay there.

Helena made herself a cup of coffee and sat down to catch-up on the weekend papers. The broadsheets all contained reviews of the Aldeburgh Festival; Helena and Simon's cello and piano recital received a five-star notice in both the *Sunday Times* and the *Observer*.

The telephone rang and it was her agent, Keith Foes. After the usual pleasantries, with Keith congratulating Helena on the Aldeburgh concert, his usual cheery though slightly cynical tone changed to something quieter and serious.

'I had Stephen Zandors on the phone this morning and he wanted to cancel your recital at his new festival. When I asked what the problem was he said that he couldn't bear to see Helena and Simon together as it was obvious that they were in a relationship. When I told him that yes, they were personally close, but as far as I was aware, there was no sexual relationship going on between them. I then asked Stephen why it was of any concern to him. And he confessed that he and Helena had been an item ten years previously but things hadn't worked out between them.'

Helena listened carefully to Keith's non-stop verbal colloquy without interrupting his flow, but responded by ignoring the personal aspects about her relationship with Simon and her past relationship with Stephen. All she said to Keith was: 'Just get back to Mr Zandors and tell him we have a contract to play at his festival and will honour our contract, as we always do with all our engagements, whether he likes it or not.'

Keith picked up on Helena's stark tone-of -voice and got the message that she was not prepared to enter into a conversation about her past or current personal life with her agent.

But later in the evening, after an afternoon of cello practice, Helena began to process the telephone conversation with Keith Foes earlier in the day and concluded that Stephen, assuming Simon and her were lovers, was insanely jealous, and that meant that he was still in love with her and wished to resume their relationship. So her anger towards Stephen for ignoring her at Aldeburgh, morphed into feeling sorry for him, as he must have seen the way she and Simon looked into each other's eyes as they made music together and made a totally wrong conjecture about their relationship.

Keith Foes, following his telephone conversation with Helena, contacted Simon Negrini – repeating what he had said to Helena about Zandors wanting to cancel Helena's recital. His accusation was that Negrini had groomed Helena to be his lover, and being disgusted with him.

The recent development of friendship between the two men was now completely out-of-the-window. Zandors had also stated that he would have found a way to cancel Negrini's contract, but now it was now too late in the day to find a replacement conductor for the two operas, at the upcoming Lough Corrib festival

Simon knew exactly what was going on and why Stephen had acted so out of character at Aldeburgh by not greeting them after the concert. If ever there was proof that Stephen was still in love with Helena and wanting to revive their affair...that was it. Otherwise, why rail so furiously against him for having a relationship with Helena, which of course was not at all what it seemed? But even if it was, Helena was not a teenager; she was a mature woman of thirty-three. A man being twenty-five years older than his lover was hardly unusual, and there was nothing disgusting about the idea of such a relationship.

Simon realised that he had to act urgently to put everything right before rehearsals for the festival – that were scheduled to commence in a couple of weeks. Simon telephoned Helena and asked her permission for what he planned to do. As Simon had an empty diary for the following few days – he told Helena that he would fly out to Galway to see Stephen and tell him the truth about their relationship, then fly to Munich for a conducting engagement and back to Galway again in time for the festival rehearsals.

 Helena was happy with Simon's plan and in any event, it was about time everyone knew about the fact that Simon and Helena were father and daughter. She would write to her parents in New York and explain everything to them; she was hoping that they would fly over to Ireland for the festival, and she also knew that her Uncle Carl, the festival's benefactor, was planning to be there, if he wasn't too frail to make the journey.

Stephen was settling into his new summer home at Tully Cross when he got word that Simon Negrini was making a special trip to Ireland to speak with him. Stephen was suddenly concerned about Simon's intentions; for him to make a special journey to see him must be of major importance. He immediately started to regret his high-horse threats about wanting to cancel Simon's contract whilst he was full of anger when speaking with Keith Foes. What if he was coming here to resign from the festival? But why make the journey to resign in person? He could have done it by letter or through his agent. Stephen feared for his festival and without Simon, the whole festival would collapse.

Simon flew to Knock airport in County Mayo and hired a car to drive to Renvyle House Hotel where he had booked a room for the night. Tully Cross was a short walk away and Simon, after checking in and saying hello to the irrepressible manager Ken Moyes, made his way to Stephen's house. Stephen had not yet had a telephone installed in his new house and Simon hoped that he would be in residence.

Simon was impressed that the house was built to snugly fit into the glorious scenery without it even being noticed by a passer-by. The design was plain, square with a flat roof and lots of large windows to give it natural light.

Stephen opened the door and invited Simon in. 'Please excuse the lack of furniture,' said Stephen after the two men shook hands. Stephen led him into a good sized room which had wonderful views of the nearby hills.

Simon sensed nervousness in Stephen that he had never noticed before. Simon had always read Stephen as a man with a privileged background who was always comfortable in his own skin. But seeing the man in front of him full of self-doubt, actually made Simon warm to him. He wanted to reassure him about the festival and also encourage his pursuit of Helena.

'Can I get you a drink, Simon?'

'I'm fine thanks and I'd prefer to get to why I'm here straight away.'

'Sure Simon... Fire away. —'

'Firstly...let me reassure you about the festival. There'll be no resignation and I'll be back at Lough Corrib in a couple of weeks – in time for the commencement of the rehearsal period.'

Simon immediately noticed an easing of tension in Stephen's demeanour as he pulled his chair up to sit closer to his host.

'On the personal side of things, I know what you've been thinking and what you've been spouting about with colleagues on the relationship between Helena and me – but you've got it completely wrong. Yes, Stephen, you were instinctive enough to notice that Helena and I were more than just musical partners, and I understood when you blanked us in Aldeburgh, thinking that you had left it too late to revive your love for Helena, as your older musical colleague had become Helena's romantic attachment and possibly lovers. What I'm about to say Stephen will shock you but also give you hope.

Simon continued...'I discovered a while back through a series of amazing coincidences – that I was Helena's natural birth father, meaning Helena is my daughter and you're one of the very first to know, and that includes Helena's adopted parents.'

Stephen just stared at Simon without saying anything, and the only words that eventually came out of his mouth were...'I need a drink.'

Stephen got up from his seat and disappeared into another room that Simon assumed was the kitchen. He came back a few minutes later with two large gin and tonics on a tray and some olives and nuts. 'You drink G and T's Simon?'

'Absolutely, Stephen – you must have read my mind' Simon said as Stephen offered him the drink. 'Cheers' they both said simultaneously as they clicked glasses.

'How did Helena react when she found out who you were to her?'

'Shock and disbelief initially, turning to anger. She felt I had discombobulated her settled life and when I told her the story of how I had met her mother – having enjoyed a fleeting sexual escapade with her in a hotel, and never seeing her again, only to find out years later that she had died in childbirth... giving birth to Helena.'

Simon continued—'the anger towards me naturally increased tenfold – as she looked upon me as the murderer of her young mother.'

'So when did Helena stop being angry with you?'

'She refused to perform with me for a while and found another pianist. But slowly she relented and the music did the rest. You see Stephen, we are a natural duo, performing as if we are one person – not two, and we got to know each other on the road travelling to all sorts of places –performing in all kinds of venues, large and small, from major cities to provincial towns in the UK and Europe. And then there were the recordings together – which bring one's own kind of intimacy with all the intricacies of getting things just right. We both found it impossible to duet with other musicians as our partnership was so very special... and a great friendship grew between us, leading to a strong emotional connection.'

'Simon... I must apologise both to you and to Helena for my boorish behaviour at Aldeburgh; now I know the nature of your relationship with Helena, I feel a fool reacting the way I did.'

'No apologies needed. After all, it was a one in a million chance that we were a father and daughter, and by reacting the way you did meant that you still had hopes for a romantic reconciliation with Helena. —Am I right?'

Stephen just nodded in agreement keeping his face down in serious contemplation.

'May I make a suggestion? I'm starving, Simon, so let me buy you dinner at Renvyle House; we can find a quiet corner of the restaurant and you can fill me in on the whole unbelievable story, whilst we stay reasonably sober. Then following dinner we can join Ken Moyes and all his cronies in the bar for some serious drinking and perhaps join in the nightly sing-song; I think we owe it to each other to let our hair down – take away the strain of all your revelations and rekindle our friendship that got rudely interrupted.'

'I'll drink to that, Stephen,' Simon said as a smile crossed Stephen's face for the first time since Simon had arrived at his house.

Stephen woke up the next morning with a hangover – having indulged in the raucousness that was a nightly event at Renvyle House. Over dinner, before the serious drinking started, Simon tried to explain everything as concisely as he could, sticking to the main points of the trajectory of events that concerned Helena's life, from meeting her birth mother in Cornwall during the summer of 1959 – to years later finding out by chance that the girl, known to him as Margo, had died giving birth, and that her baby had been adopted by a lovely family from New York.

He mentioned a bracelet that Helena had inherited from her grandmother – that her mother had worn during the tryst in Cornwall, but which had fallen on the floor after she had left Simon's bedroom at the hotel, and for some unknown reason he had made a note of the hallmark number before handing it into the reception. He had kept the note with the number over the years and that was the crunch moment when Helena showed him the note with the matching numbers, and later, seeing the actual bracelet which was rightly hers. They'd then followed up at a later date with DNA testing, which was the final proof that they were indeed father and daughter.

Stephen remembered that when he'd first met Helena and they'd been enjoying lunch at the Donizetti restaurant in Dublin – she had hardly mentioned her birth parents except to tell him that her mother had died in giving birth to her and she had no idea who her father was. But he never felt that was something that she dwelled on as she was a happy young woman who loved her adopted parents and they loved her – giving her a great start in life. She had mentioned at the time an Uncle Carl, who wasn't a relative at all, but who was almost revered by the Mentones' as he had assisted them in the adoption of Helena.

Stephen had thought at the time that this Carl character had sounded a bit of a strange individual and he couldn't understand why Helena admired him so much and why he spoiled his friend's daughter – taking such an interest in her development and well-being.

The strangest thing of all was that the very same Carl Warringson was now the financial saviour of the upcoming Lough Corrib festival. Stephen hadn't realised when Warringson was persuaded by his predecessor to support Glyndehurst in 1986, that the gentleman was the very same person known to Helena as Uncle Carl. Warringson himself told Stephen that he was a family friend of Helena Mentones, but Stephen had forgotten about this Uncle Carl and never made the connection. In any case, Stephen had expected Helena to be playing in the Glyndehurst orchestra for the festival, but as she had excused herself he thought no more about it.

Later in the day – whilst Stephen was thinking about the festival, and about *Simon Boccanegra* in particular, he became aware of art and life in parallel lines.

Boccanegra's daughter was missing and the Doge, by a chance encounter, many years later, recognised his long-lost daughter through the locket she was wearing. The daughter, Amelia, had a lover, Gabrielle Adorno. Adorno was jealous of Boccanegra, mistakenly thinking that Amelia was the Doge's mistress; but later, when Adorno wanted to do Boccanegra harm, Boccanegra admitted to Adorno that he was Amelia's father.

Was there more about life-following-art to be revealed?

Back at Lough Corrib the following day for a trustees meeting with the Donnells' and other trustees, Stephen contacted the agent Keith Foes requesting Helena's telephone number. Foes was reluctant to give it, but without divulging anything about what was the true nature of the relationship between Simon and Helena, managed to convince Foes to relent.

'Hello, Helena...it's Stephen here. 'How are you?'

'Where did you get my number from?' was Helena's sharp reply.

'Keith Foes gave it to me.'

'That was naughty of him... artists' privacy needs to be respected at all times.'

She clearly thought Keith had given the number to a stranger.

'Helena... Helena, I'm Stephen—!'

Stephen, feeling nervous, continued: 'We were very close once and despite what happened ten years ago, I've never stopped loving you. And I owe you an apology for ignoring you in Aldeburgh—.'

Helena, softening her tone slightly, responded, 'Yes Stephen – I've been aware of your mistaken assumptions about Simon and me and hopefully you now know what our true relationship status is.'

'Yes... Helena, Simon came over here to visit me – specifically to inform me about the amazing development between you two.'

'I know... it was a great shock and it took me time to process the facts, but now, through our performances together, we've grown close and affectionate towards each other.'

'That's exactly how Simon described it and I'm so pleased for you both.'

'Thanks Stephen.'

'Helena... will you be staying in London over the next few days?'

'Yes... I'm here in London until I travel to Ireland for your festival – why do you ask? '

'I would like to come over to London to see you before rehearsals start here in a couple of weeks.'

'But we'll be seeing each other at the festival, and as it's taken you ten years to re-contact me – another couple of weeks shouldn't matter?'

Helena didn't mean to sound sarcastic but she was aware that it had come out that way.

'I know what you're saying but there will be so many people at the festival and I'll have so much to do. I wanted to see you alone before the big event.'

'OK' said Helena, 'just let me know when you plan to be in London and if I'm free – we could meet.

Stephen thought what a difficult call that was, but it had to be done and all in all – it went as well as it could have, taking everything into account.

July 1993.

Stephen had rented out his London flat for the summer months, so he booked a couple of nights at the Carlton Club in St James's. Despite being a convert to the Labour Party, he had accepted an invitation to join the arch Tory Carlton Club as a token of his respect for his father. Zandors' senior, a Carlton Club member of long standing, and part of the scrutiny committee that decided who was fit or not to join the esteemed historical London political club, always stayed over at the club when in London and preferred to meet his son there than go to

Stephen's modern design flat in Notting Hill, which he considered an unacceptable area of London.

Stephen was initially rather cynical about the club when he'd first become a member, considering the membership was full of stuffed shirt Tories. But once he got to know his way around the club, he realised there was a distinct split in the club membership. There were the politico geeks, who were indeed stuffed shirt types – they did nothing else but discuss politics and to plot various political manoeuvres, but an alternative crowd of members were there for jollies and human camaraderie – to enjoy the good food and wine in comfortable surroundings. Stephen attached himself to the latter group, realising that there were Tories and Tories. On the whole, they were the most congenial of company, although he kept his cards close to his chest – as he had personally morphed from voting Tory to becoming a Labour Party supporter.

Although the club membership was exclusively male, the upstairs dining areas were open to ladies who were the guests of members, and having dinner at the Carlton Club restaurant was indeed a treat. The food was traditionally English, but in the best style, using only top quality ingredients, cooked to perfection. The restaurant staff had been at the club for many years – and knew all the names of the members, and without being obsequious, they looked after each diner as if they were the only diner there. The maitre'd, whose name was Santo, was a most genial Portuguese individual who Stephen loved chatting with. As the club was closed during the whole month of August – the staff had the month off and Santo, a very enthusiastic fisherman, always went back to Portugal to indulge in his fishing hobby – coming back to the club with many fishing stories which he shared with the club members and with Stephen in particular. He was especially proud of when he had caught a big tuna.

Helena had never entered the hallowed doors of any of London's traditional clubs and certainly had never thought of being a guest at the Carlton Club, an establishment fit for only the most conservative of English gentlemen of a certain age and renown. But as she entered the slightly austere doors, feeling nervous and out of her comfort zone, she was immediately greeted by an elderly doorman in a very smart uniform with a welcome smile.

'Good evening madam – welcome to the Carlton Club, and how can I help you?'

Helena was rather taken aback by such a friendly and warm greeting and immediately the fear at the pit of her stomach eased.

She responded… 'Good evening to you too – I'm here to meet one of the club members – a Mr Stephen Zandors.'

'Ah, yes, madam... Mr Zandors and his father are honoured members of this establishment, so let me take you upstairs as Mr Zandors junior is in the upstairs drawing room. I'm Tom... by the way'

'Hello, Tom … my name is Helena Mentones.'

'Pleased to meet you... Miss Mentones.'

Tom gave Helena a sideways glance, thinking that she looked familiar but couldn't quite place her. Tom escorted Helena up the very impressive staircase with superb portraits of various members of the royal family. He left Helena at the entrance to the drawing room, but she could not see Stephen anywhere. She took a seat and glanced around the spacious and comfortable room. It reminded her of an English country house drawing room plonked in the middle of Central London. The room was full of men with just a few women accompanying some of them – making Helena feel self-conscious without a man next to her.

The men were all dressed in suits and ties; the more senior gentlemen wore suits that were beautifully tailored, probably from Savile Row, with a crisp white shirt – silk tie and finished off with a silk handkerchief in the breast pocket. One imagined that they dressed like that every day when they were in London, whatever their occupation or activity – having a different uniform when in the country, maybe a checked sports jacket – checked shirt with a cravat – corduroy trousers and brown brogues. Amusingly, Helena noticed that the younger men wore suits that were less expertly tailored, more loosely fitted, with shirts and ties a bit haphazardly put together – giving the impression that the get-up was for visits to the club only – dressing more casually the rest of the time.

Suddenly she saw Stephen coming through the entrance. Helena smiled and waved to him.

'Sorry... It was bad timing Helena – I had been here for a while but needed to visit the gents.'

'That's OK, Stephen... It gave me a chance to look around and get my bearings. Besides, I knew you were in the building because Tom, who kindly escorted me upstairs, had said so.'

They kissed like old friends, with not a hint of their passionate past – politely complimenting each other on how they looked. Stephen had a bottle of champagne pre-ordered and once the barman, Michel, saw the couple, he opened the bottle immediately. They both savoured those first few drops of good champagne – something that could instantly clear away any anxious feelings one may have had. As they both started to relax – they looked at each other again, but this time they were thinking about what had been between them, and those past memories of passion stirred in their minds.

The maitre d', Santo, welcomed Stephen into the restaurant with a big smile and firm handshake as introductions were made to Helena.

'You're a famous classical music star, Miss Mentones... I believe... a cellist – if I'm not mistaken?'

Santo uttered in a quiet voice, so as not to draw attention to other guests who could cause embarrassment to Helena, as they shook hands. 'I have one of your recordings in my collection' he added.

'Well... Mr Santo – that's nice of you to recognise me, and thank you for buying one of my records.'

'You're welcome, and it's a great pleasure gracing your presence at the Carlton Club and having dinner with our esteemed member Mr Zandors... I will leave you the menus and the wine list and will be back shortly to take your order.

'Phew, chuckled Helena... whispering in Stephen's ear – 'I didn't expect that! Nobody recognises me around London unless I'm near the Wigmore Hall or the South Bank. After all, I'm a classical musician, not a pop star.'

'Stephen, picking up on Helena's rather amused reaction to Santo's comments, and as she was neither embarrassed nor irritated – smiled and shrugged.

'The staff at the club tend to be a bit special and Santo is a great guy with so many different interests, but I think he over-egged the compliments as he gave me a wink as he moved away from the table. These guys don't miss anything as they see lots of well-known people here. He was just trying to tell me that he approved of my choice of dinner companion.'

They ate smoked salmon, fillet of beef and apple crumble with vanilla ice cream. Finishing off the champagne they ordered a lovely bottle of a mature Pomerol wine.

They began to reminisce about their time together in Dublin and London during 1983, and laughed about the way they'd met at the National Gallery of Ireland on a sunny St Patrick's Day morning – Helena admitting that she'd fancied him from the minute she saw him in the gallery and had been thinking of a way to approach him before he had taken the initiative –

making a comment to her about comparing the sunshine outside to the sunshine on a particular painting they were both looking at – both admitting that they had forgotten the name of the artist.

They avoided talking about the pain of the break-up and how hurt Helena had been when Stephen stopped answering her letters and didn't come to see her in New York as promised.

Sitting back in the drawing room with coffees and brandies, Stephen held Helena's hand and asked her if there was any chance of them getting back together. Helena didn't say yes – but more importantly she didn't say no either.

'Stephen... It's been a lovely evening and thank you so much for inviting me to your gracious club. I must say that the dinner was superb. Let's both think things over and see how we feel when we meet again in a few weeks' time at your festival in Ireland?'

'I'm happy with that' —responded Simon.

Helena thanked Santo for his warm welcome and for looking after them so well throughout the evening as Stephen escorted her down the staircase. She said good night to Tom at the door as Stephen hailed a taxi for her. They shared a chaste kiss on the cheek before Helena climbed into the taxi – giving Stephen a wave and a smile as the cab pulled away.

Stephen went back upstairs to the drawing room for a solitary nightcap before turning in for the night – not forgetting to leave his shoes outside of his bedroom door – where they would be highly polished for him before breakfast time.

Chapter 31

Lough Corrib, Ireland, August 1993

The Irish Parliament voted to legalise homosexuality for consenting adults in June 1993. This was great news for Simon Negrini and Dov Katz, who had been a bit nervous about both of them having leading artistic roles at the Lough Corrib inaugural festival; the last thing they wanted was to be involved in some kind of scandal if their relationship became common knowledge. They meant to keep the situation between them private but in the hothouse atmosphere of a festival, people talked and gossiped; falling foul of the law was a worry for them. The legalisation was a big weight off their shoulders, although they would still be discreet about the true nature of their close friendship – as, despite the fact that homosexual activity had now been legalised, a lot of people in Catholic Ireland, especially in rural areas, were still of the opinion that homosexuality was a sin and wanted no truck with it.

Helena welcomed her Uncle Carl to the festival; he was old and ailing and was accompanied by a man in his sixties, Freddy Wakeson, who seemed to be a sort of friend and carer for Carl, and it was touching to see how much Freddy made sure that Carl was physically comfortable and was given his due reverence around the festival as its principal benefactor. Carl's wife Angela was expected to fly to Ireland and to attend one performance only of the Verdi opera, but Carl, with Freddy's assistance, had planned to stay for the duration of the festival, as he wanted to soak up all the glory that was his due.

Carl Warringson and Simon Negrini greeted each other warmly as a lot of water had flown under the bridge since the days when Simon worked for Carl's clothing company in London – starting in 1950 as a lad of fifteen. Simon thanked Carl profusely for his very generous support of the festival which wouldn't be going ahead without him.

'It's what I like to do, Simon, and to have my dear great niece Helena performing at the festival makes it extra special for me.

Carl hesitated for a moment before continuing…'I know it's a long time ago, Simon, but I owe you an apology for firing you unfairly for what happened in Paris. The dispute with the supplier was between me and him, and you got caught in the crossfire. On the other hand' – a smile appearing on Carl's face – 'I did you a favour by sacking you when I did – as you were still young enough to concentrate on your music studies, and look at you now: a renowned conductor and opera specialist who was in demand all over Europe. And Helena tells me that you're a wonderful pianist and that she adores performing cello and piano recitals with you.'

As Carl was rattling on in praise of him – Simon began to feel very uneasy – because the truth of his actual relationship with Helena and how it all unfolded over the years would soon become common knowledge around the festival campus, as well as finding out about Simon being homosexual.

How will Carl feel about his old junior employee then?

Listening to this exchange was Freddy Wakeson, who seemed to have become Carl's carer which Simon found almost comical, knowing the Freddy of old – an obsessive womaniser who was the catalyst for breaking up his early marriage to Felicity. Freddy would be someone whom he could never fully trust.

However, Dov had told him about his friendship with Freddy, having originally met each other at a dinner party given by Helena's mother, where Freddy evidently had behaved appallingly. But Dov, always seeing the good in people, said that at subsequent get-togethers' with Freddy, he had noticed a real change in his character; more thoughtful and caring. Simon was unsure how much Freddy knew of the whole personal saga, but one thing he did remember Dov telling him. Freddy had told Dov that if he ever came across the man who was responsible for Margo's pregnancy, he would punch him on the nose. Freddy, like everyone else at the festival, would shortly know who that man was – he was actually standing right in front of him at that very moment.

The rehearsals in the new opera house for *Simon Boccanegra* had begun. The conductor, Simon Negrini, and cast had assembled on the stage, together with stage director, Lizette Wakeson, the set designer, John Tern, the costume designer, Deirdre Lance, the lighting director, Nigel Ings, and the choreographer, Lindsay Dole.

It was an open rehearsal so there were a few people scattered around the auditorium, including Helena Mentones, accompanied by Carl Warringson. As Helena was not performing or rehearsing on that particular day, she decided to wear her bracelet – which she seldom wore, especially when she was performing or rehearsing with her cello, as she needed complete freedom of movement of her wrist.

Not much was happening on the stage, except lots of discussions between the various members of the production team with individual members of the cast. The orchestra players in the pit were chattering amongst themselves and the chorus members and a few dancers were gathered together at the side of the stage patiently awaiting instructions, either from the conductor, or the director. It all looked a bit chaotic and nobody seemed to be in charge.

'That's a lovely bracelet my dear,' remarked Carl. 'Where did you get it from —?'

'It's a family heirloom that was passed on to me from my birth mother.'

Helena smiled at Carl, holding her wrist up to show him the bracelet more closely. Suddenly Carl got a jolt and his expression became serious; he had an anxious look on his face as he examined the bracelet, and long ago memories stirred within him.

'Are you OK... Carl?'

Helena, seeing the look on his face, became concerned that he was unwell.

'We need to talk, Helena. Let's get out of here and find a quiet spot somewhere.'

They walked back from the lakeside to the Donnells' hotel and settled down in the lounge which was completely unoccupied. May Donnell popped her head around the room and asked if they wanted coffee – both shook their heads and said, 'No thanks'.

'The bracelet you're wearing reminded me of a bracelet that I inherited from my mother which I gave to a girlfriend during the Second World War. I'm sure it's a coincidence and I'm an old man with a faulty memory, but it looks so much like that old bracelet, that seeing it on you gave me a real shock.'

'What happened to the girlfriend, Uncle—?'

 Carl, who had always been so confident – sure of himself – and who could be rather arrogant, suddenly looked shrunken and diffident.

'I didn't behave well towards her. She was a lively and fun girl and we enjoyed wartime London together, but I wasn't in love with her. I met someone else who became my first wife and the situation was complicated because the girlfriend was pregnant and I had promised to marry her, but when I met my future wife I reneged on my promise. This caused a huge rift and consequently I was cut out of having any relationship with my daughter, Marie. Marie's mother, Wendy, tragically died unexpectedly in Cornwall, where the family lived.

Marie was a teenager at the time of her mother's death but she had run away from home and was working in a seaside holiday hotel under a pseudonym. I attended Wendy's funeral; Marie was there but she wanted nothing to do with me. I reluctantly accepted the situation – settled a reasonable amount of money on her and emigrated to California. I never heard from Marie again and when I met Angela – she would only agree to marry me on condition that I renounced my past life completely.'

Helena only responded to say that as far as she was concerned, Carl had always been a loving friend and mentor to her and her feelings towards him wouldn't ever change, irrespective of any missteps he had made in his earlier life. However, the more she chewed over Carl's lengthy soliloquy – the more a nagging thought in her head was...'*What if*—?'

Carl telephoned Angela – and, without going into detail, asked her to locate a wallet of his in a particular bureau, and said she should take it with her when she travelled to Ireland, as there were some notes in the wallet which he needed to check with his great niece, Helena Mentones, who was performing at the festival.

Helena arranged a get-together with Simon, Stephen and Dov Katz. She related what had occurred with Carl and how he thought her bracelet was familiar-looking – going on a stream of conscience narrative about his past life – in which one could make a case that he was her grandmother's lover during the Second World War, and that he was not a family friend or an honorary great uncle, but actually her grandfather!

Simon was finding it hard to take in what Helena was recounting. To think that this difficult and unlikable man, who was his boss all those years ago, could be the same man whose daughter he had slept with on one crazy night in Cornwall – then giving birth to his own adorable daughter Helena; this was just too much to comprehend. The whole personal saga had produced one incredible shock after another, and still it continued.

Stephen Zandors was on edge, because besides all the professional issues he was on hand to sort out, such as rehearsal schedules, problems with individual singers and accommodation choices, he was keen to move things on, love-wise, with Helena. They had hardly spent any time together since Helena and Simon had arrived at Lough Corrib. Helena always seemed to either be with Simon or with Carl Warringson, and there was some talk around the opera company that Simon and Helena were a couple – he thought it was about time everyone knew what their actual relationship was.

The other problem for him was that Lizette Wakeson, being such an integral part of the company as the opera director, seemed to have forgotten that the two of them had split up as lovers amicably a while back, but was still spending a lot of the leisure time around Stephen and carrying on as if they were still an item. He wished now that he had re-established his relationship with Helena when he met up with her in London. He should have asked her to stay the night with him at the Carlton Club —.

With the agreement of the others – the word got out around the Lough Corrib campus that Simon and Helena were father and daughter and that Simon and Dov Katz were in a relationship. As well as that – Stephen had a quiet word with Lizette and admitted that he wished to get back with Helena and that his love for her had never waned over the years. Lizette was most understanding and gave the couple her blessing. The rest of the company, not knowing all the background and details of the tangled relationships, took the news in their stride. After all, they were theatre people who were used to unorthodox personal set-ups and nobody was fazed; they just got on with what they were there for – to create great art.

The only two people who reacted badly were Carl Warringson and Freddy Wakeson. Warringson was disgusted with Helena for not telling him earlier; after all, he had confided in her about his past misdemeanours and had expected Helena to have been more open with him about her own situation. Helena said that she had written to her parents to tell them about Simon, but for reasons of their own they decided not to inform Carl about Helena's important news.

As for Simon – Carl thought him beyond the pale. To get a girl into trouble and taking a lifetime to find his daughter was despicable, and he told him so to his face – forgetting about his own past bad behaviour. And the homosexual aspect of the story he just couldn't abide; it was immoral and a sin, pure and simple. It took all of Stephen's persuasion to stop Carl walking away from the festival and taking his funding with him.

However, why Freddy was upset was harder to fathom; perhaps he felt left out as he always wanted to be at the heart of events, but he was also shocked to realise that the man who had got Marie pregnant all those years ago, was his old friend Simon Negrini. Simon was the man that Freddy had promised to punch if he ever found out who it was. But of course Freddy had been no angel in his past, so perhaps he shouldn't be judgemental to others.

No punch on the nose took place, but Freddy's nose was definitely put out of joint – by not being part of the inner circle for those revelations.

Angela Warringson telephoned her husband Carl to inform him that she had come down with a bad cold with a hacking cough and had decided to cancel her trip to Ireland. She was very sorry to miss the festival but felt it was best not to travel. She had the wallet that Carl had asked her to bring to Ireland. Again, without explaining any details, he asked her to look at a note in the wallet with a series of numbers written on it, and he asked her to read out the numbers. This she did on the phone – the numbers read: KLS 852269305. Carl wrote the prefix letters and numbers down. Angela apologised again and wished the festival well before hanging up.

Carl asked Helena to show him her bracelet again and he checked the hallmark with the numbers Angela had read out on the phone. The numbers matched as he had instinctively suspected they would, and he now had proof that Helena was indeed his granddaughter, and with that news – the years rolled back and he felt a young man again out to conquer the world.

Of course, there was a lot of explaining to do, and Helena, Simon, Dov and Freddy all joined Carl outdoors by the lakeside; it was a beautiful August day, sunny and warm, a rare weather day in the west of Ireland. Awkward discussions, for some reason, were easier to navigate outdoors. They sat around a picnic table and all told their stories of what they had known of the family saga. Carl repeated a lot of what he had already confessed to Helena; Simon's story was the most difficult, having to explain about his meeting with Marie, although she was known to him as Margo, and how he had tried to trace her following their sexual tryst. Through chance events over the years, and like Carl, he had kept the hallmark number of the bracelet that Marie had mislaid during their time together. Dov and Freddy both played their part in the unfolding story and both related to the group all they knew.

When all had said their piece, an exhausted five people were left with their thoughts and emotions. There was a lot to absorb with a mix of happiness for Carl and Helena in their newly found blood connection, but uneasiness for Simon, knowing that he had been responsible for setting off the whole series of events by one night's lust in Cornwall thirty-four years previously.

Dov and Freddy…both felt a certain satisfaction that they had been catalysts for the truthful unfolding of this whole story but had differing feelings towards Simon. Dov loved Simon, forgiving him for past misdemeanours, and was happy for him that all the family mysteries were now resolved. Freddy, whose allegiances were now with Carl – and having personally met Carl's daughter Marie – still reckoned that Simon had a lot to answer for – as he reckoned that Marie had been abandoned by her lover and had subsequently died giving birth.

Carl, despite his happiness at discovering a granddaughter, felt that Simon was an absolute cad – having behaved appallingly – thinking him to be the killer of his daughter.

So mixed feelings all round; but one thing they all agreed on was how uncanny it was that their personal stories had so much in common with the opera – that was currently in rehearsal at the festival grounds: Verdi's *Simon Boccanegra*.

Chapter 32

Lover's reunited

Rehearsals for both operas, *Simon Boccanegra' and The Knot Garden* were in full swing and Simon Negrini, the conductor for both operas, was struggling with jumping from the Italian high Romantic idiom of Verdi, to the more conversational style, that underpins the Englishman, Michael Tippett, and his take on contemporary relationships, including homosexual one's.

The main stage of the opera house was reserved for the Verdi – with its large orchestra and chorus. All the orchestra members and chorus were recruited locally from Galway's music college, and they were predominantly young and hugely enthusiastic. The Tippett, with smaller forces required, was being rehearsed, provided the weather was dry, in the grounds of the Donnells' hotel. Simon's time was so taken up with juggling the two operas, that he had put to the back of his head the shattering recent developments in the family saga.

Besides conducting the two operas, Simon had to fit in some rehearsal time with Helena for their recital performance. They decided that a brand new programme was needed for a brand new festival, and they talked long and hard about devising contrasting works that would be suitable for touring and recording following the festival. The programme they decided on was Benjamin Britten's cello sonata, followed by Gabriel Faure's cello sonata No.1, finishing with Felix Mendelssohn's cello sonata No. 2. For an encore – they decided on 'Danny Boy (Londonderry Air)' in a special arrangement for cello and piano.

Stephen was on the one hand, frantically coordinating everything, making sure that all the festival preparations were going to plan, but on the other hand he was desperate to find an opportunity to spend an evening with Helena. His chance came when Helena decided that she needed a night off from cello practice – asking Stephen whether he would like to join her for dinner at the Donnells' hotel, where they were both staying. Although Stephen had his new house in Tully Cross – he had decided to keep a room at the hotel during the festival period, to avoid the drive backwards and forwards.

The general plan was that all the main performing artists would stay at the hotel, taking up all their available rooms, whilst the visitors to the festival could choose to take the nightly coach to Renvyle House Hotel – which would bring them back to Lough Corrib a good few hours before the commencement of any performance. If visitors preferred to stay locally to be close to the festival campus, many of the local neighbours to Lough Corrib had been persuaded to offer bed and breakfast facilities in their homes. If visitors particularly wanted to stay at a hotel but didn't want to travel all the way to Renvyle – several hotels were located a few miles away in the small town of Oughterard – and taxis would be made available to and from the hotels. Local bed and breakfast arrangements had been made for orchestra and chorus members, as well as for all the technical crew, plus anyone else contributing to the festival.

Anyway, on Helena's practice-free night, she met with Stephen at the new bar adjacent to the opera house by the lake, and looking out to the stillness of the water with the evening sunshine glow – they both nursed gin and tonics. Finishing their drinks, they strolled up the grass verge to the main hotel building and took their place in the Donnells' elegant restaurant, for a feast of May Donnell's outstanding cooking.

The conversation at dinner was mainly chit-chat about the goings on at the campus – anyone eavesdropping could have taken them for working colleagues chewing over their professional daily tasks and planning the schedules for the days ahead.

After dinner, as it was a beautiful evening, they decided to go for a walk in the forest-like grounds surrounding the lake, and well away from meeting anyone else from the festival personnel. They walked amongst the large trees and shrubs quietly with their own thoughts, enjoying the exercise and fresh air following a large meal. Stephen took Helena's hand and gently squeezed it. Helena suddenly blurted out.

'Kiss me... Stephen.'

He turned to her and gently pushed her against a large tree trunk. He touched and stroked her face, putting a finger in her mouth. Extracting his finger, he cupped his hands around her face and looking into her eyes, said, 'I love you Helena'

She responded 'And I love you Stephen.'

He held her close and kissed Helena – slowly and lingering. Helena immersed her tongue into Stephen's mouth, with him responding in a most passionate way. They stayed by the tree continuously kissing as if to make up for the ten years without physical contact. Eventually, Stephen suggested that they should start to make their way back to the hotel and stay the night together either in his room or hers.

Helena said, 'No, there are too many prying eyes at the hotel.'

'OK'... said Stephen ...'Let's get a taxi to my house in Tully Cross and order one back to Lough Corrib in the morning.'

'That sounds wonderful, my darling Stephen,' uttered Helena with a magnificent smile on her face whilst squeezing Stephen's arm.

They cuddled up together in the back of the taxi enjoying the beautiful scenery of Connemara in the late evening sunshine, daylight remaining in the west of Ireland during the high summer months until past 11 pm. Arriving at Tully Cross – they paid the taxi driver, including a generous tip, with a promise from the driver to be back at 8 am to drive them back to Lough Corrib.

Helena thought she was in dreamland. Although all she wanted at that moment was to be naked in Stephen's arms once again – she couldn't help notice the beautiful setting of the house and how wonderful it was for Stephen to have this bolt hole to escape to – well away from the madness of festival life – but close enough to be able to get to at a moment's whim. Inside the house, it was the quietness that struck Helena as so strange but wonderful for someone used to spending so much time in busy and bustling city centres.

Although the house was sparsely furnished, everything looked clean and tidy and the bathroom that she asked to use was immaculate, with a terrific power shower and plenty of hot water.

Helena walked into the bedroom with just a towel around her. Stephen was fully clothed.

'Let me undress you, Stephen.'

She slowly undressed him – kissing various parts of his body as she did so. Once naked, Stephen whipped the towel off Helena and they held each other tightly for a few minutes, kissing – licking and stroking sensitive parts of each other's bodies.

Stephen took hold of Helena's hand and led her to the large double bed where they made love tenderly and then excitedly. Stephen's lovemaking was exactly as she had remembered it ten years earlier – confident – passionate and extremely loving. Stephen thought that Helena had matured into a sexual woman who understood her desires and was willing to express those desires with the man she was in love with.

He was even more besotted with Helena than he had been previously—.

They fell asleep in each other's arms, woke up and made love again – this time with increased passion – not wanting to let go of each other.

In the morning whilst Helena was in the shower – Stephen nipped out and picked up croissants, butter, jam – coffee and milk from the local Tully Cross shop and had a little breakfast ready once Helena was dressed. Over breakfast, Stephen proposed to Helena and Helena accepted without a moment's hesitation. This time it was for life as Stephen had learned from his Englishmen's diffidence and was in no way going to make that mistake again.

The happily engaged couple were waiting arm in arm outside the house at 8.am... as the taxi appeared to drive them back to the mad world of preparing for the opening of the Lough Corrib Opera Festival.

Chapter 33

FINALE – SCENE ONE

September 1993

Everyone was there for the opening of the Lough Corrib Opera Festival and for the first performance of the original 1857 version of Verdi's *Simon Boccanegra*. The veteran conductor, Sir Georg Solti, arrived for the opening with great fanfare and a certain trepidation from the artists – who were aware of the exacting standards from this world-famous maestro. The more relaxed and modest maestro, Bernard Haitink, also travelled to Ireland to hear Verdi's first version of the opera. The musical press were there in full and so were music agents and publishers, including Keith Foes, who represented both Helena Mentones and Simon Negrini.

The great composer, Sir Michael Tippett, born in 1905, was an early mentor to Simon Negrini, and, had been determined to attend a performance of his opera, *The Knot Garden,* at the festival. However…due to ill health he had been forbidden by his doctors to travel. Tippett sent a 'good luck' greeting card to Simon, thanking him and the festival organisers for programming one of his 'love child' operas' – that was very close to his heart.

The young up-and-coming English composer, Timothy Seda, was there to take in the whole Lough Corrib Festival set-up. He had been commissioned by the festival to write the music for the newly discovered Arrigo Boito long-held secret libretto of *Simon Boccanegra,* which was to be performed at the 1994 festival with Seda himself conducting his own opera.

Simon Negrini's most influential teacher, the conductor Sergiu Comissiona, had flown in from the US, where he was based at the time – to visit the new festival and to witness his one-time pupil's amazing musical progression. The two men had an emotional reunion, with the older conductor telling Simon how proud he was of his success and how his late mother and step-father, Mr and Mrs Flackter, would have been equally proud of how much Simon had achieved.

Mentioning the Flackters' – who Simon had been most fond of and hugely grateful to... for giving him so many opportunities to study music, gave him pause for thought to think of his own dear mother Louise, who had sadly died in 1990. Although the older 'Chalk Farm' generation had passed on, some of Simon's contemporaries from his synagogue choir days, had come to the festival to support their old friend.

Ian Monte, and his lovely wife, Ruby, were attending the festival and it was wonderful for Simon to see them again; after all – it was their wedding in Castlebar, not far away from Lough Corrib, during 1985, that had brought Simon to Ireland for the first time and led him to his reunion with Harvey and May Donnell and his meeting with Stephen Zandors. Even his old buddy, Frank Bamberg, the joker in the pack from the synagogue days, turned up at Lough Corrib with his third wife, Geraldine. Frank had no real interest in opera but he wanted to see Simon again – for which Simon was truly grateful.

A surprising visitor to the festival was Simon's ex-wife, Felicity, still very beautiful, now in her fifties. She had arrived without her husband, Frank Bailly, who disliked opera, but had come with a friend, Angela Bevan, a popular journalist, who would write an article for her paper, not about the operas, which her readers had very little interest in, but on the social aspects of the sort of people who attend that type of cultural jamboree. Simon and Felicity greeted each other warmly – Felicity telling

Simon how delighted she was at his rise in the musical world. Simon, being a bit mischievous, mentioned quietly to Felicity…

'Freddy Wakeson was there with his daughter Lizette, but without his wife, Susanna.'

He saw a reaction in Felicity which spoke of her still holding a candle for that old rogue, Freddy, after so many years since their affair.

Stephen's elderly parents, Mr and Mrs Zandors, travelled from their home in Orford, Suffolk, to visit their son in his new role running the festival. They had visited Glyndehurst several times during the time Stephen was there, but in truth, they never really got opera. For them, opera was a self-indulgent over-the-top expensive activity for arty left wingers that were run mainly by pansy types. At least their son was straight, so it was a relief to be introduced to Helena, with the news that the pair had just become engaged.

Although Helena didn't have the family credentials that they had hoped Stephen's choice of future wife would have, they showed their gracious breeding towards Helena and greeted her with much warmth and affection. What neither Stephen, nor Helena, admitted to his parents was that her newly found birth father was in a gay relationship with the leading man in the opera. In fact, they decided to keep all that side of recent personal history quiet and kept Simon out of the Zandors' way as much as possible. The plan was to keep the Mentones' and the Zandors' close together during the festival. The Mentones' had arrived from New York on the same day as the Zandors' and it was a strategy that seemed to be working, as the two couples got on really well together, despite the Zandors' generally looking down on middle-class New Yorkers.

Ricardo Negrini arrived at Lough Corrib with an assortment of relatives. All of them were keen to tell Simon what relation they were to him, despite some of them not speaking English, and Simon's spoken Italian was not as fluent as his operatic Italian.

Ricardo acted as the master of ceremonies and translated where required. They were a lovely bunch – full of warm Italian bonhomie. Ricardo was thrilled that the festival had commissioned an opera on Boito's secret libretto of *Simon Boccanegra* that he had given to Simon in Venice. The festival had already extended an invitation to Ricardo for the 1994 festival, as an honorary guest, all paid for by the festival organisers – in celebration of the extraordinary discovery which had been secretly kept in the Negrini Italian branch of the family down the years.

Stephen's ex-colleagues from Glyndehurst, whose own opera festival had just been completed at the end of August, turned up at Lough Corrib to see what their old boss was up to, at such a remote location, for a high cultural event. They'd arrived with a certain scepticism which turned to huge admiration, as they realised the professionalism of the whole set-up, and the canny choice of repertoire being presented.

Old friends of Stephen's from Cambridge University were there, mainly out of curiosity. Some were genuine opera lovers and had been regulars at Glyndehurst during Stephen's time at that establishment. Others were either just curious about Stephen's success, as they'd never seen him as a rising star during his university days, or jealous – an underlying emotion by ones who may have been top dogs at Cambridge, but whose careers, so far, had been somewhat underwhelming.

But what gave Stephen much joy – was the surprising visit to the festival of a boyhood friend, from his home village of Orford – Peter Allcote and his wife Nancy.

Big hugs all round – as the two men reminisced about their youthful frolics, cycling and hiking the Suffolk coastal areas, whilst putting the world to rights.

Nancy and Pete's life in Orford had taken the exact trajectory that Pete had described to Stephen all those years before – marriage and kids and taking over his late father's butcher shop.

However, one thing was different to the norm, and for that he had to thank Stephen. Pete had been curious about the sort of music Stephen loved, and, once Stephen moved away from Orford to start on his career path – Pete started to attend classical concerts in Aldeburgh at the Jubilee Hall, and then, at the newly built concert hall at Snape, called The Maltings, which was even nearer to Orford than the drive to Aldeburgh. Pete had slowly discovered a vast amount of the repertoire, becoming a devotee to Aldeburgh's local composer, Benjamin Britten, whose music spoke so deeply of the local Suffolk area. Pete realised that classical music was not exclusively for posh boys like Stephen, but could be appreciated and enjoyed by all sorts of people – including the local butcher. He had followed Stephen's career in the press and had always wanted to visit Ireland, especially the west coast. When he read about Stephen's new opera festival in Lough Corrib – he and Nancy decided to book tickets for both operas and see his old friend again.

Chapter 33

SCENE TWO

Dov Katz had attracted a following of opera fans that made a point of visiting wherever he happened to be singing. A whole host of fans duly arrived at Lough Corrib, and they made it clear to anyone who would listen that they were there specifically to hear and see their current favourite Verdi baritone, although they would have preferred the 1881 version of the opera, with its dramatic Council Chamber scene – giving Katz an even greater opportunity to show his star qualities. They had no intention of sitting through the Tippett opera though, but had booked all three performances of the Verdi.

Helena spent as much time as possible with her parents and getting the men in her life – her birth father and musical partner, Simon, and her fiancée Stephen – to reassure them that their status as Helena's parents would not in any way be compromised by all that had emerged in her life. She loved her parents deeply and would love them forever.

The operas – Helena and Simon's recital and the gala finale, were all fully booked, with Stephen trying to arrange an orchestral concert for one of non-opera performance nights of the festival. Having heard the young orchestra at rehearsals, he thought they were so good he wanted to show them off with a concert of their own.

Most of the audience members opted to stay at the Renvyle House Hotel – taking the nightly coach there and back where Ken Moyles looked after them extremely well. Some of them even got commandeered into the late-night singing shenanigans.

Several audience members took advantage of the local bed and breakfast houses just outside the grounds of the Lough Corrib estate. However, very few took up the Oughterard Hotel option, as it fell between the two more attractive options.

For the lucky artists who stayed at Lough Corrib Hotel, Harvey and May Donnell were perfect hosts. The meals cooked by May, and served by Harvey after the performances, were outstanding.

The new opera bar, by the lake, also served late-night meals, but a lot of the audience preferred a picnic by the lake, during the long opera interval, which could be ordered from the Donnells'... and a Donnells' picnic was always the most delicious picnic imaginable.

Simon reluctantly agreed to add an orchestral concert to the schedule despite having his hands full with conducting the two operas. Purely from a personal career point of view, although he had conducted orchestral concerts during his younger days, especially his stint with the Halle in Manchester, his international reputation in recent years had been almost exclusively built on opera – Italian opera in particular. So an opportunity in front of critics and music administrators to show his expertise in the symphonic repertory would do him no harm.

But what should they programme? It was a student orchestra, and there was little rehearsal time. Simon discovered that the orchestra had been touring around Ireland with two of Respighi's Roman Trilogy: 'The Fountains of Rome' and 'The Pines of Rome'. The pieces are orchestral showpieces and wonderfully atmospheric – a heady sound of colourful impressionistic music mixed with late Romanticism. The third part of the trilogy, 'Roman Festivals'... was less popular than the other two and playing all three would be about an hour of music – too long for what Simon had in mind for this particular concert. With a short concerto to kick the concert off – the whole programme would come in at just under an hour and it could dispense with an interval.

But what concerto to programme and who would be the soloist? Helena, resident at the festival, would be the obvious candidate, but she was taken up with learning and practising their new recital programme, and she was finding the Britten Cello Sonata especially tricky.

'What have you played previously Helena that you would like to play again?'... Simon asked over a morning coffee at the Opera Lake Bar.

Without hesitation, Helena responded, 'The piece I played as a student in New York which had a deep emotional effect on me, was *Schelomo,* by Ernest Bloch. If you're looking for a short concerto, it would be perfect – coming in at just over twenty minutes.'

'Interesting, Helena...but I admit that although I did conduct the piece once in Manchester, with the great cellist, Janos Starker, as the soloist – the cellist was full of praise for my understanding of the piece. To be honest I found it very difficult and made a mental note at the time to avoid conducting it again.'

Helena smiled at Simon and with a chuckle in her voice retorted.

'But Simon... you're a Jewish boy from an orthodox background. It's a piece I thought you would have learnt with your mother's milk—.'

'Although Simon knew that Helena was being mischievous, he still felt a bit embarrassed by her comments.

Chapter 33

SCENE THREE

Once Simon had left his home environment in north London as a young man – away from the synagogue influence – any sort of religious observance was completely shed from his lifestyle – music consuming him totally, and he began to sort of worship music as he had worshipped God as a boy. Any concept of 'the meaning of life' would come through music, which seemed more real to him than being brainwashed – believing one's own religion to be the only true one, with all other faiths false. As Simon started to go out into the world, it became clear to him that all religious life of any faith was intellectually unviable.

Of course numerous musical works were based on Christian sacred texts and Simon had no problem with those pieces; in fact, he had conducted several Mass and Requiem masterpieces of the concert repertoire himself and had felt great affection for them. One could sympathise with the sentiments of the work, especially if accompanied by great music, without believing in the core religious message. But Helena's rebuke to Simon about him not wishing to conduct Bloch's *Schelomo* again, despite his background, gave him serious food for thought. He considered himself as having spent the past thirty years in denial about his Jewish religious background.

Simon spent several nights without sleep – re-studying the score of *Schelomo* and to mug up on the Respighi pieces – which he had also conducted during his 'Halle' days. He then had several intensive rehearsals with the orchestra on day one, with Helena joining them on day two to rehearse the Bloch. The orchestra certainly enjoyed playing the Respighi, as they knew the pieces – Simon pointing out new aspects to the pieces which were different from their regular conductor. The Bloch piece, totally unfamiliar to them, they found difficult and the rehearsal did not go so well; Helena noticed the problems that both the band and Simon were encountering and actually took over the baton from Simon – working with the section leaders, to help achieve the right depth of tone required for the piece. Simon was so impressed with Helena's rapport with the orchestra that he could see for her a future career as a conductor.

'Helena... you should conduct as well as being the soloist for *Schelomo*. '

'No... Simon – I can't do that.'

'Yes you can. Let's ask the orchestra leader Luke Bennett.'

Luke put the idea to his orchestral colleagues and they unanimously approved of the proposition.

The concert itself, which came at the halfway point of the festival, was very successful – the audience loving both works with everyone surprised to see Helena both conducting and being the cello soloist. Her playing had great emotional depth, digging out those low notes depicting the old, but wise, Jewish King Solomon. The orchestra, although not technically perfect, gave Helena everything she had asked for at rehearsal – the musicians falling in love with the beautiful and gifted soloist/conductor. The audience went wild for Helena, but she made sure the young musicians shared the glory with her.

Backstage, Simon was in tears—. He'd found Helena's performance so moving – and all the emotional turmoil of recent years had just got to him. As well as that – the performance made him think about his Jewish heritage – the music reaching his soul and making him realise that although he had left Judaism many years before, it would never leave him. He was who he was whatever his rational mind was thinking.
'Simon...you need to get yourself together as there is no interval. You must get out there – the audience is waiting.'

'Yes, of course, Helena, forgive me my tears—.'

The two hugged each other tightly before Simon made his way to the podium. The Respighi performances were sensational – the orchestra was on fire and Simon conducted with pure happiness in his heart that the beautiful scores transmitted, if by magic, from Simon to the players in the most effortless and natural way.

There was another standing ovation at the close – the audience reluctant to let the orchestra and conductor leave, and only when Simon got every individual of the orchestra to their feet for a solo bow, was the audience satisfied, and the ad hoc concert, added to the schedule very late in the day, concluded.

The festival's official opening ceremony was undertaken by an Irish senator from Galway, who cut the ribbon by the entrance to the opera house. The senator made a speech about how proud he was to have an international opera festival in the county. The Irish newspapers were there in full – snapping everything in sight. Harvey Donnell said a few words and so did Stephen Zandors.

The official ceremony concluded, as the crowd, led by Stephen, sauntered into the opera bar for a celebration drink, or two, before the opening performance.

There were nerves a plenty before the opera got under way. But Simon knew his stuff and Dov Katz was the most sought-after Simon Boccanegra in the business, with the supporting cast of experienced artists, who had been rehearsed intensely.

Lizette Wakeson staged the opera in a traditional manner with atmospheric sets and colourful historic costumes, commensurate with the period of the opera. The organisers knew that some in the audience would have preferred the better-known revised version of the opera, but surely that was what festivals were for – to offer something novel from the repertoire. After all, the Wexford Opera Festival had been doing that successfully for over forty years.

Once the opera was under way, the cast and audience started to relax, the cast realising that the long rehearsal period was paying off, with the audience sensing that the new festival was presenting opera – which matched the best standards of anything in the UK and Europe.

The applause after the prologue and act one was warm but not ecstatic. Following the lengthy interval with the audience refreshed, some having picnicked by the lake, others cracking open the bubbly and saving dinner to after the performance, the atmosphere in the theatre was genuinely more festive with expectations of a great second half.

They were not disappointed, as the artists involved gave their all in acts two and three. The applause was deafening at the conclusion, despite the tragic ending in Boccanegra's death. However, the reconciliation scene between Boccanegra and his arch enemy, Fiesco, towards the end, was beautifully done and emotionally heartfelt. Dov naturally received the biggest ovation, with his supporters in the audience, but the rest of the cast were all enthusiastically applauded. Simon, the orchestra and chorus were cheered to the rafters; Simon looked absolutely exhausted.

The critics were full of praise for the whole enterprise – acknowledging the excellence of the performance but with just a few niggles here and there. That's what critics do – one would expect nothing less.

The following night, the festival performed Michael Tippet's *The Knot Garden,* which was much more of a connoisseur's piece. The critics loved it and gave it rave notices. The audience reaction was rather mixed. Those who attended contemporary opera absolutely loved it, but the more traditionally minded members of the audience were puzzled by a domestic plot and found some of the English text by Tippett himself – jarring in parts.

The cello and piano recital, given by Helena and Simon was so popular, that they had to repeat the performance the following morning. The encore of 'Danny Boy' was loved by all.

Finally, at the end of the fortnight of continuous music making, it was the time for the Gala performance. Everybody, from the organisers to the artists and the audience, some who had stayed for the duration of the festival and had attended each opera several times, as well as the concert events, were already developing a feeling of ownership of the festival. Having attended the very first one – they had started to plan a return visit for the 1994 festival.

Others had arrived specifically for the Gala night; these were mainly wealthy business-people – who had been invited with the hope of persuading them to financially support the festival in the years ahead.

Simon Negrini opened the concert with Verdi's great and longest overture, *La Forza Del Destino*. The soprano who had taken the role of Amelia Grimaldi in *Simon Boccanegra*, Karen Perian, sang the first act aria from Verdi's *La Traviata –Sempre libera degg'io* and followed up with the last act aria from *La Forza Del Destino – Pace, pace, pace, mio Dio*. The bass who took the role of Fiesco in *Simon Boccanegra*, Forbes Bineson, sang Colline's short aria from the last act of Puccini's *La Boheme – Vecchia zimarra, senti* and continued with King Philip's great aria from Verdi's *Don Carlos – Ella giammai m' amo!*

The leader of the student orchestra, Luke Bennett, stepped forward to play the gorgeous violin solo from Massenet's opera, *Thais*.

The chorus, in great voice, sang the opening chorus from Tippett's great choral opera, *The Midsummer Marriage...*

The sun! Midsummer morning! Our spirits rise towards the bright comfort of the morning light. The sun! - Midsummer morning.

The chorus were back with Verdi for the next piece. *Va Pensiero, sul' ali dorate* – the famous chorales of Hebrew slaves from Verdi's early opera, *Nabucco.*

Following a short interval, the concert resumed with Simon Negrini conducting the well-known *Intermezzo,* from Mascagni's opera, *Cavalleria Rusticana.*

The tenor who took the role of Gabriele Adorno in *Simon Boccanegra,* Riccardo Forz, entered the stage and opened his account with a Romantic Mozart aria from the opera *Cosi Fan Tutti -Un'aura amoroso* and followed that up with Manrico's challenging aria with a top c – from Verdi's *Il Trovatore – Di quella pira.*

The chorus lined up again to sing two choral numbers from Bernstein's *West Side Story; the punchy... America* and the heartfelt... 'Somewhere'

Helena came onto the stage with her cello and the whole audience stood and clapped. She was embarrassed to receive a standing ovation before performing a note of music, but they knew when they had a star artist in their midst. Thanking the audience for their appreciation, she announced that she was going to perform one of the greatest cello sonatas in the repertoire – the Hungarian composer Zoltan Kodaly's Cello Sonata Op. 8 in B minor.

Adding...'The piece is in three movements and is approximately thirty minutes in duration.'

The major masterpiece put the gala in a more serious musical light, but Helena was determined to share this music with the Lough Corrib audience. To be fair, a good number of the audience found the work a bit hard going and too long, but the musical aficionados there and the critics that were still on site, were thrilled to hear such a cello masterwork as a pleasing contrast to the more popular fare of the rest of the programme. At the conclusion of the sonata, there were a number of cheers from a section of the audience but only polite applause from the majority.

Helena thought immediately that she needed an encore, but having nothing prepared and without a piano on the stage – she improvised her 'Danny Boy' encore as a cello solo. That livened up the audience and they started to sing along with her, which Helena encouraged them to do, and as many in the audience shouted 'Bravo.' Helena – who knew how to galvanise an audience, repeated the encore – virtually everyone in the theatre sang along with her.

Up came Dov Katz to the stage and another standing ovation occurred. Dov treated the audience to the baritone aria from Verdi's *Il Trovatore – Il Balen del Suo Sorriso –* and continued with Giorgio Germont's aria from *La Traviata – Di provenza il mar il suol.* There was clapping and stamping for Katz –as he made sure the orchestra and the conductor Negrini shared in the applause.

Katz left the stage but promptly returned with the tenor, Riccardo Forz, soprano, Karen Perian, and mezzo soprano, Eithne Frele, who had taken the small role of the maid in *Simon Boccanegra.* The four artists sang the quartet from the last act of Verdi's *Rigoletto – Bella figlia dell'amore.* The applause was thunderous and only died down when Stephen Zandors came to the stage and the artists made their way off the stage.

'Thank you, ladies and gentlemen, for your warm and generous applause. Our esteemed maestro, Simon Negrini, has one more piece up his sleeve, but please be patient as we need to give our thanks to several people who have made our festival possible. The festival was the brainchild of Harvey and May Donnell, who are the owners of the Lough Corrib estate and the wonderful hotel as part of the estate. Harvey and May... please come up on the stage.'

The couple felt a bit sheepish about receiving public attention, but nevertheless were proud of their achievement. They had inherited the estate and the hotel through several generations of Donnells'. Having created an opera festival on their estate, they were assuring the continuity of the Donnell name for subsequent generations of their family.

Stephen continued... 'Harvey and May made it all happen. They negotiated with the original benefactor, who sadly passed away before things got under way, but this did not deter them, and they continued commissioning architects, acousticians and builders, as well as dealing with all the bureaucracy involved with local authorities. I came here as an adviser only, but Harvey and May had done all the heavy lifting and all I did was to help them understand the opera world in general and opera in Ireland in particular. So please... ladies and gentlemen, show your appreciation to our joint founder's – May and Harvey Donnell.'

The audience rose as one and gave a huge cheer to the Donnells'—.

Harvey Donnell stepped forward and thanked the audience for their appreciation.

He continued... 'But Stephen is too modest as we would never have got past first base without our dear friend, Stephen Zandors. Stephen had come to us from being the successful artistic director of the world-famous Glynehurst Opera Festival, and we are so lucky to have him. Stephen is our chief executive, and we look forward to Stephen driving the festival forward over the coming years.'

More applause for the Donnells' and for Stephen, as the couple stepped off the stage and Stephen continued; 'Thank you May and Harvey for your kind words, and now I would like to invite up to the stage our current benefactor, Mr Carl Warringson.'

 Loud applause as Carl made his way to the stage, helped by Freddy Wakeson.

Stephen announced...'Mr Carl Warringson, on behalf of the Lough Corrib Opera Festival, I have the pleasure of presenting you with this silver statuette with the following words carved on the front.

 "To Mr Carl Warringson, who has been awarded an honorary life membership of the Lough Corrib Opera Festival for his generous financial support."

Shaking hands with Carl, Stephen asked the audience to show their appreciation to Carl Warringson. A standing ovation ensued as Warringson bowed to the audience and indicated his pleasure in receiving the statuette. Freddy helped Carl down from the stage and carried his statuette for him.

Stephen then announced the following. 'Ladies and gentlemen, our gratitude to Mr Warringson is incalculable and there would have been no festival without his huge generosity.

Stephen then continued...'The festival plans for 1994 are incomplete but so far we can announce the following; Simon Negrini, our newly appointed artistic director, will conduct and our director of productions, Lizette Wakeson, will stage performances of *La Juive*, a French Grand Romantic opera, dating from 1835, by the composer Fromental Halevy. On appointing Simon, I asked him which opera he was most eager to conduct and immediately he chose the Halevy – which is not performed these days as much as Simon thought it should be – so that's our big opera for next year. It promises to be a hugely exciting event. Despite this year's Tippett opera not being to everyone's taste, we have decided to keep faith with the composer, and we will be presenting, as our second opera, Tippett's most recent opera *New Year,* first performed in

Houston, Texas in 1989. Glyndehurst presented the opera the following year, during my time at that festival. It's a very exciting and innovative work, and hopefully, the composer himself will be able to be with us next year, as we were so sorry poor health kept him away from the festival this year.

'For our third offering for 1994, I will leave it to Simon Negrini to make the announcement.'

'Finally...looking further ahead, we wish to explore the Grand operas of Giacomo Meyerbeer, a German-born composer who had huge successes in Paris with operas such as *Les Huguenots – Robert le diable – Le prophete and L'Africaine.* And as with Halevy, Meyerbeer, once very popular, has been unjustly neglected in recent times. Our opera production director, Lizette Wakeson, is writing a book on Meyerbeer, so that should fit nicely with our plans. But of course, these ambitious plans depend on the financial stability of the festival, but we will leave that for another day... I will now hand over to our artistic director, Simon Negrini.'

Simon hugged Stephen as he left the stage.

'Firstly... I would like to thank all the artists who contributed to this evening's concert and for you being such an appreciative audience.

'Regarding our large-scale opera production of *Simon Boccanegra,* I want to assure everyone that any dramatic parallels with the operatic characters and recent events in the personal lives of artists appearing here at the festival, is purely a coincidence. In any event, as you heard this evening, our Boccanegra, Dov Katz, is in rude health and in great voice. So you will be relieved to know that the poisoning of our Doge only occurs in the opera plot and has not been translated to real life.

'The tenor who created the role of Gabriele Adorno in *Simon Boccanegra* at La Fenice Venice during 1857 and chosen by

Verdi himself was Carlo Negrini, my namesake. I only discovered a few years ago whilst in Venice, conducting the very same opera, that I was a direct descendant of Carlo. The family tree was explained to me by a gentleman who came to see me at the opera house. The gentleman's name is Ricardo Negrini, who is a cousin of mine. Ricardo is here in the auditorium, and Ricardo... please make your way to the stage'—.

Ricardo, elegantly dressed in a three-piece suit and with the help of a cane, came up to the stage. The two men embraced warmly and Simon introduced Ricardo to the audience – asked his cousin to tell the story of the secret Boito libretto.

'Please forgive my English.' Ricardo related the story of the libretto to the audience as he had explained it to Simon in Harry's Bar in Venice.

When Ricardo finished his tale, Simon indicated for him to stay on stage – finding a chair for him to sit on.

Simon continued... 'Believe me, ladies and gentlemen, the discovered libretto is gold dust in the operatic hemisphere, and what we have in mind for next year will bring the whole world of opera to Lough Corrib. We have permission from the Boito estate to set the text, and we have commissioned the exciting young composer, Timothy Seda, to write a short opera – about ninety minutes – without an interval. The opera will have its premiere here next year – Seda conducting his own work. That will be our third opera presentation for the 1994 season.'

There were shouts of 'Here-hear' from the audience, who were generally stunned by the various announcements made by Simon and Ricardo Negrini.

Some in the audience, who had been closer to the principal characters around the campus than others, were well aware that the lives of those characters had been utterly changed by recent personal discoveries and old loves rekindled – making them think that no, Simon's dismissal of parallels with the opera were no series of coincidences. Those people who had performed for them so magnificently over the past few weeks, had actually lived a version of the plot of *Simon Boccanegra,* even if they were themselves in denial of that fact, or found it just an amusing diversion. Thank the Lord that they found the new libretto with its happy ending – otherwise, one would have been truly scared of something awful happening to that lovely man with a voice from God... Dov Katz.

Simon noticed some furrowed brows in the audience and wondered just how much they were aware of the turmoil experienced of the lives around them. Helena being his daughter was still an unbelievable positive thing for him– but for Helena? … A truly emotionally stable woman had had her life churned up completely, and to cap it all, she discovered that the rather unsavoury character of Warringson, was actually her grandfather. That was something he himself had difficulty with – the beautiful girl he had briefly known had been a creep's daughter.

The good part of their drama was that Stephen, soon to be Simon's son-in-law, had rekindled his love for Helena, for which he was thrilled about. Being wary of Stephen initially, he had grown to not only respect the man, but had become extremely fond of him.

Boccanegra and Pietro having a love affair, in the alternative libretto, by Boito, ran parallel to his overwhelming love for Dov – a truly wonderful man, with a heart of gold, whom he had loved as a boy, and unknown to Simon, was a kind and affectionate friend to Helena's mother, Marie, before her tragic death.

It would take time for all of them to come to terms with what had happened, but one decision, he made then and there, was that... he would avoid conducting *Simon Boccanegra* for the foreseeable future—.

Coming out of his reverie... Simon again addressed the audience.

'Ladies and gentleman... my apologies for keeping you so long but I beg your indulgence for just a little while longer. I have asked the soloist, chorus and orchestra to perform one more piece – my dear cousin, Ricardo Negrini, will be the conductor.

'Verdi's early life was tragic, losing a wife and children in tragic circumstances, at the start of his career. He had written a comedy opera, *Un Giorno di Regno,* that flopped badly, and then Verdi went on to write only serious tragic operas for the rest of his career. But as an old man, with the help of his friend and ours, Arrigo Boito, turned to a Shakespearean comedy, based on the *Merry Wives of Windsor.* The opera is *Falstaff.*

'I've asked my dear friends and colleagues to perform the final fugue from this great heart-warming opera. I hope you'll all agree that this is an appropriate and fitting way to complete the evening, and to close the very first Lough Corrib Opera Festival of 1993.'

There was enthusiastic applause as Ricardo Negrini lifted his arms to conduct.

> *Tout au monde est bouffonnerie*
> *L'homme est ne farceur*
> *Dans son cerveau toujours*
> *Hesite sa raison*
> *Toys des fouls! Chaque Morte!*
> *Se moque de son pareil*
> *Mais celui qui rit le mieux*
> *Est celui a qui rit le mieux*
> *Est celui a qui il est donne de rire jusqu au bout*

> Everything in the world is a jest
> Man is born a jester
> Buffeted this way and that

By his beliefs or by his reason
We are all figures of fun
Every mortal laughs at the others
But he laughs best
Who has the final laugh.

Ricardo Negrini, Simon Negrini and all the soloists, chorus and orchestra, bowed deeply to the audience, as the applause, with stamping and cheering, went on and on and on—.

Aldeburgh, Suffolk, England – 28 June 2023.

© D B Minter

Published by HAMDEN LTD

Gioachino Rossini – composer
Countess Clara Maffei – friend of Verdi
Tito and Giulio Ricordi – publishers
Michael Tippett – composer
Royal Philharmonic Orchestra
John Amis – friend of Michael Tippett
The Rising Sun – hotel
Sant' Agata, Busseto –Verdi's home:
Giuseppina Strepponi – Verdi's wife
Lough Corrib – location in Ireland
James Loughran –conductor
Sir John Barbirolli – conductor
Harold Macmillan – prime minister
Hugh Gaitskell – Labour Party leader
Harold Wilson and James Callaghan – prime ministers
O&C Butcher – outfitters in Aldeburgh
Midland Hotel – Manchester
Peter Hall – opera director
Bernard Haitink – conductor
Georg Solti – conductor
Covent Garden Opera
Halle Orchestra
Cologne Opera
ARD – Munich music competition
The Ivy – London restaurant
Andrew Edmunds – London restaurant
Harry's Bar – Venice
Renvyle House Hotel – County Galway
Tully Cross – Village near Renvyle, County Galway
La Fenice Opera – Venice
Tito Gobbi – opera singer
Wilton's – London restaurant
Snape Maltings - concert hall
Jubilee Hall – Aldeburgh
Benjamin Britten and Peter Pears – founders of the Aldeburgh
Festival
Carlton Club – London gentleman's club
Ilse Wolf – Soprano and singing teacher
Ralph Vaughan Williams – composer

Gustav Holst – composer
Elijah Moshinsky – opera director

About the author

D B Minter was born in the county of Hertfordshire, England, and is currently a resident of Aldeburgh, Suffolk. During the 1970s and 1980s, D B lived and worked in Dublin, Ireland, where he met his wife, Deirdre.

The Incidental Legacy of Carlo Negrini is D Bs first novel, but he had previously published a musical diary memoir, and written programme notes for a Suffolk classical music concert series. The diary memoir chronicled fifty seven years of concert and opera attendances – from the perspective of an audience member.

Having completed **The Incidental Legacy of Carlo Negrini**, D B is writing a second novel. The plan is to complete a trilogy of opera themed novels.

A proud father and grandfather, D B and Deirdre enjoy exploring the beautiful coast and countryside of Suffolk together, as well as attending concert and opera performances. At home, listening to music, reading books and creating delicious meals, are their preferred leisure activities.